SEABORNE

Seaborne

Katherine Irons

B
BRAVA
KENSINGTON PUBLISHING CORP.
www.kensingtonbooks.com

BRAVA BOOKS are published by

Kensington Publishing Corp.
119 West 40th Street
New York, NY 10018

All Kensington titles, imprints and distributed lines are available at special quantity discounts for bulk purchases for sales promotion, premiums, fund-raising, educational or institutional use.

Special book excerpts or customized printings can also be created to fit specific needs. For details, write or phone the office of the Kensington Special Sales Manager: Kensington Publishing Corp., 119 West 40th Street, New York, NY 10018, Attn. Special Sales Department. Phone: 1-800-221-2647.

Brava and the B logo are Reg. U.S. Pat. & TM Off.

ISBN-13: 978-0-7582-6140-3
ISBN-10: 0-7582-6140-3

First Trade Paperback Printing: April 2011

10 9 8 7 6 5 4 3 2 1

Printed in the United States of America

CHAPTER 1

The Maine Coast—July

The summer storm swept in without warning. Black clouds rolled across a lightning-streaked sky sending fishermen and tourists racing for snug harbors. Sheets of rain fell, and thunder boomed as waves and wind churned the scenic coastal waters into a deadly maelstrom.

One aging forty-footer with a crew of three—father, son, and grandson, didn't join the other boats in flight. Instead, the vessel foundered in the rock-studded waters as waves crashed over the pitching deck and gusts ripped at the open cabin and dislodged stacks of lobster traps in the stern. Aboard the old boat, one man struggled with a sputtering engine while the gray-haired captain fought the wheel, attempting to steer the foundering craft away from a looming island.

Hidden from sight by a rocky outcrop, Morgan watched the human drama unfold with mixed feelings. These fishermen were his mortal enemies. Their kind was responsible for the thousands of wire cages littering the ocean floor, ghost traps that caused the senseless death of too many living creatures to count.

Lost nets, tangles of rope, rusting hooks, and wires snagged fish, whales, dolphins, sea birds, and turtles, speeding the destruction of an abundance of sea life that had thrived for eons. Humans polluted the oceans with their trash and chemicals and spilled oil, and they decimated whole species of fish and shellfish.

Morgan knew he should hate these men, and he would have despised them if he didn't pity them for their ignorance. They didn't seem to understand that instead of destroying food sources, they should be protecting them, an act that might keep millions of humans from starvation someday.

Once, these men who breathed air and walked the earth had been brothers and sisters of his race, but no more. In their quest to leave the sea and conquer the land, humans had lost wisdom and a compassion for all living things. If these men were dashed on the rocks in their puny lobster boat, if they drowned, what was it to him? He wasn't one of them.

With a shrug, Morgan started to turn away and leave the fishermen to their fate, but before he could slip back under the blue-green water, the engine roared to life, and a third member of the crew appeared on the deck.

"Dad's got it running!" This wasn't a man, but a boy. Morgan caught a glimpse of wide blue eyes and a pale freckled face, just before a giant wave swept over the deck, knocking the child overboard.

The gray-haired captain saw him and shouted, "Joe!"

The mechanic who'd been working on the engine charged up the stairs onto the deck. Ripping off his rain gear, he leaped into the water after the boy. The old man steering the boat secured the wheel long enough to snatch a life ring off the gunnel and toss it over the side.

"Evan! Evan!" Joe swam strongly despite the force of

the waves, but there was no sign of the boy's head above
water. Morgan knew the hungry tide had claimed him,
and his death was certain.

Unless . . .

Cursing his gentle heart, Morgan plunged into the maelstrom and dove deep under the water. The tide was strong,
but he'd learned to swim in storm surges. He blinked to
clear his vision and swam under the boat to the spot where
the child had gone down. Above, Morgan could just make
out the thrashing shadow of the man, but below there was
only sand-tossed bottom. A few powerful strokes carried
him in the direction the tide was flowing. On land, he was
as clumsy and weak as a human, but in the water he could
swim as swiftly as a shark.

Even for him, the churning waves made it almost impossible to see more than a few yards, but he calculated
the direction and speed of the tide and drove on. There!
Something was there, just ahead of him, not swimming,
but tumbling helplessly in the current. Morgan kicked
hard and let the water's force carry him. In seconds, he
reached the drowning boy and seized him. For an instant,
the human child opened his eyes and stared directly into
his own, but then he went limp. Quickly, Morgan swam to
the surface with him in his arms.

Casting a net of hypnotic illusion around himself for
protection, he pushed the half-conscious child into the father's grasp. He already held the life ring, and the older
man on the boat was able to pull them both in.

Morgan lingered in the water, just out of sight beneath
the boat, using his superior hearing to eavesdrop on their
conversation. "Did you see that?" Joe sputtered as he
shoved the choking child up onto the boat. "Did you see
what that dolphin did, Pop? He saved Evan. The dolphin
saved him."

Morgan heard the boy cough and spew up a bellyful of water, before beginning to cry.

"That's it, get it out of you," the grandfather urged. "Did you see it, Evan? Did you see the dolphin? Big one, it was."

"No," the boy protested weakly. "It was a man."

"A man?" his father scoffed. "It was a dolphin, son. I wasn't three feet away from it."

"A man," the boy repeated groggily. "A blue man. He came up out of the dark."

"Hush, now, save your strength for breathing," his father said.

"Don't know what he's saying," the captain said. "We nearly lost him. No wonder he's talking foolish like."

Smiling, Morgan spread his arms wide and sank into icy depths. Human adults were easy to deceive, but human children were different. They saw and heard things that adults had forgotten. He'd been lucky. No one would believe the boy's story. He'd never attempted to use mind control on more than two at a time and never on a child. Had his spell cracked, one of the men might have seen him for what he actually was, and that would be dangerous. The security of his kingdom, of his race, depended on keeping the land dwellers ignorant of the world beneath the sea.

As he swam into deeper water, out beyond the island, Morgan almost convinced himself that he'd skirted the law and gotten away with it. . . . Until he noticed a flash of movement out of the corner of his eye.

"Going somewhere, Brother?"

Morgan turned to face him, wishing he was armed with something more than a short sword. He and Caddoc were never on the best of terms, and his half-brother had tried to kill him on more than one occasion over the years.

"I saw you."

Morgan didn't answer. Had Caddoc witnessed the incident with the lobster boat or had he seen him watching the woman?

"You're a fool. You of all people should know the penalty for breaking the law."

Morgan shrugged. "You're free to make a report to the council."

"Oh, I will. You can count on it."

Caddoc favored their father in appearance. Dark haired like his mother instead of blond, but the proud features, the high cheek bones, the broad forehead, and the square chin were identical to that of the king.

Caddoc rarely traveled alone, and Morgan wasn't surprised when two of Caddoc's cronies appeared out of the murky darkness. If an accident occurred here, no one would ever know what had happened to him, and his half-brother would be one step closer to the throne he coveted so badly.

"You'll stand trial," Caddoc warned. "Crown prince or not, you're not above the law."

Morgan waited, unwilling to provoke a confrontation, but prepared to fight if pushed into it. Three to one was not the best of odds. Caddoc was better armed, and he was known for his skill with a trident. Perhaps his half-brother was right. Maybe he was a fool to risk being seen to save a human child from drowning, but he'd make the same decision again, given the circumstances. If there were consequences, he was prepared to face them, beginning with Caddoc.

Even as the three closed in on him, he couldn't stop thinking about the woman and wondering why he'd been so drawn to her. Small hairs on the back of his neck tingled as he placed a hand lightly on his sword hilt. "Well, big brother," he said. "What can I do for you?"

"Put down your weapon, Morgan. I'm placing you under arrest." Caddoc raised his trident to shoulder height. The three razor-sharp prongs gleamed in the half-light that filtered down from the surface.

Morgan smiled and drew his sword.

Claire Bishop sat at the bay window and stared out at the rain. Wind lashed at the house and bent the tree branches, knocking limbs against the house and sending them tumbling across the wide expanse of lawn. Pitchforks of jagged lightning illuminated the sky, and the rumble of thunder echoed through the house.

"Come away from that window," Mrs. Godwin urged. "My sister knew of a woman who was struck dead as a doornail by lightning while standing at her own bedroom window."

"Dead as a doornail," Claire murmured. "I've always wondered how a doornail could be dead when they aren't alive to begin with."

"You know what I mean," the housekeeper fussed. "It isn't safe." Her Maine accent was as thick as the carpet underfoot, but Claire had been coming to Seaborne since she was a child, and neither Mrs. Godwin nor her peculiar dialect intimidated her.

"It's time for your medication."

"Leave it on the table," Claire said.

"You need to take it regularly. Once the pain gets hold of you—"

"It's not bad today." The pain in her neck was always there, waiting to grab her in its sharp teeth and shake her like a terrier would a rat, but today she felt a more dull, grinding ache rather than an all-consuming fire. "Just leave it. I'll take it in a few minutes," she said.

"You'd better. You've got to take better care of yourself."

Claire forced a smile. "You worry too much."

"Someone has to." The housekeeper brought the small paper cup with the pills and a glass of water to the side table on Claire's left. "Land sakes, but you'll catch a chill. It's like a grave in here." She picked up a sweater from the rocking chair and draped it around Claire's shoulders. "Come to the dining room and have something to eat. I've made a clam chowder to die for. Your spirits will pick up if you have something hot in your stomach."

Claire grimaced. "If your clam chowder would cure my woes, I'd gladly bathe in it. But I'm not hungry. And I'm content where I am."

"At least turn on some lights. This storm is so wicked you can hardly see your hand in front of your face." Mrs. Godwin went to the wall switch and flicked on several lamps. "I've got biscuits in the oven. Are you certain—"

"At supper, I'll make a pig of myself," Claire replied. "I'll slather your biscuits with butter and honey and dunk them in a wash basin of chowder. But for now . . ." She met the housekeeper's gaze solidly. "For now, I prefer to be left alone."

Claire turned her attention to the falling rain. Still mumbling, Mrs. Godwin hustled out of the room, leaving her blessedly alone again. The woman meant well, but she hovered over her like a mother hen.

It was raining so hard now that the large drops created a steady drumming against the windowpanes. It would probably rain all night. She hoped the storm would pass by morning. She hated the days when bad weather kept her from the beach. She was always happiest near the water.

Her cell phone rang. She glanced at the number and held down the button until the phone powered down. As much as she loved her father, she'd already spoken to him twice today. There was nothing more to be said and no reason to start the argument up again. Richard Bishop didn't want her here at the Maine house. He wanted her back in New York with him. He simply couldn't understand why she felt that she had to get away from doctors, hospitals, and his constant worrying.

But, he couldn't force her to return to the city. Seaborne was hers. Her grandmother had left it to her, along with a trust fund that insured the taxes were paid and the property was kept up for decades. Not that she needed the money, but Grandmother was nothing if not efficient. She'd loved the big rambling house and she'd known that Richard, her only son and Claire's father, hated it. He would have sold the family estate within weeks of her death. Claire had been pleased to inherit Seaborne, but she'd never realized what a refuge it would become.

The clock on the mantel chimed the hour, and Claire glanced at it. Above the clock hung an oil of Claire and her favorite gelding, Gold Dust. She wondered how he was getting on with his new owner. She'd sold him to a promising young rider when she'd given up the sport.

She wished Richard hadn't asked Mrs. Godwin to hang the painting in here. Tomorrow, she'd ask her to put it in the attic, along with the boxes of trophies and plaques that she'd acquired in her years on the international riding circuit. She didn't want to look at them anymore. All that was in the past.

Two years ago, at twenty-seven, she had every reason to expect a bright future. She had health, brains, and ambition, and she'd earned a coveted spot on the American Olympic riding team. Now, she had nothing to look forward to but a day on the beach, staring at the waves. And today, even that was ruined by the rain.

Was this a preview of the rest of her life? Years of sitting at a glass window and staring out at the world? Was she such a coward that she couldn't face the truth? What was the use of living like this?

She wasn't a quitter. When her marriage to Justin had crashed and burned, she'd acted like an adult and divorced him. Then, she'd concentrated on her riding career and made a whole new life for herself. She'd always gone into any effort wholeheartedly, full force, and taken no prisoners.

She couldn't do it again. She didn't have the strength.

Medical science had done all for her that money could buy. She'd never ride in competition again, never dance or walk . . . never be able to conceive and carry a child. The accident had left her with such unexplained gaps of memory and mental confusion that she wasn't able to safely drive a motor vehicle. In spite of all the money the jury had awarded her, she'd be confined to this wheelchair as long as she lived.

She'd never find romance again, never feel the heat of a man's mouth on hers, never make love to him, or feel the exquisite thrill of an orgasm. She rubbed her lifeless legs, unable to feel the caress of her own fingers. She, who enjoyed sex so much, would never know physical love again, never marry again, never have a reason to exist. Was it any wonder that she was depressed?

Claire buried her face in her hands and wished she had the nerve to wheel the chair out of the house, down the walk to the cliff edge, and off into nothingness. If only . . .

But she knew she wasn't that brave. All she could do . . . all she would ever do was sit here and think about what might have been.

CHAPTER 2

Morgan put a seaweed-coated boulder at his back and stood ready, sword in hand, watching his half-brother and his two comrades. The storm raging above the surface had little affect here below, other than reduced visibility. Strong currents off the coast of New England were a mild inconvenience compared to undersea. It was something Morgan had learned to deal with centuries ago.

Caddoc advanced until he was just out of reach of Morgan's weapon and took a threatening stance. He was a big man, tall and broad with powerful shoulders. Again, their father's heritage. It was too bad that he'd gotten his morals and disposition from his mother.

Morgan guessed that Caddoc outweighed him by two stone. He was a solid block of a man and what little neck he possessed was wrapped in layers of muscle. His dark hair was cut straight to fall at his shoulders, held in place with a thin gold headband. Pearls were twisted in the thin braids on either side of his face. As always, Caddoc was garbed as befitted a prince of the realm, albeit a minor one. In contrast to his own sharkskin kilt and chest bands, his half-brother's garments were embroidered with gold. Even Caddoc's sandals were set with precious stones, more suited for palace wear than the open ocean. Caddoc's eyes were small and dark with the clear and merciless gaze of a killer whale. When they were children, Caddoc's bulk and expressionless eyes had frightened Morgan.

No more.

Tora, the big Samoan, moved to guard Caddoc's right. The Pacific-born mercenary was thick and compact, hair cropped short, and hands as wide as shovels with stubby fingers. His front teeth had been sharpened to points and his wide ruin of a nose was flattened and cleaved in two grotesque halves by an ugly scar. Tora's weapon of choice was a massive coral war club, the head carved into the face of a Polynesian deity. He was equally handy with a long slashing knife, set with shark's teeth in place of a blade, that he wore on a sheath across his chest.

Tora shadowed Caddoc's every move day and night, and court gossip was that they were lovers. Caddoc, it was said was oversexed, even for an Atlantean, and would swive any creature, male or female, that possessed an orifice of a convenient size.

The ugly Samoan had been driven from his own underwater kingdom by a rebellion, and he had sought refuge bearing terrible wounds, including the loss of his tongue. Caddoc had befriended him, earning the man's loyalty, but for selfish reasons rather than altruistic ones. Caddoc enjoyed the contrast that they made in public, and he enjoyed controlling such power with a word or a glance.

The third member of the trio was Jason, Caddoc's cousin on his mother's side. Jason was close to Morgan's age, but they'd never been friendly. Jason, slim and sinewy as an eel, was armed with a sling and a broadsword. Jason's skin had a golden tint, and his eyes were large and colorless.

Caddoc motioned to his cousin, and Jason stepped left and unwound his sling. Morgan was more concerned with the sling than he was with Tora's club. Jason's missiles were deadly at twenty yards, and the Samoan had to close in to strike a blow.

Caddoc jutted his chin. His eyes clouded with arrogance. "You look pale, Brother."

Morgan tried to assume a bored expression. "You're bluffing."

"Why shouldn't I end this now? Once you're reduced to chum, our fishy friends will make certain no one ever finds a trace of you."

"Point," Morgan conceded, tamping down his temper. If he was to get out of this alive, it was his wits that would save him, not the strength of his sword arm. Some claimed the Atlanteans were immortal. Not quite true. Compared to humans, they were; but injured badly enough, he could die as surely as any land dweller.

"Are you afraid to die?" Caddoc taunted.

Heat flashed under Morgan's skin. Rarely had he ever been angry enough to want to kill one of his own kind, but he couldn't afford to show weakness. If he did, they would close in. Morgan suspected that the only reason they hadn't taken advantage of the situation was that Caddoc wasn't certain he could come through the encounter without injury. His half-brother would go to any length to avoid the slightest pain.

"The three of you could probably kill me," Morgan said nonchalantly. "It's not certain, but the odds are in your favor. But you know I won't go down without a fight. You could die or you could lose a limb. And chances are, I'll kill at least one of you in the struggle." Morgan spread his legs and took a defensive stance. "And if it's not you, Caddoc, you and I both know that you'll then have to finish off whichever of your buddies survives the fight."

Jason cut his gaze at Tora uneasily. Jason wasn't fool

enough to completely trust his cousin. Tora might appear stupid, but Morgan knew that he possessed more intelligence than Caddoc gave him credit for.

"And why would I do that?" Caddoc demanded. His face flushed. He didn't look as sure of himself as he had a minute ago.

"You couldn't leave a witness, of course," Morgan said. "You kill me, and so long as these two are alive, they'll be a danger to you and to your hope for the crown. They could blackmail you any time they wanted something from you, or they could turn you in just to see you imprisoned for eternity when they tire of your nonsense."

His half-brother scowled. "That's crap."

Morgan raised one eyebrow. "Is it?" He glanced at Tora. "Are you so certain that Caddoc wouldn't protect his own ass? Remember what happened to Deepak?"

"That was an accident," Jason said.

Morgan shrugged. "So the court decided. But some wondered. You probably wondered, Jason, especially since Caddoc took your friend's wife to his bed so soon after that."

Tora lowered his club and looked from one to the other. His lopsided grin wouldn't have convinced a child.

Jason nodded and took a step back.

Caddoc laughed. "We had you there, for a minute, didn't we, Morgan? Any longer and you'd be shitting down your legs." He turned away and signaled for his friends to follow. "Running you through would be too easy. Once the court gets through with you on the charges I'm going to file against you after what I've seen today, you'll wish we had."

Morgan watched through narrowed eyes as they swam swiftly away. He exhaled slowly, as his heartbeat slowed and his muscles gradually relaxed. They'd meant to kill him, all right. Sooner or later, he'd have to settle with Caddoc.

He knew sooner would be better. He might not be so lucky next time. He gazed upward toward the surface. He should return to Atlantis immediately and answer the charges Caddoc would make against him, but the pull of the human woman was too great. There would be time enough to explain his actions to his father and to the High Council. For now, he would return to the beach where he'd seen her.

He'd seen beautiful human women before, but he'd never found them sexually attractive. They were too weak, too fragile. But this woman on the beach was different. She possessed a strength that called to him with an irresistible lure, and he could not shake off her spell until he'd solved the mystery. He had to discover what magic she possessed that could draw him from the sea time and time again.

Cursing his own foolishness, he turned back toward the mainland. When she returned to the beach, he would be waiting.

The morning after the storm dawned bright, and by eleven Claire was able to return to her beloved spot on the beach. The house sat high above the shoreline well back from the cliff face, and the only way down was a narrow flight of stairs and the elevator Claire had ordered installed for her wheelchair. At the base of the bluff, a six-foot-wide cement walk ran almost to the water's edge, ending in a partially roofed pavilion complete with safety rails, table and chairs, and lounge where she could nap comfortably.

After many mishaps, Claire had perfected her technique and was able to reach her oasis without assistance. Once on the pavilion, she would ease herself inch by inch out of the wheelchair and into a cushioned deck chair. Or if she preferred, the concrete pathway ran down the beach parallel to the high-tide mark so she could use the chair to "walk" the beach when she wanted. Her father had been dismayed by the cost, but she would gladly have spent ten times over to have a place that was hers alone to retreat to.

This morning, the beach was alive with all manner of wildlife. Sandpipers and fiddler crabs scurried about, squabbling with seagulls and willets, and the occasional saucy common tern. The waves that had crashed and boomed against rock and shore the previous day now ebbed and flowed with a kind of orchestrated music. The air smelled of salt and wet sand and sea. The sun felt warm on her face, making her feel alive with each breath.

Claire should have been content today, now that she was on the beach again, but she wasn't. If anything, her despair was worse than yesterday's. Shortly after nine, she'd received a phone call from the private detective agency she'd engaged to search for her biological mother. When she saw the number come up on caller ID, she'd hoped that Robert Kelly had real news for her, but instead, he'd once again dashed her hopes.

Essentially, what Robert had conveyed in his brusque Brooklyn twang was a reluctance to continue the investigation at all, unless her father could provide more information on the woman who'd given her up for private adoption. Claire had always known that Richard wasn't her birth father. He'd even insisted she call him by his name, rather than "Daddy," but she'd never doubted his devotion. The only thing he'd ever told her about her mother was that she was young, gifted musically, and very, very beautiful.

Everything about her birth seemed to be cloaked in

mystery or untruth and there seemed to be nowhere to find information. Her birth certificate listed her birthplace as Seaborne, and her parents as Richard and Elaine Bishop. The attending doctor had died of a heart attack when Claire was a child, and the live-in English nurse who'd cared for her as an infant had seemingly vanished after she left Richard's employment. And Richard had been no help at all. From the beginning, her father had been against her search for her birth mother. He'd refused to provide any assistance, claiming that the woman had insisted that Claire make no attempt to contact her. He told her that going against her birth mother's wishes would only bring heartbreak.

Richard's wife, Elaine, had never been a real mother to Claire, and Claire suspected that she'd only agreed to the adoption to please Richard. They had divorced when Claire was six, and Elaine, now remarried, lived in Brazil with her fourth husband, a man even better off financially than Richard. Claire had written to Elaine twice begging for information on her adoption, but she'd never bothered to reply.

Since the accident that had destroyed her life, Claire had been obsessed with finding the truth about her birth. As a child, she'd secretly dreamed of finding her birth parents, but she'd never felt the need for a mother's love more than she did now. Robert Kelly had a reputation for being the best. With his decision to suspend the investigation, Claire's dream of reuniting with her birth mother seemed as hopeless as everything else.

Today, the sea provided none of the peace Claire sought so desperately. Hours passed, her solitude broken only by Mrs. Godwin's appearance with a lunch tray and a second intrusion when she returned with a pitcher of lemonade and the mail.

"You haven't eaten a bite," the housekeeper observed. "If you keep losing weight, none of your clothes will fit you."

"Does it matter?" Claire picked at the fruit salad to please her. She wasn't hungry. She was rarely hungry. Eating had once been a joy, and she'd been blessed with a metabolism that kept her from becoming a blimp, no matter how much pasta, chocolate, or ice cream she devoured. Now, food had no taste and eating seemed like one more unpleasant task she had to perform to keep herself alive.

On the tray was the usual container of pain medication. So far today, she'd resisted the allure of numbing her senses, despite the incessant pain in her neck. Sometimes she wished she could drown her agony in alcohol, but even when she was a teenager, she hadn't been able to stand the taste of it.

"It's warm out here," Mrs. Godwin said. "Would you like me to help you back to the house?" She shook out a beach towel and spread it over Claire's useless legs. "You wouldn't want to get a sunburn."

Claire shook her head. "No, I suppose not." It was easier to agree than to argue. She wanted only to be left alone, and the sooner Mrs. Godwin was appeased, the sooner she'd leave. "I'll be up later."

"You should lie down and take your afternoon nap." The older woman was tall and sturdy with a no-nonsense helmet of salt-and-pepper hair twisted into a fat bun at the back of her neck.

Mrs. Godwin never wore makeup, except on Sundays when she attended church. Then she exchanged her blue uniform skirt and white blouse for a navy dress with a white collar and stained her full lips and plump cheeks with a pink lipstick that Claire always thought of as the exact shade of bubble gum. Mrs. Godwin's shoes were her only weakness. Imported from Italy and hand-stitched, the low pumps with one-inch heels were expensive, comfortable, and long lasting. She polished them every evening and replaced each pair every five years on her birthday.

Claire liked to think that Mrs. Godwin had a special affection for her that went beyond the employer-employee relationship, but she wasn't convinced. And she suspected that Mrs. Godwin enhanced her salary by taking additional money from Claire's father, both to spy on her and to make certain that his rules were followed. On more than one occasion, Claire had caught the housekeeper listening in to phone conversations on another extension. The problem was that Mrs. Godwin had worked at Seaborne since she was fifteen, and she was now only seven years from retirement age. Getting rid of her, at this point, seemed harsh.

"You spend too much time down here alone." Mrs. Godwin removed ice from the small refrigerator, filled a glass, and poured lemonade over it. "You drink all of that, and I'll leave you alone until supper. Pot roast and green beans with new potatoes."

"Lovely." Claire downed the lemonade and the housekeeper bustled away. Claire turned her attention to a tern perched on the railing of the pavilion. When the bird flew off, she removed her sunglasses, turned her face up to the sun, and closed her eyes.

She might have dozed, but she couldn't be sure.

"Hello, there!"

Sleepily, she turned to see a man wading out of the surf.

"Afternoon!" He smiled and waved.

Was she dreaming?

Claire's breath caught in her throat. He was young, no more than thirty, with long, wavy blond hair caught back in an elastic, and the bronzed skin of a Greek god. She swallowed hard, her gaze captured by the sparkle of the drops of water sliding down his muscular chest.

Should she pinch herself?

He was a god. His high forehead, classic nose, sensual mouth, and shoulders were to die for. Every inch of him was good enough to eat, from the long hard legs to the flat stomach that rose just above tight, European-style bathing trunks that left little to imagination.

Guess I'm not dead after all, she thought, as barely remembered desire curled in her throat. She exhaled slowly, still too stricken to think of what to say that wouldn't come out utterly stupid.

"I hope I'm not intruding." His teeth were straight and very white, and his eyes . . . His eyes were the most beautiful blue she'd even seen on a man—on anyone. They had to be contacts. No one had eyes the color of the water off Nassau, did they?

"It . . . it's a private beach," she stammered foolishly. Her hands felt damp, her lips dry. Unconsciously, she moistened them with the tip of her tongue. She glanced past him, looking for his boat. He wasn't a local guy. He must have come off a sailboat or a yacht anchored on the far side of the island.

"I didn't mean to intrude."

The vision halted, his bare feet planted in the sand, his broad shoulders stretching from horizon to horizon . . . and his chest. She swallowed again, suddenly comprehending why some lonely older women were willing to pay any amount of money for the attentions of a young stud.

"I was hoping to find a restaurant, maybe a bar. I'm dying of thirst."

"Sorry. The nearest town is nine miles down the coast. Most of this area is national forest. Nary a café in sight."

He looked at her hopefully.

"Can I offer you something to drink? If you're thirsty?" She felt herself blush. "Something nonalcoholic, I mean. I'm afraid I don't . . ."

"Is that lemonade?" His smile widened.

She couldn't remember seeing him in any movies. He bore some resemblance to Brad Pitt, but side by side, he would have put Brad to shame. He had to be a professional model. There was something exotic looking about him. Maybe he was Italian or Greek. She'd gone to boarding school with a blond Greek guy, but he hadn't looked anything like this. "Please," she said. "Come up. There are steps on the far side."

He was tall, easily six-two or three, just the type she'd been crazy for when she'd been young and single—before she'd met Justin. Impulsively, she wished Mrs. Godwin had taken the wheelchair. Lounging here in the recliner with her legs covered by the beach towel, Mr. Dreamy might take her for just a woman on the beach enjoying a sunny day. Just a single woman like any other . . . without all the drama and pity the chair would summon. It had a way of stopping conversation.

If he noticed the wheelchair, though, he didn't mention it. He pulled out a chair beside her and sat down without being invited. She didn't mind. She didn't mind at all.

"There are chilled glasses in the refrigerator."

"All the comforts," he teased, fetching a glass and ice. She poured the lemonade from the pitcher, thankful for once that Mrs. Godwin had brought more than she could drink. It was still cool enough that it didn't instantly melt the frost on the glass. He took a long sip, and she watched the way his throat muscles flexed as he swallowed. Her mouth felt dry.

Memories flooded her mind. Once, she would have

known just what to say to a handsome stranger. . . . Once, she wouldn't have hesitated to ask him out for a night of dancing and whatever followed.

"I'm Morgan," he said. "And you are?"

His voice gave her chills. It was whiskey soft and mellow. Clearly, he was well-educated. Definitely money.

"You do have a name?" he teased.

"Claire."

"And I don't suppose *you're* trespassing on this private beach."

She suppressed a chuckle. Damn, but he was charming. She knew it, but it was too delicious not to go along for the ride. Not to pretend, just for a few more minutes, that they were just a normal couple flirting with each other. "No, I'm not trespassing," she said. "I live here."

His blue eyes sparked with mischief. She couldn't get enough of them. If she could walk, she'd just stumble into them and fall forever.

"On the beach?" He glanced around. "It's nice, but what do you do when it rains? There was quite a thunderstorm yesterday."

She took a sip of her own drink. "It was, wasn't it? Did you ride it out or head for a safe harbor?"

"I find a rough sea exciting."

He smiled again, and she felt a sharp flush of pleasure. She hadn't had this much fun since . . . Not in years. She tried to remember. Ever?

"So you're a mermaid?" he said.

"Excuse me?" She should have felt nervous. Morgan was a total stranger, and she was absolutely helpless. She should have felt vulnerable. Instead, she was having a wonderful time.

"If you live on the beach? Or maybe this dock has a basement apartment?"

She picked up a strawberry and tossed it at him playfully. He laughed, and she explained about the house on the bluff. "Seaborne. It's been in my family since the early nineteenth century."

"That old?" He retrieved a strawberry from the bowl on the table and took a bite of it. A little juice squirted on his lip and he licked it away.

"It even has a widow's walk." When she was a child, she'd loved to play there. But she couldn't climb the steep stairs now. Never again.

"I'm starving," he said, eyeing her untouched tuna sandwich. "Do you mind?"

Suddenly, she was hungry too. "I'll share," she offered. They each took half and made short work of that and the accompanying chips. Morgan snapped the pickle in two, and Claire laughed. "You eat it. I can't stand dill pickles."

"But you . . ."

"My housekeeper. She knows I don't like pickles, but she puts them on my lunch tray just the same. She reads a lot of cooking magazines, and she likes things to look proper."

"I suppose you get kale under your crab cakes too."

Claire chuckled. "I do. Are you certain you don't know Mrs. Godwin?"

"She sounds a lot like my Aunt Bella. She's always trying to feed me bananas."

"And you don't like them?" Claire supplied.

"Can't abide them."

They laughed together, and as Claire lost all track of time, she found an instant camaraderie with this handsome sea god. Before she knew it, the cliff was casting long shadows across the sand.

"Miss Claire!" Mrs. Godwin shouted from the head of

the steps. "It's getting late. Don't you want to come up now?"

"That's my housekeeper," Claire said, turning her head to look up at her. "And sometimes prison guard. Would you like to—" She broke off as she looked back to see that Morgan was gone. Puzzled, thinking he'd descended the steps from the pavilion to the beach, she waited to see him appear at the water's edge.

"Morgan?"

The only answer was the sharp twitter of a willet fluttering up from the damp sand. Claire's mysterious visitor had vanished as quickly as he'd appeared.

CHAPTER 3

"You ate all your lunch," Mrs. Godwin said. "That's wonderful." The housekeeper had come down on the elevator and joined her on the pavilion. She wore a gray tweed sweater and a headscarf, even though Claire was comfortable enough in her short-sleeve tee and shorts. Convinced that fresh air threatened her health, Mrs. Godwin hated the breeze off the ocean.

"Mr. Richard phoned," the older woman continued. "He said he'd been trying to reach you and you didn't pick up. Did you fall asleep?"

Had she? Claire was still trying to figure out what had happened to her delicious visitor. How had he slipped away without her or the housekeeper seeing him leave? Was it possible she'd dreamed the whole thing?

She shook her head. No, that wasn't a possibility. Morgan had been real enough. If she squinted, she could almost see him sitting there beside her, almost see the intense blue of his eyes.

She wasn't imagining him. He'd shared her lemonade. A second empty glass was standing there on the table. "Did you see anyone?" she asked.

"What do you mean? At the house?"

"No, here. With me. When you called down from the top of the steps, did you see someone here with me?"

"Gracious, I hope not. How would anyone be here?" She wrinkled her nose at the notion as she gathered up the glasses, plate, and silverware and put them in a picnic basket to take back to the house. Then, she paused and stared at her with some concern. "Are you feeling all right? You aren't feverish, are you? I always said no good will come of all this sitting on the beach. You're bound to catch something."

"No. I'm fine. But maybe you're right. Maybe I did fall asleep." Sometimes her mind played tricks on her, but she'd never lost track of reality. She could recall Morgan's face in detail, his voice, the way he moved, the way drops of water had sparkled on his chest.

No, this was ridiculous. She hadn't dreamed up that muscular chest. She wasn't that creative. He'd been here. A genuine hottie had been here all afternoon.

But how . . . ? Claire sighed in frustration. She took so much medication that it was a wonder her mind functioned at all. Perhaps she'd lost track of the time before Mrs. Godwin had come looking for her. Maybe she'd dozed off and Morgan had already left to return to his yacht before the housekeeper—

"Miss Claire?" Mrs. Godwin brought the wheelchair close to the lounge. "You look a little flushed to me. Are you certain you wouldn't like me to call Nurse Wrangle and ask her to stop by this evening?"

"No, thank you." She lifted her legs and swung them over one at a time. Rigorous physical therapy kept them from looking like the useless things they were, but she had no feeling from her waist down. Sweat broke out on her forehead as she used all her strength to drag herself inch by inch into the chair. "Do you suppose they have an Olympics competition for paralyzed lifting?" she quipped.

"No." Mrs. Godwin grabbed her under the arms and heaved her over as if she were a side of beef. "You poor little thing."

Claire clenched her teeth as frustration knotted in her throat, and her eyes stung with unshed tears of anger. Moving into or out of the chair alone took time and effort, but she didn't want help.

She wanted to be the way she'd been before the accident. She wanted to be the woman who'd taken first place when her university fencing team had competed nationally. She wanted to flirt and laugh with men at a singles bar and have them dying to tumble into bed with her. She wanted to ski Vail at Christmas and sky dive in Northern California with her friends from the riding circuit. She didn't want to spend the rest of her life confined to a wheelchair at the mercy of a domineering housekeeper.

She wanted her life back.

Morgan watched from the surf. Spending so long out of water this afternoon had taxed his strength, both in the energy needed to maintain the illusion that he was a human and the strain it took for him to breathe on land. He felt an overwhelming weariness of body and spirit.

Being in such close contact with the human woman should have dissolved the odd attraction he felt for her. Despite her quick wit and obvious intelligence, she was damaged, her health even more frail than the average land dweller. Although he couldn't assess her physical condition without examining her, he guessed that she was paralyzed from the waist down.

Not that it would have been a problem if she weren't human. Atlanteans had virtually no physical handicaps and possessed super healing abilities. Short of the impossibility of replacing a missing limb that had been cut off in battle or eaten by a shark, almost any injury would heal in a matter of hours. They suffered from none of the viruses, heart disease, cancers, and various illnesses that plagued humans.

Leaving the cradle of life, the sea, brought with it many challenges for the human race. The earth's force of gravity and the constant assault on the earth's surface from radiation put constant pressure on the human species. Atlanteans, who had remained in the water, were both superior intellectual and sexual beings.

The sexual part was the problem. Unfortunately, heightened sensuality was one weakness that Atlanteans suffered from, both males and females. Although some couples mated for life and remained faithful to each other, the majority, like him, took sexual pleasure where they found it. Since his kind were bound by none of the artificial human rules of morality, adults finding pleasure whenever and wherever they pleased with other adults was the norm.

Morgan reasoned that he had acquired a desire for a woman that he was forbidden to touch. It was a rare occurrence, one that he personally had never experienced, although he'd heard tales of other Atlanteans struck by this same fever in the blood. Inflamed by the unsatisfied lust for a certain object of desire—even a human one— brought weakness and both mental and physical pain.

Claire was so human that he didn't understand how he could be attracted to her. He should have felt pity for her. Instead, he wanted to take her in his arms. He wanted to touch her skin, to taste it, to nibble his way from her delicate eyelids to the tips of her toes . . . to lave every square inch of her body with his tongue. He wanted to inhale her scent until he was intoxicated by it, to run his fingers through her hair, suck her nipples until they hardened to tight buds, and cradle her in his arms. Even now, watching her at a distance, Morgan could feel his groin tightening with need. He wanted her as he hadn't wanted a female in three hundred years . . . perhaps five.

And she had been equally attracted to him. He had read the invitation in her eyes. Naturally, most sexually mature humans desired his kind. There were legends of those who walked the earth, breathed air, yet lived on the blood of their fellow humans. Vampires, they were called. It was said that vampires possessed the ability to bewitch humans with their sexuality, but the power of these bloodsuckers—if they truly existed—would be nothing compared to the sensual lure of the Atlantean race.

He sank under the waves, reveling in the powerful surge of the tide, savoring the tangy feel of the salt on his skin. This was his element; this was where he belonged. Venturing on dry land, even for a few hours, was dangerous in more ways than he could count.

But the pounding in his head and the pressure in his groin remained as strong as ever. He seemed tangled in a web of sorcery. No matter how much reason told him to leave this place, to forget her, he was incapable of doing so. He had to find a way to end this connection before it was too late.

Perhaps the only way to rid himself of his attraction was to make love to her. It would be risky. The laws against Atlanteans and humans sharing sexual favors were rigid and strictly enforced. If he were caught, he could be severely punished.

The thought that he already could have been caught watching Claire by his greatest enemy came to him. But he didn't think Caddoc had seen him spying on the woman. It was enough that his half-brother had witnessed the near drowning of the boy. If Caddoc knew about Claire, he would have taunted him about it. Caddoc never had the self-control to hold his tongue. The offense, having romantic contact with a human, would be even greater than rescuing one from drowning.

Morgan clenched his jaw. Tonight, he would go to Claire. But this time, he would take her into his element. Once they were beneath the ocean, he could use his healing powers to temporarily give her back the use of her legs. She would be able to respond to his seduction, to feel his mouth on her body, to enjoy each shared sensation. And he knew he would satisfy her more than any human male she'd ever been intimate with. But then, sadly, he'd have to wipe away her memory of the evening.

He told himself that if she came willingly, it wasn't really abduction, and if she didn't resist, what they did together would harm no one. The argument was as full of holes as the *Titanic*, but he was in no mood to be rational. As impossible as it was to believe, Claire had become an immovable obstruction. If he was to complete his mission and return to defend himself in front of the High Court, he'd have to shatter the ancient laws and seduce her first.

Claire had retired early. Mrs. Godwin's supper had not tempted her, and she dutifully swallowed the cornucopia of medications her physicians advised, all but the pain pills. Those she dissolved in her cream of tomato soup left cooling on the table with the rest of her meal.

In bed, blessedly alone with only her small reading light lit, she tried to pick up the woman-in-distress novel where she'd left off. Reading was one of her few pleasures, but tonight, even the author's creativity couldn't hold her attention. She marked her place with a sheet of note paper, put the paperback on her nightstand, and was about to switch out the light when her bedside phone rang.

She knew who it was before he spoke. "Greetings, father unit," she said.

"Hey, pumpkin. How are you? Mrs. G. said you weren't feeling well today."

"Never felt better," she answered. "Ran three miles before breakfast, and then went to the gym in Linderman. It's not state of the art, but they have decent weights. I pressed a hundred and sixty pounds."

Her father made a feigned sound of amusement. "That's my girl, always joking. How are you really? Mrs. G. sounded concerned."

"My legs don't work. I'm in constant pain. I have insomnia, and I black out without warning. Other than that, I'm top notch. I was thinking of entering the Maui Pineapple Triathlon this fall."

"I'm worried about you, kiddo. You shouldn't be alone up there, gives you too much time to feel sorry for yourself."

She could picture him, robe and slippers, McCallan scotch in hand, sitting in his high-back leather chair in his penthouse library, feet resting on the ottoman. Richard had a seventy-inch, wall-mounted plasma TV with surround sound. Her father was a channel surfer, but no matter how many programs were visible on the screen, one would be BBC America and a second the world stock reports. Unlike her, Richard would stay awake watching television until midnight.

"That's me," she agreed, wiggling up on her pillow. "It's a real pity party here. But how can you say I'm alone? There's Mrs. Godwin, her son, dear Nurse Wrangle, and an endless parade of physical therapists, not to mention the cook and housemaids. I think there are three of them."

"You should be home. With me. Where you're close to your specialists and the hospital. Anything could happen in that godforsaken place."

"Nana survived living at Seaborne for years." Claire closed her eyes, unwilling to allow herself to be drawn into the same old argument. "I'm here, Richard. I'm staying here for the time being. Live with it."

There was a pause at the other end of the line. *Here it comes*, Claire thought. *Drop the other shoe, Father mine.* As adorable as he was, Richard could be relentless.

"Justin called me yesterday."

Claire sunk a tooth into her lower lip. Her ex. Her annoying and well-rid-of ex. As civilized as their divorce had been, she wanted no part of him, and she certainly didn't want to relive the betrayal she'd felt when she'd caught him with Marla.

"Dad . . ." She rarely called Richard that. He didn't like it. Suddenly, her chest felt tight. "Justin and I have nothing in common anymore. You know how I feel about him." It had taken her a long time to stop thinking about what she might have done to make their marriage work. But in the end, she always came to the same conclusion: So long as she expected honesty and fidelity, they were much happier apart.

"He offered his services. He's concerned about you too."

"If I need a psychiatrist, I'll find one."

"Justin's the best," her father said. "And he cares about you."

She doubted that Justin had called Richard. It was probably the other way around, and in Richard's world of international corporate law, such small matters were of no consequence. "I'm good, honestly. And I have no intention of speaking to Justin ever again."

Her father's tone softened. "I'm just thinking of what's best for you."

"Me too."

"I hope to be able to get up to see you soon, maybe next week."

"That would be good. 'Night, Richard."

"Good night, Claire. Remember, I'm here for you. Always."

"I know. Take care. 'Bye." She hung up the phone, grabbed the paperback, and threw it against the in-suite wall. "Justin? I may be suicidal, but I'm not crazy."

Maybe she was, a little, but she'd sooner spill her heart out to a stranger—to Morgan—than to trust Justin Warren. She exhaled in one long breath, switched off the light, and wiggled down in the bed.

She didn't think she'd be able to sleep, not without taking something, but to her surprise, she did. And when she opened her eyes, instead of sunlight coming through the sea-front windows, she saw moonbeams dancing across the waves.

She was standing waist deep in the surf, her bare feet half-buried in the sand, with salt-foam washing against her bare waist and soaking the cotton pajama top that covered her breasts.

She looked up in surprise, her startled gaze meeting Morgan's. "What are you doing here?" she asked him.

A smile spread over his face. "I thought you'd like to go for a midnight swim."

But how? She couldn't remember leaving the house, descending the cliff face. Was she dreaming? Didn't he realize that she couldn't use her legs? Or could she? She could feel the cold water against her skin, feel the clamshell under her right foot. She wiggled her toes and felt a rush of joy as they moved. She didn't know what to say to him.

"Wouldn't you?"

"I've never swum in the ocean," she said, still afraid to believe she was standing—still not knowing how she'd gotten out of bed. "My father . . ."

"Your father isn't here, is he?"

Moonlight played over Morgan's handsome features. His body was every bit as breathtaking as she remembered. If this was a dream, she didn't want to wake up. She was standing. She had feeling in her legs. Cautiously, she took one step, and then another.

Maybe this was real and the rest was a nightmare. Maybe that speedboat with the drunken captain had never shattered her spine and skull. Maybe . . . She sucked in a deep breath of salt air. Maybe this moment was all she'd ever have. Why waste it?

"I'm not a great swimmer," she said. She felt giddy with happiness. If he'd suggested dancing naked on the beach she would have agreed.

"Lucky for you, I am."

Puzzled, she tilted her head and looked up at him.

"A good swimmer." He squeezed her hand, and she thrilled at the shivers of excitement rushing up her arm and down to tips of her toes. His hand was big and warm. He made her feel safe. She was trembling, not with fear, but with anticipation. So what if she drowned? Hadn't she been trying to work up her nerve to end her useless existence?

He was a total stranger. All her life, Richard had warned her to be wary of strangers, to beware of con men or women trying to extract something from her. Morgan might be a psychopath for all she knew, but if he was, he had certainly wrapped his craziness in a beautiful package.

He tugged at her hand and dove under, pulling her with him. Instinctively, she held her breath and closed her eyes. She'd been honest. She wasn't a good swimmer. Her lessons in the boarding school pool had only been sufficient to pass the class. No one in her family swam, and Richard had a terrible fear of the ocean that he'd passed on to her.

"Open your eyes."

She was surprised at how clearly Morgan's words came to her. She could almost hear him speaking in her head. She did as he instructed and gasped with delight at the blue and green sea bottom beneath her. Silver moonlight shimmered above them, and they slid through the water as easily as a goose flies through the sky.

She'd expected the water to be icy, but it was like warm honey against her skin. Each kick she made seemed to carry her farther, faster. They were moving swiftly now, past undersea rocks and swaying columns of sea foliage. Off to her left, Claire saw the outline of a sunken ship, the wooden skeleton glowing faintly with a ghostly luminescence. There on the right was an old lobster pot, broken loose from its float or cut free by some jealous fisherman who didn't want competition.

Claire swam beside Morgan for a long time before she realized that she was no longer holding her breath. Somehow, she was able to breathe without rising to the surface for air. She supposed that meant she was dreaming, and she felt a twinge of disappointment. She'd wanted this to be the reality. She didn't want to wake and find herself confined to the bed with legs like cold marble.

"How is this possible?" she asked. "Why aren't I drowning? Is this a dream? I can't breathe underwater."

He laughed. "It's not a dream, and you're correct. You can't. Not normally, but because I brought you into the sea, you can."

"But how?"

"Think of it as magic. Trust me, you'll be fine."

She had so many more questions, but the ocean floor spread out before her, full of marvels: giant clams, schools of cod, a small shark. How could all this beauty be here, so close to her home and she'd never seen it? Even the swirling sand formed patterns of different colors, now buff, now black as coal. Claire was enchanted. This was as much a fairyland as anything in the *Green Fairy Tale Book*.

"Duck your head," Morgan cautioned.

She did and found him leading her under a low arch of stone blocks into a narrow tunnel. She should have been afraid. The light here was almost nonexistent and the air seemed stale. She could just make out the shadows and shapes of fish and crabs swimming past. Then abruptly, they were through the passageway and into an underwater cavern lit by a shimmering rainbow of multicolored fish that glowed like lanterns.

"Ohh," she cried. "How wonderful." She had to be dreaming. How could such a place exist?

The sandy floor was littered with pieces of broken marble statuary and patterned tiles that looked almost Grecian. A waterfall tumbled from one end of the chamber, forming a bubbling stream of clear water.

"It's fresh," Morgan said. "Are you thirsty?" From a rock shelf, he lifted a crystal glass and filled it for her.

The water was sweet and cold, the best she had ever

tasted in her life. She drank until she'd drained the glass. The flavor was faintly familiar, but surely she'd never been here before. "I don't understand any of this. I feel like Alice down the rabbit hole."

He smiled at her, and the heat of that smile made her all warm in the pit of her stomach. "You don't have to, do you? Do you like what you see?"

"Yes," she cried. "Oh, yes."

"I do." He drew her closer and lifted her hand. Turning it, he pressed his lips to the underside of her wrist. "You're very beautiful, Claire."

She swallowed, marveling at the sweet sensations that had spread under her skin at the touch of his lips. "So are you," she replied.

He nuzzled her skin before releasing her, but didn't step away. They were very close, and she could see just how big he was. She wanted to touch him. She wanted him to touch her. Her breasts tingled, and a sudden rush of need filled her. She moved into the circle of his arms as though it was the most natural thing in the world, and raised her face so that he could kiss her lips.

His breath was sweet. He hadn't even kissed her, but she could feel the tension growing in the pit of her stomach. "Morgan," she whispered. "What's happening?" Trembling, she leaned against him.

He took her face between his hands and tilted it up. His mouth covered hers and he slid his hands down to stroke her throat and the nape of her neck. Heat leaped between them, and she opened her mouth as he deepened the kiss. It felt so natural, so right. She'd kissed many men in her life, made love to some of them, but she'd never felt like this.

Sweet, liquid desire melted her bones and slid through her veins. She leaned into him as her knees went weak. She was acutely aware of the corded muscles in his chest and the growing bulge of his sex. Heart in her throat, she traced her fingertips down his chest and flat belly, and down lower until she felt him tremble. Brazenly, she stroked him, growing even more excited as she felt the throbbing length and width of him in her palm.

He gasped and she clung tighter to him. How she'd missed this. She'd been afraid that she'd never feel another man inside her, never know the wild, starburst of intense pleasure that came with a climax. Eyes wide, gazing up into his face, she caught his hand and brought it to an aching breast.

His strong, lean fingers caressed her. His gentle touch set her on fire. She wanted more. Had to have more. He stroked and rubbed, finding the nipple and teasing it until she thought she would go mad with desire. Her breasts felt heavy, sensitive . . . so sensitive.

She wanted him to kiss her. . . . She wanted to feel his lips against her bare skin. "Kiss me," she begged. "Kiss my breasts. Suck them."

Groaning, he tore away her thin cotton top, lowered his head, and slowly drew her nipple between his lips. Her breathing quickened as he suckled hard enough to send ripples of pulsing joy to the growing heat between her legs.

"Tell me what you want," he demanded.

"You know what I want."

"Say it. I want to hear you say it."

CHAPTER 4

Morgan looked down at her, suddenly struck by how small, and soft, and trusting she was. Hot lust coursed through him with a liquid fire. He wanted to throw her back against the sand and possess her. He wanted to strip her naked and savor every bit of her, driving deep inside her, riding her until she screamed with pleasure. He knew he could, knew that she'd welcome him, that she'd open to take in every inch he had to give her.

Why shouldn't he? He'd brought her here for this, hadn't he? She was only human, and he was of a superior race. Why not take what was so freely offered? It would be a gift of pure, once-in-a-lifetime joy for her. And once he was satiated with her charms, he'd be free of her.

But he hadn't counted on her silken skin or the delicate female odor that filled his head and intoxicated him, a scent more powerful and enchanting than any he'd ever encountered. He hadn't guessed how holding her in his arms would cause an overwhelming feeling of protectiveness. Something deep inside stirred and blossomed, thawing the wall he'd built up to guard his emotions. He didn't know what was happening to him. He'd shared pleasures with dozens, perhaps hundreds of lovers, and none had ever been so helpless . . . so vulnerable. So what was it about this woman that was different?

Never before when he was in the throes of primal sexual desire—of the must that possessed Atlanteans at certain times of their lives, driving them almost mad with lust—had he ever hesitated. He wanted Claire with a blinding, pulsing heat. What harm would it do to quench this fire?

She was an adult with the free choice to accept or refuse him, and he would take the necessary steps to protect her from the unlikely chance that she might conceive a child. She'd not remember this night once it was over; he'd make certain of that. He was the one risking his life—it might be forfeit for this high crime—while nothing bad would happen to her. Why shouldn't he have the prize he held in his arms?

"Morgan . . . please . . ."

She was breathing hard, her beautiful eyes heavy lidded with passion. If he slid a finger inside her, he knew she'd be wet and ready for him. He groaned, fighting his own release at the thought of tasting that sweet honey. Heat seared his skin as need gripped his loins. Was she a witch that she had this power over him?

Her fingertips pressed against his chest, stroking, caressing . . . so warm, so alive. He leaned down and nuzzled her swollen breasts. What sweet breasts they were, not large, but perfectly formed with coral-colored nipples . . . nipples now taut and enticing. He caressed first one breast and then the other, licking and sucking, making her writhe and moan with excitement.

He dropped to his knees, pressing her back into a soft bed of kelp. "Claire," he murmured. "Beautiful Claire. Do you want me to love you?"

"Yes," she cried, "yes. Do it! I want to feel you inside

me!" She tugged at her pajama bottoms, pulling them away, letting him see the soft brown curls the covered her mound.

He ripped away his kilt. His cock throbbed, hard and pulsing. His need was fierce, and she was only inches away. He could so easily give them both what they wanted.

He leaned over her and covered her mouth with his own. She wrapped her legs around him, bringing her hot, wet sex in contact with his body, and making him crazy. He ran his hands over her breasts and down over her small, flat stomach where the skin was marred by a map of raised scars.

She was whimpering now, her nails digging into his back, whipping his lust to fury. He pushed her back, kissing first her mouth, and then her throat, sucking, licking, and nipping. He trailed the kisses down over her breasts to her midsection, where he kissed each raised lump of scar tissue before moving lower. Her curls were as soft as he had imagined.

Her scent was stronger now. He buried his face in her velvet folds, teasing her with his hard tongue, tasting her woman's juices, exploring her delicate secrets until she cried out and convulsed with joy. He continued kissing and laving her sex until she sighed with pleasure. Then he dropped back, breathless and panting.

Still unfulfilled, still tumescent and aching, he grasped his swollen cock and sought a solitary relief, stroking and squeezing until he reached the peak and slipped over, groaning as he found release.

Still unable to understand why he hadn't taken what was offered, Morgan cradled her in his arms and whispered Atlantean love words into her ear. She couldn't comprehend a word he was saying, but it didn't matter. He knew. The familiar words of the ancient poet seemed right for this moment and brought a little peace to Morgan's soul.

Claire raised her head and looked into his eyes. "Why didn't you . . . ?"

"It's all right," he soothed, and kissed her love-swollen lips tenderly. "It's all right." How could he answer her question? He was at a loss. All he knew with certainty was that taking her tonight would have been wrong—would have been no better than rape. For some reason he couldn't explain, it was impossible to complete his seduction. That's what he tried to convince himself, but he knew the answer all too well.

She was human. He was an Atlantean male. She had no defenses against his sexual prowess. Taking advantage of her would be wrong, even more of a wrong than bringing her into his world. She might be just a human, but he couldn't treat her with such disrespect.

He was ashamed of what he had done. And yet . . . and yet he had to admit that whatever attraction he had for her had not lessened one iota. He still desired her. What was more, he felt responsible for her in a way that he'd never felt for any other female.

How was that possible? Something like anger seeped up to mute the shame. He'd been a fool. When he'd first felt drawn to Claire, he should have found a willing Atlantean woman and sated his lust with her. It would have been easy. There was always a celebration, a party, a gathering of willing men and women eager to enjoy themselves. If he wanted a more serious relationship, there were three Atlantean noblewomen he could think of who would welcome his attentions.

So why had he chosen to become an outlaw on a whim? Maybe his half-brother was right. Maybe he wasn't fit to sit on his father's throne. Maybe he had some weakness of character, some thread of madness that would explain this deviation from the correct path. The High Council had sent him on a mission, and instead of doing his job, he'd chosen to involve himself with a badly injured human woman.

"Morgan?"

His name on her lips sent shivers down his spine. And when he met her gaze, his shame flooded back with greater intensity. "Did I please you?" he asked.

Her smile answered his question. "Yes, but I still don't understand. Why didn't—"

"It's late," he said brusquely. "Time I got you home."

She sighed and touched his cheek. "I'd rather stay here."

"No, we have to go."

She looked around. "It's so breathtakingly beautiful here. I never imagined that . . ." She paused. "This is a dream, isn't it?"

"Yes." Morgan kissed the tip of her nose. "It's a wonderful dream, isn't it?"

"Yes, yes, it is." She stroked his cheek. "I don't want it to end."

"But it has to. You have to wake up."

"How can I imagine all these things? If it's my dream . . ."

He smiled at her. "There are many things in the world we aren't supposed to understand." It was true. As old as he was, there were still many unexplained mysteries that puzzled him. He took her hand in his and helped her to her feet. "Come with me."

She smiled at him. "Anywhere."

He wondered if she would still feel that way if she were Atlantean, if she liked him because of the enchantment his kind spun over humans, or if . . . Thinking like that made him only more confused. He led her quickly back toward the tunnel. He'd return her to her home. He'd make certain that she remembered none of this. And he'd never repeat the error with a human again.

But as Claire gripped his hand, he knew that she wouldn't be so easy to forget. He might leave her, might put an ocean between them, but he had the uneasy feeling that she would continue to haunt his dreams. And he had no idea of what to do about it.

Claire opened her eyes. She was in her bedroom; she could see the familiar outlines of her dresser, the door that led to the adjoining bathroom, the table and chair by the window. A night-light burning by the entrance gave off a faint yellow glow. Her father's picture stood on her nightstand as it always had.

But the room smelled of salt and sand and rolling waves. If she closed her eyes, she could picture the ocean floor, the schools of fish flitting through the water like flocks of birds.

Tentatively, she touched her sheet, pillows, the fuzzy blanket. She opened her eyes again and saw by the clock that it was 4:30, not yet dawn. She felt confused, not quite awake and not quite asleep. Memories of the fantastic dream continued to swirl in her mind. Morgan . . . beautiful Morgan. Swimming . . . she'd been swimming in the ocean with him. They'd been together on the beach and he'd taken her under the water, led her to a magical cavern at the bottom of the sea where he'd made glorious love to her.

Well, almost. At least, he had pleasured her.

She sighed. It had all been so real . . . Morgan's kiss . . . his touch. A warm flush rose under her skin as she remembered the intimacies they'd shared. She felt no shame . . . just pleasure, and she smiled into the shadowy bedroom.

In her dream, she hadn't been trapped in a bed or a wheelchair. She'd gone down to the beach and waded in the water, felt the cold, fresh waves break around her . . . over her hands and legs. She'd felt! She'd physically experienced sensations that had been impossible for her to feel since the accident.

She clenched her eyes shut and let the memories flow over her. Like vivid scenes from a movie, they played out behind her eyelids: the sea floor, the shimmering lights and colors, the sunken ship, the fish that glowed like lanterns. She could see Morgan's azure-blue eyes gazing into hers, feel him kissing her breasts and nipples . . . feel the thrill of his hands moving over her body.

Here in this room, she was a cripple, only half alive, but the dream had made her feel alive again. Morgan's visit to the beach had given her that. If she could only live in her imagination, it was better than nothing. She buried her face in her hands. Why couldn't it be true? Or why couldn't she keep dreaming?

She could taste Morgan's lips, his sweet breath mingled with hers, smell the clean, salty scent of his skin. She could remember the feel of his long blond hair brushing against her bare breasts . . . feel the texture of his tongue against the inside of her mouth. . . .

"Why did I have to wake up?" she whispered, hugging herself in desperation. "Why?"

Abruptly, gooseflesh rose on her arms as she realized that her pajama bottoms were missing. She was still wearing her gauzy blue top with the sailboat embroidery, but grains of sand clung to the thin cotton, and it smelled of the sea.

Was she losing her mind?

By eight, Claire was ringing for Mrs. Godwin to send one of the maids up with a pot of coffee—black. Claire

wanted a clear head today. She'd finished her breakfast of
toast and juice before Nurse Wrangle arrived at eight-thirty
to assist her with bathing, medications, and dressing.

"Toast and jam is not a proper breakfast," the young
woman scolded. "You should have oatmeal or a poached
egg, perhaps prunes to—"

"Ask Cook to send a basket of fresh fruit down to the
beach, if you like," Claire replied. "I'll be on the pavilion
today."

"I don't know if that's wise. Mrs. Godwin said yesterday was not a good day for you. Bed rest until your therapist comes might—"

"On the beach," Claire repeated. It didn't do to give her
an inch.

Nurse Charlotte Wrangle was tall and model thin with
short blond hair, hazel eyes, and a white uniform and cap.
Claire guessed her to be in her mid-twenties. She would
have been attractive if it weren't for the stern expression
and the air of importance she wore like a shroud. Did anyone under the age of sixty still wear a nurse's cap on duty?
Wear a stethoscope or carry a physician's leather case with
her initials in large silver letters? Or call herself *Nurse
Wrangle*?

Claire handed back the paper medication cup. She'd dutifully swallowed every pill, except the one for pain. She
didn't want to be groggy when Morgan came again. If he
came again.

"You know you need this." Wrangle shook the cup and
smiled patronizingly.

"If I need it, I'll take it. Not before." She waved the pill
away and guided the wheelchair toward the elevator to the
first floor. "Thank you for coming," she called over her
shoulder.

"I should take your temperature. And your blood pressure." Wrangle scuttled after her in her black, lace-up, old lady oxfords.

"Tomorrow," Claire promised, reaching the doorway. Why did some nurses and doctors insist on treating their patients like small children? Had she lost her ability to make decisions when the speed boat had crushed her skull?

"But your father will—"

"My father isn't here. And you work for me, Charlotte. Keep that in mind." Claire thought that she should have a plaque made that said that very thing—*I AM YOUR EM-PLOYER. DON'T FORGET IT*! Then she could hold it up, instead of repeating herself to the staff, the physical therapists, and Nurse Wrangle.

She made her escape into the old-fashioned elevator that her grandmother had installed twenty-five years ago. "Yes!" She smiled as the door slid shut, hit the gold button, and rode to the first floor.

"Thank you, Nana," she murmured. Of course, she could have had elevators put in the house herself, if they hadn't been here. But the modern ones were all shiny metal with cagelike doors. Her grandmother's elevator was polished wood, gold framed mirrors, and spacious enough for three wheelchairs and a standing passenger or two. When the elevator reached the first floor, Claire rolled the gauntlet between Mrs. Godwin and the girl scrubbing the kitchen floor, and escaped the house.

The sun was shining; the sky was blue. And she just knew that Morgan would appear in the surf just off her beach. He had to.

Morgan arrived home just as the sun rose in the east, casting a golden glow over the surface of the water thousands of feet above the tallest monuments and rooftops in the city of Atlantis. He had arrived without fanfare, shielding his face in the folds of a cloak to keep from being recognized by passersby. He approached the palace by way of the garden and entered by a service archway that led to the kitchens.

The palace was large, but he quickly made his way past the storerooms where food and serving plates and glassware were stored. He took a narrow, twisting staircase, through a little-used door and strode past two of the palace guard. Now, it didn't matter if he was seen, and his royal insignia gave him free access.

Morgan returned the soldiers' salutes and strode down a marble-lined corridor, part of the oldest section of the complex. Few, other than the family, used this passageway, but he loved the huge blocks with their carvings that predated the earliest Atlantean colonies. He always wondered who the craftsmen had been and how they managed to lift such huge stones and fit them together so tightly that not even seaweed could penetrate the cracks.

As he rounded a corner and took a low hallway that led off deeper into the maze of living quarters, he found the way ahead in shadows. Even this area was always illuminated, and he stopped, thinking that it might be wiser to take another route. As children, he and his brothers and sisters and cousins had played here, roaming at will. He knew these passageways. At least he used to, but that was so long ago. Perhaps . . .

Annoyed at his own hesitation, Morgan hurried on. The sooner he talked with his mother, the sooner he'd—

Abruptly, a door opened and a hand grabbed his shoulder and yanked him in. Morgan reached for his sword, but not before someone else grabbed his arms and attempted to pin them behind him.

"Well, Brother, what mischief have you been up to?" a familiar voice taunted.

CHAPTER 5

"Peace, Brother, it's just us," rumbled another familiar voice.

"Orion?" Morgan swore a foul oath, and stopped struggling. His brothers! No danger here, but someone's bad idea of a joke.

Laughter burst from the man behind him as he released Morgan's arms. Morgan spun around and hugged his young brother Alexandros. "What are you two trying to do—get yourselves killed?" Morgan demanded.

Alex ignored him and wrapped him in an equally enthusiastic embrace. It was like being hugged by a giant octopus.

Orion slapped Morgan on the back with a blow that nearly caused Morgan to stumble and joined in the laughter. "You're getting slow and soft," he taunted playfully. "A year ago, we'd never have gotten away with that."

"A year ago, Alex wasn't that strong," Morgan said. "What have you been feeding him?"

"We could have sliced and diced you before you got your weapon out," Alex said. "What were you thinking to wander around the palace without hunting us down first?"

"I didn't know you were back," he answered.

"Back and ready to take you on," Alex teased.

"Take me on? We'll see about that." Morgan clutched Alex's throat and pretended to choke him. His hands were big, but Alex's throat was massive. His little brother had put on muscle as well as strength.

Orion, still chuckling, slid aside a stone panel, flooding the low-ceilinged room with light. Releasing Alex, Morgan blinked as his eyes adjusted to the brightness. His pulse slowed, and he grinned at his brothers in earnest. Although he didn't want to admit it, they had surprised him. If it had been Caddoc and his minions, it might have been a fatal error. "Slow and soft, eh?" he muttered.

"I wanted Alex to pick a different spot to waylay you." Orion gestured toward the hundreds of bright-colored runes and hieroglyphics carved into the walls and the curved ceiling. "This place always did give me the creeps."

Alex chuckled. "I like it."

"I'm with you, Orion," Morgan agreed.

"You've got to admit that it's impressive," Alex said.

Morgan gazed around. It had been years since he'd been here, and he had to agree with Alex that it was impressive.

Columns, carved in the style of great shaggy-barked trees, and glowing red with an inner fire, stood at the corners, their intertwined branches and broad leaves spreading up into the ceiling. The walls were set with fire-baked tiles, the images on each one as bright and distinct as the day the artist had painted them. Every inch of exposed surface bore rows of story runes chronicling the founding and building of a city so old that no one could remember the name of it or where it had stood.

Morgan had always had a feeling that the echoing chamber was haunted by the ghosts of lost souls. It was not the bloody scenes of battle or sacrificed victims, the stepped pyramids, the sketches of sea monsters, or the rendering of an exploding volcano that had frightened him when he was small. It was the record of flying ships from the stars and the terrifying creatures that had traveled to this planet in them.

One star beast in particular had given Morgan repeated nightmares. The alien's purple face stared out at him with huge triangular eyes that the artist had set with iridescent shells, so that the gaze seemed to follow the viewer. So realistic was the starman's penetrating gaze that it had sent seven-year-old Morgan—who had once driven off a twenty-foot squid with only a child's trident—running to his mother in tears.

Yet, this ancient room, for all its power to enthrall, remained a testament to the imagination of men. Morgan wondered what Claire would think of it. Would she be afraid of the starmen? Or would she be intrigued by the egg-shaped spheres that they had piloted through the vast distances of space—impossibly shaped ships that bore no sails or rudders. The impulse to share this place with her seized him with surprising force.

"Have you seen him yet?" Alex asked, jerking Morgan out of his reverie and back to the present.

"What?"

"Our sire," Orion said. "The king. Have you talked to him?"

Morgan shook his head. "Poseidon? No, I haven't."

He hadn't spoken with either of their parents. His father would be disappointed in him and would tell him so in no uncertain terms, but he hoped the high queen would be more sympathetic. Technically, Korinna was his stepmother, but she had filled the role of mother in every sense for so long that he could barely remember the face of the woman who had given birth to him.

"You'll have to stand trial," Alex said, laying a broad hand on his shoulder. "Caddoc made a formal charge."

"I thought he would."

"That bitch Halimeda and her clan will be after your blood." Orion scowled and tapped the hilt of his sword.

No courtly weapons for Orion; his was one of a kind, forged of some black, almost obsidianlike, metal. The hilt was silver, worked to the exact shape of Orion's hand, and the blade a yard long and the width of a big man's hand, so sharp that a human male could shave with it. Orion claimed that the sword was made of part of a starman's flying ship, but Orion was full of fancy, and Morgan never knew just what was true and what was for effect.

Lady Halimeda, Caddoc's mother and one of his father's minor wives, was a greater threat than her son. It was Halimeda who had fired the jealousy and ambition in Caddoc's heart. Morgan believed her quite capable of poisoning anyone, even Poseidon, if she thought it would advance her schemes. And she could call on a large family of allies to back her.

"Lady Halimeda after my blood is nothing new," Morgan said. "I'd be more concerned if she defended me. Then I'd know that I was scheduled for a fatal dose of something, sooner rather than later." Some called Halimeda a sorceress, but Morgan didn't think so. She was a beautiful and sensual being. It was more likely that it was the spell she spun in his father's bed rather than an alliance with the powers of darkness that gave her clout.

"Alex wanted to challenge Caddoc to a duel," Orion said, "but I told him that it might only make things worse."

"It would if you killed him." Morgan said to Alex. "You'd be banished." The murder of one Atlantean by another was the greatest sin, unfortunately one that did take place from time to time.

"Somebody's going to have to," Alex replied brusquely. "It may as well be me as you. I'm not the crown prince."

Alex's easygoing exterior masked the heart of a lethal killer. Morgan had no doubt that Alex was capable of making good on his suggestion, but he didn't want to think of the consequences.

"Let's go," Orion said.

Ducking under a low archway, Morgan followed him through a labyrinth of intertwining hallways, with Alex close behind. Some passageways led deeper into the ocean floor; others ascended stone ramps that led to glorious receiving rooms, splendid with the treasures of ancient civilizations. Now and then they passed a guard, a group of nobles, or one of those who served the inhabitants of the palace. But other than a salute, a bow, or a word of greeting, none were rude enough to disturb the royal trio's conversation.

One final marble staircase and Orion turned left into his quarters. They crossed the ornate garden with the Babylonian mineral spring pool, the massive urns that had once stood outside a king's palace in Crete, and rows of purple swaying kelp. Immediately, small sea creatures ventured out to nudge against Orion, hoping for treats. There were schools of tiny emerald-green fish, three spirited, young sea horses, and a lazy sting ray. Orion paused to scratch the scarred old ray's back and offer a tidbit, which the ray took daintily.

For a warrior of the highest rank, Orion had a love of beauty and a knack for growing things, fish, mammal, and plant life. When not engaged in defending his kingdom, he was quite happy puttering in his own yard, transplanting flowers and harvesting vegetables, fruit, and seaweed.

"You should have been a farmer," Alex teased, giving the ray a pat.

"I might have, in gentler times," Orion agreed. "Or if I hadn't been born a son of Poseidon."

Morgan shrugged. "And when were there gentler times?"

In the inner courtyard, high-backed benches surrounded a low marble table. Latticework of living coral, softened by swaying twelve-foot high fronds of kelp, formed a backdrop. Blue and yellow schools of fish swam through the coral wall and around the Etruscan marble statues, adding to the beauty of the area. As the brothers took seats at the table, several servants came rushing from the house to welcome Morgan with open arms and ask if the princes desired food or drink.

Morgan greeted them by name and exchanged hugs. They were people he had known for many centuries and were more like friends than staff. They spoke briefly and Morgan asked after their families before Orion waved them away with the excuse that he hadn't seen his older brother in months and the king would be expecting him.

When the three were alone, Orion leaned forward and grasped Morgan's forearm in a hard grip. "We were worried about you. Is it true you saved a human from drowning, or is this another of Caddoc's lies?"

Morgan nodded. "A fisherman. Just a boy. I couldn't stand by and let him die."

Alex listened intently as Morgan related his tale. When he'd finished, Alex asked, "What you did is against the law, true enough, but it's not something I haven't done. Your mistake was being caught."

"True enough," Morgan agreed. He looked from one to the other, noting the new scar on Orion's chest and the faint marks of a recent battle with a shark that bisected Alex's shoulder and upper arm.

A flicker of a smile played over Alex's lips. "Why do I

think you're not telling us everything? You're in deeper trouble than you've admitted, aren't you?"

Orion raised an eyebrow. "If I didn't know my saintly brother better, I'd suspect a woman might be involved."

"You always have women on your mind," Morgan said.

"Right. Out with it," Alex said.

Morgan glanced from one to the other again and slowly exhaled, wondering if he should confide in the two of them. They were, after all, utterly trustworthy, and three heads might be better than one in working out his dilemma concerning Claire. He had other brothers, some he loved dearly, but none were as close to him as these two.

"Well?" Orion said.

"Let's hear it," Alex echoed.

The twins were identical, blond, and nearly as tall as Morgan, equally endowed with muscle and intelligence. Both men wore the blue-and-gold kilt and insignia of the elite warrior class. Orion's chest band also bore four silver tridents, signifying an officer who had led his company into suicide missions four times, and lived to tell the tale. Alex had won his share of awards, but disdained to display them. In wartime, he was more effective working alone, often as an assassin.

Although he was the oldest and crown prince, Morgan suspected that either of these two brothers would make a better king than he would be. Certainly, both were fearless warriors; Orion was slightly more levelheaded in leading troops, but if he were pressed, Morgan's choice for the throne would have been Alex, younger of the twins, with his intense intuitive powers. Poseidon had to be strong and possess great leadership qualities, but most important, he had to be wise. Right now, Morgan felt lacking in all those attributes.

"It is a woman," Orion said. "He's thinking with his phallus. What have you done now, Morgan?"

Alex's penetrating gaze met Morgan's. "It's a human woman, isn't it?"

"By Zeus's foreskin, you're right!" Orion's eyes widened in surprise. "I didn't think you had it in you, big brother." He laughed. "How was she?"

Morgan tensed, anger rising up from deep inside. "It's not like that," he muttered. "I didn't—"

"You're a saint." Orion shrugged. "You're not the first, and you won't be the last to break that commandment. Human females can be delicious."

"Speak for yourself," Alex corrected. "I've never seen one I'd be willing to risk my career for, but I'm not the expert." Alex gestured at his twin. "He's fathered more than one half-human babe in the last century."

"I'm cutting back," Orion insisted. "I haven't been with a human female in—"

"Months," his twin finished. "What about that Maori girl, the one with the outrigger canoe? The one who tried to brain you with a club?"

"Pania is not part of this discussion." Orion scowled at Alex.

"I'm just saying." Alex rolled his eyes. "That oldest boy of hers could swim underwater longer than any human child—"

"That boy is a great-grandfather. It happened a long time ago."

"So it's not just a rumor," Morgan put in. "You have fathered—"

Orion fisted his right hand and smacked it in his left. "I just told you. It was a long time ago." His brow tightened and his green eyes took on a hard edge.

"Maybe by human standards," Alex said. "And the Maori woman did try to kill him."

Morgan could see that Orion was no longer amused by the turn of the conversation. "I didn't have intercourse with her," he said, "but I wanted to."

"I know where you're coming from. As I said, they can be very alluring." Orion's sea-green eyes clouded, as though he were remembering another time and another place. "And for the record, Pania thought I was a shark when she hit me."

"And why was that?" Alex taunted. "Could it be because you had cast an illusion over her, so that she saw a hammerhead?"

"It was a white, not a hammerhead. And it was a good spell. Three fishermen on the beach thought I was a shark, as well."

Morgan got to his feet. "I suppose I should be happy that I'm not the only sinner in the family, but I'd hoped to get your advice on what to do about my problem. And she's not a great-grandmother."

"You're mad for her?" Orion asked seriously.

Morgan nodded. "It seems that way."

"Does she have a name, this human?" Alex asked, no longer joking.

"Claire."

"And is she beautiful?" Alex nodded. "I think she is, but not in the usual way. There's something very different about her, isn't there?"

"Yes," Morgan admitted. "There is." He didn't want to share more, even with these two brothers he loved. He didn't understand what he felt for Claire, and he wasn't ready to try to explain it. "What I wanted to ask was if this had ever happened to you, and what you did about it."

"Absolutely," Orion replied. "And my advice is to take

what's offered, enjoy it, and move on. They aren't like us. They're simple beings, but they can get under your skin if you don't satisfy your itch."

"Father will take this seriously," Alex said. "Before you appear before the council, you should talk to the queen," Alex suggested. "Give her time to consult with Poseidon before your crime is discussed in the open court. Let him vent his anger privately."

Morgan's gut clenched. "They know about Claire, then?"

"Sweet Hades, no," Orion said. "Not a whisper. I have it that the charges are just those concerning the fishermen and the human boy. If they knew about your human female, my friend would know."

Alex nodded. "Pillow talk. Lady Ambrosia is very friendly with our brother, almost as fond of his sexual aerobics as she is gossip, and she shares every shred of it with him."

Morgan sank back onto the bench, his relief overwhelming. Not that he could expect to walk free on the human contact charge. But if Caddoc and his mother were aware of Claire, her life might be in danger. Or they might use her to destroy him. If he got out of his current mess, *when* he got out of it, the best thing he could do for Claire would be to forget he'd ever seen her. The farther he stayed from her beach, the better for them both.

"I say go directly to the king," Orion advised. "He'll be furious, and he'll roar like a bull walrus, but he'll think you weak if you ask for Mother's help."

"The last time we were alone together, he was so mad at me that he exiled me to the southern polar regions," Morgan said. "I was counting penguins and chipping ice off my scales for three years." He grimaced. No, Poseidon would not be pleased.

His relations with his father had never been the best. The king had been a great general and expected his heir to be a fire-breathing warrior, not a poet who preferred the quiet battle of preserving the whales, stopping oil spills, and rescuing lobsters, Morgan thought ruefully. The twins should have been born first; they were more like Father.

"You know how Poseidon feels about humans," Alex cautioned. "The sooner they die of thirst or starve to death, the better. He'd as soon be rid of them before they destroy every drop of saltwater on the planet."

Morgan didn't remind them that his father's hate for those who walked the earth went much deeper—that his first wife, their mother, had died at the hands of humans. Morgan didn't need to repeat what they'd had pounded into their minds as children. No, his rescue of a human boy would not go down well with Poseidon, high king of Atlantis. Not well at all.

In a penthouse overlooking Central Park, Richard Bishop stood with a drink in his hand and stared down at the horse-drawn carriage below. The driver was garbed in eighteenth-century costume—or at least a tourist-friendly version of the attire, including white wig and tricorn. The horse pulling the gold-and-black conveyance was a bright sorrel. The color reminded him of a five-year-old hunter he'd purchased in Kentucky for Claire when she was eleven.

"Cloud's Scarlet Tanager" had been the mare's name. Claire had adored her, and she'd taken a slew of trophies and blue ribbons in dressage. He'd had the animal flown from one coast to the other so that Claire could enter the maximum number of shows possible when she was home from boarding school.

Richard drained the drink and placed the empty glass on a tray. Claire had been born with the natural talent of an athlete and the drive to excel. He had expected her to bring home the gold in the Olympics, but that dream had died with all his others for her.

Now, he just wanted to keep her alive.

She was all he had, and he loved her with every fiber of his being. Nothing else mattered but Claire. He had to reach her, had to give her a reason to live before she slipped out of his hands forever.

Deciding that something had to be done, he picked up his cell and pressed Justin's office number. After four rings, a receptionist picked up.

"I'm sorry, sir, but Dr. Warren is with a patient. What is your call in regards to? I'll be happy to take a message," the twit said after he'd requested to speak to Justin. Richard had seen her—all boobs and no brain. He doubted if she could even remember the date, let alone how to transfer a call.

"This is Richard Bishop of the law firm of Roberts, Simon, and Bishop. And this is an emergency. Put me through to Justin immediately, or I give you my word you'll be hunting for a new position tomorrow," Richard said in his sternest courtroom voice. "Now, Ms. O'Brian."

"Please hold."

Elevator music blared in his ear. Richard waited: thirty seconds, a minute, two, before another click sounded.

"Hello, Richard, this is Justin. Has something happened to Claire?"

Richard heard a woman in the background before Justin told her to shut up. Richard switched his phone to loud speaker and poured more whiskey over his melting ice cubes. He heard the deeper murmur of a male, not Justin, but a man with an Eastern European accent. Then Justin's smooth professional voice filled the room again.

"Is Claire all right?"

"No, I don't think she is," Richard answered. "That's

why I called. Her depression seems to have taken a down-ward turn. I'm very concerned."

"Did you tell her that I'd be happy to see her?"

"I did. She refused."

Richard had never been particularly fond of his son-in-law when he and Claire were married, but Justin had a fine reputation and excellent credentials. He knew about Justin's straying, of course, but a lot of men did that. Hell, he'd done that many times before he and Elaine had finally called it quits. It was something Justin and Claire should have been able to work out with counseling. He'd always thought Claire had been hasty to seek a divorce.

"She refused?"

"Yes," Richard said. "And frankly, Justin, I don't know what to do next."

"She may not be in a position to make decisions, con-sidering her condition. Would you like to meet for dinner? Discuss this at length?"

"I'd like that. I'm afraid . . ." Richard hesitated and then continued in a rush. "I'm afraid she may be suicidal."

CHAPTER 6

Justin waved away the woman and turned his back to her and Sergei. Justin's erection continued to deflate as he exchanged a few more words with Claire's father and promised to call back with a time and place to meet to discuss her condition. Once he'd gotten Richard off the phone, he buzzed the front desk and told Crystal in no uncertain terms that he was not to be disturbed again before the next patient was due. On second thought, he told her that he would be leaving the office, due to an emergency. She should cancel his last two appointments and leave early.

"I'll be paid for the whole day, won't I, Doctor?"

"Absolutely. Now hustle Mr. Johns and Miss Farsette out of the waiting room and go. Clear the waiting room before I find something more for you to do." He ended the call and turned back to the waiting couple. "Where were we?" he said.

Obediently, the brunette dropped to her knees. Sergei resumed the position and soon was pumping away with his oversized equipment. Justin dimmed the lights, turned up the music, and returned to the couch. He liked to get in the mood by watching before they turned their attention to him.

This was a different partner than the Romanian usually worked with. Bunny? Honey? Whatever she called herself, Justin approved of her musky perfume and pouty red lips. He hoped she was as creative with that mouth as Sergei had promised.

The bitch was slightly sleazy and young, but not too young, the way he liked them. He'd threatened the agent after she'd sent him an underage girl a few months ago, and he'd had to refuse her services. The agent had provided a replacement, a Russian transsexual, but his evening had been ruined by the delay. Justin liked to gamble, but not on something so dangerous as having sex with a minor. There were too many luscious partners over eighteen to risk his career and position.

Justin moistened his lips with his tongue. Yes, this Bunny was almost perfect, dumb and innocent looking— but not too innocent by the way she was taking all of Sergei's impressive length or her quick little grunts of pleasure.

Justin applied spearmint balm to his lips and shaft and removed two capsules from the false bottom of a sculpture of the god Pan despoiling a naiad. The ten-inch statue was a museum copy that he'd fallen in love with and had altered. It had been expensive, but he thought Pan appeared quite sophisticated displayed on the dark walnut table beside the red leather couch.

Justin was anxious to talk to Richard about Claire, but not so anxious that he would ruin a perfectly enjoyable afternoon. Claire could wait. Few worthwhile things in life were gained by heedless haste. He lay back against the headrest and washed the capsules down with a swallow of energy water. He was certain that he would need all of his energy before he was finished with his latest playthings.

*   *   *

It was late afternoon, and a chill breeze was whipping off the water, sending grains of sand and the occasional gull feather swirling across Seaborne's beach pavilion when the housekeeper appeared at Claire's side. "You've been down here all day." Mrs. Godwin scowled and clutched her tweed sweater around her. "The sun has gone in."

"It's June," Claire reminded her, noticing that Mrs. Godwin had tied a green-and-orange checked wool scarf around her head. The woman hated ocean wind blowing in her ears and always swore it gave her an earache.

"I don't care if it's August. If I'm cold, it's too chilly for you in your delicate condition."

"I'm not pregnant."

The housekeeper narrowed her eyes. "There's no need for sarcasm. You know what I meant. You aren't strong."

"I'm as strong as a horse. Just a crippled one." Claire turned her gaze back to the ocean. She didn't like scarves or hats, and she'd never had an earache since she was a small child. She loved the wind off the ocean, the stronger the better. It made her feel alive.

"They used to shoot horses when they broke their legs," she continued. "Now they just use an injection to put them down. I'm not sure it's any more humane."

"We're not talking about horses," Mrs. Godwin said. "Your father wouldn't approve of this. You're not behaving sensibly."

Claire didn't answer. She was cold, but she wasn't about to admit it. She'd been here on the pavilion since morning. She'd waited and watched, straining her eyes, hoping to see Morgan stroll up the beach or rise out of the waves like a merman, or a silky, or one of those mythological beings her *Green Fairy Tale Book* had been full of.

She'd been a fan of fairy tales when she was a child: *Red*

Fairy Tale Book, *Yellow*, and *Green*; she'd cherished them all. Books and horses had meant everything to her. And now, she'd never feel the beautiful majesty of a horse under her, or possess the concentration to read again.

She tried to lose herself in the magic of novels, but after a few pages, she'd find that her eyes were playing tricks on her. The words were beginning to blur and there were white spaces scattered across the text. She began to forget if she'd read a paragraph or not. Instead, she found herself reduced to scanning magazines and watching DVDs.

She wanted Morgan to return with every fiber of her being. She'd tried to tell herself that she hadn't imagined him, that he'd appear, just as he had before. She could see every feature of his handsome face, the width of his brow, and every curve of his lips. She pictured herself laughing with him, sharing the lunch that now stood wilting on the table. She'd forced herself to take a bite of her salad an hour or two ago, but it had tasted like hay. When he had been here with her, she'd been ravenous. Whatever she'd put in her mouth had seemed heavenly.

"Miss Claire? Are you listening to me?" Mrs. Godwin took hold of her wrist. "Your pulse seems erratic."

Claire pulled her arm out of the woman's grasp. "I'm fine. My pulse rate is normal and, in any case, you aren't a medical professional."

"Please, Miss Claire. You've got to stop this childish behavior. It's not my place to question your—"

"Exactly, Mrs. Godwin, it's not your place. My body may be a wreck, but I have enough sense left to know what I want. Please, leave me alone. I'll come when I'm ready. If you'd like, take the evening off. You and Nathaniel go to town and see a movie or catch up on your shopping. I'm perfectly capable of getting something out of the refrigerator if I'm hungry later."

* * *

Morgan didn't come that day, and he didn't come the next. Claire was late getting down to the beach on the third day because of physical therapy, but again, she waited in vain for him to appear. Hope had dimmed. Now she was bargaining with herself.

Certainly, all that nonsense about swimming to a cave and having him kiss her and touch her . . . the lovemaking . . . that had to be a dream. She could see that. But Morgan hadn't been a dream. He had been here.

When her cell rang, she had the crazy idea that it might be him on the other end, but she quickly realized that it was her father calling. "Hi, Richard," she chirped, trying to sound cheerful.

"How are you?"

"Fine. Stop worrying. You're as bad as Mrs. Godwin."

"You must be bored to death up there. When's the last time you talked to someone other than Mrs. G. or one of the staff?"

"For your information, I've been bird watching. I've identified four new species in the last two days. I got a really great book online."

"I meant human interaction, Claire, not birds."

She made a sound of amusement. "Not just birds. I met a fascinating man two days ago." Oops, she hadn't meant to mention Morgan to her father. It just popped out. Now, she was in for it. She steeled herself for the lecture.

"Where? Who is he? Did he come to the house?"

"Stop," she protested. "You're not questioning a trial witness. My visitor wasn't a salesman, and he wasn't collecting for a charity. I met him here on the beach, and he was perfectly respectable." Not exactly the entire truth, she admitted to herself, but close enough. After all, the whole underwater scene and the hot sex was a dream. Morgan wasn't responsible for that.

"How did he get on your beach? And where was Nathaniel? What do you pay him for, if not for security?"

Claire drummed her fingers nervously on the table. What was wrong with her that she'd brought Morgan up with Richard? She must be losing her marbles. "Nathaniel is a gardener and handyman besides security. I imagine he was mowing the lawn. But, you aren't listening to me. In case you've forgotten, I'm not a child anymore."

"Your insistence on distancing yourself from me and your friends makes that quite clear."

Claire felt her cheeks growing warm. He knew how to push all her buttons. "What friends? My real friends have gone on with their lives. They have careers, husbands, children."

"You could have a career."

"In what? Teaching? My degree is in Classical Greek and Roman History. I might be able to roll my wheelchair into a classroom, but my short-term memory would make my lectures dull to say the least. Or maybe I could go into research. Oops, I can't read for more than ten minutes at a time, can I? Wait, I could write a book. 'Twelve Steps to Losing Your Mind.' "

"That's enough," Richard snapped. "You're making a career out of self-pity. As for marriage, you had a husband, and you were unhappy then too."

"Great point."

"I'm sorry." His voice cracked. "I know Justin did things that you found—"

"Deceitful? Disgusting?"

"You're right, I'm out of line. I shouldn't have brought Justin into this."

"No, you shouldn't."

"I thought you two had a civilized divorce."

"I don't hate him, if that's what you mean."

"Then you should consider seeing him. He's concerned about you."

"I'm sure." She was so angry with Richard that she wanted to hang up on him, but that would be immature. Adults had disagreements with other adults, and they talked it out. "I should never have mentioned having a conversation on my own beach with a pleasant and educated man. It's what women my age do. It's what women of any age enjoy doing."

"You're an innocent. Don't you realize that you're a very wealthy woman in an extremely vulnerable position? This isn't like you, Claire. You could be taken advantage of. How do you know this man isn't staking out the house for a burglary?"

"I suppose he must be." Now, she couldn't keep the sharpness out of her voice. "Why else would he bother to talk to me? What could I possibly have to say that would interest a man who didn't want to rob me?"

"That isn't what I meant at all, and you know it. Don't cry, pumpkin. I didn't call to upset you. I think you should come home. We'll try another specialist."

"No, we won't. And if you can't rein in your wild imagination, this conversation is over," she said.

"Claire . . ."

"Claire, nothing. I love you, but I'm finished with this father-daughter chat, and I'm not taking any more calls from you until tomorrow. 'Bye." She hit the end button and dropped the cell phone on the table. She was so upset that her hands were trembling.

She loved her father. She really did. But since the accident, he'd tried to control her life, and she was sick of it.

If only she could find her birth mother . . . Deep inside,

Claire knew that she hadn't given her up because she didn't love her. Whoever she was—wherever she was, her mother would understand.

At least Claire hoped her biological mother would be more loving than Elaine had been. The most she'd ever received from her father's wife was a cool indifference and strict rules about not leaving the nursery wing unless she was accompanied by her nanny. If Richard was in residence, which was rare because her father had traveled extensively during her childhood, he spoiled her rotten. He insisted she have breakfast and supper with the adults and be introduced when there were guests. When Richard was away, Elaine preferred her to be invisible.

When she was very small, Claire could remember a beloved stuffed pony that she'd slept with every night. She toted Nay-Nay everywhere and carried on endless conversations, where she spoke for both herself and the toy. But one afternoon, when she was five, her nanny took her shopping for new riding boots. She was so excited about the purchase that she'd forgotten Nay-Nay and left him on the bathroom floor.

When they returned to the penthouse, Claire was feeling out of sorts and feverish. Badly wanting her snuggle buddy, she ran to find Nay-Nay, but the stuffed pony was nowhere to be found. She remembered racing from room to room, crying and calling his name. She'd been so upset that she'd vomited all over the new black leather boots and one of Elaine's prize Tibetan prayer rugs.

Her mother had so been furious that she'd smacked her across the face. Claire could still remember the shock of being struck for the first time. She barely remembered being bathed and banished to bed. The following day, Richard came home and called a pediatrician who confirmed a severe case of German measles. Her father had sat rocking her for hours while she wept, still inconsolable over the loss of her favorite toy.

Later, she'd learned of the pony's fate when she overheard the maid and cook discussing Nay-Nay's mysterious disappearance. Elaine had discovered the toy on the bathroom floor, carried it to the garbage chute, and tossed it, saying that it was high time that Claire learned to not to leave her belongings carelessly strewn around the penthouse. She had never forgiven Elaine.

Now, staring out over the white caps, something still ached deep inside for that child. She'd imagined many fates for Nay-Nay over the years. Maybe a garbage collector had rescued him and taken him home to his own little girl, who'd loved him and slept with him every night. Or, perhaps, Nay-Nay hadn't been a stuffed toy at all. He might have been magic, as Richard had said. The pony might have come to life, scrambled out of the garbage truck, and set off on a world of adventures. He might even have made it back to the North Pole where Santa's elves had sewn up his boo-boos and given him a new mane and tail. It was possible that Nay-Nay had flown in Santa's sleigh and ended up under a Christmas tree for a second time. Every Christmas morning, Claire had hoped that she'd find Nay-Nay there, all new and soft, and smelling of pine boughs, but he never was.

She'd waited in vain for her stuffed pony, just as she was waiting in vain for Morgan to return to her. She was a woman now, not a small child, but she felt just as helpless and every bit as heartbroken.

"Do you realize the position you've put me in?" Poseidon demanded.

"I do, Father," Morgan answered, "and I'm sorry, but I couldn't stand by and watch the boy drown."

The two stood on a balcony off his father's private apartments overlooking the wide, columned avenue that ran from the walled palace gardens to the forum. One of the most beautiful sections of Atlantis spread before them: the Library of Light, the Hall of Justice, the Old College of Science, and the twin Centers for Healing. In the distance, Morgan could make out the stepped pyramid that housed the Hall of Poetry and the great Silver Tower.

The city was immense, spreading out for three miles in every direction.

Morgan always felt humbled when he viewed Atlantis from these heights. How could anyone expect him to rule over this ancient civilization with the wisdom and dedication his father had?

"A human?" the king shouted. "The race that murdered your mother? You have pity for one of them?"

Morgan nodded. "For a child, yes."

"Have you forgotten her death?"

How could he forget? His mother had taken him on a journey to see the splendors of the land of ice at the top of the world. He might not remember her features, but he could recall her soft voice as she'd shown him icebergs and glaciers, powerful white bears, and a myriad of sea creatures that lived under the pack ice.

She'd taught him how to control his body so that he could leave the sea and walk on the surface. And when a whaling ship appeared, she warned him of the treachery of humans. The ice was too thick to dive to safety, and the hole they had come up through was in the distance. In desperation, his mother had cast a net of illusion, so that the men wouldn't see them in their true forms, but as seals. It had been a fatal mistake. The humans had fired a harpoon that pierced her heart.

She could have used her healing powers to maintain her

life force until she could scramble back to the water's edge. Instead, she ordered him to flee. Her spell protected him until he reached safety, but she could not protect herself. Her illusion wavered, and she returned to her true form.

Crying that they had shot a mermaid, the sailors dragged her body onto the ship. He supposed that the humans meant to take his mother back to their own land to display as a trophy, but he couldn't allow that. Too small to sink the ship himself, Morgan had summoned up a pod of killer whales.

Although the killer whales were another race not to be trusted, the human hunters were a greater enemy. The leader of the pod directed his strongest males to ram the hull of the ship. It had not taken many blows to crack the timbers and send the frigid water pouring into the hold. The ship and all hands were lost to the deep, but there was no reviving his beloved mother. She, queen of Atlantis, most beautiful and gentle of all mothers, was lost to him.

"Have you forgotten?" Poseidon repeated.

Morgan blinked back stinging moisture. "Never."

On any other subject but humans, his father was reasonable. But he had more patience with a flesh-eating bacteria or a primeval slime slug than a land dweller. Morgan had mourned his mother; in some ways he still did, but he didn't blame all humans for those who had murdered her. And he didn't want to imagine what his father would think about his desire for a human woman . . . for his emotional attachment to Claire.

"Do you believe that I can treat you differently than I would treat an Atlantean who wasn't my son? My heir?"

Morgan shook his head. "I didn't come here to ask for special treatment or to beg forgiveness." He hadn't seen Poseidon in months, and he was surprised to see that much of his father's beard was now as white as his long,

curling locks of hair. He was by no means old, not by Atlantean standards, still strong and virile with the stamina
of a man half his age. Alex had mentioned that their father
had just taken a new wife, number seventeen, and she was
already quickening with child.

"It's a good thing you didn't, for you'll not receive it,"
Poseidon declared. "A king must not put himself or his
family above the law. You're not my only son, you know."

"Yes, my lord." Morgan nodded his head slightly in
agreement. "Doubtless, you have many sons more worthy
than I."

"By Zeus's shaft there are! A quiver full."

Of that Morgan was well aware. He acknowledged
twenty-two sisters and more than thirty brothers. Boys
outnumbered the girls, although most of the younger children were girls. Not all were in line for the throne. It
would be a male who assumed Poseidon's throne when his
father grew too old to govern. In some of the far-flung
colonies, among other species of water dwellers, women
could inherit the crown, but not in Atlantis. It was their
custom that a king pass on the crown while he still lived,
so that he could be certain of his heir. The eldest was the
usual choice, but not always.

"Look at me when I speak to you."

Biting back his resentment, Morgan turned to face his
father. Dressed in full court attire, Poseidon was an impressive sight. His toga was gold, his sandals set with glittering emeralds. He wore a wide golden torque and
armbands, each covered with ancient and mystical symbols.
For formal occasions, such as the hearing before the council, he would don a magnificent crown, but he didn't need
a crown to mark him as king. His carriage, his steely expression, his utter confidence left no doubt as to his rank.

But when Morgan's gaze fixed on his father's face, he

saw tears trickling down his cheeks. Shocked speechless, Morgan's breath caught in his throat.

"More worthy, perhaps. Sons wiser or bolder," Poseidon said, dropping his voice to a low growl. "But none that I love as I love you." He threw out his massive arms and hugged Morgan. "For all my hard words . . ." The king cleared his throat, hugged his son once more and released him. "But you're still too soft where humans are concerned."

"Perhaps not all humans are our enemies."

"All!" Poseidon stepped away from him. "You are as stubborn as always. May it give you consolation when you are found guilty and imprisoned for ten years in some ice block in the Antarctic."

CHAPTER 7

The Hall of Justice was crowded with Morgan's brothers and sisters, his aunts and uncles and cousins, as well as nobles and public officials of every rank, all garbed in their finest attire. Of all the state buildings, Morgan had always thought this one the most beautiful.

Sixty-foot pillars carved of glistening, black marble supported an arched ceiling decorated with scenes of coral reefs and sea life. The white marble walls framed swirls of white marble flooring, accented with black. Great filigreed, oval-shaped windows stretched from floor to ceiling, paned with sheets of iridescent shell that cast waves of shimmering light across the vast interior. So carefully had the vast building been engineered, that the acoustics were a marvel, making certain that every word spoken from the royal dais or the High Council's round stage could be heard in the farthest row.

Across the chamber, in the raised boxes reserved for Poseidon's wives and children, Caddoc's mother, the Lady Halimeda, sat among her family and supporters. As usual, she wore not the customary white for the Hall of Justice, but all black. Glorying in her attentive audience, she pretended nonchalance as she fed tidbits to a red octopus that undulated over one shoulder and wrapped thin tentacles around her body. Since the box and railing were white marble and the others in her group were garbed in white, Lady Halimeda and her pet drew the gazes of all who entered.

Morgan knew that she had noticed him as well. He made a point of halting and nodding to her with exaggerated respect. She glared back at him, turned her head sharply, and murmured something to her nearest lady-in-waiting. Her companions snickered.

Many courtiers considered Halimeda a great beauty with her long, ink-black hair and sensual body, but Morgan never had. Her smile was too artificial, her pale blue eyes too cold. She was younger than his stepmother, but Morgan had always felt Queen Korinna the more attractive of the two. Certainly, she was more loved by her subjects. One thing Halimeda lacked was a kind heart. *Perhaps*, Morgan thought, *the lady has no heart at all.*

Caddoc was there in the front row, with Jason beside him. Morgan didn't see the Samoan, but he may not have been admitted as he couldn't prove his rank. In the trial of one of the royal family, only those of noble blood were admitted. Morgan spotted Alexandros and Orion with his favorite sister Morwena. She waved, and threw him a kiss.

The king's throne sat empty, but the queen had already taken her place on the dais and was talking to the vizier. Morgan had visited her briefly after he'd seen his father, and she'd welcomed him as though he was of her own blood. The queen had given birth to four girls and three boys over the years. Morwena was the eldest and Morgan adored her.

On either side of Queen Korinna stood priests, priestesses, and other dignitaries. In the center of the chamber on a raised platform sat the revered members of the High Council, the wisest noblemen and women of the kingdom who would hear the charges, his guilty plea, and decide his fate.

Morgan knew every person on the council, including the Lady Halimeda's brother, Lord Pelagias. Morgan didn't particularly like him, but his judgments were always fair. A guilty or innocent vote had to be unanimous but, in sentencing a defendant who pleaded guilty, the majority ruled. Sitting next to Lord Pelagias was the chief justice, the lovely Lady Athena. If there was one vote in his favor Morgan could be certain of, it would be hers. She was his mother's cousin and well-liked for her gentle heart and willingness to stand firm when she believed in a decision. In addition, the Lady Athena was known for her sympathy toward humans.

Today, Morgan had put aside his sharkskin kilt and sandals. Instead, he wore pure white, a short toga in the same style that the Greeks had copied from the Atlanteans long ago. This was a solemn occasion, and one not even royalty could take lightly. In Atlantis, Poseidon was king, but the monarch's duty was to serve his people and see that laws were obeyed. If the court decided against Morgan, his father's wishes counted for nothing. Not that Morgan looked for any leniency from the king. Despite his father's rare show of affection today, Poseidon was still displeased with him. So it had been since he was a child.

Sentinels announced the high king's approach with a blast of conch shells and a roll of drumbeats. The queen glanced up and smiled as Poseidon strode across the chamber and took his place beside her. No palace guard or warriors accompanied him; they were forbidden to enter the Hall of Justice unless they were noblemen or women witnessing the trial as citizens.

Morgan waited impatiently as the vizier made a speech

welcoming Poseidon and his queen and telling everyone present what they already knew. They had assembled to witness the sentencing of the crown prince for a serious violation of the law against consorting with humans.

Zale, a tall, dignified man with dark hair and eyes of a particular violet hue, had the voice of a lion. He used his full range of vocal talent to remind those present that although the people of earth originated in the sea, the two races were now divided by eons of history. He recounted the facts that the humans had lost their glittering blue scales and assumed a smooth, nearly hairless skin—that their hands and feet no longer aided them in swimming, and they had lost the ability to breathe underwater.

"All these things the humans have lost, and yet they consider the Atlanteans, their sea cousins, to be monsters. Living on the surface of the earth has made humans weak of body and sick in spirit. Some of them even consider us to be nothing more than myth. This falsehood must be encouraged because the safety of every man, woman, and child in Atlantis depends on keeping the kingdom a secret from the land-dwelling barbarians."

Morgan choked back his impatience and waited respectfully for Zale to finish his speech. The vizier was a good man, intelligent, pure of heart, and faithful to the crown. He also loved to hear the sound of his own voice. Any other time, Morgan would be more forgiving, but he wanted this over with. Even today, facing disgrace and possible imprisonment, all he could think of was getting back to Claire.

"Humans are ignorant creatures," the vizier continued. "Polluting the earth and sea, killing for killing's sake, plundering without conscience. . . ."

After Zale had covered all the sins of human mankind and moved on to the dangers of trusting them, the queen interrupted him by rising to her feet and beginning to clap. One after another, the assembly stood, applauding and calling out their approval of the vizier's words. Drowned out by acclamation and praise, Zale smacked his staff of state three times on the floor and bowed to the High Council.

"Thank you, Vizier," Poseidon said. "Well said, well said." He signaled for another round of applause, and Zale returned to his place behind the king's throne, obviously well-pleased with himself.

Lady Athena, current chief justice of the High Council read the formalities of the charge and Morgan's plea of guilty. She waved him forward, asking him to explain, as concisely as possible, what had happened and why he had chosen to break the law to save a human.

Morgan complied, explaining how he'd used illusion to protect his identity and finished with the simple truth, the same statement he'd made to his brothers and father: "I couldn't stand by and see an innocent child drown needlessly. Under the same circumstances, I would do exactly the same thing again."

"Do you ask for the High Council's mercy?" Lady Athena demanded.

"I do," Morgan replied. "Not for me, but for the boy. He isn't our enemy."

"But he will be!" shouted Caddoc. "Prince Morgan has broken the law and shows no remorse."

"My nephew, Caddoc, speaks the truth," bellowed Lord Pelagias.

"Is Morgan above the law because he is a prince?" cried Lord Baeddan, another member of the council.

Other voices called out, some in Morgan's favor, others against. It was the custom that any nobleman or woman could speak before a decision and chaos often reigned before a vote was taken. But no one, least of all Morgan, expected the king to make a statement.

"I say he is guilty," Poseidon declared. A wave of shocked gasps, whispers, and cries of disbelief passed through the ranks of onlookers. Even the queen went suddenly pale.

Morgan kept his features immobile, trying to maintain his dignity, hoping the pain that knifed through him didn't show. *Father,* he thought. *Father* . . .

"I say my son is guilty, for this is not the first time this sort of transgression has occurred," the king continued. "Guilty of having a tender heart. Whether this is a good thing in a future monarch or not, that's for each of you to decide. For me, I have my own thoughts. I have never interfered in the High Council's trials before, and I, Poseidon, will not do so today. But as a father, who loves his firstborn, I ask for mercy. Perhaps, next time, he may allow his head to rule his heart."

There was a moment of stunned silence. Then the nobility and court alike rose and clapped to show approval. Morgan, alone, did not shout out the king's name. His throat tightened with emotion. He knew what the act had cost his father, and he loved him all the more for his courage.

"Poseidon! Poseidon! Poseidon!"

The decision, once order resumed, was a foregone conclusion and Morgan let out a sigh of relief. Lady Athena pronounced a formal admonition that Prince Morgan was found guilty, but worthy of mercy. This time he would face no punishment, but if he broke the law again, he would pay in full measure for his crime.

Two hours later, Morgan saluted his father, kissed his mother's cheek, and hurried out of the royal suite. His brothers Alex and Orion, and five of their friends accompanied him out of the palace.

"We're going to Heron's to celebrate," Alex said. "Come with us."

Morgan shook his head. "Another time, Brother." He felt dishonest, returning to Claire so soon after receiving mercy on the charges of consorting with humans, but he couldn't wait to see her again. He couldn't eat or sleep, could hardly think straight. He could hear her voice in his head, smell her scent. He had to go back. He could not live if he didn't see her again . . . find some way to get her out of his system . . . find a way to cool his fever for her.

Orion grimaced. "I hope you're not doing what I think you're doing."

"And that is?" Heron asked.

"Don't ask," Alex said, draping an arm around his neck. "Better not to know."

Morgan embraced his brothers, exchanged hugs and handclasps and slaps on the back from his friends. He was about to take his leave when Caddoc, the Samoan, Jason, and two more young men swept into the courtyard on horseback.

"There he is," Jason said loudly, gesturing toward Morgan. "The *prince*." His voice was slurred, as though he'd had too much to drink.

"My esteemed brother has to hide behind his father's throne." Caddoc yanked back on his sea horse's bridle and the creature tossed its head and twisted its great, curved tail. The beasts the group rode were giants of their species, reaching twenty hands at the withers. The cost of such a stallion was three years' salary for an officer of the palace guard. As likely to savage their riders as an opponent, sea horses were rarely used in battle. These animals appeared red-eyed and hard ridden.

"Watch your mouth. There's more than one prince here," Alex shouted back. Then to Morgan, he said, "Maybe we'd better teach them some manners."

"No." Morgan shook his head. "We want no trouble." He had no time to contend with his half-brother and his cronies today. When he and Caddoc faced off, he wanted them both sober, so that if he killed him, it would be a fair fight. He had no wish to face the court on a charge of murder.

"Speak for yourself." Orion adjusted his sword belt. "I'd like the chance to put Caddoc in his place." He lowered his voice. "And I wonder whose mounts they're riding. Jason and Caddoc might be able to afford the down payment on one of those beasts, but not the others. Their families aren't that wealthy."

"Unless they stole them." Alex looked thoughtful. "And then it would our duty to return the animals to their lawful owners, wouldn't it?"

"Did your mother plead your case?" Caddoc taunted.

Morgan darkened. "Ignore them."

"We could make it our affair," Orion said.

"No." Morgan shook his head.

"Come with us." Alex motioned toward an archway. "If you leave now, they're bound to follow. They might catch you alone somewhere."

"I'm not afraid of them," Morgan said.

Orion shrugged. "Alone, you could probably take Caddoc and one or two more. But do you want to face that many by yourself? I might, but—"

Alex laughed. "Listen to him. If there's one thing Orion isn't, it's humble."

"I'm just speaking the truth." Orion glanced back at Caddoc, and then at Morgan. "How long has it been since you went through warrior training? Maybe you need to brush up on—"

"My self-defense skills are sufficient to deal with our half-brother."

"Good enough," Alex said. "You go and do whatever is so important, and we'll make certain that Caddoc and crew are not in any condition to track you for a day or two." He glanced at Heron and their friends. "Gentlemen? Are you with me?" Grabbing a trident from a soldier passing by, Alex reversed it and launched himself across the courtyard.

In the space of a minute, Alex had seized Caddoc by one leg, yanked him off his mount, and set the other sea horses into a bucking frenzy. The riderless stallion unleashed its horned tail, took a chunk out of Jason's leg, and attacked another beast. Alex clawed his way up onto the plunging horse's neck and swung the trident, using the staff to knock Tora and a man named Creon off their stallions. Jason, bleeding, but still on his horse, hacked at Alex with his sword.

"What are you waiting for?" Orion shouted to Morgan as he sprinted toward the chaos. "Go! Now!" Laughing, Heron and the rest followed the twins into the melée.

Morgan hesitated, but quickly decided that no one other than Jason seemed to be directing killing blows. He put two fingers between his lips, gave a shrill whistle and summoned the Samoan's runaway stallion. He came, tail thrashing, eyes rolling, and mouth bared.

He was a magnificent creature, blue-green with red gills and yellow eyes. The bony plates that served as teeth were sharp and yellow, his wicked tail thick and muscular. A low, deep trumpeting sounded from the stallion's wide chest, an indication of both his bad temper and his willingness to attack.

"Ahh," Morgan crooned. "Shh, shh." Seizing hold of a handful of mane and a trailing rein, he flung himself into the saddle. The stallion exploded under him, lashing out with his mouth, twisting and wriggling to free himself. Morgan held on until he could catch the other rein.

The fight now spread across the courtyard with sea horses abandoning their riders and heading for the open sea as Atlanteans struggled in hand-to-hand combat. Palace security shouted orders to desist and spread out to try to restore civility. Amid the confusion, it was almost child's play for Morgan to guide his stallion after the runaway mounts.

Once they had reached the outskirts of the city, Morgan would cheerfully part with his reluctant transportation, but for now he welcomed the burst of speed. He might have a knack for enchanting other underwater species, but had no wish to be arrested for horse theft . . . not to mention the difficulty of putting up with his mount's horrendous bad breath.

A thousand miles to the west, Claire lingered in her bedroom, staring out at the gray ocean and thumbing absently through one of her grandmother's old photo albums. Raindrops pattered against the windowpanes, but it wasn't the rain that had brought her up from the beach before nightfall. To her annoyance, Nurse Wrangle had called Richard, who'd arranged for an internist to stop by and check on Claire.

Annoyed, she'd submitted to only the briefest of examinations before sending the physician on his way. By then, returning to the pavilion today seemed hopeless. She tried to reach her father by phone to protest, but got only the answering machine. Either he was out, or he was sitting in his library and waiting for her to calm down before talking to her.

On impulse, she'd put through a call to the detective agency, hoping to convince Kelly to reconsider and continue the investigation. After all, if she was willing to pay him, what difference should it make to him if there were no further leads at present? She wanted to ask if he would see what he could find out about her adoptive parents. It was possible that by searching their backgrounds extensively, he might learn something about the woman who'd given up her child to them.

When she was small, Claire used to try to imagine what her mother had looked like. She'd stare into a mirror, wondering if her eyes or nose were like her mother's, or if they'd shared the same color hair. Her biological father's identity wasn't something that she'd obsessed about. She had Richard; she didn't really need another father, but she needed a mother desperately.

Today, especially since she'd waited for Morgan to return and been disappointed, she wished more than anything she had a mother to talk to. It was selfish of Richard to deny her knowledge that he must have. Finding her birth mother wouldn't affect their relationship . . . it couldn't.

Detective Kelly was out, and the receptionist couldn't say when he'd return to the office, but Claire was able to leave a request on his voice mail. She ended by asking him to return her call. Nothing today, it seemed, was going to be easy.

But there was one thing she could accomplish. And that was to get rid of Nurse Wrangle. As soon as Claire could hire a replacement, she'd dismiss the Nazi woman in white. She called a private nursing agency that provided home service and was, once more, unable to reach a human.

She left a message on voice mail for someone to call her back.

"No Morgan, no detective, and no new nurse. Strike three," she muttered. "And . . . she's out!" No, this was definitely not her best day.

The only run scored was that Mrs. Godwin had a dentist appointment and Nathaniel had driven her. Except for Jackie, who cleaned until five, Claire had the house to herself. Sighing, she turned the page of the photo album.

When she was eight, Richard and Nana had thrown her a wonderful birthday party. Her father had even invited three of her best friends from the city and provided transportation for them and their nannies and/or mothers to come to Seaborne for a long weekend. Nana, an avid photographer, had recorded every hour of the event.

Richard had arranged for a group of Native American dancers to perform, and the whole theme of the party was an American Indian powwow. There were games with lovely prizes, pony rides, a cookout, and a real buffalo skin teepee for Claire and the girls to camp out in overnight. Looking at those pictures brought back wonderful memories.

Two of the girls had drifted out of her life in later years, but Mary Remington and she had remained close. Mary was married to a junior diplomat and living in Brazil. Claire had only seen her once since the accident. Not that Mary hadn't been supportive, but she had a job, a husband, and a two-year-old son.

Things I'll never have, Claire thought. Unbidden, a tear rolled down her cheek. She dashed it away. What was it Nana had always said? "If your eggs are broken, make an omelet."

Claire's eggs were broken, all right. Broken so badly

that she'd never put her eggs back together again, and the only omelet she could make of them was bitter and worthless. Twenty years from now, she'd still be here, surrounded by cats, listening to Nurse Wrangle babble, and baying at the moon.

"I won't be that empty woman," she whispered. "I can't."

The photo album slid off her lap onto the floor. It fell facedown, and the pages crumpled. Claire tried to retrieve it, but it was just out of reach. Instead, she rolled her chair back to the nightstand beside the bed, opened the drawer, and removed a small plastic bottle of pills. She unscrewed the safety cap and poured a handful into her palm.

It would be so easy, she thought. Everyone was out of the house but Jackie, and she'd soon be gone. A few swallows with water to wash them down, and all her problems would be over.

Another tear followed the first as she reached for her glass. . . .

CHAPTER 8

"Claire!"

She froze. She'd thought she heard someone call her name. Not from inside the house, but outside.

"Claire! It's Morgan!"

She tightened her hand around the pills, dumped them and the half-empty bottle into the nightstand drawer, and slammed it shut. She rolled to the window and unlatched the French doors that led to the wide balcony that ran along the front of the house.

It was still raining, not hard, but steady, tiny needles of rain striking her face and arms. Pushing the doors wide, she went out onto the railed balcony. Someone was standing at the edge of the bluff, a man.

"Morgan?" It was impossible. How could she hear him from her bedroom? But it had to be him. The wind whipped her hair and raindrops splashed her face, but she didn't care. It made her feel alive. "Morgan, is that you?"

He waved. "Come down! Or should I come up?"

Her mouth went dry. What should she do? It would take forever for her to get out of the house. What if he got bored and left before she could cover the distance in her chair? Should she invite him up to her bedroom? Richard's warnings echoed in her head. Yet, Jackie was still in the house, wasn't she? It wasn't as if she was inviting a serial killer into her bedroom.

She cupped her hands to her mouth. "Come up! Ring the bell! Jackie will let you in!" Was he coming? Had he heard her? Heart thudding wildly, she waited. Yes! He was. He was walking toward the back of the house.

Claire moved back inside, and shut the doors. Damn the water on the floor. But what did it matter? She wheeled herself over to her closet. He'd be up in minutes, and she looked a mess. Unbuttoning her blouse, she shrugged out of it and tossed it on the closet floor. Frantically, she looked for something to replace the damp top. A much-loved Celtic Nights tee caught her attention, and she pulled it down and yanked it over her head.

Downstairs, she heard a door close, then footsteps on the stairs. She hurried into the adjoining bath. There was time to run a brush through her hair and dab on lipstick. She took a breath, saw how pale she was, and used the lipstick to add a smudge of color to each cheekbone.

She was just exiting the bathroom when Morgan knocked on her open bedroom door. "Come in," she said. Her voice sounded strained, as though she was trying too hard. She took a deep breath and smiled at him. "Welcome to my lair."

One look at him, and her heart turned over once and soared. *Oh, my God.* He was real. He was here, and he was every bit as delicious as she'd remembered. Dark blond hair, a little damp, the same bathing suit, and a Boston Marathon T-shirt spotted with raindrops. He was here, filling her doorway with shoulders that wouldn't quit and the muscular legs of a swimmer.

"I hope you don't think I'm some kind of stalker. I had fun the other day, and I was disappointed when you weren't at the—"

"On the beach," she finished. "I was, but then the rain . . ." She took another breath. "And I had—" Don't mention the doctor, idiot, she told herself. He can see you're handicapped. "Anyway," she finished lamely.

He grinned. "Yes, it is raining."

So now he saw her in the wheelchair. Of course, he saw the chair on the pavilion before, but she hadn't been in it. He might have guessed that she couldn't walk, but now there was no doubt. He didn't seem fazed.

"I guess you already figured out I'm . . . my legs . . ." She hadn't been this tongue-tied since she was in the eighth grade, and a cute boy from Saint Andrews asked her to her first dance. "What I'm trying to say is . . ."

"Yes?"

He waited, gorgeous blue eyes twinkling. Yet, she didn't have the feeling he was laughing at her. He was just a sweet guy, a beautiful ten right in her bedroom. She would have given anything for twenty minutes of being normal. Well, maybe thirty minutes. In the days when she could still make love, she'd always liked to start slow and gradually build up to fireworks.

"A boating accident."

"Your fault?" Morgan's question was matter-of-fact. No syrup. No pity. The way she preferred.

"The other guy. Drunk. Speedboat." She smacked her palms together, and then threw them apart. "Pow!" She hesitated. "I woke up like this . . . and it's permanent."

"How long ago?"

"Two years. Please, I'm babbling. Come in." She waved him to the adjoining sitting area." Before she'd moved in, she'd had renovations done, opening rooms on either side to create a spacious living suite.

Morgan glanced at the bookshelves that lined one wall, floor to ceiling. "Do you mind?"

She shook her head. "No, look all you like."

He walked over to the rows of books and scanned titles. "Obviously you're a reader."

"Mmm, was. Not so much now. I have trouble concentrating." She hesitated, before going on with the gruesome details. "My skull was fractured. It left me with some difficulties." She didn't tell him about the memory gaps. This was an ark full of information to process.

She waited for him to flash an embarrassed smile, make an excuse about a pending appointment, and vanish. And who could blame him?

But he didn't run.

"You like history?" He removed a leather-backed volume and opened it, carefully turning the pages.

"Guilty." She smiled at him. "History major. Way back when." She liked the way he handled the book. You could tell a lot about people by their behavior. He was a reader too. He wasn't pretending. Even professional actors couldn't fake the interest in his gaze.

She couldn't take her eyes off him. It wasn't that he was so handsome—well, he was that—but not in a movie star way, not like someone who'd just stepped off a modeling shoot. Morgan was real. Masculine. Obviously an outdoors type. He probably spent most of his time on a sailboat or biking. He had to work out too, but he lacked that artificially enhanced look of bodybuilders. He appeared to be the genuine article—all man.

Claire noted that he wasn't quite as young as she'd thought the other day, maybe late thirties, but nice, very nice. And different, totally different than any guy she'd ever met before. No wonder she was having wet dreams about him at night.

She wasn't stupid. She realized that this could go nowhere. She didn't expect anything but friendship—but she was starved for that. No, worse than starved . . . dying of thirst.

"Would you like something to drink? I can have Jackie bring up—"

"No, thanks, I'm good." He carefully replaced the book and scanned more titles. "You have quite the library here. Some of these are old." He took down a small green volume. "You speak Greek?"

"Read." She grimaced. "My accent is atrocious. I'm not bad in ancient Greek. Translating, that is. I don't actually speak ancient Greek. No one does."

"No?" He seemed to question that. "No one?"

Claire shook her head. "Nope. Scholars disagree on exact pronunciation. Languages change through the centuries—you can see that in American English . . . the way it differs from Old English. Words come and go. New ones are coined, and in four or five hundred years . . ." She chuckled. "I'm still babbling."

He smiled. "You're passionate about your subject, and you're prepared to defend your arguments. I like that in a woman. Still, it's hard to believe that ancient Greek has completely faded from human memory."

"Pretty much." She motioned to a leather chair. "Sit down. Please. And I have soda here. Cans." She indicated the small wet bar and refrigerator against one wall. "Just regular. No diet—not that I think you need diet. And water. I always keep bottled water."

Claire wished he'd come closer, wished she could touch that stray lock of hair that had fallen over one eye . . . wished she could run her fingers through his blond hair. He smelled so good, as though he swam in the ocean every day—clean and fresh and something more, something she couldn't put a name to. . . . Almost unpredictable—wild, like the sea itself.

It didn't seem possible that she'd been sitting here a few minutes ago with a handful of pills, considering swallowing them . . . considering . . . Considering taking her own life . . . suicide. Not that she would have done it. She was sure of that. She would have put the damned pills back in the bottle, whether she'd heard Morgan calling her name or not. Wouldn't she? What kind of nut job could be thinking of ending her life one instant and—not ten minutes later—be wishing she had the working equipment to lure a guy into bed?

Morgan moved to the chair, but remained standing behind it, one muscular hand resting lightly on the top. "I was hoping you'd come down to the water with me. Maybe go for a swim." He looked at her hopefully. "I know it's raining, but if you're in the ocean, does that matter? You're going to get wet anyway."

But I don't swim in the ocean. Never. I can't even stand, she thought. *I'd probably sink right to the bottom.* She could feel the warmth of his gaze on her, feel the intensity of it. She opened her mouth to say no, but what came out was "All right." Suddenly, the logistics didn't matter anymore.

Morgan moved toward her, held out his hand. It seemed the most natural thing in the world to take it. His fingers closed around hers, warm, strong, almost electric. A thrill passed up her arm, flooding her with excitement . . . with hope.

Maybe it was possible. . . .

"Where is he?" Poseidon thundered. "What do you mean gone?"

Alexandros and Orion exchanged glances. "We thought you knew," Alex said. "He said he needed to get back."

"To what he was doing," Orion said. "He had important work. Following your orders."

"And that was?" the king asked suspiciously. He couldn't remember what it was that he might have instructed Morgan to do. Not that he was losing his grip. His mind was as good as ever. It was just that a king's days were filled with decisions, commands, settling trivial matters, and nobles bickering when he had larger issues to consider.

He'd canceled a meeting with Zale and his treasurer to summon the twins to one of his smaller throne rooms. He meant to get to the bottom of this outrage at once. He wasn't in the mood for insubordination. First the public shame of Morgan's trial, and then a magistrate informs him that three of his sons have been arrested for attempted murder and a fourth—his heir—was being sought for questioning.

Poseidon hadn't called the queen, but Korinna had inner radar that alerted her when any of her children were in trouble. She'd appeared almost on the twins' heels and showed no sign of leaving. He didn't want her here, but didn't know how to get rid of her without appearing ridiculous.

"Counting ghost lobster traps, wasn't he?" Korinna took a seat on his throne on the low dais. "Morgan was counting traps, I'm sure of it." It was a primitive chair compared to some in his greater throne rooms, crudely carved of rose quartz that glowed with an inner fire.

Poseidon grunted his disapproval. She hadn't broken any rules by commandeering the only chair in the chamber, but it put him out of sorts. This was his domain, where he often met with his closest male friends and advisors. His wives rarely came here, let alone took his throne, leaving him to pace back and forth a step below like a worried bureaucrat.

He glared at her.

Korinna favored him with one of her sweeter smiles. "I'm sure that's what you sent him to do, dear." She held up a string of pink pearls, a necklace that had come down to him from his great-grandmother. The pearls were much larger than normal, rare even in the finest collections and had been collected around the islands now known as Japan by the land dwellers.

"Could you fasten the catch on these, darling? I can't manage it, and I wanted to wear these pearls with this gown." She smiled up at him again, seemingly oblivious to his disapproval. "I distinctly remember that you were so concerned about the numbers of traps left abandoned on the ocean floor by humans that you wanted an accurate count. And you are so right. It's terrible, the loss of sea life from those awful ghost traps. So many lobsters, even crabs, climb inside and can't get out. They starve to death, Morgan says. Terrible."

"Call one of your women to fasten your necklace," he thundered. "I have more important things to do than fiddle with your jewelry."

He wheeled on his sons. By Zeus's hairy balls, both were in sorry condition, with eyes blackened, faces and bodies bruised. Orion had what looked like a sea horse bite on his arm, healing fast, but still black and blue with traces of torn flesh. "You're telling me that Morgan had no part in this disgraceful affair?"

"Morgan?" Alex seemed to consider the question. "I don't think so. I believe he had left by the time the guard arrived."

"Three of my sons arrested for brawling! And when I summon you from the prison cell, I find you unrepentant and smelling of cheap wine."

"Hardly cheap, Father," Alex replied. "It was that Argentinean red that you acquired for your last—"

"Great Hera, no," the queen interjected. "Didn't that

come off that sunken vessel? What was the name of that ship? *Madre . . .*"

"Stay out of this, woman!" Poseidon pointed at Alex. "I want a full explanation. Now!"

"We were celebrating Morgan's win in court, Sire. And we may have made somewhat merry."

"Lady Halimeda tells me that Morgan attacked Caddoc and his friends without warning. His cousin Jason suffered a broken collarbone and a dislocated shoulder. Valuable horses were lost to the open sea."

Orion met his gaze. "Not Morgan. He couldn't have. Morgan left at the first sign of trouble. It was Caddoc who started it. He and his followers insulted us and tried to provoke Morgan, but he wanted us to ignore them. They kept it up, and Alex lost his temper."

"Alex?" Alex assumed an injured expression. "You're mistaken, Brother. I'm not at fault. I simply went to offer assistance when Caddoc fell off his mount. He's a terrible rider, no seat at all. He shouldn't go within twenty yards of a stallion. I thought maybe he was hurt and—"

"Jason tried to take Alex's head off with a sword," Orion said. "Naturally, I—"

"A sword?" Korinna's eyes widened and she clapped hands over her mouth.

"Enough!" Poseidon threw up his arms. "Out of here, both of you. I don't want to see your faces until your units are ready to move out. You're lucky I didn't leave you locked up for the next decade."

The twins bowed respectfully to their mother and then to him and made a quick departure. Poseidon glared after them. "I don't believe a word of it."

"Then you shouldn't believe anything Caddoc says either, especially secondhand, through his mother. Halimeda is such a liar." Korinna toyed with the string of pearls she'd manage to fasten around her neck unassisted. "I don't know how you put up with her. I know why, I just don't know how. Did you see the spectacle she made of herself in the Hall of Justice? Bringing that octopus with her. It's common."

"Don't start with me," he warned. "Caddoc was badly hurt. He could have been killed."

"Is that why you're only angry with Alex and Orion?"

"I will deal with Caddoc soon enough. And I'm still furious with Morgan."

Korinna studied the nails on her right hand. "Oh, dear, I think I may have broken one, trying to close that catch."

"Did you come here for something, or simply to annoy me?" he demanded. He loved Korinna. She was his favorite of all his wives, but she took full advantage of his good nature and full advantage of her position as queen. She didn't deceive him at all. She'd arrived in his apartments to keep him from doing something he'd regret to the twins. Or Morgan. She was far too forgiving of everyone but Halimeda.

"I don't like her. I've never liked her or her son."

"My son," he reminded her.

"But Morgan is your heir." She rose and came to him. "Caddoc has always been jealous of Morgan. He and his mother probably concocted this whole story because they were angry over the High Council's decision. And now, you see Morgan wasn't even part of the disagreement."

"More than a disagreement. I won't have my sons trying to kill each other. I'll disown them all. The younger boys are much more disciplined."

"Morgan is heir and rightly so. He takes his duties seriously. Didn't he attempt to defuse the situation? Didn't he leave his brothers to return to counting his lobster traps?

As you ordered? You should be proud of him." She smiled. "I was proud of you when you defended him in court."

"I didn't defend him," Poseidon said.

"Whatever you call it, it was a noble thing to do." She tugged affectionately on his beard. "It doesn't make you less a warrior king to admit your love for your children— for any of them."

He caught her around the waist and pulled her to him. She smelled of something nice. He nuzzled her hair. "Marrying you was either the wisest or the most foolish thing I've ever done. You have no respect for my position."

She pressed her cheek against his bare chest. "I have the greatest respect for you, my lord. But as queen, part of my duty is to see that you remember that you are high king, not a god. And you are a father with the responsibilities of every father."

He hugged her against him. She was warm and soft. "You know I adore you, but that doesn't mean that I'll allow you to make war against my other wives."

"Only the ones that I believe are bad for you and for the kingdom."

"Halimeda."

"See, even you admit it. Enjoy her talents in your bed, but never trust her. She would see any of us dead to put her son on the throne of Atlantis."

"Not possible." He pushed aside her hair and kissed the nape of her neck. "Too many ahead of him."

"But Caddoc is the eldest."

"Her eldest, but not the eldest of the queen's body. First comes Morgan, then Orion and Alex. And after that, your sons."

Korinna slipped her arms around his neck. "I have been wanting to talk to you about that, my lord."

He gathered her in his arms. "And what is it that you wish to say, my sweet?"

"That we have made another child between us."

"What?"

"Is it so strange? Neither of us are in our dotage. And you are still as virile as a sperm whale, are you not?"

His heart swelled with pride. "I am pleased. Atlantis can never have too many royal princes."

She lifted her face to be kissed. "Or princesses," she murmured.

Claire clung tightly to Morgan's hand as they swam deeper. She tried to remember how they'd gotten down to the water, but it seemed hazy. She almost thought she could picture herself standing, walking over to him in her room—but that was impossible. Being in the ocean with him was wonderful, and if it was a dream or something else, she didn't care.

She had always supposed that it was dark at these depths. Instead of murky blackness, the water here was illuminated by a rainbow of iridescent golds, pinks, and lavenders. The colors seemed to seep into her body so that her skin took on an inner glow.

"Here." Morgan released his grip. "Don't try so hard. You're fighting the water, when you need to swim with it."

"I'm scared," she admitted.

"You'll get the hang of it. Just kick and stroke. See, you're doing it."

Was she? Were her feet kicking? Did she feel the water against her legs? Could she really wiggle her toes, or was it all in her imagination?

He laughed. "You're better than you thought. You told me you were a terrible swimmer."

"I am . . . I was." Boldly, she rolled onto her back and

kicked hard, sending her shooting ahead of him. How deep were they? Why didn't she need to go up for air? She had so many questions she wanted to ask him, but she was afraid that if she did, this all would disappear and she'd find herself back in her wheelchair. She realized now this was all a dream. She must have fallen asleep after she threw the pills into the drawer. But so what if it was a dream? She was going to enjoy every moment of it.

"Look." He pointed to the remains of a wooden lobster trap, half buried in the sand. He swam toward it, and she doubled back to follow him.

When she reached the trap, Morgan was hovering just above it. He wrenched open one side. Inside were three, no, four lobster shells. He brushed them aside to remove a smaller lobster. "Is it dead?" she asked.

"Almost." He placed the creature in the sand, and after a moment, one claw raised. "Go on," he urged. "Go find your dinner." The tail moved, then wiggled, and slowly the lobster swam away.

"The others starved to death, didn't they? Why didn't that one?"

"It probably lived on their remains."

"Uggh."

"No." Morgan shook his head. "That's life. You eat lobster, don't you?"

"Love it, but I'm not a cannibal. I wouldn't eat human flesh."

He shrugged. "You might if you were starving. You never know."

"I know." She shuddered.

"It's what I do."

She stared at him. "You're a cannibal?"

CHAPTER 9

Morgan laughed. "Am I a cannibal? No, I guarantee you that I'm not. Do you always take everything so literally? I count abandoned crab and lobster traps up and down the northeast coast of America. That's what I was talking about."

"Oh." She flushed, feeling foolish, though why she didn't know. It was a dream, for heaven's sake. It wasn't real. But she played along anyway because she *wanted* it to be real. "You're an ecologist or some kind of oceanographer?"

"Something like that." A small shark swam by, paying them no heed. Morgan glanced at it before turning back to her.

"Who do you work for?" she asked.

He took two strong strokes and held himself almost motionless in front of her. "My father. Actually, I have a lot of people that I answer to. But I don't do this for what they pay me. I really believe in protecting sea life."

"I'm impressed."

"Did you think I spent all my days beachcombing for interesting women?"

She joined his laughter as warm sensations bubbled up from the tips of her toes. Morgan thought she was interesting. She hadn't received a real compliment from a man since the plastic surgeon told her that she was a fast healer.

Morgan caught her hand again, and together they swam along the ocean floor. She was shocked at the amount of trash she saw amidst the beauty: truck tires, beer cans, a Vermont license plate, two more abandoned lobster traps—both with lobsters caught inside. In the first, four lobsters were dead, but the second trap produced two live ones.

Again, she noticed how much tenderness Morgan showed the creatures as he released them and destroyed the traps. "You don't suppose I could take one home for tomorrow's dinner?" she teased.

"Not much meat on them. If you're serious, we can pick up one or two in a feeding area near here."

"You don't object to people eating seafood?"

He shook his head. "I love lobster. What I object to is the useless destruction of life. Everything dies sooner or later. But with the world on the brink of starvation, it's wasteful to kill fish or crustaceans out of carelessness or stupidity."

Morgan's hair had come loose and floated out behind him like the mane on a running horse, and she was struck by how natural he seemed in this element. On the beach and in her bedroom, he'd moved with a lazy grace, but here, he seemed as much a part of this underwater paradise as the solitary shark.

"So you're against overfishing too?" she asked, wanting to learn as much as she could about him. Her dream man.

"Absolutely. Whole species have been wiped out. Look at the blue fin tuna, more than seventy-five percent of the world's supply gone. Not to mention the devastation of your New England fishing industry, all because greedy people harvested too many fish."

Claire nodded. "And the whales. Conservation has always been a serious concern for my family. My father's a big contributor to Tomorrow's Green Planet."

"I'm glad some people are concerned." He beckoned to her and swam on through a forest of waving sea grass and a sandy bed of gleaming white clams. They reminded Claire of the stones in a rocky stream not far from Seaborne.

Just ahead, she noticed a barnacle-encrusted form rearing out of the ocean floor on their right. "What's that?" she called to Morgan. It was oddly shaped for a boulder, almost cigar-shaped, about thirty feet long and shrouded in seaweed. "It looks like . . ." Surely, she was wrong. "It can't be a submarine, can it?"

"German. World War One."

"Here?"

"You're looking at it. This is where it went down."

The gray shape appeared more ominous as they swam closer. "I never knew that there were subs this close to our coast," she said. "What happened to the crew?"

Morgan tugged at her hand, and they swam around to the other side of the craft, where he pointed to a seven-foot ragged hole. "We're deep," he explained. "More than fifty fathoms. Once the hull was breached, the crew never had a chance."

"How awful." She shivered. "Are the bodies still inside?" she asked, unconsciously speaking in a hushed voice. "They must have had families—mothers . . . wives." A lump of sadness rose in her throat as she touched the cold metal. "So long ago." She could picture a young woman standing on the beach, staring out at the Atlantic, waiting for word that never came.

"If you're curious, we could go inside." Morgan's tone was flat. "I warn you that it's close quarters and dark."

"No." Claire shook her head as gooseflesh rose on her

arms. "It would be like swimming inside a coffin. Let them rest in peace."

"You have compassion for the crew, but they were enemies of your country."

"They were men, just people." And then she realized the significance of what he'd insinuated. "My country? Isn't it yours? You're not American?"

He smiled. "Greek."

She couldn't hide her astonishment. "Your English is wonderful," she said, switching to modern Greek. "You don't have a hint of an accent."

"Thank you," he answered, also in perfect Greek. "My tutors had doubts. American slang is particularly tricky for non-English speakers." His eyes gleamed with amusement. "And your Greek isn't bad, either. A little scholarly, but you might pass for a native of Athens who was educated in London."

Surprise, surprise, Claire thought. The more she learned about Morgan, the more impressed she was. Greek or American, he was still a honey. It troubled her that he'd said that they were so deep. That wasn't possible. The pressure at fifty fathoms—that was about three hundred feet—would be too great on her body. Her organs would be crushed. But anything was possible when dreaming, wasn't it?

Abruptly, a dark shadow with a white underside passed overhead. Her mouth gaped as she stared up. The thing was huge, clearly not a boat because they weren't anywhere near the surface. A chill ran up her spine. "What's that?" She pointed. It wasn't a shark or a whale. More like a floating Volkswagen.

"That's Lilura. She's a friend. Let me introduce you." Morgan brought his fingers to his lips and whistled.

The thing, whatever it was, slowed, circled, and then

glided lower. Claire's heart pounded against her chest as she realized what was coming toward them. It was a black-and-white manta ray, at least twenty feet in length. Claire clutched at Morgan's arm. "Did you call that thing?"

"Hey, Lilura," he crooned. And then to Claire he said, "Don't be afraid. She's friendly. Her name means 'enchantment.' " The creature glided closer until it hovered an arm's length away.

Claire had seen smaller rays, but nothing of this size. She was awed by the large intelligent eyes and the way it moved through the water without making a sound. "Plankton, right?" she asked nervously. "It eats plankton? They aren't dangerous to humans?"

"Plankton and small fish. She doesn't even have a poisonous spine on her tail." Morgan reached out and stroked the manta, and she practically purred with pleasure. "Claire, meet Lilura. Lilura, this is Claire . . ."

"Claire Bishop," she supplied. She was still nervous, but excited too. "You named her?"

"Mantas are very intelligent. The ancient Peruvians worshipped them."

Claire nodded. "Some other civilizations as well." She couldn't believe it. The ray nudged Morgan, and he scratched her under one flipper.

"Were you aware that they mate for life?"

Claire looked around. "Where's her—"

"Probably not far away." He climbed up on Lilura's back and offered his hand. "Are you up to taking a ride? It's fun."

"On a manta ray?" She shook her head and backed away. "I'll pass."

"Coward."

The ray continued to inspect her. Claire could almost

see her big brain working. Still trembling, but curious, she touched the massive white belly. "She's scratchy, like sandpaper."

"Have you ever ridden a ray?"

"Hardly." She kept rubbing Lilura's belly, and the creature continued to study her with what almost seemed amusement.

"Come on," Morgan urged. "It might be your only chance. The big ones don't usually come this far north. It's safe, I promise."

She couldn't walk. She couldn't swim, and she sure as hell couldn't breathe underwater. Yet, somehow, she was doing all three. Maybe she *could* ride this thing. Tentatively, she offered Morgan her hand. "If I fall off and die, I'll kill you," she warned.

"I'll keep that in mind. Now, put your arms around my neck and hold on tight." He mounted the ray, flattening his body across its back.

Squeezing her eyes shut, Claire wrapped her arms around him. "What are you going to hold on to?"

"Let me worry about that." He clicked softly, as though to a well-schooled horse, and the manta began to swim, slowly at first, and then faster. Claire kept her eyes shut and savored the sensation of water flowing around and over her . . . savored the feel of this magnificent man beneath her.

Lying on top of Morgan, feeling his body against hers gave her warm chills of excitement. She was acutely aware of every breath he took, the contours of his hard, muscular body, and the tantalizing scent that was his alone.

"Are you watching?" he asked.

"No."

"Chicken. Look around you, Claire. Don't be afraid. Live a little. Experience what it feels to be one of them."

She opened her eyes, blinked, and swallowed. Four more manta rays had come out of the depths and were swimming with them, one alongside, two above, and one following. Two of them were even larger than Lilura.

Oh, my God, she thought, *I'm calling a fish by name.* But the name did fit. At least the manta wasn't named Killer.

"The big brown one beside us is Joji, her mate," Morgan explained. "I can move over onto his back if you'd like to ride Lilura alone."

"No, this is fine," she said. "I'm fine, right where I am." She tightened her death lock on his neck. No teeth, she reminded herself. Mantas have no teeth. They couldn't bite me if they wanted to.

"Suit yourself."

Light sparkled around them. The color of the water changed and the temperature grew noticeably warmer. Claire supposed they were nearing the surface. The rays began to swim faster.

"Hang on," Morgan cautioned.

Suddenly, the rays launched themselves out of the water, flinging themselves up into the air. Claire cried out with joy as she felt the salt spray on her face, the wind in her hair, memories of taking a high jump on a hunter engulfing her. In that instant, she felt more alive than she had in years. She had a brief glimpse of white foam, blue-green waves, clouds, and a misty shoreline before the rays dove down into the waves again, taking her and Morgan with them.

The ocean closed around them like a mother's embrace, cool, sweet, and comforting. But before her heartbeat could slow to anything like normal, Lilura flexed her great body, speeded up, and broke the surface again. This time, the manta soared even higher. All around them, it seemed the other rays had taken flight as well.

"We're flying!" Claire cried ecstatically.

"How do you like it?" Morgan shouted.

"I love—" Her words were drowned in the splash as Lilura plunged deep into the depths, but Morgan knew something of what she was feeling. He, too, was captivated by the experience. Not just the thrill of riding the manta, but the thrill of having Claire's soft breasts pressed into his back, her thighs and legs molded to his.

He tried not to think of why he'd come back, of how he was certain that seeing her again would convince him that whatever attraction she'd held for him had faded. Breathing air and walking on land, maintaining the illusion for her that he was human drained his life's energy. It couldn't continue. If he kept leaving the ocean and going to her, he would sicken and die.

But those facts meant nothing compared to the way she made him feel. Seeing her again hadn't changed a thing. He wanted to make love to her even more, if that were possible. He was glad that he was facedown on Lilura's back, because if he were the one on top, there would be no hiding his physical condition from Claire.

The woman fascinated him—her spunk, her wit, her keen intelligence. He loved the way her short, reddish-brown hair bounced against her shoulders, the freckles on her nose, and the way she looked at him with bright, expressive eyes. Everything that he took for granted was new and wondrous to her. Not only did he have an overwhelming desire to possess Claire, he wanted to protect her, to teach her, to share his underwater world. He didn't want to just make love to her—he wanted to claim her as his own.

Impossible.

She was not his kind and he was not hers. Atlanteans and those who walked the earth were enemies, and if his people discovered that he was seeing her, no plea of his father's would save him a second time.

As the rays leaped high again, Claire squealed, lost her hold on him, and tumbled off. He dove after her, searching frantically for her in the water, but when he reached her, she was swimming strongly and laughing. "You didn't tell me it would feel like that!" she exclaimed.

"What is it they tell a cowboy when he falls off a horse?" he asked as he caught her in his arms.

"Get right back on." She laughed, wrapping her legs around his waist.

He leaned close, closer. Her lips were so beautiful. He kissed her, forgetting everything else but how good she tasted. He'd lost count of the sexual encounters he'd had, of the number of his lovers, but he'd never felt so out of control with a woman.

Claire had captivated him. He was completely in charge; she was in his world. Yet, she held the power in her small hands . . . in those pink lips . . . in her touch.

She snuggled against him, tangling her fingers in his hair, pressing herself so tightly against him it was almost as if they were one. The sweetness of her kiss made him giddy, and they sank down and down. . . . Until, abruptly, he felt the sandpaper skin of Lilura rise up under them.

Claire didn't seem to notice. She parted her lips, opening to him, and he touched his tongue to hers. His need for her soared; he could feel his pulse pounding, his staff growing hard as stone. He couldn't get enough of her. Her scent drove him wild.

"Claire . . ." he groaned. "My Claire." She was as hot for him as he was for her. She wanted him with every ounce of her being. He caressed her breasts, the soft skin of her waist, the sweet curves of her buttocks. There was only one way to end this . . . only one way to satisfy the need that pounded in his blood.

"Justin." Richard opened the door to his apartment. "Thanks for coming."

Justin stepped inside, handed his former father-in-law his umbrella, and removed his raincoat. "It's pouring out there."

"I'll take your things. I gave the housekeeper the afternoon off."

"Sorry I wasn't available the other day. Patients."

Richard ushered him into the living room. "Coffee? A martini?"

"No, thanks." Justin sensed a change of attitude in the older man's greeting. They'd never been close, and he'd always felt that Richard considered him not quite good enough for Claire. Things were quite different now that Claire was damaged goods. He glanced around the room, noting the oil over the fireplace. "That's new, isn't it? Not a Picasso?"

Richard shook his head. "Afraid not. A Damario. He was a student of Picasso who obviously copied his master's style. But I thought it might be a good investment."

Justin studied the painting. The colors were good, but overall, it was an inferior piece. He'd hoped that Richard had bought it believing it was a Picasso. Personally, he abhorred modern art. He much preferred the French Impressionists.

"Sit down, sit down. You don't mind if I have a drink?"

Justin shrugged. "Your house." He took a seat and leaned back, steepling his fingers. "Now, what's all this about Claire being suicidal?"

Richard leaned forward, the glass gripped tightly in his fingers. "I'm afraid she is. I'd like to have you talk to her."

"You said she wouldn't see me."

"I know that's true, but what did you tell me? She may not be in a position to make those decisions in her condition. I'd like you to talk with her. Evaluate her."

"She's in Maine, correct?"

"Yes, at Seaborne."

"I made a lot of mistakes during our marriage," Justin said, with what he hoped was the proper amount of regret in his voice. "The divorce was entirely my fault, and I take all the blame, but I've never stopped loving your daughter. It took losing her to make me realize what was truly important."

"So I can count on your help?" Richard asked. He put his glass on a coaster.

"Absolutely. Anything within my power."

"I've been thinking of going up to Seaborne. If you could go with me, maybe the two of us . . ."

"When were you planning on making the trip?"

"Next week, at the latest. I've made inquiries about a private clinic in Switzerland. They're making some wonderful progress in stem cell research—specifically spinal cord regeneration."

"So there is hope that she could regain use of her legs?"

"They've agreed to see her, but if I can't get her out of Maine, I can't get her to Switzerland."

"You're certain this clinic is legitimate?"

"Yes, I am. They can't give any guarantees, but Claire might be a candidate for their program."

"But not if she's emotionally unstable."

Richard nodded.

"What makes you think she's capable of suicide?"

"Not one thing, but everything together. Her willingness to bury herself up there—to spend her days alone on the beach." Richard got to his feet. "She's so depressed. And the things she says. We've always been close, but now she's walled me out of her life."

"I won't sugarcoat this, Richard. It does sound serious. I can't tell you how much this disturbs me. I still care very much for her. And I had hopes she could find it in her heart to forgive me."

"I suspected as much. That's why I felt free to contact you, that and your stellar reputation."

"I'd need to see her to confirm your opinion, but, if it were me . . ."

Richard rose to the bait. "Yes? What would you suggest?"

"I'd have her committed to a good hospital until she's stable enough for treatment."

CHAPTER 10

This couldn't be real. Claire was floating through a fabulous dream, an adult fairy tale more intriguing, more intense, than any she'd ever read in a children's fairy tale. The most beautiful man in the world was holding her, kissing her, wrapping his strong legs around her as he whispered love words into her ear. And it was all taking place, fathoms under water, on the back of a giant manta ray. . . .

But she wanted more. Morgan's caresses had whipped her to a fever pitch. His mouth and tongue on her breasts . . . his lean, seeking fingers touching her most secret places had brought her to the precipice of sexual ecstasy. She needed him inside her, filling her, plunging deep. She clung to him, her nails digging into his bare shoulders, hips arched to press against his hard erection. "Please . . ." she whispered. "I want you. I have to . . ."

Without warning, the ray undulated, the raspy skin rippled, and the creature uttered what could only be described as a long hiss. Claire felt Morgan tense, and she sensed that something had drawn his attention from her. She opened her eyes. "What . . ." she began. She blinked, trying to clear her mind of the sensual haze that clouded it. "Why—"

"Shh." He pressed two fingers to her lips and rose off of her, before pushing her flat against the manta's body.

Again, the massive bulk rippled as the ray glided through the water, swimming upward through blue halos of shimmering light. From the corner of her eye, Claire glimpsed the big male manta. The dark eyes were no longer friendly, but had taken on a fierce expression.

"*Melqart,*" Morgan muttered between clenched teeth.

"What? What's wrong?"

"I'm taking you back to land," Morgan said. The man who had held her so tenderly seemed changed as well. Morgan's mouth thinned, his lips were hard, and his skin stretched taut against bronzed cheekbones. From somewhere, he had produced a sword—not just any sword, but the replica of a two-thousand-year-old Greek warrior's sword she'd seen in the British Museum.

He crouched beside her on the manta ray's back, weapon gripped in his right hand, no longer her mysterious lover, but some fierce warrior from another time.

"No," Claire protested. This wasn't right. This was her dream, not a nightmare. She wanted Morgan to make love to her, not turn into Ulysses and fight sea monsters. "I don't want to go home. I—"

"Quiet! Your voice will carry." He peered into the shadowy depths, and when she tried to see what he was watching, she caught the faintest hint of several white, wispy, formless shapes.

"Tell me what's wrong," she insisted. She didn't like this twist in the dream. "I want . . ."

Morgan turned his gaze on her. For a moment her brown eyes felt the force that seemed to pour out of his, and then she was caught in a tumbling tide of sights and sounds. It was the same as falling off a bucking horse. One moment her seat was secure, the sky above, the saddle under her, and the next, she slammed into the ground. Hard.

Shaken, Claire lay there, hoping nothing was broken, trying to remember where she'd been, what mount she'd been riding when she'd been thrown. She opened her eyes, afraid of seeing hospital white, smelling the acrid odor of antiseptic, and hearing the rhythmic beep of a monitor or an overhead speaker blaring "Code blue. Code blue! Stat!"

She waited for the familiar rush of pain, the deep ache that accompanied a broken bone or the pulsing red agony of a shattered neck. Nothing. She touched the sheets, the pillow, wiggled her hands, arms.

For an instant, she couldn't remember a single thing, not even her own name. Scenes flashed across the screen in her head like a black-and-white slide show. A splash of waves. A Vermont license plate. *Click. Click.* A lobster swimming along the ocean floor. *Click. Click.* A huge manta ray flying out of the water. *Click. Click.* Morgan holding a Greek sword.

She brought her palms to her face and breathed deep. One word echoed in her head, a nonsense word, over and over. *Melqart.* Melqart? What was that? "Melqart?" she said aloud.

"Did you call me?" Jackie pushed open the bedroom door and peered in. "Did you need something?"

Jackie. The dominos fell into place, one by one. Claire took another breath. She was in her own bed. It was morning by the way the light was flooding through the French doors, a sunny day, later than she usually slept.

"You all right?"

"Yes, yes, I'm fine," Claire said. As fine as someone can be who's paralyzed from the waist down. Someone who can have the best, most vivid dream in the world and manage to screw that up too. "Come in."

Jackie, somewhere in her forties, was short and stout, with features that could only be described as plain. She wore blue jeans, high-top sneakers, and an oversize T-shirt. Her streaked blond hair was caught back in a no-nonsense ponytail, and her caramel-colored skin bore not a trace of makeup. Jackie was the only employee in the house who refused to wear a uniform, and Claire loved her for it. Jackie was prompt, hardworking, and also the only one at Seaborne who never treated her as though she was handicapped.

The maid only worked part-time, but she was such a whiz at cleaning that even the indomitable Mrs. G. tiptoed around her. Jackie had an accounting degree from the University of Maine and had worked at a high-powered advertising firm for ten years before chucking it all to return to her hometown and marry her childhood sweetheart. She was the mother of four, all active in school and church, and all honor students. Jackie was a woman who knew her own mind and cut life to fit her own pattern.

"I'd appreciate it if you didn't mention my visitor," Claire said, remembering that it was Jackie who'd let Morgan into the house yesterday. The fuzz was clearing from her brain now. She could remember Morgan coming up to her room. She didn't remember what had happened after he'd gotten here or when he'd left, but she was sure that would come.

"Who?" Jackie placed a bouquet of yellow rosebuds on the table in front of the window. "Aren't these pretty? Don't know who sent them. No card. Petal's Petals brought them out early this morning."

"My friend. The man you let in yesterday. Just before you left?"

Jackie frowned. "I didn't see any man. If you had a gentle-man caller, maybe he sent these flowers."

"Are you sure they're for me?"

Jackie nodded. "Miss Claire Bishop, Seaborne. Can't be any more specific. But I didn't see anybody here yesterday. 'Course, I left a little after four. Carmen had t-ball prac-tice. I told Godwin I had to pick Carmen up. The coach wants the parents there on time or the kids sit on the bench. And Evrard couldn't get off work."

"Oh." She supposed Morgan must have let himself in. Funny he hadn't said anything about it. She wondered if he'd sent the roses.

"Is there a problem?"

"Problem, no." Claire smiled at her. "Did the new uni-forms come in?"

Jackie nodded. "Nice. Really nice. Those old ones were a disgrace. When we went to play the Juniper Honeybees last year, our kids almost got laughed off the field. It was good of you to buy new ones for the team."

"My pleasure." Claire glanced at the clock. "What time is it?"

"After ten." Jackie waved at the breakfast tray beside the roses. "I brought that up at nine. Your coffee might be getting cold by now. I'd be glad to run downstairs and—"

"No, that's fine." She'd overslept. She hadn't heard a sound until a few minutes ago. "Didn't Nurse Wrangle come—"

"Oh, forgot to tell you. Jane will be coming in Wran-gle's place. Seems the white tornado drove her SUV into the marsh last night." Jackie grinned. "Nurse Wrangle and the principal from the high school. Together."

"Were they hurt?"

"Nobody was hurt, but they shot so far out into the muck that it took the fire company in a boat to rescue them." She winked. "Of course, Willihand might be in worse shape this morning after his wife found out who'd he'd been with at eleven o'clock at night."

Claire tried to appear interested. She wanted Jackie to leave her alone, so that she could have time to sort out what had really happened with Morgan, but Jackie loved her gossip. And she was too nice a person for Claire to want to spoil her newsflash for the day. "I'm really not a fan of Wrangle's."

"And who is, other than Mrs. G.?" Jackie chuckled. "They gave some story about them planning a special jobs fair for health professionals at the school, but nobody believed it. If they were, they would have been at the school and not on the road to Woody Point. Nothing out there but teenagers making out. And one *willing* principal, if you get my meaning. Anyway, Jane will be here this afternoon to help out."

"Thanks, Jackie."

"Do you need any help?"

"I'd appreciate it if you'd bring my chair over here." Her wheelchair was near the window. Someone must have moved it from its normal place by the bed. She certainly hadn't left it there last night.

Of course, she didn't have the faintest idea what she'd done last night. All the same, walking probably wasn't one of the possibilities. But Morgan had been here. Just because Jackie hadn't seen him didn't mean she'd imagined him. Did it? The chances were, they'd talked, maybe even had a soft drink, and he'd gone on to do whatever it was that he did.

"One more thing," Jackie said.

"Yes?" She'd been thinking about Morgan so hard that she'd almost forgotten that Jackie was still in the room.

"There was a phone call for you a few minutes ago. I

looked in, but you were still sleeping. It was a Mr. Kelly. I wrote it down by the kitchen phone, but he said you didn't need to call back. He was mailing you a dossier. Priority mail. Should I have woke you?"

"No, no, that's fine." Kelly. He must have discovered something. But, she wasn't going to get her expectations up. She'd wait until the information arrived. "Do you know when Wrangle will be back?"

"Next week. Her SUV was totaled. All that mud in the engine. Water up to their—" Jackie grinned. "To their waists. Messed up the seats, ruined the sound system, not to mention the engine. She'll be driving a rental until her insurance comes through."

"And maybe by then, I'll have found a replacement for her."

"I hope you do. Personally, I can't stand the woman." She tapped her forehead. "A little wacko, if you ask me, but of course, I'm just the maid."

"Uh-huh," Claire said. "I hear you." She chuckled. "You, Jackie, are not just anything."

"That's what I tell Evrard. If he hadn't swept me off my feet, I'd have a corner office overlooking the harbor and I'd be driving one of those foreign sports cars instead of baking brownies for Boy Scout Troop meetings." She picked up the breakfast tray and carried it over to the bed. "Peaches and blueberries. They're still good. Call me if you want anything. I'm going to start on the downstairs' bathrooms."

Once Jackie had gone on to complete her chores, Claire lay back on the pillow and tried to figure out what had really happened to her the night before. She could remember parts of a swimming dream, but most of it was hazy. Only Morgan's face was clear, that, and an image of his hair, all loose and flowing in the water. If it hadn't happened, it should have.

She took a sip of black, cold coffee, a bite of the fruit, and then set about getting out of bed and into the shower, never an easy task.

Morgan watched the beach, not certain if he wanted Claire to come down to the pavilion this morning or not. Yesterday had been a close call. He didn't want to think what could have happened if he hadn't sensed Melqart's outriders before they'd found him. He'd glimpsed four, maybe five, but they were illusive ghostlike creatures, about six feet in height and eel-thin, with glowing red eyes and gaping maws. They generally hunted in packs, and humans were their favorite prey.

If he'd been alone, he would have remained with the mantas and taken his chances. But it would have been impossible to protect Claire and hold the pack off at the same time. He'd put her in mortal danger to satisfy his own needs, and he was ashamed of it.

Normally, the hordes hunted the more populated beaches, riding the undertows and pulling down lone swimmers, often children or those who ventured into the sea at night, and sucked the life out of them. Sometimes they ripped victims apart with their teeth, causing humans to assume it was a shark attack. Other bodies they simply abandoned once they had their sport. Those corpses washed up on the shore or out to sea, seemingly accidental drownings. Melqart's minions fed off Atlanteans and other humanoid species as well as humans, but generally were too cowardly to take on even a single armed warrior. Not that Morgan considered himself a real warrior; Orion wouldn't have thought so.

Morgan had trained as a king's son. He'd gone into battle and killed his share over the years, but he didn't have the twins' ability to forget the enemies he struck down. His father was probably right. He wasn't the stuff to make a Poseidon, high king of Atlantis. But he had no qualms about seeking out and destroying Melqart's followers wherever he found them.

They were an ancient evil, neither fish nor mammal, but all too real. Like colonies of insects on land, the shades seemed to think and act collectively, rather than as individuals. So far as he knew, each was both male and female in the same body. They communicated by rudimentary groans and shrieks and some sort of telepathy, but spirit or flesh, they could be killed only by slicing them in half. Cutting off a clawed appendage or what appeared to be the head and jaws didn't appear to be fatal.

So long as this scourge prowled the Maine coast, it wasn't safe to bring Claire into the water. He should go. He'd known it was best for both of them. Still, he hated the thoughts of leaving the beaches open for such scum. He remembered the face of the lobster fisherman's son he'd saved from drowning. A boy like that, a child who'd grown up as much in the water as on the land, would think nothing of swimming at night with his friends.

It wasn't his fight. He'd saved the boy once. It wasn't his responsibility to hang around and chase every flesh-eater away from the coast of North America. He was getting soft.

The truth was that he wasn't cured of Claire's enchantment. He couldn't break free of it until he'd possessed her . . . until he'd drunk enough of her charms that his thirst was satisfied.

He was here to count lobster traps, but even Poseidon

would approve of his straying from his mission to hunt down the essence of evil. Alex and Orion and their friends had been eager for a fight the day he'd left his father's palace. If he summoned them, they could do a little hunting of their own. Once the horde had been killed or driven off, then he'd be free to seek out Claire again—providing he still wanted to. Maybe he wouldn't. Maybe he was simply bored, and a little manly sword play would cure his fever for a human woman. It wouldn't hurt to try.

He glanced back at Claire's beach. Still empty. Nothing moved on it but a single willet scratching the sand for crabs. "Maybe I'll be free of you," he murmured as he turned to swim away, but in his heart of hearts, he knew differently. Whatever hold she had on him, she'd not loose his soul so easily.

Claire's physical therapist had just left and she was wheeling her chair toward the kitchen, intending to finally get a cup of hot coffee when she heard the phone ringing.

"It's for you," Mrs. Godwin called.

"Who is it?"

"A man. He didn't give his name. Do you want to talk to him?"

"Yes, I'll take it." *Maybe it's Morgan*, Claire thought.

The housekeeper handed her the receiver. "I'll be in the laundry if you need me."

"Hello?" Claire said.

"Claire?"

Her heart sank. Justin.

"Are you there?"

"Yes, Justin. I'm here."

"How are you? Did you get my flowers?"

Claire groaned. "The roses?"

"Yes, yellow ones. I remember they were your favorites."

Jonquil daffodils, Claire thought. *Yellow, but not roses. Jonquils.* "Thank you, Justin. They're lovely."

"What are you finding to do up there in the wilds of Maine?"

She sighed. "I do a lot of water skiing."

"Water skiing?" There was a pause and then he laughed. "Same old Claire."

"Absolutely." She was disappointed. She'd wanted the flowers to be from Morgan, or from Richard, if not Morgan. She'd thought maybe her father had regretted their argument and was trying to apologize,

"It's good to hear your voice."

"It's about the only thing that hasn't changed."

"I've changed," he said. "I've had a lot of time to think."

"Both of us," she agreed. She wondered if he wanted to borrow money.

"Your father's worried about you."

"I'm fine, Justin. Really. It was sweet of you to send the flowers, but I'm just in the middle of—"

"Wait, don't hang up on me. It took a lot for me to get the courage to call you. It's only fair you let me finish."

"I'm not sure what—"

"Claire, I know I hurt you, and I'm sorry. I need to see you."

"Justin, we don't—"

"Please, Claire. I know I have no reason to hope that you'd be able to forgive me, but I still love you. And . . . I want us to be together again."

CHAPTER 11

"You want us to get back together?" Claire was in shock—they hadn't talked in months. "You've got to be kidding."

"I've never been more serious," Justin insisted. "I realize how much pain I caused you."

Claire felt her stomach clench. "Do you?" She'd thought once that she loved this man, but that had been a long time ago. She'd been wrong. Now, she didn't feel anything for him. She didn't love him. She didn't hate him. She just didn't care about him at all. "What about Inga?"

It all seemed like a dream now, but the scene was still clear in her mind. She'd taken an early flight home, walked into the apartment, and caught Justin and his receptionist in the act.

She could remember seeing articles of Inga's clothing scattered across the floor . . . the scent of her own perfume thick in the air . . . and the unmistakable rasping moan of her husband's climax.

"Are you pretending that you didn't screw her in our bed?"

"It was a mistake."

"A damned big one," Claire declared. "She was wearing my favorite negligée."

"I'm not denying that I did something stupid, but . . ." His voice took on the charming tone he used on women patients. "It's over, Claire." Now Justin sounded sheepish. "Inga and Joe have reconciled."

"My sympathies."

"No, it's not like that. We broke up years ago."

"Really."

"Really. She went back to her husband, and I understand they've had another baby."

"My sympathies to the baby. Having a slut for a mother." Claire was in no mood to be generous.

"Don't be bitter. I take full responsibility for what happened."

"I would hope so. I wasn't the one who cheated, you did." She was beginning to wonder what had prompted this bizarre phone call. Surely her father wasn't at the bottom of this. He wouldn't dare invade her privacy this way, by talking with her ex. Would he?

"You're the best thing that ever happened to me. I admit that I destroyed our marriage by being unfaithful. Now, I'm trying to mend it."

"It's a little late, for both of us," she said. "Considering my physical condition, I'm hardly your type anymore."

Justin had always favored athletic women. He wasn't adverse to nice breasts, but he preferred a tight rump and legs that wouldn't quit. Inga had possessed the entire package, plus a husband, and a four-year-old son. Her sport was tennis, and she looked smashing in tiny white shorts.

"Think about it, will you? I'd be willing to go to marriage counseling."

"There is no marriage. We're divorced. Remember?"

"We could correct that."

"Please. We made each other miserable, Justin. You cheated on me, and I suspect that Inga wasn't the first."

She'd been so young when she married him. He was twelve years older and divorced. He'd swept her off her feet with his wit, his sophistication, and his willingness to discuss anything from politics to first-century Roman sculpture. She'd been so smitten that she'd been unrealistic as to who he really was. What he was.

Claire thought she was well over the sense of failure the divorce had brought but, hearing his voice again, she realized the scar was still tender.

"Maybe I had to lose you to know what you meant to me. I'm human, with human failings, but I love you. If you'll come back, we could make a good life together."

Her mouth was dry. She was the one with the head injury. How could he think she was so stupid as to fall for his lies again? "What's in it for you, other than my money? You're a man who likes sex, a lot of it, and I'm not capable of having a normal marital relationship—unless you like making love to a—"

"Don't be crude. You were always a lady. It's one of the things that I always admired about you. And I don't need your money. My practice is doing quite well."

She exhaled softly. "I walked away from the accident with millions, and that was after my attorneys got theirs. If we can't have normal sex, and you don't need money, what's in it for you?"

"I love you. And you may not always be paralyzed. There are new developments in medical science every—"

"This isn't a movie, Justin. The heroine doesn't rise from her wheelchair and dance into the sunset. As long as I live, I'll be in this chair." Except in my dreams, she thought, smiling faintly. If this was reality, who needed it?

"We could have a good life together. Plays . . . museums . . . music. We could travel. We could adopt children, as many as you'd like. You always wanted to be a mother."

Sharp pain stabbed through her. "Low blow."

"I'm serious. What does it matter if you can't give birth? It's a messy process, and lots of children need families."

"As if. What agency is going to give a child to a woman in a wheelchair?"

"You're wrong. Many physically challenged people adopt. It's not as though the child wouldn't have a full-time father, nurses, nannies. Do you think those Hollywood stars change diapers or get up in the night when baby is teething? We can hire all the help we need—the finest."

"Thanks for the offer, but . . ." She wondered again if her father had talked to him, if he had warned Justin of the dirty details of her life, the lost moments in time, the pain, the mind-numbing meds. Not to mention her waking dreams when she imagined she swam with a beautiful man at fifty fathoms below sea level.

"Tell me you'll at least consider it?"

"No, I won't. Find someone else. Maybe Inga's ready for another go-round. Maybe you could make your perfect life with her."

"Claire, please."

"Thank you for the roses, but my answer is no. Goodbye, Justin." He was still talking when she pushed the button, cutting him off. She laid the hand set on the table and stared at it, letting her gaze drift out of focus.

She'd meant to go down to the beach, but she was suddenly weary. Instead, she took the elevator to the second floor and returned to her room. She wasn't fooled by her ex's sudden declaration of love, and whatever his reasons for saying he wanted her, she didn't want him back.

Justin probably knew to the penny how much she'd been awarded after the accident. No matter how successful he was, he'd covet her fortune. The chances of him remaining faithful in a sexless marriage were somewhat less than the chances of her winning the lottery without buying a ticket. And even if his cheating wasn't an issue, she'd lost respect for him. Justin was nothing more than an educated bag of wind.

As Claire pushed open the elevator door, she saw Jackie polishing the big hallway mirror. Jackie glanced up and removed her headset, spilling pop music into the passageway. "Sorry. Can I get you anything?"

"No, thanks." Claire smiled. "But you can take those roses home with you when you go."

"You don't want them?" Jackie dropped her dust rag and bottle of glass cleaner into her divided bucket with the assortment of sponges, sprays, and brushes. Her supplies were as tidy as she was.

"I started sneezing after you left them. I think my allergies are starting up again."

"Are you sure? I could put them downstairs in the entrance hall."

"No, you take them. You like roses, don't you?"

"Love them."

"Good, enjoy." Claire pushed open her bedroom door. She wasn't fool enough to fall for Justin's line, but it was impossible to forget what he'd said about adopting children. As usual, he'd honed in on her soft spot.

Since she was small, she'd wanted to be a mom, someday. Secretly, knowing she was adopted, she'd wanted someone who looked like her, someone who was part of her. After her marriage to Justin, things became chaotic, and it never seemed the right time for her to get pregnant. And after the accident, it wasn't possible.

Over time, Claire had come to believe that never being a mother was the worst loss she'd suffered . . . worse than losing the use of her legs . . . of never riding again. Eventually, her father would grow old and die, leaving her alone with no one but paid staff. Maybe she was just being selfish, but that wasn't an existence she liked to contemplate.

Claire went to the French doors, opened them, and rolled out onto the balcony. Her beach was hidden by the cliff. But she could see the ocean and several wooded islands in the distance. The water looked a deep blue, frosted with puffs of white.

She couldn't see the beach, but at least she could see the water. Or could she? Was she here in this room, or was she locked in a hospital somewhere? Had the accident left her a vegetable, dependent on a machine for nourishment and oxygen? Or was the true world the one she dreamed of under the sea with Morgan? What was real and what was imagination? Maybe Justin's offer was as much a dream as flying through the air on the back of a giant manta ray.

"Find him," Lady Halimeda said. "Find him and kill him. I don't want to know how. Just do it."

"And what does that get me?" Caddoc nudged one of his mother's repulsive pets aside with the toe of his sandal. He hated octopods unless they were served in a stew with olives and onions, and her apartments were always crawling with the creatures: red ones, green ones, tiny black ones with yellow spots, enormous purple ones with sticky appendages. They gave him the creeps. When he was a child, he'd always been afraid that they would wrap their tentacles around him and smother him.

"What is it you want above all else, Caddoc?"

She had just risen from her bed. Her hair was unbound and she wore only a transparent black shift. His mother had always been comfortable with her own body, and she had no qualms about displaying it to him. He supposed it was a good body for a woman her age, but he wished she'd save her charms for her lovers. Her full breasts with their protruding brown nipples did nothing for him, and the shadow at the apex of her thighs was disgusting.

"Are you stupid as well as incompetent?" she demanded. "Kill Morgan and you'll be the next high king."

Caddoc felt his face growing hot. He had respect for her witchy abilities, had seen her perform tricks that he couldn't explain, but even she couldn't make him Poseidon's heir. "I may be your eldest son, but after Morgan come those annoying twins, and then that brood of Queen Korinna's. Do you expect me to murder them all? It might make the royal couple suspicious. Let alone the people."

"Hold your tongue until you have something worthwhile to say," she snapped. "You're useless. You always were. I should have exposed you on shore when you were born. I doubt very much if you have a drop of royal blood in your veins."

He winced. He was a man grown. He'd fought battles against killer whales and giant squid; he'd killed men, even some who deserved it. He shouldn't have been afraid of his mother, but the truth was that he did fear her.

"Spineless sea worm."

Caddoc stood as bile rose in his throat. He'd never let anyone else speak to him this way. "If you've summoned me here for more of your abuse, I have better things to do than listen to this."

"Stay where you are."

"Hades take you! You'll give me orders no more."

She slapped him hard across the face.

Hot fury made him want to lock his fingers around her blue throat and choke the life out of her. Instead, he made a rude gesture and took one stride toward the door. Then something odd happened. Caddoc found himself rigid, unable to move so much as a finger. He opened his mouth to shout, but could not speak.

"Do you doubt my power?" his mother asked. "Do you?"

A green octopus brushed against his cheek, one tentacle probing his open mouth. Caddoc struggled to clench his teeth, to knock it away, but he might have been carved of solid coral. The repulsive thing slid over his lips, leaving a trail of thick slime. He tried to scream as the octopod flowed into his mouth, gagging him, then wiggled and squirmed, down his throat.

Sweat broke out on his forehead. Blood infused his head so that the sound of it beating became a pounding drum in his ears. *Mother, please! No! No! I don't want to die like this!* His silent scream echoed in his head.

"Do you doubt me?"

"No . . . no." Caddoc, ripped at his throat, trying to rid himself of the octopus that writhed and curled in his gut.

She extended her hand. "Down on your knees, you ungrateful boy."

He did as she ordered. Bowing his head, he kissed her ring. Tears sprang from his eyes. "Forgive me, Mother," he sobbed.

She laughed. "Get up. You're fine. Are you such a child that you don't know illusion from reality?"

He didn't answer. Who knew what she might do if he said the wrong thing, offended her even more?

"Do as I say," she ordered. "If you are too stupid to think, at least recognize that I am not. Track down Poseidon's heir and kill him. Let no one see you do it."

"But, how . . . ?"

A red octopus wrapped around her arm and slithered

around her throat. "Leave the rest to me," she said. "First the king will name you as the new crown prince, and then he will die."

A sound in the doorway drew their attention. Caddoc turned to see a serving girl, clutching an ivory comb, her eyes wide with fear.

"Come in, Mgoc," his mother said. "I've been waiting for you to do my hair."

Caddoc studied the wench. She was a naiad-mermaid cross, neither one nor the other. As often happened, her flat face was more fish than humanoid and her tail was more decorative than practical. And as usual in such cases, Mgoc was not the brightest whale in the pod. Such creatures were timid and made relatively good servants, if the master didn't expect too much initiative. Taking one into service was considered an act of charity as they were considered outcasts by both naiad and mer folk. Abandoned at birth, most went the way of all chum, quickly eaten by scavengers. This one was plump, so she'd obviously been eating well, at his mother's expense.

"Were you eavesdropping on me?" his mother asked the girl.

"No, Lady."

Her speech was slurred, and came out more "Nah, Iddee." If Caddoc remembered correctly, the cross couldn't pronounce "Halimeda." Something about their lack of a proper tongue.

"You heard nothing we said?"

The monster shook her head.

"Good. Come here and comb out my hair."

Hesitantly, still terrified, the cross hurried to obey. His mother signaled Caddoc to wait while the maid attended to her toilet.

It took the better part of an hourglass for the cross to

finish and his mother to dismiss her. "Wait in the garden," she ordered. "And speak to no one. Your garbled voice gives me a headache."

"Yes, Lady."

"My father, the king, hates me," Caddoc said, the instant the girl left the room. "He'd never name me his heir over Orion or Alex."

His mother smiled. "Leave that to me. Now go. Don't let me see your face again until you bring me his severed head." She grasped his arms and pulled him to her. "When you wear Poseidon's crown, I'll give you Morwena to be your concubine."

"My own half-sister?"

"You think I haven't seen the way you look at her?"

"Look, yes. I'm flesh, not stone, but to take her to my bed . . ."

"Don't be so particular. She pleases you, doesn't she?"

"Yes, but—"

"Then that is all that should concern you. Didn't I just tell you that you may not be the king's get at all? I can think of two or three who are more likely your sire."

"I've no objection to killing Morgan," he said. "He's earned his death many times over. But I don't know where he is. It may take some time to locate him."

"Then you're wasting time standing here, aren't you?"

"What will you do with his head?"

She grasped his shoulders and kissed him full on the mouth. When she drew back, it was all he could do not to gag. "I'll make a feast of his brains for my pets," she said. "Who knows, it might even lend them some bit of immortality."

With a sour liquid rising in his throat, he started to leave her apartments.

"One more thing, Caddoc," she called after him.

"Yes, Mother?" He gritted his teeth. "What is it?"

"Make certain your blade is sharp enough. Take the head off that creature in the garden, as you go out."

His mouth gaped.

"You heard me. We can't have her sharing our little secret with the help, can we?"

"But if I kill her in your . . . How will I dispose of her body without anyone seeing?"

His mother sighed and stroked the nearest octopod, a large red one. "Bring it back in here, if you must. My darlings haven't fed yet today, have you, my sweets?"

Again, Claire waited for Morgan to return. The afternoon passed and then the evening. She had lain awake far into the night, unable to read, unable to concentrate on any of her DVDs or television. As hard as she tried, she couldn't remember what had happened after he'd come to her bedroom. Sometime after two, she finally drifted into a fitful sleep. She'd hoped to dream of the ocean again, but she knew nothing until Mrs. Godwin came with her coffee in the morning.

Jane arrived promptly. The woman was pleasant, quick, and professional. Since this wasn't a day for the physical therapist, Jane helped Claire to exercise her legs and massaged her neck, assisting her into the wheelchair-friendly shower. Afterwards, she gathered Claire's hair products and laid out clothing for the day.

Claire liked the nurse enough to ask if she'd be interested in becoming Wrangle's replacement. Unfortunately, Jane had a full schedule and had come this week because her regular patient was having surgery.

Later, a thick manila envelope arrived from Kelly's agency. Eager to open it out of Mrs. Godwin's curious gaze, Claire took it into the east parlor, closed the door, and tore open the package. Quickly, she scanned the folder, but was disappointed to find little about her parents' history that she didn't already know: birth dates, immediate family, high school, and college. Both were only children, and both had attended university at opposite ends of the country: Richard at Stanford, Elaine at Colgate. They'd met two years later at Harvard, marrying just as her father graduated from law school.

Elaine had been born when her mother was forty-five, and her father nearly sixty. Her parents had passed away of natural causes while she was in grad school. Richard's father had died when he was four, but his mother Sophia had lived until Claire was twenty. It has been Sophia, her nana, who'd left her Seaborne.

She flipped through the pages until she came to copies of several newspaper articles. Most concerned Richard's rise to partner in his prestigious firm, but one photograph was a picture of her father accepting a gold medal at a swim meet. An accompanying article proclaimed numerous breast-stroke records that Richard had set during his college career.

There had to be a mistake. This had to be some other Richard Bishop. But when she looked closely, she realized there was no mistake. She clearly recognized a younger version of her father, grinning and proudly displaying his medal. Richard had obviously lied to her about his fear of the water. But why would he do such a thing?

Confused, she picked up the phone and called him. "Why would you lie to me?" she asked when he picked up. "You told me you were terrified of the water, that you never learned to swim and in reality, you swam competitively in college?"

There was a moment of silence on the other end of the line. "Claire, darling. You must have misunderstood me.

What I said was that I used to be on a team, but after I was caught in an undertow and nearly drowned off Seaborne's beach, I gave up swimming. I was my mother's only child. She was terrified that something would happen to me, and honestly, it scared me."

"That's not the way I remember it," Claire said. "You never let me swim in the ocean. You distinctly told me you had a fear of the ocean as a kid."

He cleared his throat. "You're making too much of this, pumpkin."

"I just want a straight answer."

"Don't get yourself upset. You know that . . . since the accident . . . your memory plays tricks on you."

"So that's your answer. I'm crazy." She slid the photo and the articles back inside and closed the folder.

"I didn't say that." His voice hardened. "I don't like this attitude, Claire. I'm coming up to Seaborne this weekend. We need to have a heart-to-heart talk."

"All right," she agreed, wrestling with a sea of emotions. She wasn't crazy. She wasn't wrong about this. But why would Richard lie to her? He was right. She had been mistaken about other things. Her memory wasn't good. Maybe she wasn't remembering correctly. She exhaled, feeling defeated for some reason, but still not ready to totally give in to the idea that she was mistaken on this subject. "That's probably what we need. To talk." *Because if you lied to me about not being able to swim,* she thought, *what else have you lied to me about?*

CHAPTER 12

Neck pain kept Claire from sleep. Twice, she slid open the drawer in her nightstand, tempted to take the medication that her physicians and nurses urged her to use. And twice, she closed the drawer without weakening. So much of her life was out of her control. After two years, it was difficult to tell what the accident had done to her and how much of her mental confusion was the result of overmedicating.

The days before and after the accident remained a black void. She'd been spending the July weekend with friends on Cape Cod. She and Willa had been with Willa's fiancé, Max, on his Hobie Cat when Jeremy Smith had hit them at a speed nearing sixty knots with his high performance boat.

Claire didn't know if any of them had ever seen Smith's speedboat before it hit them. Max claimed he'd seen it, but there was so much television and newspaper coverage that it was difficult to tell what was firsthand and what was hype. In seconds, the Hobie Cat was shattered fiberglass, rope, and tattered sail. Willa died instantly. It was Max, who'd been thrown clear with a dislocated shoulder, a broken wrist, and facial lacerations, who'd saved her from drowning at great risk to his own life. Smith's motorboat continued on, fleeing the scene, and later colliding with another sailboat and killing the lone occupant.

Smith, the son of a presidential candidate and heir to his grandfather's billions, had a record of alcohol and drug abuse, driving under the influence, and felony manslaughter, both by automobile and watercraft. He'd pleaded guilty, and—due to his family's influence and a lenient judge— was committed to a luxury rehab for six months, followed by a period of community service. His father's lawyers had settled quietly out of court with the survivors, and Richard had seen to it that she received lifetime medical expenses, as well as her cash award.

Max was discharged from the hospital the day that he and Willa were scheduled to be married. He dropped out of his doctorate program at Yale, began drinking heavily, and when Claire last heard from him, he was backpacking through Nepal and India. Everyone told Claire how fortunate she was to have survived, but she wondered if Willa hadn't been the lucky one.

Claire had never considered herself a quitter. She'd fought through the months of rehabilitation, learning to speak, to feed herself, to brush her teeth. She endured long nights when pain consumed her, until she was nothing but a hollow shell, and even opening her eyes seemed too difficult to achieve. But she'd never felt pain below her waist. The crash had made graham cracker crumbs of her lower spine. Like Humpty Dumpty, the orthopedic surgeons had put her back together again, but she had no sensation below her waist.

Her shoulders hurt a lot, especially when it rained, as did the places in her arms and hands where the bones had been fragmented and were wired, pinned, and plated back together. She suffered no pain in her head, not even where some brain matter had been shaken to pudding and had to be removed. Mostly, it was the fiery throbbing in her neck that made sweat bead on her forehead and kept her from sleeping more than a few hours at a time.

But the pain medication left her mind fuzzy. Claire didn't like that. It was bad enough that she had permanent brain damage; she didn't intend to stifle what wits she had left by numbing herself with pills. She'd rather deal with the pain—at least it gave her something to fight.

Until Morgan had appeared in her dreams and given her hope . . .

So much of her life that had been full was empty. Grass grew in the paddocks where she'd kept her beloved horses, and her Australian cattle dog, Jinx, no longer woke her with excited barks. Her father had found a good home on a farm in Vermont for Jinx, a few months after the accident, but she still missed the way he'd paw at her face to get her out of bed in the morning.

Before her life had changed, she'd loved to run, and she'd often risen at dawn so that she could get her exercise in before she began her day's activities. When she wasn't riding, she rode mountain bikes, played handball, and tennis. Once, she and four friends had hired a guide and spent a week climbing in the Alps. Being cooped up inside four walls made her restless and now, short of wheelchair basketball, there was little she could do in the way of sport.

A large part of the income from her invested fortune she'd directed to children's charities and others that provided homes for neglected horses. Although she was glad to help, it did little to comfort her on lonely nights. She wanted to feel like a woman again, to be held by a man who cared for her.

And for a little while, Morgan had made her feel that way again. Morgan, her mystery man, the guy no one else saw . . . the guy who appeared and disappeared without a trace. Maybe he was just a figment of her desperate imagination, but it didn't matter. He filled the emptiness in her soul.

Lying there, staring at the ceiling was maddening. She wiggled up to a sitting position and used the remote to switch on the TV. A late-night local news station was re-running footage she'd seen earlier in the day about a female college student who'd drowned.

"This is the second accidental drowning in the area this week," the reporter said as the camera panned a deserted beach. "Tuesday morning, a surfer was apparently struck by his own board. Local resident, Tyler Clement, age twenty-two . . ."

Claire winced. She didn't want to think about the senseless deaths of two young people. She flicked the channel, surfing through old sit-coms, sales pitches, and a diet program that would change your life. She didn't watch much television, so she hadn't bothered purchasing a satellite package. Now she regretted that decision. Unable to find anything worth watching, she hit the power button.

"Where are you, Morgan?" she called into the shadowy bedroom. "I need you. Please come back to me. Please . . ."

Justin hated Central Park in the daytime, always crawling with screaming children, crazy bike riders, and barking dogs that did their nasty business wherever they pleased. He hated it worse by night. Who but a lunatic or a junkie would walk there alone after dark? The police didn't like to go in there after the sun went down, and they usually traveled in pairs and carried heavy artillery. But when dealing with Carlos, it had to be Central Park. Justin thought it must fulfill some made-guy fantasy of Carlos's.

Carlos Reyes was a former patient with connections to the underbelly of the city. He was rumored to have a lengthy juvenile record, as well as the conviction for the murder and mutilation of an associate when he was seventeen that had sent him into the state mental health hospital for nine years.

Whatever he'd done, and for a patient, Carlos was remarkably closemouthed about his past, he'd gained considerable success in the prostitution and weapons trade since his reentry into the free world. Carlos didn't traffic in drugs, or at least he'd always insisted that he hadn't. A particularly interesting sexual deviation had brought him to Justin's practice, and both had profited from the lengthy therapy sessions.

Justin considered Carlos to be more trustworthy than most. The man had never disappointed him, and he'd remained discreet. But Justin wasn't pleased to meet him in such an isolated area, especially when he was carrying so much cash. He would have preferred the subway at rush hour. Nuclear weapons could be bought and sold there, and if they didn't detonate, no one would be the wiser.

He checked his watch. Quarter past three. He'd entered by the West Eighty-sixth Street entrance, where he noticed a streetlight out, and he'd given himself exactly twelve minutes to reach the grove where Carlos would be waiting. If there was one thing Carlos was precise about, it was meeting at an exact time.

Rain dripped off the trees, dampening Justin's clothes and threatening to do mortal damage to his athletic shoes. Not that it mattered. He intended to drop them and his clothing into a trash can as soon as he could get home and change. It was a miserable night, drizzling rain with the occasional clap of thunder.

The foul weather made this exchange more difficult, but certainly cut down on the homeless riffraff that usually prowled here, feeding pigeons or trapping them. Justin didn't care. He didn't like pigeons any more than he did dogs or horses. He'd suffered the creatures, at least the dogs and horses, when he'd been married to Claire. Never again.

He wore black slacks, a navy tee, a black sweatshirt, and an oversize blue ball cap. The agreed-upon sum in twenty dollar bills was folded neatly, wrapped in aluminum foil, and stowed in a brown lunch bag with grease stains and the remains of yesterday's cheese steak. Carlos had told him that he would be carrying a pizza box. The trade would be easy, Justin's cash for an untraceable Glock.

A man on a bicycle pedaled past. Justin kept his head down. It was important that no one see him tonight. Any witness was a liability, and Justin didn't believe in taking unnecessary chances. He hoped that his attire and purposeful stride would keep any park predators from thinking he was an easy target. Tucked into his deep sweatshirt pocket was a can of wasp spray, just in case.

The cyclist circled around and came back. "Sellin' or buyin'?" he asked.

"Get lost." Justin patted the spray can and the lump and the clink of metal was sufficient to send the would-be merchandiser on his merry way.

The city was a sewer. It took a real man to know how to deal with the sewer rats. He walked on, ignoring the fast approaching thunder and lightning. He didn't deviate from his planned route, and he arrived to find Carlos waiting. He was standing in the shadow of a big tree, a lit cigarette in his hand.

"Freddie? I've got your lunch." The name was Carlos's idea and Justin felt foolish using it, but until he had what he'd come for, he had to play the game Carlos's way.

"Do you know who's pitching Saturday?"

Justin bit back an oath. Carlos had to recognize him. Who else would be fool enough to walk up to a total stranger in the middle of the park in a thunderstorm?

"Doctor?"

Justin sighed. "Babe Ruth."

Carlos laughed. "Just being careful. You never know. It's a jungle out here." He held out his hand.

Justin passed him the lunch bag with the money. Carlos dug out the sandwich, tossed it away, and hefted the weight of the twenties.

"Always a pleasure to do business with you." Carlos handed him the pizza box.

"Is it loaded?"

"Not much good if it isn't. It's good to do business with you, Doc."

"Same here," Justin replied. "How's the therapy going?"

"You know, slow. Hard to change old habits."

"The important thing is a desire on your part to try to get past this."

"I know, I know." He pointed to the box. "Take it out, get the feel of it in your hand. It's a beautiful piece."

"Not traceable."

"Nope. I guarantee it."

"Good." Justin opened the box, took out the handgun, and emptied the first shot into Carlos's midsection. Carlos cried out and grasped his gut.

The second bullet he put between the man's eyes, and as Carlos collapsed, Justin fired a third time into the base of his skull. After the second shot, Carlos was beyond caring. Bloody business but efficient. Justin took care to stamp out Carlos's cigarette before he walked away. Smoking was a nasty habit.

* * *

According to the evening news, an unidentified body had been discovered in Central Park, obviously the victim of a mugger, since the deceased's wallet was missing. Justin was amused that he hadn't thought of robbing the body, other than taking back the bag of money. A dangerous place, the park in the wee hours of the morning. Gang members, drug dealers, all sorts of undesirables. With Carlos's record, Justin doubted the authorities would try very hard to locate his killer.

Morgan hadn't found the pack. He could cover great distances through the water quickly when he wanted to, but Melqart's shades were elusive and there was a lot of inhabited Maine coastline to search. If he'd come upon them, he would have destroyed as many as he could, but he knew it was wiser to wait until he had his brothers and friends to fight beside him. He was torn between his desire to rid these waters of the demons and his overpowering need to be with Claire.

The monsters had fed; Morgan didn't need to be psychic to feel the dark energy on the tide. The schools of fish felt it, as did the turtles, and even the flocks of sea birds. The salt air thrummed with tension, and the sea creatures reflected the evil presence in their nervous behavior. The horde had taken down a human, perhaps more than one, and they would hunt and keep hunting until their lust was sated, or until their master summoned them home.

Melqart, the Phoenician god of war, was ancient and rarely took part in the blood sacrifice he set in motion, but Morgan was certain he took pleasure in the killings. Some Atlanteans believed that the life energy sucked from humanoids by the horde was what kept Melqart alive, but that was only conjecture. All Morgan knew was that

Melqart represented the darkest face of evil beneath the waves.

Deciding that he needed backup, Morgan had traveled as far to the east as the edge of the Georges Bank where he'd hoped to find someone to carry word to his brothers. Returning to Atlantis himself might mean explaining his actions to his father or crossing swords with Caddoc again. He preferred to avoid both if he could. He couldn't lie to Poseidon. If the king asked the right questions, he'd be forced to admit that he was seeing Claire.

Morgan found fishing boats, but no dolphins or Atlanteans. He thought he'd caught sight of one of the North American serpent-folk garbed in the outward form of a shark, but when he called out, he got no response. The water was murky and visibility poor, so he couldn't be certain. It was doubtful that he would have received assistance if he'd made the contact. The serpent-people were recluses, never friendly to any but their own kind, having no sympathy for humans or Atlanteans.

Morgan was about to give up and start the journey home to Atlantis when a deep sound vibrated through the water. Immediately, several large schools of panicked herring swirled past. Acting on impulse, Morgan swam toward the surface and waited, scanning a vast expanse of moonlit ocean. The seas were calm, waves no more than thirty feet from crest to crest. As far as he could see, there were no fishing boats in sight, nothing but dark sky, blazing stars, and a low-hanging, yellow crescent moon.

Morgan paddled lazily in place, waiting. Tiny splashes around him showed the presence of small baitfish. Again, he felt, rather than heard, a dull, thrumming noise. The ocean seemed to go silent for the space of a heartbeat, and then a massive humpback whale exploded out of the water, mouth agape.

Spray flew into the air as the whale dove and breached, rising high and splashing backwards, gulping mouthfuls of fish before plunging deep to begin the process again. Although he was far too large to become whale dinner, Morgan kept well away until the bull's feeding frenzy slowed to a playful slap of the great wavy tail and a relaxed circling on the surface.

Each humpback possesses a tail fluke pattern all his own, and Morgan recognized this animal as Lodar, one he and his brothers had met nearly a half century ago off the south coast of Iceland. Tonight the whale was alone as he was that day when a pack of killer whales had separated him from his pod. Morgan and his brothers had intervened in the hunt, and their swords had made the difference. The young bull had returned to his family group, battered and bleeding, but wiser.

Now, Lodar had reached his prime. He was over fifty feet long, and the numerous scars on his powerful body proved that he'd learned to defend himself from predators, both human and otherwise. Adult humpbacks were too large to fear Melqart's demons, but the shades were not above sucking the life out of a whale calf if the mother was young and inexperienced.

Lodar had lost his mate to a Japanese factory ship off Iceland more than two years ago, but he was still mourning her and thus not attached to a pod. Whales in general were reluctant to involve themselves in human or Atlantean affairs, but they possessed a sense of fairness and honor. Conscious of this, Morgan addressed the whale, not in speech, but telepathically.

I see you, Lodar.

The humpback circled again, displaying his black-and-white tail fin, and blowing a fountain of spray.

Morgan listened, willing his mind to accept and translate the message of another species.

Who calls to me?

The picture-words formed with infinite slowness, almost as if they were dredged from the sea floor and constructed of sand, one grain at a time.

Morgan, prince of Atlantis, greets his friend, the mighty Lodar. Whales were highly intelligent, but touchy. They gave way to few species with good reason.

Ah, I remember.

Morgan clenched his jaw against the lightning bolts of pain that ricocheted through his head. It required intense concentration and all his mental ability to communicate with whales, and it always gave him a hell of a headache. His brother Alex had the gift. It was a lot easier for him, but Alex wasn't here. *I heard of the loss of your mate,* Morgan thought. *I'm truly sorry.*

The whale drew near, an eye focusing on him. *As am I.* And then, almost apologetically, Morgan heard: *I remember you as larger, prince of Atlantis.*

He laughed. *You were younger then, Lodar. We were both younger.*

Yes.

The huge mouth opened in what might have been a yawn or a smile, and Morgan saw shreds of fish and seaweed clinging to the whale's hundreds of baleen plates that substituted for teeth.

Morgan swam closer, noting the barnacles clinging the humpback's knobby head and scarred and rough body. He was anxious to ask for Lodar's help, but knew better than to risk insulting the whale by rushing into the request. As difficult and time consuming as the process was, it was necessary to discuss the availability of krill and the number of human fishing-shells that he'd sighted. They asked and exchanged news of other humpback family groups and the attributes of unmated cows in the Atlantic before finally turning to business.

At last, Morgan was able to explain his dilemma and was rewarded with a favorable reply. To settle his debt, Lodar agreed to carry Morgan's message back to Atlantis to his brothers.

. . . Which left Morgan free to go where he wished.

"Claire."

She opened her eyes.

The night-light cast a yellow glow across the floor. Morgan could barely make out her features framed by the pillow, but he could smell her special scent and his heart opened in a rush of joy.

By Atlantean law, it was wrong of him to be here. By law and thousands of years of warfare between Atlanteans and humans, they were enemies, but he didn't care.

"Morgan . . ."

He could feel the warmth of her smile . . . could feel himself being drawn into her net.

He went willingly.

Leaning over the bed, he brushed her lips with his own. He wanted desperately to transport her to the sea where her body would be whole, but tonight, it was impossible. He had no right to carry her to an element where he couldn't protect her.

Melqart's shades were still out there. For all he knew, they waited just beyond the surf . . . hungry . . . fangs bared . . . claws honed. Claire was only human and might easily fall prey to their vicious attack.

Her body might be wounded, but her life force was strong. She would be prime bait for death's shadows. No matter how difficult it was for him to maintain the illusion of being human in her world, he couldn't risk taking her to his.

"I called to you," she murmured sleepily.

Her eyes were heavy lidded, her lips full and soft. Her beauty . . . her vulnerability tugged at him. His throat constricted, and he wondered for the hundredth time if she was the innocent she appeared, or if she possessed the power to lure him to his own death.

There could be nothing between them but a brief time of passion. They were of two different worlds, and they should never have met. As a prince of his people, he had a duty to fulfill, but Claire made him question everything that he thought he knew about humans.

The fever gripped him, burning into his bones, making him desire her as he'd never desired another female. His flesh seemed on fire. He had to possess her. If he didn't . . .

Morgan pitted his will against his sexual need. His muscles strained; his loins ached. A sheen of sweat glistened on his body. His mind rebelled at the notion that he couldn't have her, and his physical body paid the price. It was a struggle to maintain the illusion of a form Claire could accept. If she saw him as he truly was, she might feel terror, and he couldn't bear to scare her.

But his spell held and so did her human innocence.

"Are we going to swim tonight?" She stretched, catlike, and a smile of anticipation lit her eyes. She was alive, this human female, alive in every cell of her body. But her beautiful legs lay as still as marble columns, her lovely hips unmoving.

He shook his head, trying to keep his voice from showing the passion he felt. "Not tonight."

"You look tired."

He felt as though he'd swum from the Pillars of Hercules, but he would do that and more to be here with her.

He forced himself to take what would seem like normal breaths, but it was difficult. The earth's gravity weighed him down. With no water to buoy his body up, each step was a struggle. "Would you like to go out on the balcony?"

"That would be nice." She pointed to her wheelchair. "I'll need that."

"No, you won't." He gathered her, blankets and all, into his arms and carried her across the room. In seconds, they were outside, the sound of the surf crashing in the distance, and the great dome of the night sky above them.

"The stars are bright," she murmured.

"Not as bright as your eyes." He settled into a wooden reclining chair and cuddled her against him, reveling in her scent and the feel of her in his arms. "Now, I've got you," he teased, nestling his face into the soft curve of her neck, savoring the brush of her hair against his skin. "You're my prisoner."

She laughed. "Am I? It's my dream. I think you're my captive." She pulled his head down and kissed his lips.

Desire shot through him, and he shuddered at the intensity of his need for her. Maybe she was right. Maybe, for all her paralysis, she was the one in control. He felt his loins tighten, his staff harden. He wanted her as he'd never wanted anything, but there could be no question of intercourse tonight, not when she lacked sensation below the waist. The Atlanteans had few rules regarding sexual satisfaction, but one that was cast in solid bronze was that all parties must have the capacity to enjoy the act.

Having Claire here in his arms, feeling the heat of her body, inhaling her scent, yet unable to satisfy his longing was a sweet torture.

Since he'd come to full sexual maturity, Morgan had never denied himself. When he and another wanted each other, there was no need to wait. He'd been attracted to many women in his lifetime; a few he'd thought he loved. But this was different—she was different. Tonight, he didn't think about himself. Tonight would be about Claire, about what he could do to please her, and if he had to sacrifice his own physical needs, so be it.

He traced the line of her mouth with his tongue, catching her lower lip between his own lips and sucking gently. She groaned and pressed her mouth to his.

"That's nice," she murmured when they finally broke for air. "But, as much as I want to . . . want you . . . I'm not able to . . ."

"Shh." He kissed her again, tenderly, letting the sweet sensations flow through him, enjoying the holding, the touching, letting down all his defenses. "Beautiful, Claire . . . beautiful, mysterious Claire . . . Do you have any idea what you do to me?"

CHAPTER 13

He lowered his head and kissed her mouth. His lingering caress filled her with sweet tendrils of pleasure and made her giddy with joy. It was impossible that Morgan could be here, holding her as if she were an ordinary woman, not caring that half her body was dead. She pushed away those thoughts. Kissing him back, feeling the texture and heat of his body were too precious. She wouldn't trade one second of this miracle for reason.

He brushed his tongue against her closed lips and she opened, taking him in, feeling the thrill of intimacy with a man. She gripped him tightly, running her fingers through his hair, inhaling the scent that was his alone, all brine and sea and virile male.

He was a very good kisser.

"Claire, Claire," he murmured when they'd broken apart long enough to draw breath. "You're something special."

She nestled her head against his chest. She wanted to tell him how much his touch excited her . . . wanted to beg him to stroke and kiss her breasts, but she couldn't. If she tried to speak, she'd choke with tears.

It didn't matter who he was or why he'd come to her. She didn't even care if her father's warnings were correct.

If Morgan was dishonest, if he'd only approached her for her money, it didn't matter. All that mattered was feeling alive . . . feeling like a woman again.

As if he could read her thoughts, he nuzzled her throat and kissed the ticklish spot behind her ear. She laughed, and he moved lower to brush the tip of his warm tongue along her collarbone until she shivered with delight and arched her back, offering her breasts to be kissed and fondled.

He didn't disappoint her. Slowly, he unbuttoned her pajama top, one tiny button at a time, parting the silken fabric and kissing her skin until she was breathless.

"Are you real?" she whispered. "Or are you a dream?"

"I'm real enough," he answered. "It's you I can't believe. You seem like some enchanted princess imprisoned in a high tower, waiting to be rescued."

Have you come to rescue me, Morgan? Or will you fade away in the morning like dew on the grass? She wanted to ask him, but she didn't have the nerve. All that was important was this moment. If he was gone in the morning, if she never saw him again, she'd have this memory to cherish.

He threaded his fingers through her hair, and glanced up at the dark heavens. "Lots of stars tonight."

"Yes."

"When I was small, I never wanted to go to bed and my mother used to tell me stories to make me sleepy." He brushed his lips against her eyebrows, one after another. "We have a legend that tells how the stars came to be."

"Tell me." She moved her fingers in slow circles over his chest, tracing the lines of hard muscle and caressing the base of his neck. "I want to hear this story."

"I'm sure I can't tell it as well as my mother, but I'll try. Once, long ago, when the world was young, and the seas were clean, there was a mermaid, braver and more beautiful than any of the others. This mermaid never feared the storm tides as they plunged over the rocks of her island home. She didn't fear the giant squid that rose out of the depths to hunt, and she wasn't afraid of the dark hordes of—"

"Claire!" A woman's strident voice and the sound of loud rapping cut through Morgan's story.

"That's my housekeeper," Clare said. Why was Mrs. Godwin banging on her bedroom door at this hour of the night? Had she locked her bedroom door? She never did, in case she needed help. "It's Mrs. Godwin," she whispered to Morgan. "I don't want her to know that you're here."

"It's all right. The door's locked."

"But how do you know—"

He shrugged. "I locked it. I wanted to be alone with you. Was I wrong?"

"No, but I've got to let her in. You'll have to hide out here until I get rid of her."

"All right." Morgan rose from the chair with her in his arms and quickly carried her back inside. He placed her gently on the bed, kissed her, and drew a sheet over her, covering her legs and waist. "My chair," Claire whispered. "I need . . ."

He nodded and pushed the chair to the side of the bed. He blew her a kiss, then returned to the balcony, closing the door quietly behind him.

"Miss Claire!" Mrs. Godwin shouted before knocking again. "Are you all right? Your father is here."

"In the middle of the night?" Claire called.

"Claire!" That was her father's voice.

"I'll get the master key," Mrs. Godwin said. "It's by the elevator."

"Just a minute," Claire said. "I'll let you in if you give me time to get into my chair."

"Are you all right?" Richard demanded. "Is there someone in there with you? I thought I heard—"

"I'm alone," she answered, crossing her fingers. That was a lie. Well, not exactly a lie. No one was in the room with her. Morgan was trapped on the balcony. Not that anyone would have reason to look out there, but it made her feel foolish. What single adult woman couldn't have a man in her room if she wanted? "Do you want me to unlock the door?"

"Never mind," her father said. "Mrs. Godwin has a key."

Claire heard the sound of a key in the lock. The knob turned, and Richard pushed the door open. "That will do," Richard said. "Go back to bed, Mrs. G."

"Would you like anything to eat? Drinks?" the housekeeper asked. Claire saw the woman peering anxiously around her father's shoulder. "I could—"

"We can make do for ourselves," Richard assured her. "You'd better stay out here."

"Call me if there's anything suspicious."

Claire sat bolt upright. That wasn't Mrs. Godwin's voice. It wasn't Mrs. Godwin's son, and it certainly wasn't Richard. But she knew that voice all too well.

Her father came into the room. "Are you all right, pumpkin? Sorry to pop in on you at this hour of the night, but there was an accident that shut down traffic for hours. We were caught on the Petersburg bypass and—"

"We who?" Claire glared at him. "Who's with you?" she asked, although she knew perfectly well who was standing outside her bedroom door. "Not—"

Her father approached the bed, stopped, and threw up his hands in a sign of surrender. "Don't get excited. You know that drives your blood pressure up and—"

"Richard. Who did you bring with you?" She groaned and dropped back on the pillows as Justin stepped through the doorway. "You didn't!" she protested.

Justin looked exactly as he had the last time she'd seen him. Not his clothing, but his hair . . . his face. Justin wore only designer fashions, and he'd changed little in appearance since the day she'd married him. Either he had a very good plastic surgeon or he'd made a pact with the devil.

"I made it clear that I didn't want to see him. Didn't I?"

Ignoring her outburst, Richard glanced around. "You're alone? I was sure I heard voices."

"Why are you here?" Claire fisted her hands under the sheet. "You have no right to come to my home uninvited."

"Blame me," Richard said, leaning to brush a cool kiss on her forehead. "I invited him."

"We were both concerned about you," Justin said as he approached the bed. "You've lost weight. You don't look good at all. And you're flushed." He glanced at her father. "I'll take her pulse."

"Like hell, you will." Claire pointed at him. "Out of my bedroom, Justin. I don't need you playing doctor at my bedside." She had every right to be angry with them both. Her pajama top was half-unbuttoned. Her hair was a mess, not because she was ill, but because she'd been making out on the balcony, an excuse she could hardly give either of them.

"All right. All right. It's upsetting, I know, seeing me like this." Justin smiled reassuringly. "We really didn't mean to arrive at this hour, but your father thought—"

"He was wrong!"

What would Morgan think? Please, please, she prayed silently, as she tried to deal with these two without their getting suspicious of her behavior. Keep Morgan on the balcony. The last thing she wanted was to have him confront her father or Justin in her bedroom, in the middle of the night. How she'd get Morgan out of the house without being discovered, she didn't know. But she didn't want a scene. It wasn't that she was afraid of Richard, but he could make her life difficult if he took a notion that she was behaving foolishly.

"We have only your best interest at heart." Richard pushed the wheelchair away from the bed and sat on the edge of the mattress. "I apologize for startling you, but I'm not sorry I brought Justin. You're obviously having a bad time of it, and—"

"I wasn't having a bad time of it until the three of you starting banging at my door. Now, can you please let me get back to sleep?"

"You're right," Justin agreed. "You do need your rest. There will plenty of time for us to talk in the morning."

She glared at him. "No, there won't, because you'll be leaving right after breakfast."

The following morning dawned hot. There was no breeze, and the temperature was already in the high seventies by eight o'clock. At Seaborne, Nathaniel was mowing the west pasture, near the entrance lane, and Mrs. Godwin and a maid were busy in the kitchen. Claire, her father, and Justin slept in after being up so late the night before.

In the small town of Coffin's Cove, fifteen miles north along the coast, four-year-old Misty Tucker had been awake for more than an hour wanting her breakfast. The black-and-white TV on the dresser was playing a cartoon about a cat and a dog, but Misty had seen the show a lot of times. She was hungry, and the picture on the TV rolled so that it was hard to tell what was happening. It was hot, and her Tinker Bell pajamas were all sweaty.

"Mommy!" she called.

No answer.

Her mother's bedroom was next to hers, and she could hear someone snoring. Mommy got mad if Misty woke her too early. Mommy worked nights, and she liked to sleep until lunchtime, but Misty hadn't had anything to eat since the egg sandwich Hester had given her before dark.

Hester was old, so old her hair was all white and she walked with a cane, but she was her friend. She lived in the trailer behind Mommy's, and looked in on her while Mommy was at work. Hester had a little poodle named Cookie that Misty liked to pet. Someday, when she was big, Misty would have a dog just like Hester's, only pink. She would name her Queenie, because that was the best name she could think of.

Misty pushed open her bedroom door and listened. The TV in the living room was quiet, and she couldn't hear the coffeemaker. If Mommy was awake, she liked to watch TV while she drank her coffee. The trailer was quiet, except for the loud snoring coming through the wall.

As quiet as a mouse, Misty sneaked down the hall in her bare feet. Mommy's door was broken. It never stayed closed. Misty peeked in. There was Mommy and a strange man in her bed. A big pair of cowboy boots lay on the floor by the door. Misty was sure the man wasn't Uncle Mike because this man had hair and Uncle Mike was bald.

With a sigh, Misty retraced her steps, past her bedroom, and down the narrow hall to the bathroom. She made "tinkle," washed her hands, and brushed her teeth. When she got down off the stool by the sink, her tummy made a funny growling sound that reminded her how hungry she was.

Maybe there would be some cold pizza in the refrigerator, or maybe Mommy had gone to the store last night and got cereal. Misty liked the kind that was all colors and crunched. As she hurried through the living room, she saw that somebody had made a tower out of beer cans on the coffee table. There was a pizza box on the floor, but it was empty.

No grocery bags on the table. That wasn't good, because the milk that had been in the refrigerator had gone sour, and Misty had poured it down the sink. Hopefully, she opened the refrigerator door. No pizza. No milk. No juice. She pulled open the lunchmeat drawer. There was the plastic that the bologna came in from the store, but it was empty too.

Misty stood on tiptoe and peered way in the back behind the beer. There was a carton of rice that Mommy had brought home from a date last week. Misty found some pink sweetener and sprinkled that on the rice. Yesterday, she'd found ants in the sugar bowl and she didn't want to eat ants with her rice. She got a spoon and went out on the carport to eat.

Maybe Hester would come out of her trailer and talk to her. She might even ask her to come in and have pancakes with her and Cookie. When Hester got her "security," she always bought lots of groceries, cookies, potato chips, and tuna fish. Hester's pancakes were the best Misty had ever tasted, better even than at Mary's Diner.

If Hester didn't have pancakes, she always had good kinds of cereal and milk that was never sour. There wasn't much rice, and Misty was still hungry when it was gone. She was thinking about going to Hester's house and knocking on the door when something wonderful happened.

A duck walked by Mommy's car. It was a duck with a green head and tail feathers that curled up in the back. Misty wanted a better look at the duck, so she ran after it. "Here, ducky. Here, duck."

The duck stopped quacking and pecked at the dirt.

What if she could catch it? Its head looked really fuzzy. Maybe Mommy would let her keep it, and she could make a bed for it in her room. Nobody in her Head Start class had a pet duck. She could take it to school and show her teacher and the other kids.

But the duck wasn't easy to catch. Every time Misty thought she was going to grab hold of it, it flew up in the air or waddled faster. Misty trotted after the duck down the rutted drive that ran around the back of the trailer park where nobody lived and the trailers were all surrounded by junk and spooky. "Here, ducky," she coaxed as it stopped to eat a worm.

This time, Misty got a lot closer. She got so close she could see its black eyes. She started to sneak up on it, and then the duck ran down the path through the tall reeds that led to the beach. For a while, Misty just stood there trying to decide what to do. The reeds were way taller than her head and scary. And there were mosquitoes. But she could hear the duck quacking just around the bend, so she went a little farther.

And then, after she was a long way from the trailer, the duck just disappeared into the reeds. Misty sat down. She was still hot, hotter than ever. She was thirsty too. She'd never come this far by herself, and Mommy would be mad. But she remembered that this path led to the bay. There would be white sand and water and cool breezes.

Maybe, she'd just go and look at the beach. Sometimes, Hester took her there in the morning while Mommy slept. She fished and Misty got to play in the shallow water. Hester never caught any fish, but Misty didn't care because the old lady told her stories of when her husband had a boat and they went out on the water every day.

"Never go into water past your chest," Hester said.

"There are monsters in the ocean that like to gobble little girls for dinner." Mommy said that Hester was a silly old woman. There was no such thing as water monsters, but Misty wasn't sure.

A mosquito buzzed around her head and she swatted at it. She had lots of mosquito bites on her arms and legs and she didn't want any more. They itched almost as much as chiggers. Misty decided that since she'd come this far, she would just go down to the beach for a little while. Maybe the duck would be there waiting for her.

Suddenly, the reeds opened and there was the water. Misty scrambled over a few rocks and onto the shore. No one was on the beach but two seagulls. She didn't like gulls because they always sounded mad and looked like they might bite if they got too close. She sat down in the sand and looked at the waves. They looked so cool and wet. Maybe if she just waded in up to her knees, she wouldn't be so thirsty. After all, Mommy should know if there were monsters or not. Mommies knew everything.

At Seaborne, Claire joined Richard and Justin in the breakfast room at nine. The room had once been a spacious porch that ran along the eastern wall of the original house. Nana had brought in an architect who transformed the space into a charming informal eating area with ceiling-to-floor French doors, Mexican tile floors, an antique fountain, and space for lush greenery that included lime and lemon trees. It was Claire's favorite place in the house, other than her apartment. And not even Justin could dim the pleasure of sipping Columbian coffee, and eating blueberry scones and fresh strawberries at the round table that had once graced a Spanish monastery.

Claire felt immensely surer of herself this morning. Somehow, Morgan had made good his escape from the balcony. She supposed he must have climbed down to the first-story roof and then found a way to jump the last fifteen feet without breaking his neck. She'd waited a good hour before getting into her wheelchair and going out to tell him the coast was clear and everyone had gone to bed. To her surprise, Morgan was already gone. She'd imagined all sorts of things, the worst being that he was lying sprawled in a boxwood hedge with a concussion. But since the alarms hadn't gone off and Nathaniel hadn't discovered him when he was mowing, Claire supposed that Morgan had been as inventive as usual.

She was expecting her physical therapy aide at ten, which left an hour to get rid of her ex and settle things with Richard. She loved her father dearly. Any other time, she would have been delighted at his company. But, first, she was still annoyed with him because he'd lied to her about being on the swim team in college, and second, he'd gone against her express wishes and dragged Justin to Seaborne.

She wanted them both gone. She wanted time with Morgan. If Richard remained, her mystery man would stay away. And, if she could help it, that definitely wasn't happening.

"You really should have protein in the morning," Justin said. His breakfast consisted of unsweetened bran flakes, a poached egg, a handful of vitamins, and a protein shake.

In defiance, Claire spread clotted cream on her scone and took a bite. She rarely ate more than a few mouthfuls at breakfast, but she had no intention of letting Justin give her orders. Childish, maybe, but she'd earned the right to be immature where he was concerned. Childish wouldn't be adding empty calories to her scone; it would be spilling the pitcher of fresh-squeezed orange juice in his lap. She wouldn't do it, but the thought that she might made her feel better.

"I hope the traffic is better on your way back to the

city," she said pointedly. "I'd hate to see you stuck on I-95 again."

Richard looked hurt. "I'd hoped you'd see things differently today. I know it was a surprise, showing up without warning, waking you—"

"Out of a sound sleep," she finished. "You know very well, Daddy, dear, it's not you I object to." She looked directly at Justin, and he had the decency to flush, just a little. "It's him."

Her father set his cup on the table and leaned forward. "It's not good for you to be alone here, Claire. I want you to at least read this brochure from the clinic I mentioned in Switzerland. You can't ignore the chance of regaining more of your life." He removed a glossy booklet from his briefcase and pushed it toward her. "Please. Say you'll at least consider it."

"I'm sick of hospitals, doctors, sick of physical therapy that doesn't—"

"Do it for me, Claire," Richard begged. "Please."

"Listen to Richard," Justin said. "You're young. You have years ahead of you. Why would you turn down the possibility of walking again?"

Claire's throat constricted. What if her mind was playing tricks on her? What if Morgan only existed in her imagination? "I'll read your brochure," she said. "But I'd really like you and Justin to leave Seaborne after breakfast."

Her father half-rose in his chair, leaned, and put his hand over hers. "I know you want us gone," he said. "But I have to do what I think is best for you. I'm staying, at least through the weekend. And if you don't want me, if having Justin in the house upsets you so much, then you'll have to call the police and have us escorted off the property."

CHAPTER 14

"You can't continue this," Alex said. "A prince of Atlantis hiding on a human's balcony? It's embarrassing. And for what? It's not as though the two of you can be together for more than a hot interlude. They're fragile, these earthlings, and your Claire sounds more delicate than most."

The twins had joined Morgan a few leagues off Seaborne's beach in a forest of kelp no deeper than forty fathoms. His brothers had come in answer to his plea for help against the horde, but they'd taken one look at him and pronounced him unfit for battle.

"Look at you," Orion scolded. "You've aged a decade since we saw you at the palace. We aren't adapted to breathe on land. We can do it when we must, but it drains the life force. And you, big brother, are drained. How did you think you could take on Melqart's shades if you came upon them? A dozen of them would devour you. A waste of a crown prince, I'd say."

Morgan brushed away their concern. "I'm fine. Tired, but nothing more."

Alex drove a fist into his shoulder, knocking him backwards through the water an arm's length. "Right, just tired. Weak as a clown fish. Mother would have our fins if we let you dash around playing hero for a few humans. And humans you don't even know. How much danger would they put themselves in for one of us?"

Morgan rubbed his shoulder, knowing he'd be black and blue for hours. His little brother carried a mighty punch. He always had. But Alex wasn't nearly as callous as he pretended. "I thought you two had your fill of playing games with Caddoc and his buddies. Of course, if you're reluctant to take on the outriders . . ."

Orion arched a blond eyebrow. "And who said we were?" He drew his massive black sword and arched it dramatically through the water.

"No need to impress me," Morgan said. "I know how lethal you are with that."

"It's you we're worried about," Alex supplied. "Nothing wrong with either of us."

"We were just saying that it had been too long since we'd had any serious hunting," Orion said. "The shades have been decimating young mer folk off the Isle of Skye. My friend Dolaidh lost a niece and nephew, nothing left of them but bloody skins."

"Not to mention the attack off Crete," Alex added. "Eleven dead there, one an Atlantean warrior. You may have known her, Morgan. Iphigeneia? An older woman, but fit, very well respected as a fighter. Her crack team of dolphins died beside her, one an alpha. They held their own for hours, but there were just too many, and then the sharks moved in. We wouldn't have known what happened if it hadn't been for a naiad cross who was wounded and left for dead. He managed to take shelter under the keel of a wreck. Poor thing succumbed later, too badly injured to recover."

"This probably is a different pack," Morgan mused, "but it doesn't matter. One outrider is as bad as another.

Unfortunately, there's a lot of New England shoreline. I've been hunting for them, but I don't know where—"

"Alex knows," Orion said. "We passed a school of wild dolphins a few leagues away. He asked them. You know he has the knack for inter-species communication. And they were eager to share. It seems the horde killed another human this morning. The dolphins were leaving the area. You know how humans are. A little blood in the water and they start hunting sharks with guns and depth charges."

"Which includes anything with fins or flippers," Alex said. "Melqart's crew is still here and still up to mischief, not far north."

"So we're wasting time," Morgan said. "When we should be cleaning up the trash."

Alex smiled. "A man after my own heart."

After her disturbing exchange of words with her father and Justin, Claire left the breakfast room for her regularly scheduled pool workout. Three days a week, physical therapists came to Seaborne to provide the exercises she needed to prevent her legs from atrophying and to maintain upper body strength. Two of those days were scheduled for water therapy, and she'd had an indoor pool addition built adjacent to the main house after she'd come to Seaborne to live.

The therapist, Paul, was a new one from the agency. He was pleasant but efficient, and the hour went quickly. As she left the pool house, she wheeled herself along the passageway and took the elevator to the second floor. As the elevator door opened, just down the hall from her bedroom apartment, Justin was standing there waiting.

Surprised, she frowned. "You."

"Were you expecting someone else?"

She'd almost forgotten that he was still here. She'd been

thinking about Morgan, hoping to get down to the beach alone, thinking of what she'd say to him if he appeared there . . . hoping to explain her father's unannounced arrival in the middle of the night. "I'd hoped you'd taken the hint and left."

Justin effected his best clinical expression of concern. "We can't leave you when you're in this state." He moved behind her and pushed her chair down the hall, away from her suite, to a book-lined sitting room. "I was hoping we'd have a chance to talk about my offer."

"Your offer." Claire tried not to let him know how annoyed she was. The library was cool, and she was still in her bathing suit under the robe. She was chilled and wanted a shower. She didn't want to contend with Justin now.

"Marriage counseling," he said. Smiling, he took a seat in a leather lounge chair a few feet away.

This was a family room, full of comfortable furniture, pictures. When she was a child, she and Nana had come here to watch home movies on a pull-down screen. She'd rarely come in here since her accident. Justin wasn't part of this room, and she didn't particularly want him here.

"Us getting back together. Perhaps even considering a family."

"Just like that." She wanted to smack him. Instead, she focused her gaze on a silver-framed photograph of her grandmother and Richard standing beside his first car, a gently used but aging green Volvo, a gift for his sixteenth birthday.

"Claire?"

She glanced back at him, trying to control her temper. "And you expect me to forget everything that happened, buy into your 'happily ever after' fairy tale, and say 'I do'?" She shrugged one shoulder. "I may be brain injured, but I'm not a fool."

He folded his arms over his chest. "This isn't like you, Claire. It's simply further proof of your depression. You used to consider all your options before you slammed the door in my face."

"You're blaming me for our divorce?"

"I did things I shouldn't have. I admitted that, but I was provoked. If you think the breakdown of any marriage is the fault of only one partner, you're deluding yourself." He took her hand in his, and it was all she could do not to flinch. "I love you. I don't think it's too late for us to have a second chance."

"At my fortune?"

He blinked, once, twice, but his lips remained soft.

Good recovery, she thought. *You always were a cool one, Justin.* "The award was something over thirty-seven million, but I've been fortunate in my investments."

"You've changed, Claire. You were never so crass. And you didn't mind spending my money when we were married. Designer fashions. Imported shoes. Trips to Brazil and Germany to one horse show or another."

She sighed. "I was young, and that was a long time ago. I don't see how we could possibly—"

"There's more. Something that may interest you."

He steepled his beautiful hands, hands that were as manicured and cared for as carefully as any society chairwoman. Justin had never favored rings, not even a wedding ring, but she noticed that he wore a diamond that must have three carats. *Expensive,* she mused, *if it wasn't cubic zirconium.*

"I doubt it," she answered.

His eyes narrowed. "Hear me out, darling. A colleague

of mine mentioned that he knows of a student at Julliard who is interested in making an adoption plan for her baby. She's of Korean heritage, with a fantastic future in modern dance, and being a single mother isn't an option. The father, I'm told, is doing his residency in orthopedics, Caucasian, and fully invested in placing the child. The mother doesn't drink or smoke, and the baby seems to be growing normally."

Claire was stunned. It was one thing for Justin to talk about a theoretical adoption and quite another when there was an actual child involved. For a moment, she found herself speechless, and then, she asked, "How far along is she?"

"Five months, nearly six. If we're going to do this, we have to act quickly. You can imagine how many couples would like to adopt this child."

"Are you telling me the truth?"

"Of course." He removed his cell phone from his shorts' pocket. "If you don't believe me, I'll ring my friend. Or you can reach him through his office. I wouldn't lie to you about this."

"Just about being faithful?

"For a woman who pretends not to care, you're carrying far too much baggage."

Claire shivered. Why did Justin always strike where she was most vulnerable? "All right. I'll try. But you have to be honest with me. How much of this sudden desire to raise our marriage from the dead is inspired by my rosy financial situation?"

"Didn't your mother ever teach you that discussing money is poor manners?" He rose and strolled to the window, staring out across the rolling fields.

Claire ran a hand through her damp hair. "As a matter

of fact, she didn't. I can't remember much she did teach me, other than which fork to use for seafood."

"I'm sorry." He glanced back, his smooth features again composed. "I forgot that your relationship with her wasn't ideal."

"Not ideal? You could say that. I was an intrusion on her life, an unwanted annoyance, or a rival for Richard's attentions. Take your pick."

"Self-pity doesn't become you, Claire. I thought you'd resolved your issues with your mother a long time ago."

"My adoptive mother."

"Yet, you entertain the idea of motherhood yourself, and you claim to want to adopt. Is that how you see yourself? As something less than a biological mother?" He scoffed. "If you feel like that, then the child in question would be far better off with someone else."

"You missed your calling, Justin. You should have been a trial lawyer. You can draw blood without using sharp objects."

He returned to the chair and leaned forward, his gaze intent. "Since you're determined to make this difficult, I'll play devil's advocate. What if I did want to marry you for your money? We have a history. We enjoy many of the same pleasures, and I genuinely like you, Claire. At least, I like you when you aren't wallowing in self-pity."

"What are you proposing? A business arrangement?"

"If you care to put it like that. Since you refuse to believe that I still hold strong feelings for you—which I do. Your maimed body doesn't revolt me. I'm more concerned with your mind, your opinions, and your interests. We did have good times. Can you deny it?"

She shook her head. "No. But to marry just for selfish reasons . . ."

"You need someone to take care of you. No, don't deny it. Your father won't live forever. Then what? Do you want to sit here alone, old and forgotten? You're hiding from life. You've been dealt a bad hand, true enough, but you can make the most of it."

"With you?"

"Yes, with me. To begin with, we'd investigate these specialists in Switzerland. We'd do everything humanly possible to make certain you're taking advantage of the best science has to offer. And you could have the child you seem so desperately to want."

"You've stated your case. Now, if you don't mind, I'd like to get in a hot shower."

"You will think about what I've said? You won't close your mind to the possibilities? To the advantages?"

"And if we did marry, what's to keep you from deciding to place me in an institution? To shut me away somewhere, leaving you full access to my fortune?"

"Do you think Richard would allow such a thing? You could take legal precautions, an iron-clad pre-nupt. Unless you believe that I'm some sort of psychopathic monster? Why stop at imprisoning you in some hospital? Why not murder?"

She chuckled. "Even I never thought you were capable of murder, Justin. Dirty dealings, perhaps, but not violence. You aren't a violent person. That was always something I admired in you. My father has far too much of the killer instinct when it comes to getting something he wants badly."

"That's reassuring, that you don't believe I'm capable of murder."

"Seriously, if we did marry again, and I'm only saying *if*, why would the mother choose to place a child with me, in my 'condition,' as you put it?"

"Money."

Claire's eyes widened. "Don't tell me that you offered to buy her baby?"

"No, nothing of the kind. We'd pay medical expenses, assist with college tuition. She's practically destitute, a scholarship case, and she's struggled in life. It's my understanding that she wants her child placed in a financially stable home, one where if she or he chooses to follow a dream, the child won't be held back by lack of funds."

"So you think she'd overlook my lack of legs in exchange for a fat portfolio?"

Justin shrugged. "In a nutshell, yes."

"And you? What kind of father would you be to the child?"

"Probably no worse than most. I have a fondness for children, and I'm certainly not a pedophile. I have no attachment to my genes, and I like the idea of providing a home for an unwanted baby. I don't promise to change diapers and learn the words to all the nursery rhymes, but I could take an intellectual interest in a child's education."

"Hardly an emotional response."

"You asked for the truth, Claire. Richard is a rare father. He'd probably be an excellent grandfather. Our child might get the hands-on trips to the zoo and kiddy movies about lost puppies from him. I'm more the parent to take him or her to the Met or the symphony, and to sign off on a school-break trip to France or Italy when our heir is of suitable age. Not necessarily less, simply different."

"What makes you think I'm capable of being a good mother? After all, aren't I wallowing in self-pity and hiding away from the world?"

"A baby might give you exactly what you need."

"Is that fair to a child? To be exactly what I need?"

"Life is give and take, Claire. Would it be better for this

child to be adopted by some garbage collector and his cashier wife? We could give a child every advantage. And you would shower it with love. That's the type of person you are. You have a big heart, larger than mine, I admit."

"What you haven't addressed are your other needs. Am I to go into an arrangement, knowing that you'll have affairs with other women?"

"You do insist on dragging out every painful detail, don't you?"

"It's a pretty large detail."

He smiled. "Thank you for the compliment."

"We both know how well endowed you are," she said. "And how much a part of your life you devoted to satisfying your needs. I wouldn't expect that could change."

"I learn from my mistakes. I would be discreet. And if you didn't pry too closely into my personal life, you'd never have to know."

"Honest, at least. I suppose that's something that many wives learn to live with."

"All I ask is that you think about my proposition. Just don't think too long. My contact said that we have weeks, no more. If we don't step up, some other couple will."

Misty laughed as the waves broke over her belly. The water was cool and all foamy like the whipped cream that Hester squirted on her hot chocolate. Misty scooped up handfuls of water and splashed it on her face and neck. It felt so good that she squealed with delight.

And then, just as she was having so much fun, something even better happened. The duck flew out of the reeds, over the beach, and landed in the water, just a little ways from where Misty was standing.

"Hey, Duck!" Misty shouted. The duck was paddling in the waves, using his bill to smooth his feathers, and sticking his head underwater. He looked so silly. "Hey, Duck, it's Misty! Do you want to play with me?"

The duck was so close. Misty waded out a few more feet. Water rose to her bubbies, but she was still standing on the bottom, so she knew she wouldn't drown. The beach was right there. She took another few steps.

Suddenly, the duck flew up with a startled squawk.

Misty stared up at it. The duck looked scared, but what was there to be scared of? Misty looked all around her, suddenly feeling all shivery. The sun, that had been shining so bright, was gone, and dark clouds made the air cold.

Frightened, but not knowing why, she took a step back toward the beach. Abruptly, something grabbed her ankle and jerked her feet out from under her.

Misty screamed as the water closed over her head.

CHAPTER 15

Water filled Misty's nose and throat. She kicked and struck out with both fists, trying to dislodge the *thing* that bit into her ankle. It hurt! Bad! Raw terror seized her. She couldn't breathe! Something was eating her! Choking, she fought with every ounce of her strength to get away.

Monster! One of Hester's monsters had her. It was going to gobble her up. It hurt worse than when she'd spilled Mommy's hot coffee on her chest and had to go to the hospital. Misty could feel her flesh ripping, her skin tearing.

A red tide flooded her thoughts. Now the monster was chewing her arm. She could feel his hot breath and sharp teeth. She tried to scream, but the water kept pouring into her mouth. Her chest felt like it was going to explode. She was slipping . . . slipping into blackness. Terror strengthened her will. Thrashing, she raised her head above water, gulped the air and waved frantically. She coughed up lungsful of water and managed a strangled cry for help before the biting thing pulled her under again. . . .

Waves closed over Misty's head. She clawed at the smothering thing that pulled her down. And then she felt teeth clamp onto her throat. With a long moan, she sank beneath the waves, letting the tide drag her deeper, letting the monsters carry her away.

On the beach, Hester shouted and waved her cane. The small white poodle barked frantically and ran up and down on the wet sand. A fisherman came running. The old woman pointed to the place where she'd seen the struggling child go under. "Shark!" Hester screamed. "A shark attacked Misty! Help! For God's sake, help!"

Beneath the water, the horde crowded greedily around the human child. Snarls and growls gave evidence of the current possessors' determination to retain their prize and others' fierce drive to claim her. Distracted by their fresh prey, the shades failed to keep watch.

Orion and Alex descended on the pack from either side, while Morgan slashed a path through the center. Howls and yips of dying shades alerted the school too late, and fully half were dead or mutilated before the innermost realized that they were in deadly peril of being overrun.

To his left, Morgan was aware of Orion's legendary blade cutting a swathe through the savage abominations. On his right, he sensed, rather than saw Alex, but he had no fear for his little brother. Against such an enemy as this, Alex was in little danger. And while Orion bellowed an ancient Atlantean war cry in the heat of battle, Alex remained as silent and lethal as a Pacific tsunami.

A shapeless form arose out of the churning mud, teeth bared, eyes glowing. Morgan sliced it in half with a single backhanded stroke. Another seized his thigh. He disabled that one with a downward thrust of his Phoenician dagger. Two more clung to his back, biting and clawing. Blood streamed from a dozen gashes on his torso and neck.

"Morgan?" In the shower, Claire started bolt upright in her chair. "Morgan?" Her heart hammered against her ribs. The hairs on the back of her neck prickled, and she gave a deep shuddering sigh. Without warning, without reason, she was shaking. Her chest felt as though a heavy weight was pressing on it. It was difficult to breathe, and she felt stinging pains in her arms and legs.

Tears blurred her vision, and she began to sob uncontrollably. She leaned against the side of the shower, weak and confused, trying to make sense of this. How had she suffered phantom pains in all her limbs when she had no feeling below the waist?

What was happening to her? Was she suffering a seizure? No, in spite of her weird physical sensations, she instinctively knew that it wasn't her—it was Morgan. Something terrible had happened to Morgan.

Not had happened. The crisis was happening now. She could taste it—feel it in the pit of her stomach. Morgan was in terrible danger. Worse . . . there was nothing she could do to help him. Nothing . . .

Morgan twisted and slashed at the two shades on his back, beheading one and sending the second shrieking away, missing most of what passed for an arm. Blood spilled from Morgan's throat, but he judged the wound to be not mortal.

A strange buzzing sounded in his ears. He glanced from side to side, oddly expecting to see Claire's face materialize out of the swirling water. Impossible! Had he lost more blood than he'd thought? What was wrong with him that thoughts of Claire would cloud his mind at a time when he needed all his concentration to deal with the task at hand?

The child. He had to reach the child in time. He and the twins had been almost within sight of the horde when the shades had attacked and dragged her under. He'd smelled the little girl's fear, caught only a glimpse of small white legs and a terrified face, before the outriders swarmed over her.

There was only a brief window of time. Even now, the child might be saved. With a mighty effort, he pushed Claire and his need for her to a shadowy recess of his mind.

The outriders had not all feasted on the victim's life force, not if they followed their usual methods. The one who'd struck the first bite, that predator would have taken precedence over his comrades. Slowly, while she yet lived, the shade would suck out the child's soul and living essence, taking long minutes to drain the last spark of energy. To kill her too quickly would mean the loss of that which Melqart desired most, and to displease their master meant extinction for great swathes of the damned creatures.

He had to get to the child before she expired of drowning or loss of blood, before her soul was stolen. If he couldn't save her life, he might yet preserve that which was hers—that which she would use in a future life beyond this existence. Had this been an Atlantean or a mer youngster, his chances would have been better. Humans were so terribly vulnerable—so frail of body and spirit. And this one, in particular, was so small, so young.

It was that helplessness that tugged at his too-soft heart and would not allow him to abandon her. . . .

Abruptly, a grimly smiling Alex loomed at his side. Together they descended on the remaining four monsters that pressed the child down in the sand and fed off her. The first never realized what hit him as Alex's blade ripped through its midsection. The thing beside it squealed and withdrew its fanged maw, dripping blood . . . so much that the saltwater was stained pink with it. Morgan cut that shade in two while Alex dispatched another.

The remaining fiend seemed so intoxicated by the child's life force that it could not release its prey, even to preserve its own existence. Morgan finished it off, and then gathered the convulsing girl in his arms.

Her throat was torn in two places. Gashes gaped on her arms and legs. White rib bone gleamed through the mud-churned water. Her head hung back, her eyes rolled up, only whites showing, her small mouth open. Her blond hair streamed out behind her in the tide like so much seaweed.

"Too late," Alex said.

His gruff tone didn't deceive Morgan for an instant. Inside, he knew his brother was screaming with rage for the loss of such an innocent to the likes of Melqart. Of all his brothers, Alex was the most tenderhearted when it came to young things, be they silkies, naiads, or a hammerhead shark. A veritable Achilles, Alex rarely showed mercy to his enemies on the battlefield, but no small and vulnerable creature need fear him, only those who would take their lives.

"A pity." Orion joined them, his great sword, hands, and arms stained with the stinking blood of the unclean creatures he had slain and maimed.

"She was lost from the moment she walked into the water," Alex said.

Morgan lifted the child, pressing his ear to her mangled chest, listening for the faintest proof that her heart still beat, but there was only silence. A great sadness welled up inside him, as again he thought of his Claire. She had been such a child once, laughing, full of life and curiosity. It wasn't Claire's fault that she'd been born human and weak, nor this little girl's fault. And it was unfair that this tiny humanoid should die in such a way on such a beautiful day.

Save her. Claire's voice echoed in his head. *You know what to do. Do it quickly, before it's too late.*

No, he thought. Not in *his* head. He was reading her thoughts as he had the sperm whale's. He wasn't hearing Claire's voice, but absorbing the plea she sent out to him across the sea. *Save her for me.*

Alex's eyes narrowed. "No, Morgan. Don't. You can't."

"I can," he answered, shaking off the hand his brother placed on his shoulder.

"Think of the consequences," Orion counseled. "Aren't you in enough trouble at home? Father might not be so forgiving this time."

Morgan bent his head over the dead child and breathed into her slack mouth. She stirred faintly in his arms.

"Don't do it," Orion advised. "You'll live a thousand years to regret it."

Morgan concentrated on the girl, shutting out everything else: his brothers, the red tide swirling around them, the doubts rising in his mind. He gently pinched her nose closed and gave her the breath of life . . . the energy not of a human, that time was past, but that of an Atlantean.

Shock stunned him, nearly knocking him off his feet. He could feel the strength draining from his limbs, feel his bones soften, and his muscles become water. Weak . . . he was so weak that the child seemed to weigh a ton in his arms. He staggered, barely able to hold her.

Orion swore a mighty oath.

Salt tears sprang from Morgan's eyes. He sank to the ocean bottom, the little girl still cradled against his chest. And once again, he pressed his lips to hers, not as he would a woman, but in a last-ditch effort to hold back the extinction of a precious life.

The little girl coughed and sighed heavily. Her eyelids flickered.

Yes, Claire murmured faintly in his heart. *Yes.*

It was nearly impossible for Morgan to hold his eyes open. They burned with fatigue. His muscles ached, and his head felt too heavy for his neck. "Help me," he managed.

Orion shook his head. "This is your doing, Brother. I'll have none of it."

But Alex couldn't resist the helplessness of the child. He knelt beside Morgan and helped to hold her up as Morgan breathed once more into her mouth.

This time, she gave a gasp and her eyes opened, no longer blue and human, but green as the sea. Her hair, so thin and stringy, so limp, thickened and turned from pale white to a shade of molten gold. Life returned to her face, her body. Limbs that hung limply plumped and grew strong. The thin face grew round cheeked, and her wounds began to turn from raw gaping holes to pink and then to healthy flesh.

The force thrummed through Morgan, making his skin and scales vibrate, sending burning sensations through him. His own injuries were healing as well, but much slower than normal. Blood loss and the vast exertion of energy that he'd breathed into the child had made him nearly incapable of holding up his own head. He curled on the sand and closed his eyes, too weary to think of the consequences, too weak to care.

It was the right thing to do, he heard Claire murmur. *I love you. I'm proud of you.*

Claire? His last thought was of his Claire as he drifted into unconsciousness, leaving Alex to take the whimpering child into his arms.

"Shh, shh, little one," Alex said.

"Monsters," she wailed. "Monsters trying to eat me."

"They can't hurt you now," Alex soothed. "You're safe now. Safe here with your father."

"But I don't . . . have . . . don't got a daddy," she managed.

"You do now," Orion said. "He's here, sleeping beside you. He'll love you and care for you always."

Her eyelids fluttered and she sighed. "For real?" she whispered.

"For real and forever," Alex said. "So long as you both shall swim."

"Morgan? Where are you?" Claire called into the wind. Her only answer was the lonely shriek of a gull swooping overhead. The sound pierced Claire's skull, making her migraine worse. She felt queasy, her stomach in turmoil, her head throbbing with a white-hot pain.

What had happened to her in the shower? Was Morgan safe or had something terrible happened to him? She'd suffered strange symptons since her accident, but nothing like this.

If she closed her eyes against the bright sunlight, scenes of dark water and white shapes swirled across the back of her lids. She could almost smell blood, a sweetly-acrid scent she'd never forget from the awful weeks and months in the hospital.

It hadn't been easy to wheel her chair out of the house and down to the cliff edge without being seen. Every moment, she'd expected to hear her father's voice or see Justin coming after her. The elevator had jammed as she'd made the descent, and she'd spent long moments pushing buttons, her heart in her throat, until finally, with a creaking of gears, it had begun to move again.

She had no reason to believe that Morgan would be

here. She'd only hoped. The thought that he might not be real was always with her. She needed to see him, needed to touch him, desperately needed to know that he wasn't a figment of her imagination.

And she had to know that her earlier fears were only a product of her brain injury. Nothing had happened to him. He was alive and well. Wasn't he?

She wasn't ignorant of her condition. The doctors had warned her of possible blood clots in her brain . . . of hallucinations and seizures. It was why she could never legally obtain a driver's license. It was why being paralyzed from the waist down was the least of her problems.

There were also the foreign substances that remained lodged in her brain, pieces of metal too deep and too dangerous to remove by surgery, objects that could move and kill her in an instant. Is that what had happened? Had her fears for Morgan been only the movement of a minute shard of metal? Would her condition now become worse? And if there was that possibility, it would be wrong to take on the responsibly of a child. It wouldn't be fair to bring a baby into her damaged world, would it?

"Morgan!" she shouted again. "Where are you?" *Please, please,* she begged silently. *Please come to me. Take me under the water with you. Hold me in your arms. Keep me safe.*

"Claire?"

She turned, hoping against hope that he was here with her. But even as she twisted in her chair, she realized that the man striding toward her wasn't Morgan but Justin. Her heart sank.

"What on earth are you doing here?" he demanded. "Your father and I have searched all over the house for you. Haven't you noticed the storm moving in? We're in for a gale, a bad one, according to the weather channel. A child was caught in the undertow this morning and swept out to sea not far from here. It was all over the news."

She blinked. "A storm?" She swallowed. Yes, the wind had risen. Dark clouds raced in from the northeast, and the beach was free of birds. White caps churned and crashed against the shore. "I . . . I hadn't noticed."

"Do you know what time it is? You missed dinner. Mrs. Godwin thought you were sleeping, so we didn't disturb you." He leaned down and kissed her forehead. "You feel warm to me, Claire. I hope you aren't feverish again."

It was after dinner? She tried to grasp the loss of time. She must have been down here for hours. Her migraine had faded, but she felt oddly disoriented. She could feel the tight prickle of sunburn on her face and arms. Had she even bothered to apply sunscreen? Surely, it hadn't been this dark when she last noticed.

"Are you all right? You look confused."

"No, I think I dozed off." She forced a chuckle. "I suppose I lost track of time."

"Another seizure more likely." He pushed her chair down the walk toward the elevator. "We're calling your physician, and I won't take no for an answer. You've got to take better care of yourself."

She glanced back over her shoulder at the ocean. Was he out there somewhere? Would he ever come to her again? Or had it all been a wonderful and terrible illusion?

CHAPTER 16

As the hours after the battle with the shades passed and Morgan showed no signs of recovery, Alex and Orion's fears for his safety grew. Not only was their brother's condition growing worse, but the child he'd sacrificed so much to transform from human to Atlantean was failing as well.

Far above, the waves whipped to storm heights, crashing against the rocks of nearby islands, and driving vessels from the sea. The whales dove deep, and the birds took shelter amid trees or craggy outcrops. Gale winds howled and the water churned from blue-green to inky black, while below, all remained calm and quiet.

Alex had carried Morgan into the shelter of a tall seaweed jungle. Nothing moved here but summer flounders and a single juvenile lobster, all more concerned with hunting dinner without becoming one. Rough water on the surface mattered little on the ocean floor, but Morgan was better protected here from schools of marauding sharks and other predators.

He and the child lay side by side on a cushiony bed of sea grass. She remained restless, only half conscious, tossing and crying out as if she was in pain. Morgan lay like a stone. Since they'd carried him from the site of the struggle, he hadn't stirred.

"If we're not careful, we could lose both of them," Orion said. "He's obviously in no condition to give her the strength she needs to survive the process. I think one of us should take her to Atlantis."

Alex nodded. "Yes, Mother will know what to do with her. She has a soft heart. She'd defy Poseidon to see that the girl gets to the temple for care. And it will take more than healing her body. To be merciful, it's best if she forget everything in her old life."

"I agree." Orion glanced at the child. She no longer looked human, not entirely, but neither was she Atlantean. Her gills were rudimentary, and her fins nonexistent. Her color was a pale green. It was a wonder that she hadn't drowned. "Do you think he fully realized what he was taking on? That he'd be responsible for her for the next eight hundred years? I could never picture Morgan as a single father."

Alex sighed. "I was tempted to do the same. It's hard to see little ones die senselessly. Even humans."

"But you didn't do it, did you?" Orion paced in frustration. "How long has it been since anyone's done this? Transformed a human? Centuries? No good will come of it, I promise you."

Alex bent over Morgan and pressed a hand to his brother's brow. "I think he's worse. He needs more than we can give him, and he needs it now. He wouldn't live to reach Atlantis."

"If we delay, she'll die. And if we try to move him, we'll lose him. What option do we have?"

"You take her," Alex said. "Shar-nehey-wah isn't far. I'll take him there and beg mercy from the serpent-folk."

Orion looked unconvinced. "Shamans' Caverns? Good luck with that. The serpent-people would as soon see him gull food on a mud flat as to share their healing secrets."

"They're unfriendly to our kind, I'll give you that. And theirs is a primitive society, but their medicine is powerful. If I can persuade them to help, I think he'll have a better chance than just sitting here and hoping he'll recover on his own."

"Or die. But you don't expect me to take the child back to Atlantis? You're the one who's good with young things. What am I going to do with her?"

Alex glanced from Orion to the girl. He was torn between doing his best for the half-human child and staying here with his brother. Orion was right. He was better with young ones than he was, but he'd have to manage. "Keep her alive until you get her to Mother."

"And how much do I tell the queen? You know how she is. She'll want to know where Morgan is."

"Tell her the truth. Go now. We don't have much time. Look at Morgan's color. He's fish-belly white and barely alive. Spending all that time on the surface with that human woman didn't help. His life force was already depleted."

Orion hesitated. "What if the youngling dies on the way back to Atlantis? Why do I have to be the one to take her?"

"Because you don't have the faintest clue how to speak serpent." Alex felt bad about this. No matter which task he took on, the possibility for failure was present.

"Right."

"Have faith, Brother. Whatever it takes, you'll get her there alive."

With a grimace, Alex gathered the little girl in his arms

and passed her to his brother. "Go, and go quickly. Take the shortcuts. Use any means you can to get there fast."

"I'll do it," Orion grumbled. "I'll be back as soon as I can with reinforcements." His jaw tightened. "It's all the fault of that human. If she hadn't—"

"Morgan should have known better, but when did he ever take the easy path?"

"Take care of him," Orion said. "If anything happens to him, I'm next in line for the throne, and that's one honor I'm not seeking."

Alex nodded as he picked up Morgan. "Either of us, Orion. Either of us."

"You're ill," Richard said to Claire. "And being here so long, squirreled away like some recluse, hasn't helped your mental outlook. What were you thinking to sit down there on the beach for hours? Look at your face. You're sunburned and dehydrated. When the doctor comes, I'm going to ask him to give you a sedative."

"I don't need a sedative," Claire protested. "And I think I know whether I'm ill or not. Maybe I just wanted to be alone to think."

"Or maybe you were expecting that con man again. I've asked Nathaniel to keep an eye out for him. If he shows, Nathaniel has instructions to forbid him entry to the property."

"You have no right to say who can and can't come to my home," she answered hotly.

"Yes, I do. When your safety is concerned, I do. You're not capable of managing your affairs. I want you to return to the city with Justin and me. Justin's told me that he's asked you to consider marriage counseling. It sounds reasonable to me. I think you should go."

Claire's stomach clenched. Her headache had returned, and she wanted nothing more than to crawl into her bed and sleep for twelve hours. Instead, she had to deal with the physician that her father had called, and she had to contend with both Richard's and Justin's insistence that she leave Seaborne.

It wouldn't do to lose her temper with Dr. Chou, the young physician that Richard had engaged to come to the house. She couldn't imagine how much her father must have offered the man to come out in a nor'easter for less than an emergency.

But Dr. Chou was on his way, and if she appeared less than competent, who knew what the three of them would do? She'd not give them an excuse to treat her like a mentally challenged patient. She'd asked Justin if he intended to put her into an institution. Now, if she weren't careful, it might be Richard who took that step.

She forced herself to eat the chicken soup that Mrs. Godwin had prepared for a light supper, and she'd drunk a glass of orange juice and a second one of water. She finished her meal with a fruit salad and an almond cookie, none of which she wanted. But when the young Dr. Chou arrived, soaked through despite his all-weather slicker, her vital signs were good, her temperature and blood pressure were normal.

Actually, she liked Chou. In a parade of doctors—she'd seen so many over the past two years that she'd lost count—he was both competent and reasonable. He'd prescribed rest, liquids, and a sensible diet. He promised to call again in a few days.

After Dr. Chou's departure, Claire turned her attention to her father. "You've made your point. I think you may be right."

"About what?" Richard asked suspiciously.

They were in her bedroom suite. Where Justin was at the moment, she didn't know and didn't particularly care. Richard was enough to deal with. "I'm going to consider Justin's proposal," she blurted out. "Not marriage. I'm not going that far yet, but I will think about it. It would mean a big change in my life, and I'd like privacy to decide what's best."

"You're asking us to leave Seaborne?" He glanced toward the windows where needles of rain drove against the glass panes and the shutters banged and groaned in the onslaught of wind. "In this?"

"No, not in this," she said. "When the storm passes."

"It could last three days. The roads may be impassable."

"Dr. Chou got through."

"He was driving a Land Rover. And he nearly got stuck a mile from the driveway coming in."

"You know I wouldn't throw you out in the middle of a storm."

"Well, that's something. I'm glad to hear it." The lights flickered, and something crashed and rattled across the patio below.

"Now who's being juvenile?" she asked. "I need time to think."

Richard's face fell. "I never thought the day would come when I'd be unwelcome in your home."

"You know I love you more than anyone on earth. It's just that with the two of you here, I feel . . . bullied."

"Bullied?" He cupped her cheek with his hand. "How could you ever believe that I—"

"For starters, you brought Justin here against my wishes." Another gust of wind hit the house and the lights blinked out and then came back on in seconds.

"Why you want to live here so far from civilization is beyond me," he said.

"Don't change the subject. Both of you would like to wrap me in swaddling cloth and tuck me into a rocking chair. It's my life, Richard. As messed up as it is, I have to figure this out for myself."

"All right, we'll leave as soon as the roads are passable. But I want you to call me. Every day. And if I don't hear from you, I'll be on a plane back here ASAP." He frowned. "And I want you to agree to fly to Switzerland and be evaluated at the clinic."

"One demand at a time," she said. "Isn't that what you always taught me?"

"You're insufferable. You always were. I've spoiled you rotten and now it comes back to slap me in the face."

She ignored his whining. "A few days, maybe a week. Justin knows of a young woman who's seeking adoptive parents for her unborn child. If I'll marry him, he believes we can be that couple."

"A baby? Do you really think your health would allow—"

"That's something I need to consider, isn't it? Wouldn't you like to be a grandfather?"

"It's not something I've given much thought."

A knock at the door caught Claire's attention. Mrs. Godwin entered with a kerosene oil lamp and a flashlight. She placed both on the nightstand beside the bed. "Just in case," the woman said. "We do have the generator, but that could fail too."

"I doubt it," Claire said. "It never has." If there was a power failure, the generator could be activated by flipping a switch in the utility room. Newer models were automatic, but this one was large, dependable, and expensive.

"Always a first time." The housekeeper glanced at

Claire's father. "Mr. Justin wants you to know that he's retired for the night."

"Thank you," Richard said. He looked at the door
pointedly. "It's late. You probably want to get to bed as
well."

She nodded. "Breakfast at nine, sir?"

"Yes, thank you," Claire said, dismissing her. When
they were alone, she looked back to Richard. He'd pulled
up a chair and taken a seat.

"Have you ever thought of marrying again?" she asked
him.

"God, no! Why would you ask that after all these years?
One wife like your mother was enough. Why would I want
to put myself through that again?"

"My feelings exactly," Claire said. "I know Justin all
too well, and the only reason I'd ever consider remarrying
him would be to adopt a child. My life feels so empty, that
the trade-off might be worth it."

Claire woke to the sensation of being carried. For a moment, she was certain she was dreaming. Her eyelids felt
heavy, almost impossible to open. Around her, she could
smell the sea. Salt air blew against her face. Hope surged
in her chest. "Morgan?"

No answer.

Strong arms held her. She felt the surf rise over her legs
and waist and breasts. She steeled herself for a rush of
water in her mouth, but it didn't come. Instead, she found
herself swept along in the powerful grasp of a blue man.
Fear mingled with awe.

She blinked, wanting to pinch herself. This wasn't the
way the dream was supposed to go. "Morgan, wait," she
said.

192 Katherine Irons

But the eyes that stared into hers weren't Morgan's. The handsome face wasn't his. And the touch of his skin against hers was that of a dangerous stranger. She began to struggle, and immediately had the sensation of choking. She gasped and cried out.

"Be at peace," rumbled a deep voice. "You're in no danger." She wasn't hearing it, not as she did Morgan's familiar timbre. Rather, she heard the words in her mind, each word carefully enunciated.

"Who are you?" she demanded.

"Shh, shh, it will all be clear soon enough. Trust me."

Trust him? She pushed against him, but his arms were like steel bands. His hands . . . Sweet Mother of God! For the briefest space of a moment she was sure she saw webbing between the fingers of his large, beautiful hands. This is a dream, she told herself. I'm dreaming. Morgan didn't come back, so I've dreamed up another one.

Immediately, her breathing relaxed and the terror faded. She should have been afraid of this new phantom, but she wasn't. Hadn't she called him up? With a sigh, she let her body go limp, molding her limbs against his, opening her eyes wide to take in the glorious scene around her.

A school of cod swam by, hundreds of them, their scales flickering iridescent colors through the water.

"Morgan needs you," came the voice in her head. They were going deeper. She could tell by the way the light faded. She could still see well enough, but the water here felt cooler.

"Morgan needs me?"

"I'm taking you to him."

"Who are you?" she demanded. It was her dream, after all. She should be in control, not this Nazi fish man. "Do you have a name?"

Amusement vibrated from his chest. "I do, but there's no need for you to know it."

She reached up and touched his face. What had she been thinking? He wasn't a monster. He was a man, clean-shaven, high cheekbones, square chin, lovely, classical nose. What had made her think he was other than human? She glanced down at the big hands that held her. No webs, simply strong, broad hands, the hands of a man who did manual labor, rather than sat at a desk.

"I insist you tell me your name," she said.

He laughed. "You're not in a position to demand anything of me, Claire."

"You know my name." He dove even deeper. Strange fish that she didn't recognize drifted past. There was a squid and, not far away, a small shark. "Who are you?" she repeated.

"What's important for you to know is that Morgan is ill. He's been calling for you. If you will help him to the best of your ability, I'll return you safely to your home."

He stopped swimming. Just below and to the left, Claire saw what appeared to be the opening to a large conduit or tunnel. Water rushed into the mouth of the hole, swirled, and was sucked down.

Suddenly, she was afraid. "Tell me that we're not going down there."

"Close your eyes and hold tight."

In an instant the current caught them. Claire screamed as they were caught in the whirlpool, tumbled over and over, and were pulled down into utter blackness.

CHAPTER 17

The force of the water was so great that Claire could hardly bear it. She'd always hated the dark, and this plunge into the roaring abyss seemed endless. Disoriented and terrified, she clung to her guide, too frightened to cry out. Down and down they plummeted, twisting, tumbling, carried on by the intensity of the powerful current.

If this was a dream, it was time to wake up. And if it wasn't, she was lost beyond redemption. Her heart galloped and bucked as though it would burst, and her courage wavered. She was seconds away from total surrender to the nightmare, ready to let the rushing water suck her down, when they splashed into a calm eddy. Rays of light warmed Claire's face as they bobbed to the surface, and she opened her eyes to see a broad river bathed in a kaleidoscope of ever-changing colors.

She gazed up, expecting to see sky and clouds, but there was no familiar sun and no blue heaven. Instead, the vast curving roof of this strange world shimmered a pale emerald swirled with ribbons of jade. Shining gold stars, larger and closer than any star she'd even seen, drifted across the emerald sky, borne on an unseen tide. On either side of the river, great forests of towering trees crowded the banks, gnarled roots sprawling down the mossy banks to vanish into the cool, clear water, massive limbs twisting and stretching toward the distant stars. The leaves of these trees were of varied shapes and sizes, some whimsical, others starkly beautiful. Not even in Ireland had Claire seen so many shades of green.

She bit her forefinger, first to make certain she was solid, and second to find some point of reference to counter the odd sensations she was experiencing. What seemed like air around her moved and flowed like water, but liquid so clear and transparent it was invisible. . . . Water that she breathed as easily as she'd inhaled the ocean breeze on the cliff at Seaborne. How soft this water felt against her skin, how comforting. It seemed to her like some magical cream that would wash away all traces of fear and sorrow.

"What place is this?" she asked as she twisted to face her mysterious escort. She could see him all too well in the radiant light. He bore some resemblance to her mysterious Morgan. This man's hair was as blond, though longer, his features as magnificent, but his eyes were not Morgan's eyes. There was more than a hint of predator in these icy green eyes, and she instinctively sensed that beneath the mask of protector coiled a waiting menace.

"The worst is over." His gaze bored into hers, probing, searching out her deepest secrets. "You did well," he said. "Don't fail Morgan now."

"Do you make a practice of never answering questions?"

The corners of his sensual mouth turned up in a faint smile. "Not if I can help it."

She waited.

"This is Shar-nehey-wah, the sacred caves of the serpent-people."

"Serpents?" A ribbon of fear curled in the pit of her stomach. This was definitely a nightmare, and she wanted to wake up. The sooner, the better. She shivered. "You mean serpents as in snakes?"

He glanced to her left. She followed his line of sight and recoiled as she caught a glimpse of a face peering up at her from beneath the surface of the river. For the space of a heartbeat, black, almond-shaped eyes stared into hers. And then, with a splash, the face was gone. She looked back at her guide, wondering if her mind was playing tricks on her. The water seemed deep, but it also appeared that she could see a long way down into the green depths. If there had been someone or something, how could they vanish so quickly? Impossible in reality, less so in a dream, she supposed.

"They're curious, but none will hurt you here," came the amused voice in her head. "We are as strange to them as they are to us. Just don't expect a welcoming basket of fruit. There is a saying among my kind that those of the serpent race are born old and cantankerous. Each can tolerate no company but his own. How they make peace long enough to breed is a mystery to me."

The river had grown noticeably narrower, and now Claire could make out shapes moving among the trees. Sinewy bodies, some green, some silver, others brown with yellow patterns. She couldn't tell what sort of creatures they were, whether humanlike, reptile, or animal. She saw dark, piercing eyes . . . glimpsed muscular arms, but no legs. Instead they appeared to have thick, trunklike tails that ended in fins like a mermaid's.

If these were the serpent-people, they wore little or no clothing, and every inch of skin appeared painted or tattooed in fantastic and multicolored designs. Most wore close-fitting hoods that made them appear even more snakelike. But as she stared at them, they were inspecting her, so much so that her skin prickled with the burning sensation of being watched.

She'd been studying the serpent-creatures so intently that she hadn't realized that her protector had carried her out of the river and onto a white-pebbled beach. Beyond, a path through the trees opened up, and he followed it, striding along as though her weight was nothing to him.

"Put me down," she said. "I'm capable of walking." And she was. How or why, she couldn't fathom, but she knew that she'd left her paralysis behind at Seaborne. She wanted to feel the joy of walking under her own power, longed for it as a thirsty plant needs rain.

"It's not much farther. We'll make better time, this way. And no one will snatch you off the path for a better look."

"Right." She exhaled softly. That made sense, she supposed. The serpent-people were here as well. She could catch glimpses of spooky eyes peering through the foliage. They gave her the shivers.

As her captor walked on, she stared wide-eyed at the unfamiliar, large-leafed trees, the shaggy trunks that seemed enveloped in thick moss, and the curtains of hanging vines that bore an odd-looking but sweet-smelling purple fruit.

"Don't touch it," he warned. "And whatever you do, don't eat it. Your legs will fuse into a swimming tail."

Her mouth gaped. "You're not serious?"

"No." He laughed. "The fruit is wabi, and it's delicious." He plucked one from a low-hanging branch and handed it to her.

Claire accepted his gift warily. The pineapple-shaped object was thin-skinned and gave off a delightful odor, something between vanilla bean and strawberry. She wanted to taste it, but . . . She wasn't sure she could trust him. What if she did grow a tail?

As if reading her mind, he chuckled, leaned close, and took a bite. Purple juice ran down his chin and he wiped it away. "Coward," he teased. "And I was beginning to think you were an exception to your race."

Claire took a deep breath and nibbled at the wabi. It was wonderful, irresistible. Quickly, she took another bite, chewed slowly, and savored the rainbow of exquisite flavors.

"What do you think?"

"Mmm." She finished off the fruit and licked her fingers.

"It does have one side effect," he added. He met her gaze and arched one perfect gilded eyebrow.

"Yes? And what is that?"

He grinned wickedly. "It's said to stimulate the sexual appetite."

Claire opened her eyes. Strange, because she couldn't remember closing them, couldn't remember feeling sleepy. They were no longer moving through the trees with golden starlight sparkling through the leaves. Instead, the trees were gone, and she was surrounded by a misty, dark haze. From somewhere in the distance, she heard an owl hooting, and nearby, the muffled cadence of a drum. Her guide still had her in his arms, but he was standing, muscles tense, alert for what she couldn't tell.

She felt strangely relaxed, as though she'd slept for hours. One by one, her senses came alive: touch, hearing, smell. She stretched and peered up at her guide through heavy-lidded eyes, suddenly aware of the scent of his hair and skin. . . . Suddenly she was all too conscious of the feel of his warm flesh pressed against hers.

"You really should tell me your name," she coaxed.

Okay, so this was her dream, and she'd been kidnapped

from her bed in the middle of the night by some strange superhero. Or villain. Whether he was her hero or a dastardly evil ogre was yet to be proved, but he had arms to die for, washboard abs, and shoulders too wide and glorious for any flesh-and-blood man. Not to mention that he smelled good, sexy good, curl your toes and scream for mercy good. All sorts of X-rated fantasies began popping up in her mind like bubbles in a glass of expensive champagne.

She slipped an arm around his neck. Muscles there too, not football line backer solid-as-a-brick-wall, but panther-quick, I-can-bench-press-a-jillion-pounds-and-never-crack-a-sweat muscles. Danger radiated from him, but she sensed that she had nothing to fear. Claire nestled her cheek against his chest and smiled up at him.

He groaned. "I warned you about that."

She giggled. "About what?" She trailed her fingertips down over his collarbone. If he was a superhero bad guy, he came in a nice package.

"Cut it out."

She ignored his warning. "I have to call you something." She teased his chest with the tip of her tongue. "Don't I?"

"Claire!"

She stiffened. Someone had called her name from the surrounding darkness. Not someone—Morgan! "I'm here," she cried. "Where are you?"

A fur-swathed figure glided from the shadows, a turtle-shell rattle in one hand. She couldn't tell if the newcomer was one of the serpent-people or not. He wore some sort of long robe that brushed the white oyster shells carpeting the floor. If he had a tail rather than legs, it was hidden.

As he grew closer, Claire made out fierce black eyes in a masked face, a towering headdress of fur, shells, and bone.

The drumbeat and the primitive garb suddenly made sense. Not a snake-creature, she realized, but a Native American tribesman in full regalia. A little hazy on his time period, perhaps, but a man, nevertheless. She breathed a little easier, suddenly aware of the smell of wet fur, scorched feathers, and fresh-turned earth.

"The high shaman," her escort murmured. "It wouldn't hurt to be on your best behavior. He could transform you into a giant oyster if he took a mind to."

"Right."

Her companion's expression remained stern. "Absolutely accurate."

She looked around, ignoring superhero and the masked Indian's bobbing head and the rattle being shaken in her face. "Morgan!" she called. "Where are you?"

Seemingly satisfied, the shaman shuffled aside, motioning to an alcove in the cavern wall. For this was a cave, Claire realized, thinking that they must be deep in the earth, perhaps even under Seaborne itself. The surroundings were cooler here than in the forest, and it smelled damp and musty, like the caverns she'd explored in France where she'd visited a Neanderthal burial site.

Abruptly, Claire's guardian lowered her to the ground and released her. She wobbled, got her balance, and stood solidly. Once she was certain she wasn't going to fall on her butt, she glanced back at him, but he'd already vanished in the thick fog, stealing away without a sound.

She didn't need him anymore anyway. Her dream had moved on. Hadn't it? Morgan was nearby. All she had to do was find him in this dark fog. "Morgan!"

"Claire."

His voice, weak, but his voice. She moved toward the sound, breathing a sigh of relief as she made out a faint glow directly ahead. "Keep talking," she urged. The floor

was uneven under her bare feet. There were shells everywhere: oyster, clam, mussel shells, conchs, some large ones
she didn't recognize. Shells were pressed in patterns into
the wall and enormous shells held bubbling water.

"Here."

She took a few more steps and saw him in the semi-
light. He lay stretched out on a thick bed of green moss
with only a fur blanket covering his lower half. It was her
Morgan. There could be no doubt. But he looked terrible,
his face lined, his blond hair and brows streaked with
gray. He seemed stricken by some sudden and virulent ill-
ness making him appear far older than he was.

"Oh, Morgan." She went to him, kneeling beside him.
She grasped his hand, as tears clouded her eyes. He felt
cold to the touch, almost damp. "What's happened to
you?" She pressed light feathery kisses to the back of his
knuckles. "What are you doing here? Why aren't you in a
hospital?"

She knew how foolish that sounded the moment she
said it. He was a dream. She'd conjured him up. A dream
man didn't need a hospital. She was all he needed. Just like
in the fairy tales. All she had to do was kiss him to bring
him back to life.

A lump rose in her throat, and she was overcome by her
desire to touch him . . . to feel him warm and solid. She
knelt on the edge of the bed, took his face between her
hands, and kissed his mouth. "Oh, Morgan. I've missed
you." His lips were cool, but they molded to hers, warm-
ing as the seconds passed. And as they kissed, the magic
rushed back, filling her with an overwhelming desire for
this man.

He uttered a soft moan. "Claire. Are you real?" He
stroked her cheek, caught a lock of her hair and brought it
to his lips. "Is it you? Not some trick of my mind?"

"It's me," she assured him. "I'm here and everything will be all right now. I promise you."

It seemed the most natural thing in the world to lie down beside him, to put her head on his shoulder and wrap her arms around him. "I waited and waited," she whispered, "but you didn't come." Her heart pounded; her pulse raced. She couldn't lie still, had to get closer. She wanted . . . yearned . . . "Morgan, Morgan, I thought you'd gone away for good."

"Better for you if I had," he said. "Maybe better for both of us."

"No, don't say that."

He embraced her as she showered his cool face with kisses. "I wanted to come," he admitted, "but circumstances . . ."

"Don't talk, just hold me."

He kissed away her tears. "Don't cry, Claire. I can't stand it if you cry."

"It's just that I'm happy . . . so happy."

He kissed her mouth, and she thrilled to the sweet sensation of his caress. She felt so safe in his arms, so loved.

"I was afraid that . . . after what happened?" she managed. "After my father came and Justin, and I told you to hide on the balcony, you might think that I was—"

He cut off her explanation with another lingering kiss, one that seared her lips and sent eddies of warmth washing through her body. Her pulse quickened and her nipples hardened into sensitive buds. "Shh," he murmured.

"We're divorced," she said as a heavy-limbed aching made her all-too aware that he was naked under the light covering. "Justin and I haven't . . ."

"To Hades with him. I don't care about him."

She gasped as Morgan slipped a hand under her pajama

top, gently cupped her breast, and teased her nipple with the base of his thumb. "Haven't seen him in a long time," she finished.

"It doesn't matter. I don't want to talk about Dustin."

"Justin," she corrected.

"Dustin . . . Justin." He unbuttoned her top and kissed her breast.

Was it her imagination or were his lips warmer? Heat flashed under her skin, and heady excitement washed over her as she pressed herself even closer. "Morgan, Morgan," she gasped. He drew her nipple between his lips and suckled until she cried out with pleasure. In some crazy way, their lovemaking seemed to make him stronger.

"How did you find me? How did you get here?"

"Later," she said, ripping open the last button on her top and sending it flying against the wall. She closed her eyes as he laved her nipples and drew them deep into his hot mouth. The sensation was unbelievably and excruciatingly wonderful, and she could feel the tugging of connecting silken cords deep in her woman's cleft.

Vaguely, she was aware of flickering lights set into niches in the stone, illuminating the moss bed in a faint yellow glow, as she lifted her other breast for him to kiss and lick and suckle.

The drums still sounded in the mist, primeval, sensual, striking a chord deep inside her, pulling her back and back to another age. Around them, the thick curtain of swirling mist gave an illusion of privacy. The moss was soft, the heat of Morgan's mouth, the feel of his hands and tongue on her body intoxicating.

This was right. She knew it. With each kiss he grew stronger.

Growing desire made her bold. Her breath came in quick,

sharp gasps as she trailed damp, warm kisses over his throat and chest, using her teeth to nip his skin, her lips to caress him. He tasted of salt and sea and virile male.

This was her dream. There could be no shame in a dream, could there? His hands were everywhere, moving over her, stroking, caressing. And every spot that he touched fueled the need inside her. The fluttering sensation that would not let her be still became an incandescent drive. Her pulse pounded in her ears, her need became a hunger.

She pushed away the fur covering and slid her hand lower, stroking and exploring, teasing, feeling his growing need for her. Suddenly, she wanted to please him, to give him the gift that he'd bestowed on her in that other cave, soon after they met. Tendrils of hair fell forward over her face as she inclined her head and pressed damp kisses down the swollen length of his phallus.

Morgan groaned, and the sound of his desire added to her own growing need. All too aware of the throbbing heat between her damp thighs, she used her tongue to moisten the head of his shaft before drawing it between her lips.

He arched and moaned. His fingers sunk into her flesh as his arousal whipped into a white hot flame that arced between them.

Laughing, he grasped her hips and lifted her on top, so that she sat astride him, clasping him with her thighs and rubbing her wet and swollen sex against his tumescent shaft. "Enough of that," he gasped. "Any more and I'd not be able to . . ."

She laughed. "Love me, Morgan. I want to feel you inside me."

A few minutes ago, he'd looked like death. Now he was whole and strong again.

He groaned. "Do you know what you're doing, Claire? Do you have any idea how wrong this is?"

"It's not wrong," she whispered hoarsely. "How can it be wrong? It's making you better." Damp heat glistened on her skin. Her heart was pounding, her breath coming in quick, hard gasps. "I love you."

"You don't understand," he protested, rolling her over onto her back. "I'm not who you think I am. It's a lot more complicated."

She looked into his heavy-lidded eyes, so blue, so beautiful, eyes so deep and full of desire she could drown in them. "Are you married?" she asked.

"No. Hades, no. I've never been married."

"Gay?"

He laughed and guided her hand to his throbbing erection. "What do you think, Claire? Am I?"

"Hell, no." She gasped, raised her hips, and clasped him to her. "I want you to live, Morgan. More than anything, I want you to be well and safe."

CHAPTER 18

As Morgan plunged deep inside her, Claire arched her body, wanting every inch of him, wanting them to become one being. Immediately, an intense orgasm, lasting longer than any she'd ever felt, rocked her body. Rainbow tremors radiated out to every cell in her body, falling like so many shooting stars, causing her to cry out with joy as she felt him fill her again and again.

Despite Morgan's size and power, there was no pain, only greater pleasure, and she clung to him, urging him on. She lost all track of time, but twice more, waves of exquisite sensations swept over her before Morgan groaned and she felt the hot rush of his seed fill her womb.

For the space of half a heartbeat, it occurred to her that neither of them had used protection, a risk that she'd never taken in her life. But then she remembered that this was only a dream, and any danger imaginary. Those passing thoughts lingered for only seconds before they vanished in the aftermath of sweet satisfaction. Laughing, they clung together, kissing and touching, pressing damp skin against skin, hearing the quick, deep rasp of each other's breathing and the pounding of two hearts as one.

"Claire," he murmured. "My Claire."

He kissed her mouth, her face, her throat. His strong

fingers caressed her shoulders and spine. He nibbled and nuzzled the back of her neck down to the hollow of her back. And all the while, he murmured sweet words of love. At least, she thought they must be. It wasn't Greek that he spoke to her. She wasn't certain what language he was uttering, but she didn't need a translation to understand what he was saying.

Morgan stroked and fondled her buttocks and her thighs, planting warm damp kisses on the backs of her knees and making her laugh. He caressed her calves and ankles, massaging and rubbing her feet, treating her as if she were a precious gift. Claire had never felt so desirable, so loved, or so beautiful.

But then caution intervened and she said, "We didn't . . . I'm not on birth control and you didn't wear a—"

"Don't worry," he soothed. "I swear to you on my mother's soul that I'm free of disease."

"But . . ."

"Shhh." He kissed her mouth, teasing her bottom lip with his tongue, catching it between his lips, and sucking gently, until the warm sensations stirred in the pit of her stomach again.

She opened her eyes and looked full into his face. He'd changed, she realized. In the space of their lovemaking, however long they'd been at it, he had made a full recovery. Better than full, she thought as her heart skipped a beat and then gathered speed. Surely, she'd been wrong. The light had deceived her. He wasn't ill, wasn't old. He couldn't be above his mid-twenties. The gray pallor was gone from his face, and his eyes flashed with life . . . with desire.

"This is a dream, isn't it?" she asked.

"Do you want it to be a dream?" He pulled her against his naked body, cradling her, kissing her hair, and wrapping his strong, muscular arms around her, making her feel safe. She laid her head on his shoulder and let the high sweet sound of a flute wash away her fears and worries.

When had the Indian drums become the haunting refrain of a primitive flute? She didn't know, didn't care. All that mattered was Morgan, being here in his arms, knowing at last the joy of fully making love to him . . . of being loved.

Her eyelids felt heavy, but she fought the urge to close them. These moments were too perfect. If she drifted off to sleep, she might wake in her own bed, might never find her way to this dream again. If she slept, she might wake in a wheelchair, imprisoned in her own body.

"If we did make a child, I'd claim it as my own," he whispered into her ear.

"Our own," she corrected him. What was she thinking? Not even a dream was powerful enough to make her a mother. Her shattered body could never conceive a baby. Despite what she'd thought she'd felt when Morgan had ejaculated inside her, she no longer had a womb or ovaries. The accident had claimed her ability to ever be a biological mother.

Pain, sharp as a sliver of broken glass, pierced her heart. Her own mother had given her up at birth and any hope of ever carrying a child was a fool's dream. Tears welled in her eyes and spilled down her cheeks.

Morgan kissed them away, one after another. "Don't cry, my darling," he said. "What's wrong?"

"I wanted a baby . . . so badly. When I was younger . . . when Justin and I . . ." She choked back a sob. "I had a husband once. I could have been a mother, but I wasn't ready. There were other things more important . . . horse shows . . . trips . . . parties. I let the precious time slip away, and now it's too late."

"Why is it too late?"

"I'm crippled. Can't you see? I can't walk? Can't care for myself. How could I care for a child?"

He rolled onto his back and pulled her with him, lazily running a hand over the hollow of her back and cupping one cheek in his big hand. "These legs are perfect, aren't they? These hips? These feet?" He rubbed the arch of one bare foot, then massaged it with strong fingers. "Not much good for swimming, I'll admit, but very pretty."

She laughed as he tickled the sole. "Be serious."

"Why?" He bent and kissed the toes on the foot he'd been caressing.

"Morgan!" Still chuckling, she pulled her foot free. "Men don't do that for real. Only in romance novels."

"No?" He shot her a long, sexy stare that made her shiver inside.

"You don't understand." She was suddenly babbling, more to herself than to him. "None of this is real. You're not real. I made you up, and when I open my eyes again, you'll be gone."

His chest rumbled with amusement. "You made me up?"

"Yes." She nodded vigorously.

"And Alex, did you make him up as well?"

"Alex?" Was this a joke? She peered at him suspiciously. "Who is Alex?"

"My brother. He brought you here. Surely you haven't forgotten Alexandros. He's a little hard to miss."

She pushed him back against the bed of moss, brought her knees up and sat astride him. "You mean the superhero? The blond Adonis?"

Morgan rose up lazily on one elbow and used his tongue to tease her right nipple. She shuddered with pleasure and closed her eyes, savoring the ripples of desire that tugged at her most secret places.

"Adonis?" he murmured huskily as he cupped her breast in one hand. "He'll like that. Although he might prefer Achilles. He's a bit bloodthirsty, my baby brother."

"I dreamed him up as well," she said, offering him her other breast to be pleasured. "He's no more real than you are."

She was wet for him again, wet and hot. She couldn't remain still and she moved seductively against his growing sex.

"You're insatiable, woman." Morgan's breathing quickened as his hands claimed her body.

"Am I?" She was ready for him again, and wanted to feel his raw power. Wanted him hard and fast and deep. Wanted him . . .

And once again, her dream lover fulfilled her every fantasy and invented a few of his own.

"Please, Athena, you must help her," Korinna cried out. "She's dying." Deep in the labyrinth beneath the Temple of Healing, the high queen of Atlantis rushed into the secret chamber, cradling a small limp figure against her breasts.

Startled by the queen's appearance and her desperate plea, Athena rose from where she'd been kneeling by an ancient freshwater spring. She scattered the remaining stardust in her hands on the bubbling water and quickly finished her prayer before turning her attention to her friend. Athena's dark eyes widened in surprise as Korinna moved into the light, and she could make out what Korinna was holding.

"A human child? Here?" Athena hurried across the polished crystalline floor of the sanctuary to meet them. Access to this section of the temple was strictly limited to priestesses of higher degrees than Korinna possessed, but she was, after all, high queen and Poseidon's favorite. Doubtless, someone had allowed her to pass, and that someone would have to answer for it. Athena glanced back at the spring. All seemed as it was, so the spirits were not angry. Relieved, she met Korinna's anxious gaze. "Tell me," she said with quiet concern. "What do you do with a human child here?"

"Not human. Not anymore." Korinna held the child out to Athena. "My so— The one who rescued her," she quickly corrected, "did all that was necessary, but the little one isn't strong enough to complete the successful transformation without assistance."

Athena touched a lock of the girl's blond hair and felt a rush of pity for this lost one. Always, she'd felt compassion for all young things, fish, or bird, or mammal . . . even land walkers. "You want me to make her an Atlantean?"

The queen nodded. "It has been done before. You know it has. There are legends—"

"Legends are not always true." She stroked the girl's arm. She was cold, so cold. "It is an irrevocable decision, one not made easily."

"But not on your conscience," Korinna said. "Another began the process. He breathed life into her drowned human body, but their young ones are so fragile. And most swim like stones."

"That can't be disputed. As intriguing as they are, those who have abandoned their mother the sea are helpless in the water."

"I didn't know who else to ask. You're a powerful priestess of the Light. You can give her life."

Athena sighed. "And explain to the council why I did so, I suppose." She held out her arms and the queen passed the child to her. How little she weighed. Her throat constricted. How could she refuse her friend's request? If they waited for official approval, it would be too late. The girl's grip on life was fading fast. It might be futile to attempt to save her, even now.

"Please," Korinna whispered.

Athena retraced her steps to the side of the holy pool and sat on a marble bench. Sparkles of stardust glittered on the floor like so many electric jewel fish. "Are we doing the right thing, I wonder?"

From the depths of the spring came a murmur of sound, not quite speech, more song, but not uttered in any language that still existed on the planet. The sound was sweet, peaceful . . . approving.

"Yes," Athena answered. "I ask your permission and your blessing for this act of mercy." She listened for an answer and it seemed to her that she heard the word "*Danoo.*"

A life size stone figure of Danu, mother earth goddess of Eire, one Athena had seen centuries ago on the seabed rose in her mind and she smiled. Washed and worn by eons of waves, toppled by men, Danu's features had retained a gentle grace and haunting beauty.

"Yes," Athena agreed, "yes, I will." She glanced back at the queen and Korinna's face went pale. "It's all right," Athena assured her. "They approve. And they have instructed me to give her a new name to begin her new life."

She bent over the child and kissed her lips, breathing into her tiny mouth. "May you live and grow strong," she whispered. "Be no more of the earth, little Danu, be a child of the sea."

For what seemed a long time, there was no change in the girl. But then, her features blurred and shifted. Her starfish hands opened and closed, and her long, dark lashes fluttered and then opened wide. She stared into

Athena's face with bright, curious eyes, green and clear as
polished emeralds.

"Welcome, precious," Athena said. She smiled down at
the child.

"Mommy?" Confusion flickered in her gaze. "Mommy?"

Athena leaned down and kissed the little girl's forehead.
"No, sweet one. I'm not your mother, but I'm sure she'll
come for you soon."

Danu blinked. "I didn't catch the duck."

Athena shook her head. "They fly, don't they? But we
have other wonderful things for you to see and play with.
Have you ever held a baby starfish?"

The little girl shook her head, and Athena saw how tangled her golden locks had become. "I think someone needs
to brush your hair."

"I'm hungry."

Athena laughed. "Children usually are." She motioned
to Korinna. "This is a good friend of mine, a very nice
lady."

"Will she take me to Mommy?" Danu slid off Athena's
lap and swam toward the queen. "Hello. I'm . . ." She
paused, as if trying to remember. "I'm four."

Korinna knelt down and caught the child in her arms.
"Yes, you are four. And your name is Danu. *Dan-oo.* Can
you say it?"

She giggled. "Danu. I'm Danu and I'm four."

"And I'm Queen Korinna, and I'm a lot older than
four."

Danu giggled again. "Where's your queen hat?"

"In a safe place. I don't wear it unless it's a very important day. It's heavy and it makes my head itch."

The child's arms went around Korinna's neck. "Is my
daddy here?"

"Not right now, but he'll be here soon," Korinna said. "And I'll tell you a secret. Can you keep a secret?"

Danu nodded solemnly.

She leaned and whispered in the girl's ear. "Your daddy is my little boy. That means I'm your grandmother, but we can't tell." She hugged Danu tightly. "You can call me—"

"Queeny!" Danu declared. "Because that's the bestest name of all!"

An hour later, after being escorted out of the temple through a private passageway, Queen Korinna and Danu were tucked into a curtained conch-style conveyance drawn by dolphins. They reached a private family entrance to the palace and left the carriage. Once inside, Korinna led the child across an atrium and through a series of passageways toward the royal apartments.

The child's presence drew only a few curious glances. Danu's transformation was complete. For all intents and purposes, she was an Atlantean, beautiful, strong, and full of vigor. Her color was lovely, and despite the untidiness of her hair and her common dress, she could have been one of many noble children who made their home in the palace. But Danu would never appear completely Atlantean. Since she had been born human, she would always retain traces of her ancestry. She was not less attractive than one born of the sea, but slightly different. And whether that difference would be an advantage or a challenge, only time would tell.

There were regulations to follow. Danu's transformation must be recorded in the Akashi Records as her birth date. The fact that she was already four in earth years was hardly worth mentioning. As an Atlantean, she could expect to live for thousands of years, and four more or less didn't matter. Parents must be noted as well as her lineage.

As Morgan's daughter, Danu would be as much a descendent of his parents and grandparents as any of his brothers and sisters.

The only snag might be whom to write down as the mother. Morgan had no mate, and some woman must agree to stand as Danu's female parent. That law was nonnegotiable. Morgan would have to choose, but in doing so, he would link himself to the woman for all eternity, not necessarily as wife or mate, but as mother to his child. Danu would have a long childhood, and Morgan and the woman in question would be responsible for her education, her nurturing, and her safety. Being a parent was not to be taken lightly among the sea dwellers. It was a sacred task, and those who failed from lack of devotion would pay a high price.

And, there was the matter of the king. How would she explain this to Poseidon? How could she tell him that the son who'd so recently been on trial for saving a human from death by drowning had disregarded the High Council's warning and done it a second time? And this action was much worse. Morgan had interfered in the natural order; he had taken it upon himself to transform a human into an Atlantean. Zeus alone knew how her beloved stepson would get out of this.

"I'm really, really hungry," Danu said. The small fingers held tightly to Korinna's as they moved through the brightly tiled hallway. Clear blocks of crystal were set into the walls so that the inhabitants had a glorious view of one of the planet's greatest reefs, all massed coral, magnificent plant life, fish, crustaceans, and Korinna's favorite, a sheltered nursery for the palace dolphins.

Guarded by faithful nurse sharks and elderly dolphins of both sexes, tiny dolphins dove and rolled and splashed in complete safety while their parents were at work. Since

Atlantis was far too deep for dolphins to reach the surface to breathe, other provisions had been made, and even the little ones could find oxygen when needed.

Danu would have her own dolphin, naturally. All Atlantean children did. But today was not the day for dolphins. Settling her in and introducing her to her new grandfather in a manner that would ensure his support and affection was what was important.

And protecting Morgan . . . always. For she loved her reckless stepson as much as those children she had given birth to. She'd loved him from the first moment she'd laid eyes on him as a mischievous boy. Morgan had climbed in her lap and given her a sticky kiss, washing away all her anxiety and selfish fears in an instant.

Korinna and the child had reached the top of a flight of stairs and were about to turn left down the grand corridor when Lady Halimeda suddenly appeared. Inwardly, Korinna flinched. Not Halimeda. Not now. Involuntarily, she moved in front of Danu.

"So, it's true!" Halimeda drew herself up to her full height and fixed Korinna with a black stare. "Orion did bring a human child here. Let me see her."

"Not now," Korinna said. "We were about to—"

"Poseidon!" Halimeda sank into a deep curtsey. "Husband. I've only just learned . . ."

"Korinna."

The queen turned to see the king coming toward them and forced a smile. Let the witch curtsey and pander to Poseidon. He'd get no such foolish adoration from her. Korinna genuinely loved their husband, but she was ever mindful of her own position and considered herself his equal. "Poseidon," she began, "this is—"

"A human child illegally transformed by your son Orion," Halimeda cried. Quick as a moray eel, she darted in and snatched up Danu. "Look at her. See with your own eyes. She is not Atlantean born."

Danu began to whimper and struggle in Halimeda's arms. "I feel," Halimeda cried. "I see more. Through touching her, I see the truth. She is linked psychically to another."

"Put her down," Korinna ordered, reaching for Danu. "This is not the place or time to—"

"No! This is the time. You must know. This is not simply Orion's sin!" Halimeda screamed, thrusting the child toward Poseidon. "I see everything. It is both Orion and Morgan! Orion may have helped in the crime—he brought the child here to Atlantis. But my powers tell me that the real culprit is Morgan. Your precious crown prince has spat in the faces of the High Council and defied the law once more."

CHAPTER 19

"Are you madwomen?" Poseidon roared. "To make a public spectacle of yourself? Halimeda, give that child to me. You're scaring her half to death. Have you never seen a changling before?" He took a now wailing Danu from her grasp and held her aloft.

"Give her to me," Korinna said. "You're both frightening her."

"Not a chance," the king snapped. "Aphrodite!" Servants and passing officials vanished by the nearest portals, leaving the four of them alone in the corridor. "Aphrodite!"

A mermaid appeared in the doorway Poseidon had just entered through. Hastily adjusting her bodice and attempting to make some order of her tumbled locks, she swam to the king. Her hair was long and dark. Her cheeks were red and her mouth appeared bruised as if it had recently been kissed quite ardently.

"Take this child!" Poseidon bellowed, offering the little girl to the mermaid. "Take her to the nursery and find someone to look after her."

"She's hungry," Korinna said. "I'll take her. She knows me. She doesn't need to be thrust among strangers."

Poseidon glared at Aphrodite. "Have you lost your wits along with these two?"

"No, Your Highness."

And before Korinna could make further protest, the mermaid whisked Danu away. The king had many diversions, but Korinna hadn't seen this one before. She doubted the wench's name was Aphrodite. It was a term that her husband used when he didn't want to bother memorizing mermaid names. They were long and difficult to pronounce.

For the most part, mermaids were not particularly bright creatures, but entirely self-centered and exceedingly vain. Like fish, they rarely tended to their own young, simply laying vast amounts of eggs and leaving them to the mercy of the sea. A mermaid was hardly one that Korinna would entrust an Atlantean child to, especially her own grandchild. For that was what Danu was now; Morgan's impulsive act had made it so.

And brought them all a storm of trouble, Korinna feared. "My lord," she began in a soothing voice. "Is there somewhere we could talk in private so that I could explain—"

He scowled at her. "Explain? What is there to explain?"

Halimeda fluttered her long fingers helplessly. "Your Majesty, you must not allow this travesty to go unpunished. Both Orion and Morgan are involved in this disgrace, but Morgan is the one who began the transformation."

"You have proof of those accusations?" He whirled on Halimeda.

"You know I have the sight, husband," the witch replied. "When I touched the creature, I could feel her connection to the crown prince. He's to blame for this. Never doubt it. And to do so after you made such a plea before the council for his release, my heart goes out to you. You will be shamed before your subjects, great king. They will say that you have one set of laws for them and another for your own children."

"Don't listen to her," Korinna said.

"You knew and you tried to cover up what they did," Poseidon accused, turning on Korinna.

"When has she ever supported you, Your Highness?" Halimeda wheedled. "She rejects your authority as much as your heir does. Neither is fit to wear the crowns of Atlantis."

"Careful," Korinna warned. "You go too far, lady. Doubtless you think my crown would look better on your head." She looked at Poseidon. "She has always been jealous of Morgan. She wants to put her son in Morgan's place. That's what this is about."

"Not this time," the king said, his voice husky with anger. "Too long have I excused my sons' actions as boys' pranks. I won't be made a fool of and I won't be defied by—"

"There's no defiance," Korinna insisted. "Morgan saved a child's life. How can that be evil?"

"Not a child's life," Halimeda put in. "A *human's* life. He ignored the law and put us all in jeopardy."

"Go to my blue grotto, Korinna. We'll discuss this further in private." He motioned to another stairway leading up to his apartments. "Now!"

"Command this slut or others of your many bedmates, if you wish," Korinna said, "but I'm high queen of Atlantis. I'm not a servant to be ordered about on your whim. I'm going to the nursery to see that Danu is properly cared for. Later, when you're in a more reasonable mood, I'll be happy to tell you anything more that I know."

"You see," Halimeda said. "I told you that she's not

worthy to sit the silver throne. She believes that she can obey or not—"

"Will you be still, Halimeda!

Halimeda curtsied low to the floor. "As you wish, sire. But don't forget Orion's part in this nasty business. He should be placed under arrest. He brought the monster here to Atlantis."

"I believe I am capable of dealing with Orion."

Poseidon's voice dropped to a soft and reasonable tone. Korinna knew the signs. She'd seen him in a royal rage before and knew him capable of violence. Without another word, she attempted as dignified a retreat as possible. She'd nearly reached the bottom of the stairs when she heard the king's shout.

"Guards! Find Prince Orion and place him in irons. Then bring me Morgan and Alexandros."

She hurried on, not looking back.

"Korinna!"

She hesitated, wondering it would be better to give in or continue on her own course. "Yes, husband, what do you want?"

"I want you and your brood to leave the city. Go at once to the old palace off the north shore of Crete and there await my pleasure."

Anger flared in her chest. How dare he? Was he so under the thumb of the bitch that he'd threaten her? "And if I don't?"

Poseidon came to the head of the staircase, his features rigid, his face a mask. "You will go as I bid you, woman, and you will go now. Unless you prefer to be escorted by my guard and placed in custody as your precious stepsons will certainly be."

"May I take the child with me?"

"What child?" He descended the stairs and came to tower over her.

Korinna held her ground. "Little Danu. May I take her with me?"

"The changling?"

"She is an Atlantean now, my lord. No matter her beginning, she deserves your mercy."

"Take her, if you wish, but be gone within the hour. I've had enough of your undermining my authority." He stroked his beard thoughtfully. "And take all you need with you, for you may remain there indefinitely."

Korinna met his hard gaze with equal force of will. "Are you divorcing me? Placing that crazed sorceress on my throne?"

"I might. Time will tell. She at least—"

Korinna's expression softened, and she reached out a hand toward him. "Take care, 'Eidon. And don't trust Halimeda. You know you can't. Remember how her first husband died."

"Enough of your jealous accusations. Begone."

She shook her head. "Never trust her. In my heart, I know she means you no good."

"What is this place?" Claire asked Morgan as she lay on her back, her head on his shoulder, his arm around her. "I know the name, but I don't know where it is . . . or why."

Morgan chuckled and nestled her closer. "Is it important?"

She sat up and stretched, raising her arms over her head and sighing. "Am I mad or sane?"

"Do you care?"

"Stop that." Playfully, she punched his chest. "I want to know. I don't understand this. I don't understand you."

"Oww." He groaned dramatically. "Have you no pity on a man near to death?"

She laughed. "If you're near to death, I'd hate to have you make love to me when you were whole." She ran her hand across his throat and down over his massive chest. He was not a hairy man, but what hairs grew on his chest and below his flat stomach were slightly curled and golden. She decided that she'd never seen a more beautiful man . . . not even Alex could match him.

She turned and leaned her elbows on his chest and stared into his eyes. His lashes were long and thick, the irises of his eyes so hauntingly unique that she felt she could drown in them. "If I dreamed you up, I've outdone myself," she teased.

"You still believe that this is all a dream?"

"Isn't it?" Lazily, she brushed her fingers over his cheek and mouth, imprinting the lines of his face in her heart's memory. "But you make me happy, Morgan . . . happier than I've ever been."

A look that might have been regret flickered in his eyes, and abruptly, he sat up. White, even teeth flashed, as he smiled down at her. "Would you like to see more of this world besides this bedchamber?"

She nodded.

"Come then." Taking her hand, he led her toward the stone wall, and to her amazement, the stone parted before them—not opening so much as vanishing like mist. On the other side, she found herself standing at the edge of a fog-shrouded cliff, much like the one at Seaborne, but higher.

They were so close to the edge that Claire felt a little frisson of fear, and she clung tightly to Morgan's hand. "Trust me," he said. "I won't let you fall. I'll keep you safe."

"Always?"

He squeezed her hand. "Sometimes, it's best to live for the moment and see what life has in store for us."

He waved his free hand and the haze parted. Claire gave a small sound of wonder. Far below lay a vast lake or inland sea. Instinctively, she felt this was not the ocean but something different. The surface of the water shimmered in the starlight, for when she glanced up, she saw the same strange sky that she had observed before.

Swimming on the lake were myriad and unusual creatures, some almost dinosaurlike in appearance, others beyond anything she could imagine. Schools of giant fish in rainbow colors leaped and splashed in the slowly moving tide, and fantastic schools of fish of every size mirrored the creatures of the water.

"Do you like it?" Morgan asked.

Claire opened her mouth to answer, but she could find no words to describe such serene beauty. Joy bubbled up inside her. She felt so happy that she wouldn't have been surprised if she'd grown wings and flown off into the sky. "Yes, yes, I do," she managed, and she circled his neck with her arms and pulled his head down to kiss him.

"Then, you may like this as well," he teased. Tugging her hand, he led her a few yards in the opposite direction, back the way they'd come from their love nest. But when Morgan waved away the mist again, there was no rocky outcrop of stone but another valley, this one not filled with water but oceans of blue grass and marvelous trees. Waterfalls tumbled from the surrounding cliffs, and streams twisted and flowed over rocks to form a swift-flowing river.

Herds of animals grazed in the distance, and here and there, she could see what might be small encampments. Smoke rose from rounded huts. If the villages were inhabited, they were too far away to see the people, other than as tiny moving figures. Of modern civilization there was no sign: no roads, no power lines, no train tracks. This Eden spread untouched before her.

"Would you see more?" he asked.

She shook her head. "Not now." She struggled to take in the tranquil beauty, the colors and scents, the sound of the falling water and the wind. She wanted to wrap each image in memory and lock it away to take out and cherish on the days she sat alone at Seaborne's shore and stared out at the ocean.

He nodded, understanding, and led her back to their secret chamber where he held and kissed and caressed her all that long afternoon.

It was the blond Adonis who brought their lovemaking to an end. Morgan was feeding Claire bits of a sweet treat that tasted like a cross between licorice and honey when Alex returned.

"I hate to break this up," he said brusquely, "but I need to talk to Morgan, alone."

Morgan covered her naked body with a seaweed blanket of the softest weave. "Your timing is off, Brother. We were—"

"I said *alone*." Alex's handsome face was expressionless.

Morgan nodded. "Stay here, Claire. I'll see what—"

"This can't wait," Alex said, grasping Morgan's arm. "I'm glad to see you so greatly recovered, but we've no time to waste."

"Is it the child? Did she . . ."

"What child?" Claire asked. Gathering the blanket around her, she rose on her knees. "What is he talking about?"

Alex turned his gaze on her. "Go to sleep, Claire."

"You can't . . . can't," she began. But, suddenly, a great weariness came over her. She sank down onto the moss. "I don't want to . . ."

"It's all right," Morgan said soothingly. He returned to the bed and placed a palm on her forehead. "Shhh, sleep. It's all right."

She closed her eyes, so dizzy that she thought . . . That she thought . . .

Abruptly, she heard the sound of surf. Waves crashed around her. She could taste the salt on her lips, hear . . . hear . . .

Nothing. Blind and deaf, she felt the tide lift and carry her.

When she opened her eyes again, someone was shaking her arm.

"Claire. Claire."

"Richard?" She blinked. Not again. Sorrow welled up inside her. No, this couldn't be happening to her again. She must be losing her mind.

"We've called for an ambulance," Justin said. "Lie still. Don't try to talk. You've had some sort of seizure."

"No, I'm fine. I was asleep," she managed. What time was it? Sunlight streamed through the windows. Morning? Afternoon?

"We couldn't wake you," Mrs. Godwin said, patting Claire's hand. "We called the doctor, and he suggested an ambulance."

"No ambulance. I'm not sick," Claire protested, pulling her hand free.

"Not this time," her father said. "You could have an embolism in your brain. We're taking you to a hospital, and if I have my way, we're transferring you back to the city, to your own physicians, not these quacks who—"

"There's nothing wrong with me. You can't force me to go. . . ." The wail of a siren cut through the windowpanes.

"Maybe you should listen to her," Justin said. "I'm not certain that you can simply ignore her wishes."

"I can and I will." Her father stroked her hair. "I'm sorry it has to be this way, but you're no longer in any condition to make decisions about your health. We're going to take good care of you. Whether you like it or not."

Knowing that arguing with him was useless, Claire lay back on the pillow and closed her eyes. *I want to go back*, she thought in desperation. *Back down the rabbit hole to Morgan and Alex and my own personal funhouse of pagan drums and serpent-people and flying mantarays. I don't want to be here anymore.*

"Please," she begged. "I don't need a doctor. Richard . . . Don't do this to me."

"You know how much he loves you," Justin said. "Just trust him to do what's best."

"Whatever it takes, we'll find the finest doctors for you," her father said. "And when you're better, you'll realize it was for the best."

The piercing sound of the ambulance grew louder.

"We won't leave you," Justin said. "I won't leave you. I'll stay with you every step of the way."

"That's what I'm afraid of," Claire whispered. And once again, she began to weep.

Four days into Claire's hospital imprisonment, Morgan, Alex, and Orion stood side by side, their hands bound in silver chains, awaiting the verdict of the High Council. The twins' fate was irrevocably linked with Morgan's. Whatever his penalty was, their sentence would be the same. Their stepmother, Queen Korinna, at the palace off Crete was beyond the reach of the court and no charges were brought against her. Poseidon had forbidden her to return to Atlantis until the case was settled.

The child, Danu, was held innocent of any crime. She was an Atlantean, and as such, every citizen of the kingdom was pledged to her welfare. If Morgan and the twins were entombed in coral, as the king expected, someone would take the child into their family. She wouldn't suffer for the crimes committed in her name, and she wouldn't suffer for being born a human, despite Halimeda's ire.

When Morgan and Alex had joined Orion in prison, they'd been questioned at length by representatives of the court and by high priestesses and priests. Morgan had bargained in vain for his brothers' release, admitting that he was responsible for Danu's transformation from human to Atlantean and confessed his attachment to a human woman. His sacrifice was useless. Additional charges were placed against all of them, and no leniency was offered to Orion and Alex because they had been aware of Morgan's crime and not reported him.

Poseidon had wept and raged, then refused to see any of his three accused sons. He was here today to hear the verdict, but Morgan knew that he could expect no mercy this time. His father was adamant. Morgan would be found guilty and sentenced, and once he was declared beyond the law, he would lose his position as heir to the throne of Atlantis.

The first member of the court stood and the hall grew silent, all but Orion, who leaned close to Morgan and whispered, "I hope she was worth the loss of the throne, Brother. It will be a long time before you hold another woman in your arms."

"I never wanted to be king." Morgan knew that he

should be thinking of his brothers, of what he'd brought them to and how they would suffer for his sins. But it was Claire that he regretted. She would never know why he'd abandoned her. She'd grow old and die on her small stretch of beach waiting for him. The pain of his betrayal was almost more than he could stand."

"Yes, but you're the best of us," Orion said.

"Silence!" a chamberlain ordered. "Silence before the High Council."

The respected elder, an Egyptian by birth, cleared his throat. "It is with great sorrow that I cast my vote against Morgan, crown prince of Atlantis. Guilty."

Orion grimaced. "One down."

This was a waste of time, Morgan thought. Nothing more than a spectacle to appease the masses. They would sentence him and his brothers to a hundred years entombed in coral. By the time he was free, Claire would be dust and his heart and soul with her.

And Claire would not be the only one he'd let down. Danu would grow up an orphan without father or mother. Maybe they were right. Maybe it would have been better to let her die. Who was he to go against thousands of years of law and civilization?

"You'll love it, Brother," Alex joked. "They say coral is good for the bones. It adds centuries to your life."

Lord Pelagias, Lady Halimeda's brother was next to pronounce judgment. "Guilty."

"Guilty."

"Guilty as charged."

Morgan forced himself to give the High Council the respect due them. He was guilty. He deserved to be punished, but Claire didn't, and little Danu didn't, and his brothers' only crime was in keeping faith with him. He felt his father's gaze on him and looked up to meet the king's stubborn glare. Morgan raised his head higher and stiffened his shoulders. He wasn't sorry, and if he had it to do over again, he'd do exactly the same.

"Prince Morgan."

Lady Athena's soft voice broke through his thoughts and he saw that she was standing and addressing him. He fixed his attention on her and nodded slightly in salute. "My lady."

"I found this case to be a most difficult one," she said. "You aren't the first to secretly romance a human. In searching through the Akashi Records, I find that there have been more than a few."

A rumble of dissent rippled around the vast chamber.

"No!"

"Blasphemy," Lord Pelagias muttered.

"Lady Athena," Poseidon said. "Is this a delaying—"

"Not only has this crime occurred before," she continued, boldly interrupting the king, "but it was repeated so many times that a statute was enacted to deal with it, a statute that has never been repealed and stands as law today.

" 'From the *Scrolls of the Silver Tide, Volume Sixty-six*," she said, unrolling a seaweed parchment. " 'Law eighty-seven: If a subject of Atlantis commits the crime of love with a human, he or she can plead guilty, accept the sentence and be entombed in coral without light or sound for one hundred years, or he or she may risk all for the chance to continue the union.' "

"Rubbish!" Prince Caddoc leaped to his feet and shook a fist. "What jest is this? Sentence the criminals."

"Quiet," hissed his mother. "Do you forget where you are?"

Morgan glanced at her. Lady Halimeda as the voice of

reason was a new occurrence. Today, she was garbed all in scarlet with a diamond-studded crystal coronet gleaming against her night-black hair. She met his gaze, inclined her head, and smiled.

A nobleman cried out, "This is a trick to evade the law!"

A dozen of Lady Halimeda's supporters rose to echo the sentiments, but she urged them to quiet. "Hush, please, hush. Let us hear the Lady Athena."

Poseidon stood and slammed his fist down on the arm of his throne. "Silence! Unless you wish Prince Caddoc to suffer the same fate. I've had enough of disobedient sons."

Caddoc sank into his seat and scowled at his mother.

" '. . . He or she may risk all for the chance to continue the union,' " Lady Athena repeated.

Morgan was struck by how much authority Lady Athena radiated in her robes of state. The king bellowed and roared, but she commanded respect without theatrics. Morgan preferred her method of leadership. Had he ever become Poseidon, he would have . . . He smiled at his own foolishness. Since he was a boy, he'd protested that he didn't want to inherit the crown. Now, he was getting his wish, so there was no need to consider how he might or might not have ruled.

" 'The accused has the right to see their human lover one final time," the lady continued. " 'The accused may ask the human to join him or her in the sea forever. If the human chooses to become one of us, he or she will never breathe air or walk on land again. The two may marry with the court's blessing, a transformation will be granted by the High Council, and all charges will be dropped.' "

Morgan swallowed, not certain that he'd heard what he'd thought he'd heard. Was it possible? Was there a chance he could be with Claire? That he and his brothers would be set free? That he could act as as father to Danu? A tiny flame of hope sparked in his chest.

"Don't get happy yet," Orion whispered. "There's got to be a *but* in there somewhere."

Alex remained as motionless as if he had been carved of stone.

" 'The accused may ask the human to become one of us,' " the lady continued. " 'But if the question is asked and the love is not strong enough, if the human refuses, the sentence will be carried out.' "

Muscles twitched along Orion's square jaw. "I told you so."

Morgan's fists clenched.

" 'Under no circumstance may the human be told about the consequences,' " Lady Athena pronounced. "That section of the law is clear. Any infraction and the supreme penalty shall be enforced."

"Here comes the punch line," Alex hissed.

" 'Imprisonment in coral will be not a hundred years,' " Lady Athena continued. " 'Either the human joins her or his lover under the sea or the accused suffers the extreme penalty. The Atlantean will not be put to death, but will be entombed in coral in darkness, forever.' "

CHAPTER 20

Morgan felt a rush of shame as he looked at his brothers. How could he do this to them? No matter how much he wanted to take the chance, risking his life was one thing, but placing their lives in the balance was an entirely different matter. It was bad enough that they'd have to suffer a hundred years imprisonment for him, but if Claire refused him, Orion and Alex would be equally condemned for what amounted to an eternity. How could he think of sentencing the twins to a living death for a human woman?

But he wanted her . . . wanted her more than life.

More than his brothers' lives?

"What are the odds?" Orion asked cheerfully. "We've survived worse."

Alex shrugged. "He's in, I'm in."

Morgan felt his gut twist. He needed time to think. Too much was at stake here. Claire had kept asking him if she was dreaming. It was what he'd wanted, and what was easier, but if Claire knew the truth, could she give up everything for him? Was what they had more than intense sexual attraction?

As if reading his mind, Zale, the vizier spoke. "I would ask a boon of the court."

Halimeda gasped, snapping her head around to glare at him.

The vizier rose and rapped his staff of office. "If I may have leave to address the council?" he asked.

Lady Athena nodded. "I yield to Zale, our esteemed vizier."

The man cleared his throat and waited until it was so quiet in the Hall of Justice that you could have heard a conch shell open. "We have much at stake here, Your Highness and respected council. The lives of our three greatest princes may be lost, including that of Crown Prince Morgan." He waited while the audience had time to let that statement sink in.

"Morgan's stubborn," Poseidon interjected. "He doesn't deserve your pity. He's shown willful disregard for my orders and the laws of the kingdom."

Zale nodded. "As His Majesty says, our crown prince is headstrong. But, isn't that a trait of all kings? Your Highness is the exception, of course."

The king scowled.

Zale went on. "Prince Morgan is still young. He may not fully realize the ramifications of this sentence. I ask the court to seal Prince Morgan, Prince Orion, and Prince Alexandros in coral until the moon comes full again, twenty-one days as the humans figure time. Allow our royal princes a taste of what awaits them. Then when they fully understand the penalty, allow them to decide."

Lady Athena glanced at her fellow council members. "Your thoughts?"

"I object," Lord Pelagias protested. "Prince Morgan is his father's favorite. Too long have we forgiven his transgressions. This nonsense about giving the human a chance to trade the earth for love of an Atlantean is an old law, one that hasn't been invoked in a thousand years, perhaps longer. It's nothing but romantic nonsense. I say there's no need for the council to waste more time on this affair. Sentence the princes and be done with it."

"I disagree, Lord Pelagias." Lady Jalini, clothed elegantly in cloth-of-gold in the Egyptian style, raised a palm to be heard. She was one of the youngest members of the High Council and one who rarely spoke out. "This plan sounds most sensible to me," she said in a gentle voice. "I believe the vizier's suggestion is a good one."

Pelagias frowned at her. In theory, all members of the High Council were equal, but length of service and age added to a justice's prestige. By custom, the newer judges were there to listen and learn, and few challenged Pelagias's decisions.

One by one the others nodded. "It's fair," Lady Athena said, "but our decision must be unanimous. Lord Pelagias, would you reconsider your position?"

He tightened his mouth into a thin line. "All right," he said grudgingly. "It's against my better judgment, but I will agree with the majority."

"Thank you, Lord Pelagias. Your generosity is noted and most appreciated." Lady Athena clapped her hands twice. "Lord Zale's request is granted. Sentence to be carried out immediately."

Guards stepped forward to escort the prisoners to the coral prison many leagues from Atlantis off the island of Cyprus. Poseidon rose and strode away without looking back at his sons. Quickly, the court followed. The members of the High Council remained until the hall was nearly empty before filing out.

Morgan paid them little heed. All he could think of was Claire. She wouldn't know what had happened to him, and she'd believe he'd abandoned her. "Lady Athena," he called after her. "Am I permitted to send a message?"

Athena paused on the stairs, one hand on a marble railing, and shook her head. "When this time is past, if you still want her, then you may go to her. Until then, I'm sorry. No contact."

"I'll make an attempt to tell her," Alex said quietly.

The nearest guard shook his head and frowned. "No talking."

Morgan nodded. Alex possessed unusual powers for telepathy and intuition, but humans had forgotten the gift. He doubted that Claire, for all her intellect, could interpret his brother's mental communication. He gritted his teeth as a padded hood was drawn over his head, making him effectively blind and deaf.

If it were not for his worry for Claire, the monthlong sentence would not be impossible to serve. He'd survived in total isolation before. But he didn't need a month to make up his mind. There had been only one decision he could make and thirty days or thirty years would make no difference.

No matter what it cost him, no matter what it cost his brothers, he had to try. And if Claire could accept him as he was . . . accept his world . . . then they would share centuries of love and companionship. And if she couldn't . . . if she couldn't give up the earth for him, then he would accept his fate. The bitter dose would be the sacrifice of his brothers' lives for his forbidden love.

A week passed and then a second. Despite her tears, her anger, and her pleading, Claire was subjected to endless medical tests, interviews by social workers, psychologists, physicians and, finally, lawyers. She was poked, prodded, scanned, and studied. She spent hours discussing her emotional state with strangers and hours on the phone with her lawyers.

"Do whatever's necessary," she said to Mitchell Cole, her lead attorney. "I'm being held here against my will. It's little better than kidnapping, and I intend to bring suit against the hospital if I'm not released."

"I understand your frustration," Cole said. "But your medical condition complicates things. We're bringing in our own specialists to challenge your father's. We'll win this, but you can't hurry the system."

"You'd better try," she insisted. "Or I'll find someone who will."

On the fifteenth day, her legal team prevailed over the best her father could hire, and a Portland judge declared her competent to manage her own affairs, including her medical and financial decisions. Finally, after an emotional roller coaster and a huge fight with her father, Claire was able to secure her release from the hospital to return to Seaborne without Richard.

Her father approached her outside the hospital entranceway where nurses prepared to assist her into her specially equipped van. "Claire. Wait, please listen to me, baby," he called. "You have to realize that we had only your best interests at heart. Don't hold this against me."

Nathaniel moved to her side. "Miss Claire—" he began.

"No." She waved him away. "I'll speak to him." She took a deep breath. "The truth is I do hold it against you," she said to her father.

"Claire, try to understand my position."

"If you love me as you claim, you'll let me go," she said. "Don't call me. I'll call you."

"Will you?" He took hold of her hand. "Will you call me?"

"In a week or two. I promise." She pulled free of his grip.

"No hard feelings." He'd followed her to the van, and watched as Nathaniel helped her into the front seat. "You're all I've got, Claire."

She closed the door and rolled down the window. "I know that. It's why I will call. I can't say when."

"You're angry with me."

"I am, but I'll get over it in time. Just make sure this never happens again, or . . ." Breaking her ties with her father would be the most difficult thing she'd ever have to do in her life, maybe worse than waking up after the accident and finding that she was a basket case. But Richard had to understand that she was an adult. If he couldn't respect that, she'd have to learn to go on without him.

"Take me home, Nathaniel," she said.

Richard was saying something else, but she pushed the button to roll the window up. She'd heard enough of his excuses. Knowing that he had forced her into the hospital because he loved her was the only thing that kept her from making a permanent break here and now. But what kind of love was it? He'd shattered her self-respect, and if she hadn't had the fortune she did, she had no doubt she'd be sitting in some very expensive psychiatric hospital for the foreseeable future, and she didn't know if she could ever forgive him.

"And what if this human woman agrees to enter the sea? To become one of us?" Halimeda demanded. "Stranger things have happened."

She, Caddoc, and her brother Pelagias were closeted in Pelagias's library with guards outside the door to insure privacy. "What if Morgan brings her to Atlantis, they have a court wedding, and all is forgiven? What are your chances of becoming king then?"

Caddoc shrugged. "What are my chances now? Slim, at best. Who's to say my esteemed father won't live to reign for another five or six centuries?" He drained the last drops of wine from the crystal goblet and set it down on a marble sideboard.

He'd rarely been in his uncle's private rooms and this one made him vaguely uneasy. It was in the old part of the palace and the ceilings were low, the wall carvings ancient and dark. Rows of niches along one wall held scrolls. How many he wouldn't attempt to guess. The floor was some sort of clear crystal, and it gave him the feeling that he might tumble through it and keep falling forever.

His mother dropped her voice and leaned close to stroke his arm. Caddoc tried not to flinch at her touch. It was bad enough to see her behavior toward her brother. Most Atlanteans were sexual beings, but his mother went beyond normal custom. It was whispered jokingly in some parts of the palace that she would copulate with a white shark if one could be found that didn't fear her.

"I say that Poseidon won't make old bones," Halimeda said. "On the appointed night, I'll join the king in his bedchamber. We'll share a late supper. He's quite fond of Chilean pickled eels and the thin wine of Cyprus. I've never cared for either, myself. Later, he will become suddenly ill."

Caddoc struggled to conceal his surprise. "You would . . ."

"Poison? Are you too cowardly to say the word, let alone administer the dose?" She folded her arms and raised her chin defiantly. "Poseidon must die if you are to inherit the crown."

Pelagias arched a shaggy eyebrow. "You are the eldest born. You should be the next king."

"I should have been named high queen long ago," Lady Halimeda said. "Not that milksop Korinna. Even the king regrets it now."

"With the princes imprisoned, now is the time to overthrow the king's party," his uncle said. "Three precise strikes, and the throne is yours. Do you have the nerve to claim it?"

"You know I do," Caddoc said. "But it's not enough to have Morgan, Alexandros, and Orion under arrest. So long as they're alive, we'd risk civil war."

"They will be released at the proper time," his mother said. "Just days from now Morgan will go to fetch his woman, and the vizier will send the twins to retrieve their mother from banishment. I will deal with Poseidon."

"We must strike at the same instant," Pelagias said. "It will be your job to ensure that Morgan and his human lover suffer some accident. He will be weak when he reenters the sea. That will be your opportunity to finish him."

"But . . ." Caddoc glanced back at his mother. "If something should happen to Poseidon, wouldn't Queen Korinna assume—"

"Korinna won't be an issue," Pelagias said. "Once Alexandros and Orion reach the old palace, the guards will arrest her, Orion, and Alexandros on charges of treason. Obviously, they were part of the plot to murder Poseidon and place Morgan on his father's throne."

"But to merely arrest them—"

His mother slapped his face. "Fool! Would that I had another son. You are so stupid that it's a wonder you aren't devoured by the carnivorous flowers outside the palace gates."

"I'm not stupid! I merely asked—"

Halimeda curled her lip. "Imbecile. How anyone could believe that you are Poseidon's son is beyond me."

Caddoc rubbed his cheek. He was trembling with anger. He wanted to strike back at her, to hurt her, but he was afraid. He knew what she could do. He backed away. "What are you saying? Isn't the king my father?"

Pelagias laughed.

Halimeda shook her head, then glanced slyly at her brother. "Did I tell you he was stupid?"

"You did," Pelagias agreed with a sigh. "But I didn't want to believe it."

"I don't believe either of you," Caddoc growled. "You're lying again, Mother. Of course, I'm Poseidon's son. I look just like him."

"Do you?" She laughed. "Stare into a mirror, and then look at your uncle. You will see a resemblance."

Caddoc shook his head. "No. You're making a joke at my expense."

"Would we do that, my son?" Pelagias asked. He moved quickly, closing the space between them, and seizing Caddoc's right hand. He raised it, and pressed his own left against Caddoc's fingers. "Do you see how the middle finger is shorter than those on either side? How the nail is flatter? It is the mark of the men of our line. One of your feet has a similarly shaped toe."

"Your own brother? How could you?" he demanded of his mother.

Halimeda shrugged. "It was common in ancient Egypt. Doubtless among our royal ancestors as well."

"It disgusts me," he flung back. "And you could be lying. I could have inherited the strange finger and toe through you and not my uncle."

She smiled. "If it pleases you to think you bear Poseidon's blood, then continue to deceive yourself. It doesn't matter. As to my actions, tell me you do not lust after Morwena? You would have made the beast with two backs gladly with her, believing her to be your half-sister."

"She isn't?"

Halimeda covered her face with her hands and sank onto a backless couch. "Have you heard nothing we've said? What should it matter who fathered you, if all believe you to be the eldest born of Poseidon? You will be king once he and Morgan are dead, and you will take the sweet Morwena, princess royal as your bride."

"And my son will be Poseidon," Pelagias said, joining Halimeda on the couch. He caught a lock of her hair and rubbed it between his fingers.

"Our son," she said, leaning close to kiss him.

The kiss was not a sisterly one; it was openmouthed and lecherous. It turned Caddoc's stomach, and he decided that once all this came to pass, once he was high king, he would find a way to make himself an orphan as soon as possible. Doubtless his mother would take delight in futtering a shark and then cutting its throat once she'd reached sexual satisfaction.

"After you've taken the twins and the queen, what will you do with them? Why are you placing them under arrest instead of killing them?" Caddoc asked. "Why wouldn't the High Council allow the queen to reign until—"

"Don't be ridiculous," his mother said. "Of course, they will die. They are arrested in front of witnesses, treated with respect, and transported back to Atlantis for an official inquiry into the king's death."

"Sadly, Korinna's family and the guards will be attacked by Melqart's minions a few leagues from the old palace," Pelagias explained. "They will put up a gallant fight, but all will perish. Prince Alexandros and Prince Orion will be chained with no chance to defend themselves or their mother."

"The guards will know that there was no attack by shades," Caddoc said. "Even if you paid them handsomely, how would you prevent them from talking?"

Halimeda leaned back against her brother, allowing him to fondle her naked breast. "Didn't your uncle just say that all would perish?"

"Even our soldiers?"

"A regrettable necessity," Pelagias said. He pulled Halimeda into his lap and kissed her again, running his long fingers over her lower back and buttocks.

Caddoc thought he would vomit. He choked, swallowed his gorge, and forced himself to think of Morwena. She had beautiful breasts, high and round, with small pink nipples.

He could imagine himself sucking those nipples until she screamed with passion. "You promise I can have Morwena?"

His mother nodded. "Taking her as your queen will stifle any gossip and bind Korinna's followers to you. Later, if you tire of her . . ." She shrugged. "Who know what might become of her? It's a small matter."

"And if she refuses to marry me?"

"You will be Poseidon," his uncle reminded him. "You may do what you want."

Caddoc's heart beat faster. He could see Morwena's sensual mouth and her taut buttocks in his mind's eye. She would be his to do with as he pleased. Heat curled in the pit of his stomach, and he felt his cock grow hard.

"You will have to be strict with her," his mother said. "She is willful. You must not allow her to come between you and your true family."

It was true. Morwena was spirited. She felt herself superior to him. That would have to be mended. He would force her to his will if he had to, but better if she leaned on him in her grief . . . if, after they were wedded and bedded, he gained her trust and devotion.

Morwena had a soft heart, especially where her younger siblings were concerned. She would take their deaths hard. He'd come upon her playing ball in the courtyard with her sister Tatiana not long ago. Tatiana was just ten, beginning to change from a child to a woman. In time, she might be even more beautiful than her older sister. He wondered . . . "You say that Queen Korinna's offspring will die with her. Even the little ones?"

Halimeda smiled. "Children grow up, my son. Haven't you? If your throne is to be secure, Korinna's whelps must die with her."

CHAPTER 21

Danu woke slowly. For a few seconds, she couldn't remember where she was. She had fleeting memories of another bed in a tiny brown room in a long boxlike house, but they quickly vanished as she stared around her. Her bed was a giant shell, round and pink and white with pearly insides, but it wasn't hard like a clam shell. Her mattress and covers were green and silky, so soft that they reminded her of a kitten's fur. Danu liked kittens almost as much as she liked puppies, but she'd never had one of her own.

"No kittens," someone had shouted at her. "Fleas. They climb on the table." Not here. Not in this place, but a long time ago. She tried to remember who the grown-up was who said that, but she couldn't. She did remember the part about the fleas.

Danu wasn't certain what a flea was or why it would climb on the table. But she hadn't wanted a flea. She'd wanted a little black kitten to sleep with. If not a real kitten, maybe a toy one, like a teddy bear. She lay on her back and stared up at the high roof. This was such a big room, but it wasn't dark. Light shone from the floor and from the sparkly white icicles that hung from the ceiling.

If she listened hard, she could hear pretty music all

around her, and best of all, lots of tiny little fish swam around the icicles. Some were yellow and blue, others purple and green. It was fun to lie on her back and watch them playing tag with each other.

Danu slid down out of the round bed and was surprised at how warm and smooth the floor was. She looked down at her toes and wiggled them. That was funny. She had little skin things between her big toes and her next toes. She couldn't remember seeing that before, but it didn't hurt and didn't feel like a boo-boo.

Her tummy was making noises. She guessed she was hungry. She was always hungry, but Queenie gave her good things to eat. Everybody here was kind to her, but she still felt a little bad. Her daddy hadn't come to take care of her like he said he would. And she missed someone else so bad that she had a big lump in her throat and she felt like she was going to cry. The trouble was, she couldn't remember who it was she wanted to see.

There was a little squeak at the door and her dolphin swam into the room. In her mouth, Echo carried a basket of breakfast. Danu laughed. "Echo!"

Echo wiggled her tail and looked just as happy to see Danu. Echo had slept beside her shell bed last night. Wherever Danu went, Echo went, and sometimes, when Danu was tired of swimming, the dolphin carried her on her back. A dolphin was a good friend, Danu thought, almost as nice as a kitten, but a lot bigger. She didn't have fur like a cat. Her skin was smooth.

Danu had eaten most of the food in her basket when Morwena and Tatiana came in. Shyly, she smiled at them, and they both came to give her a hug. She liked them. Tatiana was a big girl and Morwena was a grown-up, but she didn't act like most grown-ups. She liked to play games, and she'd taught her a song yesterday.

"Is my daddy here?" Danu asked. "He said he would come."

Morwena shook her head. "Not yet, but Mother is going to search for pearls in the garden. Would you like to help?"

Danu nodded. Morwena's mommy was Queenie, and Danu liked her best of all. "That's silly." She wrinkled her nose. "Tomatoes grow in a garden and sometimes moles."

"Moles?"

Danu nodded again. "Moles are like mouses, only big. Hester didn't like moles in her . . ." She paused and nibbled her lower lip. Hester? Who was Hester? She didn't know anyone by that name. "Can Echo help too?" She didn't want to leave the dolphin behind. Sometimes friends went away and you never saw them again.

"Of course," Tatiana said, giggling. "She's your nurse dolphin. She goes everywhere you go to protect you from sharks and squid and . . ." She wiggled her fingers in a scary way and made a face. "Sea monsters!"

Danu's eyes opened wide and she looked to Morwena to see if her sister was just teasing about the monsters. Morwena was smiling, so Danu laughed too. "If any monsters come, Echo will eat them up! Won't you, girl?"

The dolphin squeaked and rolled over twice, always a good sign. Queenie had promised that after a while Danu would learn to talk to Echo. She didn't understand that. She talked to Echo now, but the dolphin just squeaked. She didn't talk at all. It had to be another grown-up story that they told little kids.

Morwena took her hand. "Come on, sweetie. Let's go. You'll love the garden. There is another school of baby starfish and I think I saw a blue sea horse just the right size for you to ride."

Danu swallowed the sad, missing-daddy feeling and

moved along with them. Her tummy was full, her friend Echo was coming, and there were exciting things to see. Best of all, Queenie would be there, and she would hug her and tell her what a good girl she was. It would be a fun day . . . if only Daddy could come like he promised.

On the beach at Seaborne, Claire rolled her chair down the long cement walkway that ran along the high tide line. Metal railings prevented her from taking an accidental tumble into the sand, but even sturdy construction required constant work to keep the path from being washed away by waves and storms.

The week since she returned from the hospital had been a restless one. Every day, except for two days when it had poured rain, she'd come to the water's edge to wait for Morgan to return. She'd watched the waves, staring out to sea, straining her eyes to see him appear out of the surf. And at night, in her room, she'd lain awake in her bed, listening for his step, waiting in vain to hear his husky voice.

It was good to be home. She'd never appreciated Seaborne more; the tranquility of the house, the beauty of the grounds, the beauty of the ocean. She couldn't imagine ever leaving this place, ever wanting to live anywhere else. All the examinations, the CT scans and the interviews had tired her, and she'd slept eight or ten hours a night over the last few days.

The only thing that had troubled her—other than her separation from Morgan—had been the reoccurring migraines. At least, she thought she might be experiencing migraines, but the intense pain never came. Three or four times, she'd seen a bright light in her bedroom, a light with no source, a light so brilliant that it had hurt her eyes. And twice, she'd been certain that she heard a voice in her head. Not Morgan's voice, not a voice that she could identify, just someone calling her name, and once, the word "wait."

Okay, so this wasn't something she was prepared to share with anyone else, especially any of her doctors. People who heard voices were crazy, weren't they? But this voice was oddly reassuring. It wasn't telling her to blow up anything or alert the neighborhood to an invasion by space aliens. The voice usually came shortly after the incidents of the light, but once she'd awakened in the middle of the night, certain that there was something important she should remember but couldn't.

It wasn't that she hadn't tried to understand what was said. She desperately wanted to make a connection to the dream world she'd shared with Morgan. What if that was something similar?

She didn't know how or why Morgan had come to her in the first place, but she'd decided that he was real. Whether he came from outer space or another dimension, it didn't matter. Morgan existed. All she had to do was to find him again.

She tried to recall every trace of the strange experience she'd had the last time she and Morgan had been together: Alex, the man Morgan said was his younger brother, the whirlpool that had sucked them down into an alternative world of fantastic trees, green skies, and Indian pipes, and Morgan's passionate lovemaking. Never had she given so much of herself to a man, and never had a man pleased her so much. If it was a dream place, it was better than this existence.

She and Richard had barely spoken since the hospital. She wasn't ready to forgive him, didn't know if she ever could. She still loved her father. Nothing he could do or say would ever change that, but she had taken a step to independence that she'd never taken before. She'd no longer live her life according to Richard's suggestions. For better or worse, she'd make her own decisions.

By forcing her to undergo mental tests and physical examinations she didn't want, he'd almost stripped away what little she had left of her self-worth. This was her life, and if she died, so what? Didn't every human being die sometime? Not that she was looking for an escape. Maybe once, in a dark period of her life, but not now. Morgan had opened windows to possibilities she'd never dreamed existed. And even if she never saw him again, she was through being a victim and done feeling sorry for herself. She'd find a way to make her life—what there was of it— count, and she'd treasure every second of it.

She stopped pushing the chair to watch the antics of two willets fighting over a tiny crab. They were long-billed sandpipers, about sixteen inches tall with black-and-white wings. Each was so intent on capturing a scurrying sand crab and keeping the other from having it that a seagull swooped in and carried off the prize, leaving the willets staring suspiciously at each other.

Something about the larger of the two sandpipers reminded her of Justin and she laughed aloud. He'd been in contact several times since she'd been home, but this morning's conversation had been their longest talk, and it made her think. At first, after she'd returned from the hospital, she'd refused Justin's attempts to reach her. She hadn't wanted to speak to him any more than she had Richard. But, as Justin pointed out, in all fairness, he had tried to talk her father out of sending her to the hospital against her wishes.

Not that she had any silly illusions about Justin. He was definitely after her money and still trying to convince her that she'd be better off married to him than sitting here alone. He'd reminded her that if she had a husband,

Richard would be unable to make medical decisions for her. There would never be a repeat of what had just happened.

"Unless it was you," she'd flung back at him. "You could have me committed if we were married."

"I would never do that," he'd insisted. "No matter how much I wanted to have you get the best care, I couldn't take away your right to make your own choices."

He'd reminded her of the baby that was available for adoption. "This opportunity might never come again," he said. "Not for a child of this mental and physical potential."

Thinking about the baby was emotionally wrenching. It was hard to accept that she'd never give birth . . . never hold a child born of her own body. Although, why the desire to be a mother was so overpowering she didn't know. It wasn't as if she'd had any experience with babies or ever been in close contact with a newborn.

As the two willets flew off, followed by the screeching seagull, Claire wondered if she was being foolish. Was she trading motherhood and a somewhat normal life for the existence of a hermit here at Seaborne? And what if Richard was right? What if that clinic in Switzerland could give her back the ability to walk again? Was she slamming the door to her own future for a dream man who swam with fish?

And what if her dreams had vanished as quickly as they'd come? "Then I'll just have to dream new ones," she murmured into the wind.

Using her cell, she made the call she'd been planning on all afternoon. She needed to give Justin an answer concerning his marriage proposal. His office was closed, and the recording said that they would resume normal hours on Monday, which was odd. It wasn't a holiday. She wondered if he had taken a vacation and why he hadn't mentioned it when they'd spoken.

She tried Justin's apartment and got voice mail there as well. She didn't leave a message. What she had to say could only be said to him. Undaunted, Claire looked up Justin's new cell number and punched that in. He'd always changed his personal number when he acquired a new phone. It was one of his many quirky traits, such as checking his car door twice whenever he locked it. *Typical psychiatrist*, she thought, *crazier than his patients*.

This time, she was successful. Justin picked up on the third ring.

"Claire. Darling. What a nice surprise. I was just thinking of you. I have copies of the sonogram. The baby's a boy."

A boy, she thought. Somehow, she'd pictured herself the mother of a little girl. She shook off the notion. Trust Justin to extract every drop of her emotions. "I tried the office first," she said, forcing her voice to be cheerful, "but I got the recording."

Someone was laughing in the background. It sounded like a woman. She wondered if Justin was in a bar or having a late lunch in a restaurant. "Is this a bad time?" she asked.

"No, not at all. I thought I'd told you when we talked. Crystal, my receptionist, had her tonsils out," he explained. "I'd had two cancellations, and one of my favorite patients is having a facelift. It was easier to take a few days off than to deal with a temp from the agency."

She resisted the urge to ask why he hadn't called Inga, the woman she'd caught him cheating with, to see if she was available. Justin had always insisted that Inga was a top-notch office manager. But, there had already been enough bad feelings between them. There was no sense adding salt to the wounds.

"Everything's all right, isn't it? You aren't sick?"

"Never better."

"It sounds like I hear the ocean. You're down on the beach alone again, aren't you? Do you feel safe there alone? What if you fell out of your chair?"

"Then I'll get back in it. I work out, Justin. My upper body strength is probably better than yours."

He gave a polite chuckle. "You always were the athlete of the family. So, what do you think? Shall I fax you these sonograms? The mother still hasn't chosen a family. If we act quickly, I believe I can guarantee you—"

"No."

"You don't want to see the—"

"We tried. Whether it was you or me, it doesn't matter. We couldn't make a go of our relationship before I was paralyzed, and I'm not willing to compromise. There's someone out there for you, Justin. It's just not me. Honestly, I wish you well."

"You're making a mistake."

She blinked back tears. There was no way to explain it to him, no way to explain it to anyone. With Morgan, she'd known real love and passion. She couldn't settle for less. If she never saw Morgan again, she'd live on her memories. "You are who you are," she said softly. "And I'm still me. I might be a wreck, physically, but . . ."

"You're a fool, Claire." He couldn't hide the bitterness. "You'll be old and sick and all alone. Richard won't live forever, and then you'll have nothing but your precious settlement."

She tried to think of a come-back line, something that would deflate his ego, but in the end she said, "Good-bye, Justin," and pushed the end button on her cell. Strangely, she had no more urge to cry, and she felt as though a weight had been lifted off her chest.

No more Justin. No more marriage of convenience . . . and no sweet baby to cradle in her arms in the dark hours of the night. She'd chosen her path and she'd follow it without regrets. Or at least she'd give it the old college try.

Justin threw his cell down on the nightstand so hard that it bounced off and fell onto the carpet. "Stupid bitch," he muttered. "Damn her." He needed her fortune more than ever. His practice was sliding downhill. His hobby was expensive, but he couldn't stop.

"What's wrong, honey?" The woman on the bed shoved aside her male partner and sat up. She was naked except for the red, patent-leather dog collar and an oversize copper nose ring.

"Shut up!" Justin snapped. She laughed and watched him through cat-eye contacts as he retrieved his trousers and fumbled in the left front pocket for a bottle of blue pills. He swallowed one and washed it down with Scotch. To hell with his practice and his creditors! He needed Gi-Gi and Brad and all the others.

"Get it." He pointed to a strap-on phallus that lay abandoned on the floor.

Gi-Gi smiled and threw him a coquettish look. He wasn't fooled. She was laughing at him. He didn't know why he'd ordered her from the agency. She hadn't been particularly enticing the last time they'd partied, but Brad was different, and he could only have Brad if he took Gi-Gi as well.

He glared at her as she slid down off the bed and waddled over to the pink sex toy. She was so short that she might have been a dwarf and she was grossly fat. Not a single hair gleamed on her toffee-colored body. She strapped on the apparatus, and Justin felt a surge of excitement. This was more like it.

Gi-Gi's mouth was candy-apple red, not with lipstick,

but a cartoon-style tattoo of luscious lips, and her fat tongue was pink and extremely talented.

"Dance for me," he ordered as he poured himself three fingers of the Scotch and reached for an oyster on the half-shell. They'd been at this all afternoon, and he needed time to recover his strength. He turned up the music, some kind of polka-rap, but it had a beat and Gi-Gi's rolls of blubber undulated with obscene skill.

He walked over to the bed, stripped back the sheet, and slapped Brad on a bare buttock. Brad rolled over, disclosing an engorged member that would have done justice to an Angus bull.

Heat seeped under Justin's skin and his nuts contracted. Brad was a thing of beauty, six-foot-seven, a former WWF contender, and all of two hundred and fifty pounds of sheer muscle.

The scrape of a plate caught Justin's attention and he snapped his head around to see Gi-Gi slurping one of his oysters. She laughed and tilted the shell up, letting the gray meat slide into her scarlet mouth.

"Keep dancing," Justin said. "Did I tell you to stop?" He was feeling better now. Seeing Brad stretched out on the bed waiting for him lifted Justin's mood. What did it matter if Claire had refused him? He'd have her money just the same. It was wasted on her. He, on the other hand, would know how to spend it. He could pay his debts and he'd never need to work again, never need to see another crazy patient.

He leaned down to nibble one of Brad's big toes and Brad giggled, a high-pitched womanly laugh that spoiled Justin's rising desire. "Don't talk," he warned. A silent Brad was much, much sexier than his voice insinuated.

Justin picked up a bottle of scented oil and began to massage it into one of Brad's size-fifteen feet. Justin wasn't about to allow Claire to spoil his party, not one iota. He had paid five thousand dollars for an afternoon of fun, and he meant to enjoy every minute of it.

Morgan tried to picture Claire's glowing face as they'd stared out over the inland sea. Her lips had been parted, her eyes wide with wonder. If he willed it hard enough, he could remember her sweet scent.

How brave she'd been . . . how accepting of worlds and creatures that she'd never seen or imagined. His father was wrong when he said that humans were lesser beings, stupid, and uncaring. Morgan had never known a more sensitive woman or one who took such pleasure in making love.

He loved her. As impossible as it seemed, it was true. She was everything to him, more than father, mother, brothers, sisters. If he couldn't have her as his own, he didn't care if he spent eternity locked in this black tomb. Being parted from Claire brought a pain as sharp as raw coral slicing through living flesh.

He'd tried to keep track of passing time, but it was impossible. He might have been here hours or weeks. There was no light, no sound but the beating of his own heart. How he longed to reach through the walls to take his brothers' hands. As bad as it was for him, he couldn't imagine the pain Alexandros must be feeling.

Alex was wild, even for an Atlantean. He'd been high-spirited and fearless since he was a child, but even Alex had a weakness. He was afraid of being confined in a dark place. In the darkest corners of the ocean there were always glimpses of florescent creatures and endless freedom.

This dark prison was blacker than the greatest depth, blacker than a moonless night on the Sargasso Sea. Here the coral pressed so tightly around them that it was difficult to flex a muscle, let alone move a finger or a toe. Morgan's dearest brother, who at eight had faced a hungry hammerhead shark armed only with his wits and bare hands, had sobbed and wept when he'd accidently locked himself into a small pantry beneath the kitchens.

Orion would survive. He was strong and bold, but the thought of Alexandros's suffering tore at Morgan's heartstrings. He had brought this terror to his brother and he couldn't regret it. For Claire . . . For Claire, he would do anything. She was his weakness, and he needed her with every fiber of his being.

The coral pressed around him so tightly that he could barely breathe. The water here was dank and fetid; it burned his skin like acid. A man imprisoned here for life would surely go mad. Or, if he retained his sanity, he would die for lack of open ocean and salt spray and hope.

"Claire!" he screamed wordlessly. "Claire!"

There was no answer. There could be no answer. Tears gathered in his eyes and trickled down his cheeks.

Was she well? Did she believe that he'd abandoned her? What if her father had taken her away from Seaborne? What if he went to her and asked her to become his wife and she refused him?

What if she only existed in his dream, and that dream had faded away with the rising sun?

CHAPTER 22

Some hours later, in Poseidon's bedchamber at the palace, Halimeda grew weary of the entertainment and waved away the mermaid and naiad dancers, the sensual performers, and musicians. "His Majesty wishes to be alone with me," she pronounced. "Inform the guards that if we are disturbed, it will be their heads that roll."

Poseidon laughed, drained the last drops of wine and set the empty chalice beside his bed. He wasn't nearly as stupid as Halimeda believed him to be. He knew her faults very well, but she amused him. For a king, a man of great and varied needs, a truly wicked woman every few centuries was a delight. And this minor wife of his never failed to keep him intrigued.

Some called Halimeda a sorceress. Who knew? They might be right. But he had no fear of witches. So long as she didn't attempt to harm him or his, he didn't care what mischief she brewed up in her lair.

Short of his experiences on his five-hundredth birthday with a particularly talented mermaid and intoxicating substances, no other woman had led him such a merry chase, blending both pain and ultimate sexual gratification, in more than a thousand years. Had Caddoc shown half of her ambition and imagination, he would have showered the boy with signs of his favor. Sadly, he didn't.

Halimeda had it fixed in her mind that by desire or magic, she could convince him to overturn the secession and make Caddoc his heir. It was as likely to happen as it was that he, the high king of Atlantis, would leave the sea, become an air breather, and take up cabbage farming in the Australian desert.

He was Poseidon. He could neither be bribed nor tricked, and no amount of fawning or coaxing would ever make him advance Caddoc's career. His oldest son was a petty, small-minded youth without the barest qualifications to be a prince, let alone king, other than courage. And even his reported recklessness in battle was suspect. Whether Caddoc's supposed bravery was truly an attribute of character or proof of his stupidity, Poseidon wasn't certain.

Neither the youth nor his mother had any affection for him, beyond what material goods and powers he could give them, and neither had a scrap of honor. It was just as well. Considering what a disappointment Morgan had turned out to be, had Caddoc been a better candidate, he, Poseidon, might have been at pains to choose between him and Orion as next in line to the throne.

Halimeda clapped her hands, and the lights in the chamber dimmed. Strains of mating whale songs filtered through the thick draperies, sounds that always stirred Poseidon's loins. He had always been larger than life, and he felt a great kinship with the leviathans of the deep. They too were highly sexual and sensitive creatures with vast wisdom and a sense of both mystery and sadness about them.

Poseidon breathed deeply, waiting, anticipating what was about to happen. She came to him, thick, black hair loose around her shoulders, and clad only in filmy purple veils, her woman's mound and her shapely breasts tinted red to accentuate her sex. She smelled of jasmine and oysters, and he found the scents alluring beyond belief.

"What would you have of me, husband?" she purred as she rubbed her cleft suggestively with two slender fingers. Halimeda plucked the hairs from her body so that she was smooth and bare all over except for the tattoo of an thin black octopus that sprang from her navel and stretched one tentacle down to vanish between her woman's folds.

He drew in a deep breath and brushed the hair out of her face so that he could see her eyes. Dark as ink, dark as Melqart's heart, full of secrets that Poseidon longed to uncover, but suspected he never would.

"You know what I want," he answered. Halimeda always knew what he wanted—she was a woman who understood a man's needs. It was one thing about her that never failed to please him.

Laughing, she dropped to her knees and began to caress his inner thighs. He closed his eyes and tilted his head back, shuddering as her hot mouth pressed against his flesh and her tongue flicked against his sensitive scales. He caught handfuls of her hair and pressed her head against his groin.

With teeth and tongue she moved from thigh to staff, teasing him to full arousal, before opening her red mouth and taking him in. He was a big man, heavily endowed, but she could swallow more of his length than any Atlantean woman. He groaned and writhed with pleasure.

She made small, urgent whimpers as she suckled him. He could feel the pressure building, and fought it to prolong the delicious torture. Then, with a cry, he ejaculated, pumping his hot seed down her throat. And as he came, he

felt her sharp teeth bite into his flesh. Once again the pleasure mixed with hurt, and she laughed as he threw her
down upon the polished stone floor.

Pinning both wrists, he flung himself on top of her, feeling his virility build again. It was always thus with Halimeda. Lust fed lust, and he felt himself swelling again. He
parted her thighs with his knees and drove his cock into
her, hammering until she screamed, and he felt the gush of
his release.

He bit her mouth, her throat, her breasts, drawing
blood but not biting deep enough to cause actual harm.
She struck out at him, clawing him with her nails, gouging
him with her teeth, but it was all part of the game they
played together. Later, others would join them, willing females or males, and he would taste unfamiliar joys.

This was not the sort of ribald evening he could plan
when Korinna was present. She was as eager a partner as
any red-blooded Atlantean female, and was willing to try
almost anything, but she preferred that they not include
others in their lovemaking.

He catered to her whims because he did love her. She
was dearer to him than any of the others, perhaps even
dearer than his first wife, Morgan's dead mother. Korinna
had an innate dignity which befitted a high queen, and he
had no doubt that she cared for him, not because he was
king, but in spite of it. What he could not tolerate was Korinna's inability to accept his word as law. She was too
stubborn to suit him, and thought nothing of going behind
his back to get what she wanted.

Korinna wasn't selfish or vain or grasping. She was a
good mother and a faithful wife, so far as he knew. And
she understood that as Poseidon, he couldn't be satisfied
with a limited number of wives, mistresses, and passing

sweets. Other than her unreasonable dislike of Halimeda, she showed no jealousy of his other women.

However, this matter of Morgan and the humans was beyond his ability to forgive and forget. Korinna had been caught aiding Morgan and the twins, as well as attempting to hide the changling. He'd had to punish her as an example. The high queen must be beyond reproach, and it made him look foolish if he couldn't control her.

As he tumbled Halimeda in the big bed and called for more wine, he gave a few final thoughts to his high queen. He would bring her home from Crete in a few days. After all, she was breeding again, and he didn't want her to worry herself until she became ill. He would have to remember to ask the royal jeweler to fashion something special. Gifting Korinna with a new emerald necklace or ruby bracelet would go a long way toward smoothing over this tiff.

He and Halimeda had finished the wine and enjoyed another romp amid the piled cushions, this time with her facedown, and him on top. It was one of his favorite positions, and she had a lovely ass. As he caught his breath and caressed those round globes, two stunning women entered the room from the private stairway.

The tallest, with golden hair and skin, Poseidon recognized as a voluptuous Valkyrie noblewoman from the cold waters off Norway. Her companion, who hailed from the Bay of Bengal, was slender as a reed with a river of black hair that fell straight to her ankles. Her satin skin was so dark as to be blue-black, and her eyes and gills glowed with an inner fire.

The golden girl carried a short leather whip, but it was the second with the great, liquid eyes that promised the most delight. Her nails were long and curling, like talons, and her small white teeth came to sharp points. Rumors were that she carried the blood of one of the old gods and possessed unique powers.

Halimeda clapped again and the lights extinguished. With the darkness came the haunting odor of a strange perfume that mingled with the scents of females in heat. Poseidon roared a welcome and opened his arms to the newcomers. It would take the stamina of a king to satisfy these three, but this was one sport at which he had never failed.

Sometime in the night, the Valkyrie wandered off and the Indian beauty curled up to sleep at his feet and morphed into a river otter, leaving only Halimeda to amuse him. Poseidon was tired himself, but he would have cut off his own arm rather than admit it. "Bring me something to eat," he commanded. "Even a king needs food to keep up his strength after pleasuring so many females."

"I have your favorite wine from Cyprus," she said. "Thin and sweet, spiced as you like it." She waved toward a curtained alcove. "Come!"

Immediately, a five-foot blue octopus swam into the room, a golden bowl of pickled Chilean eels nestled in purple seaweed from the Russian Arctic waters, more raw oysters, and a jar of wine clutched in his suction-covered tentacles.

"Your wine," she said as Poseidon reclined against the bolster and nibbled a small black eel.

"You know I hate to drink alone," he reminded her.

Inclining her head, she found her goblet from where it had rolled under a table and took some for herself. The octopus lingered near her, sliding over one shoulder and coiling its tentacles around her arm. "I'll only have a little," she said, ignoring the creature. "Last time we shared a bottle, it gave me a migraine. You must have Cyprian blood."

"Where have you been for the last millennium, wench?" he teased. "Haven't you heard? Poseidon is the god of the sea. The spirits haven't been distilled that would bother me."

"Of course." She chuckled.

He waved a hand at the octopus. "Away with you. How can you bear the things always touching you?"

Halimeda motioned and the creature glided away.

"I don't know why you love them so," he said as he permitted her to feed him, bite by bite. "I don't like the way they stare at me. They never blink."

"Ah, my lord, but they make the best servants because they never talk, and above all I require discretion in those who serve me."

"You require a great deal for one not born to the palace."

"It's true, Majesty. I was not born a princess. But you yourself chose me from the pool of concubines and made my brother and father lords of the realm."

He laughed. "Because they were useful to me, as you are. Do not ever change, Halimeda. I like you just as you are."

"Thank you, Highness. My only wish is to do your bidding." She brushed her hair back from her eyes and peered up at him through thick dark lashes.

He sighed with contentment. The dish were perfect, the vinegar tasted sharp, the eels just old enough so that they crunched between his teeth but the meat was still tender. He yawned. "Even the wine has a bite to it."

"Isn't that the way you like everything?" she asked as she refilled his cup, licking her upper lip mischievously. "Spicy enough to die for?"

* * *

The light hurt his eyes. Morgan suppressed a groan and stretched, trying to work the kinks out of his cramped muscles. "Is it time?" he asked. He'd been surprised when the coral vault was opened. He had lost track of the days, and his mind seemed dull. "Are the twenty-one days up?"

One of the two guards grunted. Morgan didn't recognize either of them. They weren't Atlanteans. Most prison attendants were drawn from the pool of hybrids; they were *Turklins*, a cross between early European Neanderthals and a hard-shelled reptile that had gone extinct during the last ice age

Turklins were taller than Atlanteans, heavily muscled, and bore a tough, ridged shell on their backs, chests, arms, and legs. The fibrous covering was harder than bone and acted as a natural armor. Most Turklins were born in the Black Sea and were known for skill with weapons, taciturn personalities, and ability to go for weeks without sleep or food. Round hairless heads, snubbed, almost nonexistent noses, and small round eyes made the Turklins unattractive in the opinion of the more highly advanced humanoids.

It was said that the species kept their females at home in caves, and that they were amphibians like their turtlelike ancestors. The males enlisted as mercenaries or prison guards for five-year terms of service, and they were invaluable in positions where they could follow orders and not have to do any original thinking. Morgan had known some Turklins, but never any that he felt a real companionship for. If he were high king, he'd not employ them, as they had a tendency toward cruelty and seemed to have no code of honor among themselves.

Shielding his eyes, Morgan looked around. The low-ceilinged corridor was empty other than himself and his two escorts. "Have my brothers been released?" His voice sounded husky after so long without speaking. His throat was dry and he felt weak from lack of food.

The first guard, a hulking creature with a scarred face and three fingers on his right hand, instead of the usual four, gave Morgan a shove and motioned with his chin for him to move along.

Morgan stiffened. "Careful, Ulryk," he said, reading the name tag on his uniform collar. "As far as I know, I'm still a prince of Atlantis." Neither of the guards carried weapons other than thick staffs, but they were capable of beating him to death with them if the notion took them.

The yellow eyes narrowed. "Go. Prince," he spat in badly accented Atlantean, which was garrulous for a Turklin, before striding off down the passageway toward a lighted archway.

Morgan followed, taking in the locked doors on either side and wondering how many prisoners were held here. He'd never had much to do with this prison, being more familiar with the larger and less confining one in Atlantis. As they passed, he could hear mumbling and an occasional moan, and he vowed that once he was able, he'd make it his affair to examine the system and see if all who were held here deserved it.

Now, all he could think of was getting to Claire and asking her to be his wife. He hoped that she'd forgive him for staying away, but he wasn't certain he was prepared to tell her exactly why he couldn't come. She was tender-hearted, and the thought of his coral imprisonment might terrify her so that she would refuse to accept his proposal. He refused to consider the consequences if she chose to remain earthbound.

His gut clenched. No, Claire would agree. She loved him as much as he loved her. She'd want to be with him in his world. There was no other option for them. And once his father came to know her, he would realize how special she was. He might never inherit the throne with Claire as his wife, but he would retain his title of prince and she would be a princess. Their children would carry no taint of her human blood. They would be as royally born as he.

Had he been taken this way when he'd entered the prison? He didn't think so. The coral walls grew closer on either side of the tunnel and the ceiling lower. They were deep beneath the surface of the sea. He could tell by the pressure against his skin and the stagnant water. Here the doors to the cells stood open and the spaces inside were empty. "Where are you taking me?" he demanded. "I've served my sentence. I'm entitled to have my weapons returned to me and to be set free."

When neither Turklin answered, Morgan stopped and looked up at the second guard. His wrinkled face appeared impassive; he didn't seem particularly on edge as he might have been if a trap lay ahead. "Have you seen my brothers? Are they all right?"

Again, no answer.

Morgan's head throbbed and he felt sick to his stomach. When a prisoner was locked in coral for more than forty-eight hours, drugs were administered to put him into a semi-coma. Otherwise, the lack of fresh saltwater, the constant pressure, and the force of the tides might cause an Atlantean to sicken and die. But the drugs had left him groggy. Each step was like wading through molten lava.

Had the Turklins carried swords or even a trident, Morgan might have attempted seizing a weapon from them. Unarmed, he was no match for them. He had trained with a club as a youth, but as powerful as he was, he knew better than to take on two Turklin guards single-handed. At least, Morgan thought he knew better, but as they wound through the labyrinth, going ever deeper, he began to wonder if he'd made the wrong decision.

Just as he was about to throw caution to the winds, turn and rip the club from the guard behind him, they climbed a flight of narrow stairs and moved into a busy corridor crowded with both Atlantean soldiers and civilians going about their daily routines. Ulyrk stopped before a wide porthole opening in the wall and motioned for Morgan to go in.

To his relief, Morgan recognized the waiting room. He'd passed through this area on his way into the prison. Along the walls were stations where uniformed prison staff filled out records, checked identification, and directed visitors and incoming and outgoing prisoners to various destinations.

The first person Morgan saw was Alexandros standing near a door at the far side of the chamber. Morgan shouted his brother's name, and Alex's worried expression turned to one of joy.

"Morgan!" Alex crossed the room and threw his arms around him. "You're safe. I feared—"

"Where's Orion?" Morgan hugged him tightly. Alexandros was wearing his bow, sword, and knives, so he'd obviously been set free. He was pale and thinner than when they had last parted three weeks ago, but other than the worried expression in his eyes, he seemed well. "Is there some holdup with his release?"

Alex drew him aside. "No, there's no holdup. They'll call your name in a moment. Processing is immediate." He turned toward the Turklin guards. "Your job is complete," he said. "My brother will be free in minutes. I'd advise you to go about your business."

Ulryk's mouth quivered as though he was about to speak, but his companion tapped his shoulder and spoke to him in their crude language. Ulryk scowled, threw Morgan a hard look, then left the reception area with the other guard.

A clerk called Morgan to his station, and shortly afterwards, Morgan was duly marked on the underside of his left forearm with a release stamp, and handed the weapons and personal belongings that had been taken from him when he was arrested. As he strapped on his sword, he glanced around. Still no sign of Orion. "What's taking so long with Orion?" he asked Alex. "Why do you think—"

"I'll explain everything," Alexandros said. "First, let's get out of this hole." He led the way swiftly through several more hallways, through a guard station where a quick showing of their release stamps passed them through barred gates, through two more ports, and out into the open sea.

Morgan paused and let the clean water run through his gills. He took a deep breath and felt the fog clear away in his head. "You seem no worse for the experience," he said, glancing back at the prison complex. Little showed above the sea floor, and what was there would have been easily overlooked if he hadn't know what to look for. But he didn't understand why they hadn't waited for Alex's twin. He looked at his brother for an answer. "Why didn't—"

Alex gripped his arm. "When they opened Orion's cell, he was unconscious. The antidote produced no results. When they couldn't wake him, they called a prison healer. I spoke to him after he'd treated Orion. The man seemed honest enough, but who can tell? He couldn't or wouldn't tell me what was wrong, but he seemed to think Orion would wake on his own in a few days. My guess is that someone administered too strong a dose when he was locked away."

"Where is he?" Anger flared in Morgan's chest, and he threw Alex's hand off. "Why are we leaving without seeing him? We should be with—"

"Easy, easy." Alex moved to block him. "Do you think I'd walk away and leave him there? I saw him myself and insisted they take him back to Atlantis for healing."

A bad feeling washed over Morgan. "Who took him?"

"It's all right. Palace guard. All Atlanteans. He's in good hands. Heron was in command of the detail. Orion's vital signs were strong, but I think he was still in coma. The temple physicians know what they're doing. I told Heron to send word to Poseidon and to Lady Athena. They'll put him right."

"All the same. We should follow them and make certain no harm comes to him. I'd intended to go directly to Claire, but—"

"That's the thing." Alex grimaced. "Sorry, big brother, but you'll have to make a change of plans. I have orders from our father to go to Crete at once to bring Mother and the children home. Morwena and your little changling are with them."

"He's not sending an escort?"

"He is. We have twenty of the elite guard waiting a few leagues from here. But I need you. Orion was supposed to accompany me, but . . ."

"Mother has her own guards. How many does she need to—"

Alex shrugged. "I could go and fetch them alone, but Melqart's shades have been hunting in the area. There are seven confirmed kills. I'd feel better if I had you at my back."

Morgan nodded. Claire would have to wait a few days longer. "Of course, I'll come," he said. "So Poseidon's forgiven her and wants her home."

"I suppose. I imagine he just wanted her out of the city during the trial. Maybe he thought she'd break us out of jail."

"She might have," Morgan agreed, only half in jest. "Zeus knows she's capable of it. She can be a terror when it comes to protecting her children. Including us."

"I didn't forget to try what you asked about your woman," Alex said, hovering in the water only an arm's length away. "I tried to get a message to her."

"Did you succeed? Do you think she heard you?"

"It's difficult to tell. Humans aren't very developed when it comes to receiving psychic messages. I'm afraid I might have done more harm than good."

"How could that be?"

"I think she was frightened."

"Still," Morgan said, more to convince himself than Alex, "she might have heard you and understood." He didn't want to think of Claire being alone and afraid. Not going to her troubled him, but the safety of his stepmother and the little ones came first.

Claire would have to understand that he had duties to his family. At least he didn't have to worry that she was in any danger. When he did get to Seaborne, she'd be there waiting for him. They would be together, and he would spend the rest of his life showing her the wonders of his world.

CHAPTER 23

Justin sat at a booth in the back corner of a bar in Brooklyn, nursing a beer and nibbling stale pretzels. It was a Wednesday night, and relatively quiet in the establishment. Montana Mike's was a single public room, long and narrow, with paneled pine walls and dark floors. Only half the tables were full, and other than one loudmouth in a ball cap who was well on his way to being stewed, they seemed a quiet crowd.

Justin glanced at his watch and wished he'd picked up something at a used clothing store to wear tonight. He'd deliberately dressed down, but his docksiders, Yankees' tee, and khaki slacks made him stand out in this haven of scuffed sneakers, blue jeans, and Dickies work shirts. Not wanting to miss his contact, he'd arrived ten minutes early. It was now after eleven, and he'd been sitting here for an hour and a half. He was about to call it quits when a uniformed police officer came through the door, spoke to the bartender, and walked back toward Justin's booth.

He had the sudden urge to void his bowels. He hadn't done anything wrong yet. How could anyone know . . . ? To his surprise, the cop smiled and slid into the bench across from him. Justin felt sick.

"How's it going, Bill? How's the wife and kids?" the cop

asked. He waved and the bartender pulled a beer for him. "Got any nachos to go with that? I like the spicy sauce."

"Excuse me," Justin said. "I was just going to use the men's room." He stood up, and his knees felt like rubber. There was a short hall with bathroom doors on either side that he'd checked out when he'd first arrived. The only way to whatever lay beyond the bar and presumably a back entrance appeared to be through a curtained doorway behind the cash register. Justin might not be able to escape, but he was going to relieve himself in the proper receptacle, not in this booth.

"Take your time," the cop said. "Just as long as you don't have a gun stashed in the john."

Justin stared at him.

The policeman laughed. "*The Godfather*? The first one. Didn't you see that movie?"

Justin shook his head. "I'm not much for theater."

By the time he reached the toilet, Justin was shaking so badly he could hardly get his pants down in time. A foul slime rose in his throat, and he felt even more like throwing up, but he couldn't move off the seat. Which would be worse? Shit in his khakis or vomit on his docksiders? Hiring professional help to solve his problem had been a bad idea from the first.

After he was finished, thankfully without soiling himself, Justin took a long time washing his hands with the foamy pink soap. He thought about simply walking out, walking past the officer, and out of the bar. Maybe if he was lucky, he could get to the street . . . lose him. Maybe—

The doorknob rattled.

"Occupied." Justin grabbed for a paper towel and found the receptacle empty.

There was a clunk and the bathroom door burst open.

The cop stepped inside and closed the door behind him. Hands dripping water, Justin backed up against the sink. The single dirty bulb swayed on a wire over his head, but there was enough light for the man to see his face—to identify him in a lineup.

"There must be some mistake," Justin began. "I just—"

The cop folded his arms and leaned back against the door. He was a hatchet-faced man in his mid-forties, tall and muscular, but not beefy. It was difficult to see his face under the police cap, but his body language told Justin that he was fit and tougher than a city employee ought to be. "I don't have all night, Dr. Morgan. And I don't like wasting my time."

Justin swallowed, not sure of what to say.

"I understand that you might be nervous, but you requested our service."

Justin's mouth was dry. He tried to speak, but he was too frightened, so he simply nodded. Another of his patients with a dubious background had made the connection. Justin had assumed that he must be getting a cut of the money. He said the nonrefundable fee would be fifty thousand, twenty-five up front, and another twenty-five when the contract was fulfilled.

"Did you bring the cashier's check?"

"Y . . . yes. I did."

"Good. Now, let's go back to the booth, have a drink, and complete our transaction before people start to think we're having our own private party back here."

"All right." Justin felt lightheaded. "Yes." He wondered if this was a real cop or a disguise. He wanted to ask, but thought the better of it.

"No need to be afraid of me," the man said. "I'm not in the wet end of the business. I simply handle transactions."

"Dis . . . discretely, I hope," Justin managed. His patient had sworn no one would know his name. Obviously, he'd lied, the perverted, little, foot-sniffing prick.

"I can assure you that so long as you hold up your end of the bargain, you'll never be linked to the operation. And neither will I."

"What . . . what assurance do I have that . . . that the matter will be . . ."

The big man flashed a wide smile, but Justin guessed that the smile didn't extend to his eyes. It was the kind of smile a grifter might give a mark, just before he took him for the big score.

"We're in business to satisfy our customers. If we cheat you, you never come to us with a problem again. The people that I work for aren't common criminals, Dr. Morgan. They have standards. I could give you references. . . ."

He chuckled, and Justin realized that he was making a joke.

"Of course, if I told you who our satisfied customers were, we would have to kill you." He stepped back and opened the door. "After you, *Bill.*"

Somehow, Justin forced his legs to carry him back down the hall. A plate of nachos and two fresh beers stood on the table. He slid into the booth, keeping his head down, his face in the shadows. If this was a trap, if the cop was going to place him under arrest as soon as he passed over the check, there was nothing that he could do about it.

The man sipped at his beer, then wiped foam off his upper lip. "Have some of that salsa," he suggested. "Hot as hell but the best in Brooklyn. Andy makes it himself. Fresh Italian tomatoes and peppers. Some kind of Georgia onions."

Justin kept his hands in his lap. If he raised them over

the table, he'd be unable to hide his trembling. "You want . . ."

"I want nothing. I'm going to give you an address. Mail the folder with the photograph of the subject, his name, and physical description along with the check to a Mr. Peter O'Conner at that address. Once the contract is fulfilled, you'll receive a bill for dental work from Tri-State Dental Care. The second cashier's check goes in the mail within twenty-four hours. So long as you don't mention us and we receive the money, we won't come to your apartment in the middle of the night and blow your brains out. Am I making myself clear?"

"Perfectly." Justin shuffled his right foot back and forth on the floor. There was something sticky stuck to the bottom of his sole. Likely chewing gum. Justin hated gum chewers and their foul habit of throwing their discarded gum on the ground.

"Don't think that you could move to another city or country to evade paying. We are an international organization with contacts that would surprise you."

"I'm not going anywhere." His voice sounded high-pitched and he lowered it an octave. "My practice and home are here in New York. "But . . . the details. Where and when?"

"You'll receive instructions and a phone number. At the proper time, all you have to do is call that number and order a Philly cheesesteak. We hope you're intelligent enough to use a phone that can't be traced."

"Yes," Justin agreed. "Yes, of course."

"Excellent." He reached for a tortilla chip. "Now try this salsa. I promise you won't be sorry."

Poseidon was sick. He was often under the weather on mornings after he indulged in an orgy of sex and strong spirits. His age was beginning to show, Halimeda thought. Although his prowess in the bedchamber hadn't slackened, it would only be a matter of time before he'd be unable to satisfy her and she'd need a new partner.

A pity that Alexandros wouldn't be available. She fancied him; she had since he'd first begin to grow into the equipment that was the pride of Atlantis. He proved such a disappointment over the years, rudely rebuffing her advances. Why her stepsons disapproved of her, she couldn't imagine. It was their loss. She could be very, very good to those in her favor.

The king leaned over the edge of the bed and groaned. "I think I'm dying," he muttered. "The wine had too much spice."

"You had too much wine," she said. "You'll feel better after you eat something. I've ordered a Chilean kelp broth with shrimp and minced clams. You know the kelp is only at its best every three years. And those strange fruits you like so much. The ones from Ceylon."

He groaned again, sat up, and dragged his fingers through his beard. Blond hairs were tangled in it, and he picked them out and tossed them on the floor. "My sons are released from prison today," he said. "I suppose I'll have to receive them."

She didn't answer. With luck, he wouldn't have to. Timing was everything. She'd waited so long for this moment. She'd hidden the tiny vessel containing the powerful poison in the anteroom off the king's bedroom. When she'd freshened herself up this morning, it had been a simple thing to retrieve it and slip it into a fold of her morning robe.

Several gentlemen of the bedchamber came to dress the king and see to his toilet. He waved them away, insisting that he was capable of dressing himself. And when they reminded him that he was receiving ambassadors from the water kingdom beneath Japan, he replied that the visitors could await his pleasure. Duly chastised, the noblemen made hasty exits. Few wished to challenge Poseidon when he was in such a mood.

A mermaid carried in the tropical fruit and two bowls of the exquisite and rare soup. The identical porringers were Phoenician, fashioned of beaten gold in the form of high-prowed ships, no larger than one of Poseidon's fists. They and crates of other precious dinnerware had been salvaged not long ago from a sunken ship in the Mediterranean. Halimeda loved the bowls. Once the king was no more, she'd insist that no one but her be permitted to dine from them.

The girl put the soup on the table and looked helplessly at Poseidon.

"Well, what are you waiting for?" he demanded.

Halimeda smiled at him. "Will you come to the table, my lord, or would you prefer that I bring breakfast to—"

Grumbling, he joined her at the table. "Where is my wine cup? Am I to sup without wine?"

"By the bed, sire," Halimeda answered. "Shall I fetch it for you?" Muttering under his breath, he went to get the goblet, and as soon as his back was turned, she sprinkled the deadly poison over his bowl of soup. The kelp broth was a deep green, and the dried flakes amber. She lifted a silver spoon and stirred once, making the addition invisible.

Poseidon returned, held out his goblet for her to fill it from the jug, and sat across the table from her. He reached for his spoon, fumbled, and dropped it. It bounced off the rim of the table onto the floor. He swore.

"I'll get it, husband." Quickly, Halimeda rose and stooped to recover the spoon. It had fallen under the table. "Here." She held it out to him. "No worse for wear."

"Do you expect me to eat from that?"

She sighed. "Take my spoon then. I haven't touched it." She returned to her chair, lowered her head, and took a spoonful of the broth. "Delicious," she proclaimed.

"It had better be." Cautiously, he sampled a small amount, smiled, and then began to eat with enthusiasm. Halimeda's appetite had fled, but she continued to partake of her own portion

Poseidon ignored her comment. "You were right. This is delicious. I feel better already." He reached for a piece of fruit. "A pity we can't have this often."

When Morgan and Alexandros reached the meeting place, there was no sign of the promised escort. Nothing moved in the area but a school of small gray fish. "I don't like this," Morgan said. "Are you certain this was the spot?"

"That's the information I was given." Alex rested his hand on the hilt of his sword. "I don't like it either."

"It could be a mix-up. It took awhile for us to be released. Maybe they came early, didn't see us, and went on to the palace."

"Wait." Alex motioned for him to stay still and swam thirty yards toward an underwater outcrop of rocks.

Morgan couldn't see what had caught his brother's attention, but he waited until he returned. "What?"

"A turtle. An old one, shy, but I was able to communicate with him. He said that no Atlanteans had passed through here. He hasn't moved from his spot in . . ." Alex shook his head. "A long time. His kind do nothing in a hurry. He's seen sharks, jellyfish, baitfish, but no palace guards. There's a wormhole not far from here. I think we'd better take it."

Morgan agreed. Scattered across the floors of the oceans were portals that led beneath the earth. Once these passages, known as "wormholes," had been the digestive tracts of enormous wormlike creatures. As the earth's atmosphere changed, the seraphim had evolved into something even more alien. They no longer moved or reproduced, but their dormant bodies were used by Atlanteans as high-speed transportation.

Entering and leaving a wormhole could be tricky, as was making sure that the traveler exited at the right stop. The first three times Morgan had attempted the adventure alone, he bypassed his destination by hundreds of miles. Once, when he wanted to reach the coast of Brazil, he'd been ejected at Tierra del Fuego in South America, and spent weeks trying to catch a ride back.

Today wouldn't be as risky. Crete was only four hundred or so miles from the prison, and both he and Alex were experienced at manipulating the turns in seraphim's digestive tract while avoiding the feeding chambers. Those unfortunate enough to be sucked into a side passage ended up as worm dinner, so it paid even veterans to remain alert.

Neither he nor Alex had a trident with them, a most useful weapon for closing dangerous chute doors and tunnel grates, but they were lucky enough to find several planted in the sand near the worm's head. It was customary for riders to leave tridents for others to use once a journey was completed, but—as with many traditions—the courtesy was fast falling away.

They passed through the rushing currents of the seraphim and reached the correct dropping-off point without incident. But as they approached the old palace, which lay between Crete and the island of Kythera, Alex seemed more on edge that normal. "I don't like this," he muttered. "I don't like it at all." He looked around. "Where are the dolphins? There are usually dozens here."

As with the prison, most of the palace was hidden beneath lava flows and tumbled rock. For thousands of years, the area had been inhabited by humans, but none of them had ever discovered what superior civilizations existed beneath the waves. Many of the earth dwellers, those who didn't discount Atlantis as a myth, believed that the true site of the kingdom was the island of Thera.

It was true that in the long past humans and Atlanteans had interacted more often in this part of the world than in others, to the benefit of the humans. The Mycenaeans and Egyptians had borrowed much of Atlantean culture, including knowledge of mathematics, medicine, philosophy, and poetry. Greeks thought the Atlanteans were gods, and their own society mirrored many aspects of Atlantis, but this small corner of the world was never more than a minor underwater colony for the kingdom.

The old palace was a vacation retreat for the royal family, a place where Morgan and Alex and their brothers and sisters had come to play and relax from the more rigorous decorum of the city. Morgan had been here many times and he loved the old pillared halls and courts and the many pleasure gardens. But the palace had always been a haven for dolphins, and he'd never failed to see them.

Underground pools of molten lava spewed columns of steam, creating a natural barrier to sharks and larger predators. Here the dolphins found sanctuary for their old, their injured, and their young. If the dolphins were gone, Alex was right. Something was seriously amiss.

At the gatehouse, four soldiers kept watch. They wore the uniform of the elite guard, but neither Morgan nor

Alex knew the men by name. Two knew their faces and let the brothers pass without delay. Inside the courtyard, they saw other guards, but still no dolphins.

"Watch your back, Brother," Alex warned. "This smells like dead squid, three days in the sun."

The first man that Morgan recognized was Damasko, captain of his mother's guard. He came toward them smiling, but his eyes were wary, even frightened. "Where is everyone?" Morgan asked. "Poseidon sent us to bring the queen home. We were supposed to have an escort, but—"

"They arrived here earlier, Prince Morgan." Damasko saluted both him and Alex. "Her Majesty waits in the garden off the lion court. She's most anxious to receive you."

"She knew we were coming?" Alex asked.

Damasko nodded. He was a tall man, thin and wiry with a short, rusty-colored beard. A native of the Aegean, his skin was a dark blue, almost glossy. He was a steady leader of men and Morgan liked him. He'd been the queen's protector since she'd come to Atlantis as a bride.

As they passed over the painted tile floor of the larger reception room and through the columned archway into the garden, Morgan heard the voices of the children and the laughter of his adolescent half-brothers. Lucas, Markos, and Morwena had set up a target at the far end of the enclosure and were practicing with bow and arrows. From the shaft lodged in the bull's-eye, it appeared that one of the three was adept at the sport. Morwena saw them coming, dropped her bow on the sand, and raced to meet them.

Morgan's gaze passed over his beloved half-sister to his mother and the child she was holding on her lap. Danu they called her now. Once human, and now Atlantean and his daughter, she was a beautiful sprite of a child. For the first time, Morgan wondered what Claire would think of having a ready-made family. He'd given Danu a second life, and it was his duty to raise her with all the love and nurturing he'd received. *Oh, Claire*, he groaned inwardly. *How will I explain Danu to you?*

"Morgan! Alex!" Morwena threw herself into Morgan's arms. "Are you all right? Was the coral awful? Where's Orion?"

Morgan hugged her. "Who's the marksman?"

She laughed. "Me." Bouncing out of his embrace, she seized hold of Alex. "Are we to go home? Can't we just keep you here? No Father, no courtiers, no politics. "

Morgan smiled at her and moved toward his mother. "The king misses you," he said. "He's sent us to—"

A fourteen-year-old boy charged him. "Alex! Morgan! We need bigger bows."

"Men's bows!" Lucas shouted.

Alex caught Markos around the waist and threw him over one shoulder. Lucas, three years younger, picked up the discarded bows and stood grinning at them with shining eyes.

"Don't kill them," their mother admonished. "They just got here."

"They've grown since I've seen them," Alex said. "What have you been feeding them?"

Morwena laughed. "Anything they could stuff in their mouths. They never stop eating."

"You're the one getting fat," Markos flung back. "Not us."

"Your sister isn't fat," Morgan defended. "She's just growing into a woman."

"Growing and growing and growing," Lucas teased.

"I've been so worried about you. Are you all right?" Korinna asked, looking around. "Where's Orion? Isn't he here?"

Morgan shook his head. "Don't worry. I'll explain when this bunch quiets down."

"Let's have a look at that target," Alex said, leading the boys and Morwena back toward the archery range. "Who can split Morwena's arrow at thirty paces?"

The queen rose from the bench where she'd been sitting with one of her ladies and motioned to Morgan. "Come and greet your daughter. Danu, here's your daddy. I told you he would come for you."

Danu peeked at him and became suddenly shy. She wrapped her arms and legs around his mother and hid her face in the queen's lap.

"She's a delight," Morwena called over the child's shoulder. "She's been asking for you every day."

"She is a darling," Lady Freya agreed. "She's a favorite in the nursery." The queen's handmaiden and a female servant Morgan recognized as Gita picked up their sewing and moved discretely away to give them privacy.

Morgan took a few steps toward them before sudden movement behind him caught his attention. Armed men in the uniform of the elite guard swarmed into the garden from three entrances. "Alex!" Morgan warned, drawing his sword.

The lady-in-waiting cried out in alarm and clutched the maid's hand.

"I see them," Alex said. Catching Morwena by the waist, Alex pushed her behind him and reached for his own weapons. "Go to your mother," he ordered. "Lucas! Markos! To me!"

Morwena snatched her bow from Lucas's hand and slipped an arrow from the quiver on her back. The boys notched their own arrows and quickly obeyed. Alex moved to stand beside Morgan, and the youths retreated to protect the queen, her two women, and their sister.

"What's the meaning of this?" Morgan demanded.

An officer, bearing the insignia of a senior captain, stepped forward. "We mean no disrespect, Queen Korinna, but we are here on a matter of greatest urgency."

Morwena raised her bow and took aim at the center of the speaker's breastplate. "How dare you enter my mother's garden with drawn weapons?"

"We bring evil news, princess. The high king, great Poseidon, is dead."

The lady-in-waiting began to shriek and the queen slapped her.

"We have come to arrest Queen Korinna, Prince Alexandros, Prince Morgan, and the Princess Morwena."

Morgan flicked his gaze to Alex. His brother remained tensed to strike, showing not the slightest hint that he had heard. Their mother's upper lip quivered and her eyes grew bright with unshed tears.

"On what charge?" Morgan asked.

"High treason. The king is dead of poison. The four of you are the chief suspects in his murder."

"By whose order?" Alex's eyes narrowed. Morgan sensed his brother's fury and steeled himself for what was to come.

The captain swallowed. "By the command of Poseidon-in-waiting as commanded by His Majesty on his death bed, Prince Caddoc."

CHAPTER 24

Claire hung up the phone and closed her laptop. She'd had a productive afternoon. She'd spent a great deal of money, and she didn't regret a penny of it. A charity that she'd supported for years had an urgent plea on their new website, and she'd made a large contribution.

Mustang Haven was a nonprofit group home for troubled girls in Idaho run by Henry Grail, a former rodeo rider and high school teacher, and his wife of twenty-two years, Billy Anne, a psychologist. The staff provided sanctuary for homeless adolescents and a number of wild horses that had been rounded up and were unsuitable for placement due to age, poor health, or temperament. The youngsters who lived at Mustang Haven were between thirteen and twenty years of age, and some were pregnant. Few had attended school regularly, and none were prepared to enter the world and support themselves or their children.

Four sets of house parents lived in cabins on the two-thousand-acre ranch, as well as a team of horse handlers, a licensed midwife, and a farrier, all female. Billy Anne, a full-blooded Navaho, had grown up in the foster care system, and her dream was to provide a real home and direction for both unwanted girls and mustangs. As part of her education, each girl was assigned a mount, and as the young women learned to ride and care for their animal companions, they grew in confidence and self-assurance.

Once accepted into the program, no girl or animal was ever turned away from the ranch. If a young woman completed her high school education, she was offered either assistance for college, a paid position at Mustang Haven, or help in finding a job and living accommodations in the larger world. Those who gave birth while they lived at the ranch could choose to keep their baby in a nurturing setting or make an adoption plan. The success rate for young women and wild horses was amazing.

Not surprisingly, the cost of maintaining such a project was enormous and growing every year. Billy Anne and Henry had poured their life savings into the ranch, but due to the economy, charitable donations had slowed to a trickle. On the website, Billy Anne had described her heartbreak at having to turn away homeless girls and horses because the Mustang Haven—which had received the highest ratings—was sinking deeper into debt every month.

Claire sighed with satisfaction. She'd just instructed her financial director to set up an anonymous trust fund in the amount of seven million dollars for Mustang Haven and to transfer a donation of another million for immediate use. That should keep the horses in oats and the girls in popcorn and schoolbooks for a long time.

It wasn't enough to just write a check. She intended to inquire about volunteering at the ranch. It wasn't easy for her to travel, but it wasn't impossible. If she took a nurse with her and the right equipment, she could teach classes in financial skills, history, and riding. As physically challenged as she was, if she could be a role model for even one girl and help to improve her life, it would be worth it.

Claire loved Seaborne, but she wasn't going to sit here and petrify like a dead tree.

She'd wait a few more weeks . . . maybe a month or two. If Morgan didn't come back to her, she'd dedicate what was left of her time to something positive. With extra money, the haven might be able to open their doors to girls who were physically damaged as well as emotionally. She couldn't walk, but she could still comfort a crying teenager, see that an aging horse received love, medical care, food, and a green pasture to run in.

She chuckled as she imagined what her father would say about *wasting* so much money on *hopeless* causes. "You can't save them all," Richard was fond of saying. But maybe she could save a few . . . and in doing so, maybe she could save herself as well.

"My husband is dead?" Queen Korinna asked. Her hand fluttered to her throat and she swayed as if about to faint. "Is this true? Poseidon is dead and Caddoc named future king?"

"Prince Caddoc?" Morgan's face darkened in anger as he stared at the captain who had just announced Poseidon's death and their pending arrests. "Caddoc?" He scanned the garden, counting sixteen soldiers. There should have been twenty. Where were the others?

"What treason is this?" Alex demanded. "Where is your proof? How do we know that you aren't the traitors sent here to seize the queen and murder her?"

"Poseidon is dead, as you will soon learn," the captain said.

"Caddoc is not the heir to Atlantis. The new Poseidon stands before you, fool." Alex motioned to Morgan.

Morwena moved to steady her mother. "Prince Morgan

has been crowned," the princess said. "His name entered in the temple rolls. To interfere is to damn your souls."

"Quiet, girl," the captain ordered.

Ignoring him, she whipped around to include the guardsmen drawing closer around them. "You know what Caddoc is—what his mother is! And you would hand the kingdom to such a worthless sack of shark dung?"

Queen Korinna drew herself up to her full height. "Who accuses my sons of patricide? The witch, Halimeda? If the king was poisoned you don't have to look far to learn who the murderess is."

"Lay down your weapons and surrender to the king's justice," the captain said. "To attempt to defend yourselves would only put these young ones in danger. You will have a fair trial. Prince Caddoc gives you his word."

Morgan backed closer to his mother. Five of them armed, one a girl and the other two hardly more than children, against sixteen of the elite guard. It would be a massacre. Where was his mother's household guard? Where was Damasko? Morgan would have bet his right arm that Damasko would remain faithful.

"Hold fast," Alex warned. "If this is Halimeda's brew, none of us will live to reach Atlantis to stand trial."

The captain's gaze was hard, his features rigid. "I'll not tell you to drop your weapons again!"

"Wait!" Korinna held up a beringed hand. "Peace, all of you. There is no need for violence here. Or the need to terrify my women and the children. May I ask your name, sir?"

"I am Knut, Highness, of the clan of Magni," he answered gruffly. "I will not say that I welcomed this task, but know that I and my men will follow orders, no matter the cost."

Korinna bestowed a gracious smile on him. "Surely there is no mention of my lady-in-waiting, my chambermaid, or this infant," she said, indicating Danu. "They will only slow you in your duty. Let me send them and my two younger sons to the nursery. They can do you no harm, and we may yet settle this misunderstanding without bloodshed."

"You think me a fool, madam?" Veins stood out on his forehead and his hand rested on his sword hilt. "These pups face me down with drawn bows, and you believe I'd send them off for milk and cookies with their nannies? If they think to defy the new king's orders, they can face trial with the rest of you."

Korinna gave a little sound of amusement. "Oh, my," she said, pretending disbelief. Again she waved her hands helplessly and touched her lips with fluttering motions. "Surely not my youngest son. Prince Lucas is only ten years old. Let him and the little girl go to their school-room," she pleaded.

A white-faced Lucas opened his mouth to protest, and Morgan silenced him with a stare. Lucas was eleven, but no need to let a lad's pride of being older than his mother had claimed stand in the way of his release.

"Well enough," he said grudgingly. "Off with them. But not the older boy."

"Oh, thank you, sir. You show great generosity of heart," the queen twittered. "But my poor ladies. Neither would know what to do with a sword if you handed it to them. Surely, they are no threat to you or your troops."

"Please," Morwena begged, lowering her bow. "Have pity. They would only be a burden to you in transporting us to Atlantis."

"Let them pass," Knut muttered. "But you, princeling."

He pointed at Lucas. "Drop your bow where you stand."
He glared at the queen. "And now I will have your surrender, Highness."

"Wait," the queen said, still pretending fear and confusion. It was all Morgan could do to hold in his laughter at
her portrayal of a stupid woman. He dared not look at
Alex. If he did, Alex would give all away.

"Wait but a moment," Korinna begged. "Until the children and my women are safe away. I could not bear it if
they should be frightened." And to her lady-in-waiting,
she whispered, "Take them into the treasure room and
lock yourselves in. You will be safe there." She picked up
Danu and handed her to Lucas. "Care for her as you
would me," she murmured.

"No talking!" Knut waved to the guard at the door.
"Call Damasko."

Lucas cast a last look at his brother Marcos and reluctantly carried Danu toward the nearest archway. The
weeping women hurried after them.

Damasko, commander of the queen's palace guard, arrived swiftly. "Sir?" He made no eye contact with any of
the royals, but Morgan noted that he was not wearing his
sword belt and assumed that he must be a prisoner as well.

"Take the women and children away and set a watch
over them. Let none harm them unless they attempt to escape or send out a message. If you fail me, you and your
men will suffer for it."

"Yes, sir. I understand, sir." Damasko saluted and vanished through the archway into the interior reception hall.

"My patience is at an end," Knut said to Morgan. "Lay
down your weapons or I will take no responsibility for
your—"

"Shoot him," the queen ordered.

Morwena raised her bow and released her arrow. "Shoot, Marcos!"

Knut jerked, gasped, and stared down at the feathered shaft that had suddenly blossomed in the center of his chest. His eyes widened in surprise and, gasping, he staggered forward and dropped to his knees. His sword fell from his fingers. Blood poured from his open mouth and he sank full-length on the sand.

Morwena drove a second shot into the commander's throat as he went down. The queen had already scrambled for Lucas's bow and taken shelter behind the high-backed bench. Alex leaped to defend them, taking the head off one charging soldier with a single swing of his sword.

Morgan met two opponents head on, sword to sword. A third rushed at him with a trident, but Marcos put an arrow into his shoulder, knocking the fight out of him. The two soldiers were seasoned warriors who knew their craft, and Morgan was hard put to defend himself. He blocked a killing blow, jabbed, and sliced through the thigh of the man to his left.

"Morgan! To me!" Alex shouted.

Morgan began to slowly retreat, all the while fighting off his two attackers. Then one stepped on Knut's outstretched arm, lost his footing and fell. His companion turned his attention for a fraction of a second and Morgan dealt him a hard blow to his midsection. He jerked his sword free and dashed back toward his mother.

One of the guards had circled around and was advancing on the queen. She was on her feet, using Lucas's bow like a club, striking the soldier as hard as she could, but it was a boy's weapon and slender. Her attacker ignored the blows to his face and head and jabbed at her with his trident. Morwena had used her last arrow and had run to Marcos to grab one of his.

As soon as his sister was clear, Morgan reversed his sword and threw it. The blade made a full circle in the water, the point piercing the soldier's spine, and sending him crashing into the queen. They both went down in a heap, but Korinna scrambled up, her tunic soaked in blood. For an instant, Morgan feared that she had taken a serious injury, but her quick movement proved her unhurt and the gore that of the dead guard.

Morgan put a foot on the man's back, yanked his sword free, and grabbed his mother's shoulder. Half guiding, half pulling her, he followed Marcos and Morwena. Alex ran in front of them, cutting a shining swathe of steel through the guardsmen with a sword in each hand.

With five soldiers in hot pursuit, they reached the shelter of the columned portico and plunged through a narrow doorway leading down a flight of slippery stone steps to a storage room beneath the reception hall. When Morgan reached the bottom of the stairs, he turned to wrest a circular stone loose from its resting place. "Alex! Help me! It's too heavy."

Together, they rolled the stone into a hollow trench in the floor, blocking entry from the staircase. "Hurry," Morgan said. "There's another passageway. It leads to the dolphin stables." He and Alex sent the marble statue of a flying horse crashing to the floor. Behind the sculpture lay another tunnel, so low that Morgan and Alex had to duck their heads to enter.

Now, their mother led the way, with Morwena behind her, Marcos following, and Alexandros, and Morgan guarding the rear. Stone pressed in on all sides. The way was dark; the water stale and thick. In some places the tunnel was so narrow that Morgan had to turn sideways to get through.

"Faster!" Alexandros pushed his younger half-brother.

"They'll know we've left the storeroom. We've got to reach the dolphin quarters before they do."

"I'm doing the best I can."

"He's hurt," Morwena said. "He took a sword wound in the chest."

Morgan swore. "Why didn't you say so?"

"How bad is it?" Alex asked.

"I'm good," Marcos said. "As you said. We have to get out of here."

Morgan could hear the pain in the boy's voice, but he was right. Wounded or not, the lad would have to remain on his feet and keep moving. It would be impossible to tend his wound or even carry Marcos through the narrow stone corridor. They had to reach the other end ahead of their pursuers or they'd all die on the sword points of Knut's men.

"Not far now," the queen called back. But a few yards later, she stopped. "There's a rock fall. The passage is completely blocked. We'll have to back up."

"And then what?" Alex asked. "Wait in that storeroom like fish in a barrel?"

"Fish in a barrel?" Their mother laughed, and Morgan wondered if she'd become hysterical. Not that she ever had in his memory, but nothing like this had ever come to pass before, either. "Go back," she said. "It's the only way."

In the king's bedchamber in the royal palace of Atlantis, Halimeda became aware of a strange sensation. The room had begun to spin and undulate.

"What's wrong?" Poseidon asked, peering into her face. "You look pale."

"Nothing, I—" She gasped as a sharp pain seized her lower abdomen.

She looked down at her golden bowl. It seemed as if the

container had transformed to a real ship and was pitching up and down. The pain in her belly intensified. "I'm ill. I . . ."

"What's wrong, wife?" Poseidon smiled down at her. "Something you ate didn't agree with you?"

"You . . . you . . ." Moaning, she clutched her middle, staggered up, and tried to run. He caught her before she's gone an arm's length, turned her towards him, and held her fast, his strong fingers digging into her shoulders.

"Do you like the soup, wife? You should. It's of your own making."

Bile rose in her throat. She choked and blood spattered her hand and the front of her robe. "No. No," she protested. "I did nothing."

"Nothing?" He shoved her and she fell to her knees.

He came to stand over her, his face a pitiless mask. "What's wrong, witch? Don't like the taste of your own brew?"

"Poseidon, please . . ." She screamed as the pain rose, rolling through her, gnawing her bones with sharp teeth. "Mercy," she begged. "Mercy! I'm innocent."

"Hades take you, you traitorous bitch. Do you think me such a fool that I could be tricked so easily? I switched the bowls. The dish you planned for me is your reward."

"Back the way we came," Queen Korinna insisted. "At that last turn, there's a hole in the roof. You can climb up on Alex's shoulders and pull us up, one by one."

"You might have mentioned that when we passed it," Morwena said.

"I didn't remember. The last time I came through here, as a child, none of us were tall enough to reach the ceiling, let along strong enough to lift someone else."

"And you're certain that's the spot?" Alex asked. "We've come a long way along this tunnel and—"

"I'm sure," Korinna said. "There's a trident carved into the wall. Not much higher than your waist, but my fingers brushed against it as we passed it."

It was Morgan's turn to lead them, and when they found the trident exactly where their mother had said it would be, he also discovered crude footholds carved into the rock. It was a simple matter to climb up to a larger passageway above. Alex came next, and Morwena was able to help Marcos. The boy was clearly failing in strength, but he made no outcry as they hoisted him up. In minutes, they stood in an ancient hallway, dimly lit by glowing shells set into the walls.

"Which way?" Alex asked, picking up Marcos. The boy offered a token protest, but it was clear that he couldn't have traveled much farther on his own.

The queen reached for Morgan's hand. "You haven't told me where your brother is? Where's Orion?" She squeezed his hand. "The truth. Tell me that he isn't dead too."

"No," Alex said. "Not dead. They gave him too heavy a dose of the sleeping drug when he was locked away. We sent him with friends to the temple. Lady Athena will restore him."

"You can't know that he's alive," Morwena said. "If someone murdered our father, they could as well murder him."

Alex shook his head. "Orion's not so easy to kill. In the temple, he'd be safe from attack."

"I wish I could believe that," Korinna said. "But I never thought that I'd see Poseidon murdered."

"Orion is alive and well," Alex said stubbornly. "You know the link we share. I feel his strength returning. He's well, don't worry your heart on his account."

"And Father? You had no inkling of his death?" Morgan asked.

"No, I didn't. I sense a bitter blackness, nothing more."

Morgan looked from Alex to Korinna. "Tell us which way to go, Mother."

"Left," Korinna said. "Take the first flight of stairs, then right at the top. You'll see a doorway ahead, at the end of the hall."

"What is it?" Morgan asked. "We haven't reached the dolphin stables yet, and I don't think we're close enough to the surface."

"Weapons storage," Morwena said. "I've been here before, but not through the tunnel from the garden. The tridents and swords are the old design, but they're fashioned of some strange metal. They never rust. And there are arrows aplenty."

"But not bowstrings, I'll wager," Marcos put in.

"No. No bowstrings that I remember. Luckily, I brought my bow with me," Morwena declared triumphantly. "And the weapons cache opens directly to the sea. We can escape that way, if we want."

"We can't leave the palace with Lucas and little Danu still prisoners," Korinna said. "But if they reached the treasure room, they'll be safe. No one can break through those walls."

"We're not leaving them," Morgan said. "I'm still not certain that Damasko betrayed you. I don't know if there were traitors among your servants, but according to my count, there can be no more than seven of the elite guard still able to fight."

"Once we have the three of you in a safe place, we'll retake the palace and rescue the others," Alex said. "You can count on it."

"The two of them," Morwena said. "I fought beside you, brothers, and I know I killed at least two guardsmen. You can't deny me the opportunity to help you save the children."

"Oh, but we can," Morgan said. "It will be your mission to protect Marcos and your mother."

"But I—"

"You heard the crown prince," Alex said. "If Poseidon is dead, he'll be our next king. You have to obey him."

"Not when he gives stupid orders," she protested.

"You'll find it's a habit of kings," Korinna said.

The light was dim in the hallway, but he could see the strain on her face. She would truly mourn his father. For all his faults, he'd been a great king and a good father. There was no time now to think of what Atlantis might be without him.

Later, he promised himself. There was Halimeda and her son to deal with and a rebellion to put down. He couldn't imagine that anyone on the High Council would believe that he or the twins or Queen Korinna would be guilty of murdering Poseidon. He hoped they wouldn't. More important right now was getting those who depended on him to sanctuary, doing what must be done, and getting to Claire.

What if she'd been with him here during the attack by soldiers? Could he have protected her? He'd failed to protect Marcos. The thought that he could bring Claire to Atlantis as his wife and still lose her turned his blood cold. He would have given half his lifetime to hold her in his arms at this moment, but it was impossible.

Wait for me a little longer, he vowed silently. *Wait for me, my love. I'll come for you—though Melqart and all his legions bar my way.*

CHAPTER 25

He's not coming back, Claire thought, as she looked out over the railing of her bedroom balcony at the sea. It was a gorgeous day. The sun was shining; the temperature hung in the low seventies, and she'd dined on freshly ripe cantaloupe and blueberries, a chocolate croissant, and a lovely Earl Gray tea. She should have been happy, but she didn't know how to end this longing for something she couldn't have ... something she might never have actually had.

She was trying not to mope, attempting to keep busy, to make plans. But the sadness remained. As the days and nights had passed since her last dream of Morgan, she'd tossed all her pain medication away. The suspicion that it had been drugs that had conjured him and his watery world lingered at the back of her mind. She still lived with the pain, and she slept poorly, but she managed.

She tried to fill the hours of each waking moment with something positive. She exercised harder, paid close attention to her diet, and did something she hadn't done in a long time. She'd taken out her makeup case and began wearing eye shadow, mascara, and lipstick again. The woman who looked back at her in the mirror was still confined to a wheelchair, but she looked younger and more ineresting. She looked like someone that she would like to know better. "I'm not dead yet," she'd said aloud. "And I won't look like it anymore if I can help it." Maybe she'd even do something different with her hair, add highlights, get a new cut.

No more poor me, she thought. No more self-pity, and no more anger. What was done was done, and the world was tough. As Jackie often said, "No matter how bad things get, you can always find somebody worse off. You've got to be happy with what you do have."

Jackie would be pleased when it came time to pay college tuition for her children or to make her next mortgage payment. One of the things Claire had done yesterday was to pay off Jackie's home mortgage, and provide funds to send Jackie's children to college and grad school, all anonymously, of course. She'd also doubled Mrs. Godwin's salary and plumped up her retirement account.

Billy Anne had phoned yesterday, overjoyed with the donation to Mustang Haven. They'd discussed ideas for improving the program, and Billy Anne had invited her to come out for an indefinite stay to see the ranch firsthand. It was what Claire had hoped for, and she was thrilled, or she would have been if she wasn't so worried about Morgan.

More than just missing him, she'd awakened in the night with the feeling that she'd heard him call out to her . . . that something was wrong—that he was in mortal danger. By the light of day, she could try to discount her fear for him, but it remained, shadowing her hopefulness. She might go down to the beach later, but for now, she was content to sit here, staring out at the green grass and the blue sea in the distance. "Be safe," she murmured. "Wherever you are, be safe."

* * *

Danu was angry. She didn't like the bad men who'd come into the garden and frightened Lady Freya or Gita, and she didn't want Lucas to take her away from her new daddy. Lucas said it was just a game, but it didn't seem like a nice game to her. Men with swords had taken them to the servants' quarters and locked them in a storeroom. There was no food here, but Danu didn't want to eat anyway.

She missed her dolphin Echo. When the bad men had come into the garden, Echo had swum away so fast that they hadn't been able to stop her. Danu didn't know where she was or when she would come back. She wanted Echo. She wanted Queenie and Morwena, and she wanted her daddy.

She and Lucas, Lady Freya, and Gita stayed in the room for a long time. Danu didn't know how long, but she had slept and awakened and slept again. Now she was awake, and everyone else was sleeping. There were no beds and the stone floor was hard against her bottom. She missed her lovely shell bed with the colored icicles and the music. She wondered if the orange and blue fish missed her.

Danu kept quiet. She was good at staying quiet when people were sleeping, but she was hungry again. She was searching the room when she heard a familiar whistle. When she looked up, she saw Echo's head on the other side of the window.

"Echo!" she cried, but not too loudly, because Lady Freya could be cross when people were naughty. In a flash, she was at the window and reaching through the bars to stroke Echo's skin. The dolphin had missed her too. Danu could tell because she made lots of little clicking sounds and rubbed Danu's hand with her long nose.

"Where did you go?" she demanded. The dolphin made a noise that sounded like a chirp and banged at the window with her nose. "Do you want to come in?" Danu whispered. "I don't think you could fit through this window, even if the bars weren't there. It's a very little window."

Echo wiggled and snorted.

"I wish I knew what you were saying," Danu said. How old did she have to be to learn dolphin talk? Morwena had promised that she would when she was older. But Danu had an idea. Lucas was big. He was eleven. Maybe he would know what Echo wanted. Danu swam back and shook him. "Lucas, wake up," she whispered in his ear.

He blinked his eyes and sat up. For a moment, Danu thought he was going to be angry with her, because you could never tell about boys. But when she pointed at Echo, he nodded and went to the window.

When Echo saw him, she made a lot of excited whistles and squeaks, and to Danu's surprise, Lucas made noises that sounded just like Echo's. "She wants you to come out," he said. "There are enemies in the palace. People who want to hurt us."

Danu sighed. "We know that."

"Echo says they are Lady Halimeda's soldiers. She wants Mother dead so she can be queen."

"Oh. I don't like her."

"Lucas frowned. "No one does but the king. And maybe Prince Caddoc."

"Why do they like her?"

"Caddoc is her son, and the king . . ." Lucas trailed off. "I'll explain when you're older. But Echo needs your help now. She's saying something about a lock, but she's so excited it's hard to understand it all. Wait, Echo," he said. "Slow down. Tell me again." Lucas stroked her beak and the two exchanged a few more whistles and clicks.

Lucas glanced back, and he looked scared, maybe even like he was going to cry, and that scared Danu too. "The soldiers killed two of mother's fighting dolphins with spears when they tried to help Damasko," Lucas said. "Echo says Lady Halimeda's men drove the palace dolphins into the stable and locked them in. She thinks they want to kill all of them, the Atlanteans and the dolphins."

"But why? Our dolphins are good, aren't they?" Dolphins had big mouths and a giant row of teeth, but she hadn't seen them bite anything bigger than a squid. "Why do they want to hurt the dolphins?"

"Because they aren't wild dolphins. They're our dolphins, and they will remain loyal." Lucas bit his bottom lip. "Do you know what loyal means, Danu? With our dolphins it means they are bonded to us, like Echo is to you. They will care for you, fight for you, remain faithful, even if it means their own death. Once a dolphin is pledged to a person, they stay with them all their life."

"But the bad men wouldn't hurt the mother dolphins or the calves, would they?"

"All of them. Dolphins know what people are thinking," Lucas explained. "They can read minds. Echo says if we don't stop them, the bad soldiers won't leave a single dolphin alive so there's no one to tell what they did to us."

"I thought Damasko was bad too."

"He was pretending. Do you know what pretending is?"

" 'Course, I do," she replied, small hands on her hips.

"Mother's loyal guard, Damasko's men, and most of the servants are in the dungeon. But Echo saw the bad soldiers throwing bodies to the sharks."

"Can't our dolphins swim away?"

"By Zeus's great toe! You're such a baby, Danu. I told you that the stables are locked. There's a key. Echo needs you to unlock the gate. Then she and the other dolphins can rescue Damasko's soldiers."

"I'm not a baby! Why can Echo let the good men out but not the dolphins? Why does she need me?"

"Dolphins can't do keys," Lucas explained. "Keys are too small for them to hold. There's just a bar on the dungeon door. If the dolphins can get past the soldiers, they can open the door. We can't waste time, Danu. The window's too small for me to fit through. Will you do it? You have to be very brave."

"I am brave," she proclaimed, spreading her arms wide. "I didn't cry when the bad men scared us. Lady Freya did."

"All right. Stand back. Echo's going to push the bars and the window casing into the room, then you can squeeze through."

With a pop and a clatter, Echo knocked the window in. Danu swam through the opening and the dolphin wiggled and squeaked.

"I think she wants me to hold on to her harness," Danu said to Lucas. "Maybe I'm starting to learn dolphin talk already."

"What are you doing?" Lady Freya sat up. "Danu, come back here."

Danu pretended she didn't hear her.

Lucas did too. He was busy propping the window casing back in the hole. Before Lady Freya could say anything else, Echo started swimming, and Danu had to hold on tight to the harness handles. Echo swam fast. It was usually fun, but today was too scary to be fun. Danu didn't want any of the dolphins or people to be hurt, especially Morwena, Queenie, or her daddy.

When they reached the entrance to the stables, Danu didn't see anyone around at all. Echo nosed open a hatchway, swam inside, and followed the hall to the big gate. Sure enough, it was locked. Danu could hear clicks and whistles from the far side. The dolphins sounded scared. Echo clicked and chattered, and the noise stopped.

The silver key was hanging on a loop of braided seaweed. It was easy for Danu to pull the key off the hook, but when she tried to fit the key in the hole a man shouted.

"What do you think you're doing, brat?"

Danu was so startled that she let go of Echo's harness and slipped off her back. Echo's high-pitched whistle hurt Danu's ears, but that wasn't as bad at the man coming after her with a long, pointed trident. Clutching the key, Danu swam as fast as she could under Echo.

The dolphin gave a cry of pain, and a stream of something red dirtied the water. Echo made a sound that Danu had never heard before and zoomed over the man's head.

"Don't leave me!" Danu cried. Terrified, she did a flip and dove into a rack of dolphin harnesses. She wiggled through a small opening and out the other side, but the man swam around the rack and jabbed his trident at her.

"Echo!" she cried. "Help me!"

He said a bad word and tried to stab her again, but she dodged the sharp points and darted back through the hole. The man was coming. The dolphins were whistling and banging into the far side of the gate. She wanted to try to unlock it and let them out, but there was no time, and there were no more places to hide. The bad soldier was between her and the hallway to the ocean.

Danu screamed as the man closed in on her.

Then there was a wave of white water and Echo came swimming fast and butted the man. He grunted, dropped the trident, and tumbled head over feet. Echo opened her mouth wide and made a hissing sound in her throat. Snap. Snap. She closed her teeth on his leg, and Danu heard an awful crunch.

The man squealed and tried to get away, but Echo

grabbed his arm and crunched that. Danu pushed the key in the hole and turned it. The gate opened and angry dolphins came flooding out.

Echo turned and nosed Danu. She grabbed hold of Echo's harness, and Echo swam down the hallway and out into the water. The dolphins came after them, bulls, cows, and calves, but the man didn't follow. Another dolphin bumped against Echo, and she made a hurt sound and shivered.

"Oh," Danu said. "You're hurt." There were three bloody holes in Echo's side where the soldier had stabbed her with his trident. "Poor Echo," she crooned.

Some of the mother dolphins and all of the babies swam with them to a seaweed jungle not far from the palace. Echo thought they would be safe there. Danu was happy that she had gotten the gate unlocked and helped the dolphins escape, but she was worried about the others. What if the bad men had come to hurt Lucas? She was afraid, but not as afraid as she had been because Echo was with her. "Will my daddy come soon?" she asked Echo, but the only answer she got was a worried whistle.

Korinna hugged Alex and then Morgan. "Be careful, both of you. I couldn't bear it if anything happened to you."

Morgan nodded. "We'll be all right. It's Danu and Lucas I'm worried about."

"They wouldn't hurt them," Morwena said. "How could they? They're just children."

But Morgan knew by the terror in his sister's eyes that she didn't really believe that. She was attempting to ease her mother's mind. "So long as you and Alex and Orion and Marcos are alive," she insisted, "there would be no reason to harm the children."

If Orion was alive, Morgan mused. Had he been slain on the way to Atlantis while he was still unconscious and helpless? A woman who would poison her own husband would stop at nothing to rid herself of her rivals. And if anything had happened to Alex's twin . . .

Morgan cast a glance at Alexandros and cold steel replaced the uneasy feeling beneath his heart. If Orion had been murdered, there would be no hiding place for Halimeda, her son, or their supporters. Alex would hunt them down, one by one, and destroy them.

Morgan was struck by the sense of loss he felt when he thought of Poseidon's death. Larger than life, he had been a man of excess in all things. His father had been a hard man, a courageous but sometimes ruthless ruler. He'd shown small affection toward his grown sons in the centuries past, yet Morgan had to admit that he loved his father and had desperately sought his approval. Poseidon was . . . or rather, Poseidon had been more than a man. He had been a legend, and if he was truly gone, there would be none to match him in the years to come.

It had taken longer to find a place of safety for his mother, Marcos, and Morwena, than he'd expected. The waters off Greece were dangerous, and without their loyal dolphins or palace guard, the women and his injured half-brother might easily become victims of Melqart's creatures or other predators. He'd had to take them to an underwater cave near the ancient land of the Spartans.

The waters here were zealously guarded by warrior naiads, and the magical humanoids would give Queen Korinna and her children sanctuary for a few days. After that . . . Morgan couldn't think past what had to be done. As he had pushed thoughts of Claire to the far corner of his mind, so he must do with thoughts of the political struggle to come. Saving Atlantis from Caddoc and Halimeda had to wait until the old palace was secure and his family safe.

The journey back was uneventful, without encountering anything more than a cruise ship of human tourists plowing through the water without heed to the watery world below the surface. Alex and Morgan had sought the relatively shallow floor of the ocean and stared up as the mammoth shadow passed by overhead.

The palace wasn't far, and they had decided that the easiest undetected entry might be made the way they had escaped, but as they neared the site, Alexander stopped swimming and got a strange expression on his face.

"What is it?" Morgan demanded, sliding his sword free.

"No." Alex made a chopping motion with his hand. "It's Orion. He's here. And he's recovered." His brother grinned. "All's well, Morgan." He set off swimming and Morgan followed, still wary. He knew Alex had good instincts, but his intuition wasn't always perfect.

In minutes, joy replaced his apprehension. Orion appeared with Lucas at his side and Danu in his arms. "If you've come to win a victory for our side, you're late," Orion said, laughing and slapping his brothers on the back. "This little one has already done it."

"Daddy!" Danu threw out her arms and leaped through the water. Morgan caught her and held her tight.

"Are you all right?"

She giggled. " 'Course, I am. I helped Echo save the dolphins, and the dolphins saved the good soldiers and—"

"The dolphins broke Damasko and the guards out of the dungeon," Lucas supplied. "There was a big fight."

"And we won. Actually, I did," Orion said.

"Don't listen to him," Lucas said excitedly. "It was all over when he got there. Our dolphins killed three of them and the others surrendered to Damasko's men. And they weren't even armed yet."

Danu clung to Morgan. "Where were you? A bad man tried to stick me with his trident and he hurt Echo, but she's better, and I missed you."

"I brought fifty men with me," Orion said, "but I could have come alone. Other than the shades. We ran into a pack of them."

"And?" Alex arched a golden eyebrow.

Orion shrugged. "Let's say they won't be a problem anymore." He grew serious. "Mother? Is she—"

"Safe with the naiads. At the Spartan caves. You can swing by and pick her up. Morwena's with her. Marcos was hurt in the fighting, but give him a few days and he'll recover."

"We were worried about you," Alex said to Orion. "How did you escape Halimeda's crew? After Poseidon was poisoned—"

"Not quite," Orion answered. "I'm well enough. I woke up in the temple with Lady Athena sprinkling flower petals over me. For a minute, I was afraid I was dead. I've a hangover you wouldn't believe, but otherwise, I'm as good as Father."

"The king?" Morgan shook his head. "He's not dead?"

Orion laughed. "No thanks to Halimeda. She tried to poison him, but you know how suspicious he can be. He switched the soup bowls on her and, apparently, she ate from the wrong bowl. As you can imagine, he's not too happy with her."

Alex frowned. "She survived?"

"She won't for long. It's a slow poison, painful but effective. You know Poseidon. He'll show her no mercy."

"Why should he?" Alex said. "She doesn't deserve it."

"So there's no uprising? Poseidon is in control?" Morgan asked. He kissed Danu and passed her back to Orion. "You're telling me that our father is alive and in good health?"

Echo crowded close and nudged Orion. He placed Danu on the dolphin's back, and Echo clicked contentedly. "Perfect health," Orion replied.

"Caddoc?"

"He and his cronies got away. So watch your back. There's a death warrant on his head, so he has nothing to lose."

"Then why did Halimeda's guards try to arrest us? If the plot had already failed. They insisted Poseidon was dead and Caddoc—"

"Poor timing, I guess," Orion answered. "They probably thought he was. Father's not so easy to kill."

"Neither is Caddoc, apparently," Alex muttered.

"So now what?" Morgan asked.

Orion grinned. "We finish up here, retrieve Mother, Morwena, and Marcos, and take this little heroine back to Atlantis. You know how Poseidon loves a rousing tale. Once he hears how Danu saved the palace, you'll be his favored son and heir again."

"Other than our pending sentence of eternity in the coral prison?" Morgan said.

Orion nodded. "Small squid. You got us into this, Brother. I'm counting on your good judgment to get us out."

"What are you waiting for?" Alex asked, turning to Morgan and giving him a shove. "I hate suspense. Go get your woman."

CHAPTER 26

"Miss Claire, please." The housekeeper tugged at Claire's arm and raised her voice above the salt wind. They were on the beach below Seaborne, and Mrs. Godwin had come down the walkway to coax her back to the house.

"You remember," she said loudly. "Tomorrow starts my vacation. There's a shower for my niece tomorrow at the parish church in Stowe, and I promised my sister that I'd help her set up. Nathaniel's taking me, and we'd like to get started this afternoon, before the roads get too bad, if you don't mind."

"Absolutely. It's a long drive." Claire settled the binoculars around her neck. She'd been watching a sailboat in the distance, half hoping that it might be Morgan. Wherever he was and whoever he was, she suspected he didn't need a sailboat to reach her.

The wind caught Mrs. Godwin's headscarf and ripped it away. It sailed up and then tangled in the wire mesh that lined the sidewalk. Grumbling, the housekeeper hurried to seize the scarf, put it back on her head, and double knotted it under her chin.

Claire covered her mouth to hide her amusement.

"No way I'm going off and leave you here on this beach,"

Mrs. Godwin said as she began to push the wheelchair back toward the pavilion. "It's bad enough leaving you alone for a week. I wouldn't go today if Jackie hadn't promised she could come out, fix your supper, and spend the night."

"Don't be silly," Claire replied. "I don't need Jackie. She has her husband and children to cook for. I'm capable of being alone in my own house for a few hours. And, the agency is sending Jane tomorrow morning. She'll be here all week."

"Jane's responsible enough, I suppose, but a little young for my taste. You know I always liked Nurse Wrangle. She was—"

"Creepy. A Nazi. I won't have her back. Ever."

Mrs. Godwin huffed and puffed as she pushed the chair against the wind. "You really need to consider an electric chair."

"I like this one. It keeps me fit." She didn't need Mrs. Godwin's help to get up the incline to the pavilion, but it was easier to accept it than to argue.

"The weatherman says that we might get hit bad by this nor'easter. I'd feel better if I was here. Maybe I should just postpone—"

"You go and enjoy yourself. I'm not helpless."

"I suppose. Now, Jackie won't have to actually cook tonight. I've left chowder, salad, and blueberry buckle."

Claire sighed. "I doubt if we'll starve. The freezers are full."

"And if the power fails, all Jackie has to do is throw the switch in the utility room, the one with the red button."

"Jackie's familiar with it. And so am I. I've done it myself, more than once."

"In the dark, it's not so easy. I've left written instructions on the kitchen counter."

She allowed Mrs. Godwin to push her chair toward the

elevator that led to the top of the bluff. Sand blasted their exposed arms, legs, and faces, and threatened their eyes as the elevator began the slow rise to the top. The bluff had sheltered her somewhat and she hadn't realized how quickly the weather had changed for the worse. Mrs. Godwin was right; she should have come up from the beach earlier.

Back at the house, Claire urged Mrs. Godwin to leave at once, and assured her that she'd be fine. As soon as she got to her room, she located Jackie's number, called her, and told her that she wasn't needed this afternoon.

"You certain about that?" Jackie asked. "I don't mind. I told my kids that it would be hot dogs and beans tonight, and it won't hurt their daddy to watch over them."

"I'm certain. Mrs. Godwin left enough to feed an army. The weather's turning nasty. You don't need to make the drive out here to heat chowder in the microwave and serve me a dish of dessert. I'll be fine, and Jane will be here first thing in the morning."

"If you say so. I can tell you. I don't care much for driving the beach road in bad weather."

"Absolutely. Try and stay dry. See you next Monday."

Claire wheeled her chair to the window and watched until she saw the van with Nathaniel and Mrs. Godwin disappear down the driveway. A fine rain was already pattering against the glass, and the clouds had taken on a darker hue. They were in for a real old-fashioned *buster*, as the housekeeper would have said, but Claire didn't mind. Storms had never frightened her, especially here at Seaborne. She'd always thought of the house as a great sailing vessel, riding the Seven Seas in search of buried pirate treasure.

Her cell ringtone announced Justin's call. She almost didn't pick up, but then she decided that she wasn't going to spend her life hiding from him. Wasn't there something she'd read about the philosophy of karma? *The best way to rid yourself of a karmic tie to an enemy isn't to hate them; rather to feel no emotion regarding them at all.*

Okay, she decided. That was worth a try. "Hello, Justin."

"I called earlier, but you were on the beach."

"You called me on the beach this morning."

"Right. After that. You must have had your cell off."

"Maybe, I was bird watching."

"Oh. I was afraid I was making a pest of myself, and you'd decided not take my calls again."

"I thought of it."

"I apologize for what I said. It was wrong. It's just that I'm disappointed that you won't consider—"

"Let's not rehash it all, Justin. I'm willing to be on friendly terms, nothing more."

"All right. If that's what you want."

"It is."

"So you really are turning into a bird watcher?"

"I've been keeping a log of the birds I see every day. Identifying new ones, looking for unusual ones."

"Sounds fascinating."

She almost laughed. By the little enthusiasm in his voice, Justin was lying through his teeth. "I caught a few seconds of the weather," he went on. "It looks as though you might be getting some heavy rain."

"I think it may be more than rain. It looks like a nor'easter is bearing down on the coast. But we'll be fine here. Seaborne's ridden them out for centuries." She pushed herself over to the refrigerator and removed a Coke. Where Mrs. Godwin found them in glass bottles she couldn't guess, but icy cold, they were delicious. She could almost hear the wheels turning in Justin's head as she took a sip of the soda.

"And you've got your housekeeper and her son there with you? When I spoke to Nathaniel earlier, he said something about driving his mother to Vermont."

"A family shower. It's her vacation week. But Nathaniel will be back, and I've got a nurse coming in the morning."

"No one with you tonight?"

She was tempted to lie. All she needed was Justin calling Richard and having him bugging her. But lying required too much energy. "I was supposed to have Jackie—she's one of the maids—but I told her not to come because of the weather."

"So you're alone?"

"Like Rapunzel in her enchanted tower."

"That concerns me, Claire. What if you should have another seizure?"

"Don't worry. Nathaniel will be back, and I feel fine."

"Well, don't hesitate to call if you need anything. I still care about you."

"I know you do." That was an untruth. She knew no such thing, but it was one of the small white lies honest people told every day to make life easier. "I've got to go, Justin. Lots to do."

He tried to prolong the call, but she uttered a cheerful "Good-bye," and hit end. She dropped the phone in her lap and slowly finished her Coke.

Outside, the wind beat at the shingles and rattled the windows. The sky had become even darker while she'd been on the phone with Justin, and the raindrops drummed rather than pattered against the house. She placed the empty bottle on the floor and pressed her fingers against the glass of the French doors. Mounds of black storm clouds piled up and she thought she saw a streak of lightning to the north. *Guess Mrs. Godwin was right*, she thought. *We're in for a real buster.*

She was suddenly hungry. She took the elevator to the kitchen, rummaged around in the refrigerator for the seafood chowder that Mrs. Godwin had made fresh this morning. Homemade whole wheat bread and a caesar salad would go perfectly with the hot chowder. Humming, she found a bowl and spoon, heated her soup in the microwave and carried her early supper to the breakfast room.

She'd forgotten a drink. Even though she'd just finished the small Coke, she was still thirsty. Returning to the kitchen she retrieved an icy bottle of Samuel Adams, opened it, and returned to her solitary meal. The rain was coming down in sheets now, and it soothed her as she ate. "Maybe I'll get a cat," she murmured aloud. Mrs. Godwin hated cats and so did Richard. *Too bad*, she thought. It was her house, and if she wanted a pet, she'd have one.

She was just finishing the last spoonful of the delicious chowder when she thought she saw movement in the corner of the room. She started, her breath catching in her throat. No one was here. No one could be here. To get into the room, someone would have had to walk past the table.

She stared into the shadowy corner as her pulse thudded. If this was a trick of her Humpty-Dumpty brain, it was a new one. She'd never seen ghosts before, not unless you counted Morgan as a—

Light as concentrated as a flashlight beam held inches from the floor flickered against the tiles. She blinked at the brightness of the pulsing illumination. Fire? Was there an electrical fire? No, this wasn't flame, more of . . . Claire's mouth grew dry as the light source grew and the image of a man wavered and materialized against the backdrop of the brick wall.

Not a flesh-and-blood man. A helmeted warrior from the far past. Transparent. Ghostlike. Maintaining an image for a fraction of a second before dissolving into gray mist, and then appearing again, this time clearer.

She wasn't a screamer, but she gasped and opened her mouth to yell. But then the face under the crested helmet took form. Strangely familiar. Suddenly, she knew who it was. It wasn't Morgan, but the Achilles who'd come to kidnap her from her bed—the dazzling apparition Morgan had claimed as his brother Alex.

"Richard. This is Justin. How's the weather out there on the coast?"

"Seventy-five and sunny. Anything wrong there?"

"No, no, not at all." Justin had pulled over into the rutted parking lot of a boarded-up seafood wholesaler just south of the Maine state line and made the call on his cell. The windows of the rental car fogged up as wind and rain beat against the windows. "I hoped I wouldn't catch you in court."

"No. I always put the phone on vibrate when I'm in court."

"How's it going?"

"Could be better."

Richard had told him weeks ago that he'd be in San Francisco consulting on a high-profile court case. The coincidence of Richard's absence and the housekeeper's annual vacation had been a stroke of luck, and Justin meant to take every advantage of it. Who knew when he'd get such an opportunity again?

"Have you spoken to Claire? She's still not answering my calls."

"Yes, I have. As a matter of fact, I just talked to her a few minutes ago. I was worried about her up there with Mrs. Godwin gone, especially with the storm moving in," Justin said smoothly. "I called and convinced her to go to a hotel in Bangor for a few days, just in case. Separate rooms, of course."

"What?" Richard demanded. "I can hardly hear you."

Justin repeated himself. "Did you get that?"

"Still scratchy but I can hear you. You say Claire agreed to go with you? That's a surprise."

"She did," Justin said.

"Say again." Richard was fast becoming impatient.

"I said, she did."

"Can you hear me?"

"Perfectly."

"I hope I didn't do the wrong thing, insisting she go to the hospital," Richard said. "She hasn't been this angry with me since I refused to allow her to sail from San Diego to Hawaii with friends when she was a sophomore in high school."

"I know. We've had our fair share of fusses, but she never holds a grudge long. I'll see if I can get her to call you tonight. Is there a number at the hotel where she can reach you?"

"She has my cell number."

"And if the connection's no better than this, you wouldn't get much out of her. Are you at that hotel you usually stay at?"

"Yes. I'm in 4210. I'm not sure of the area code, but I haven't had any reception problems other than this one. Your phone may be dying. Come to think of it, your name didn't come up when it rang."

"Didn't it? That's odd."

Justin heard a man call Richard's name, and then he hurriedly said, "Sorry, I've got to go. But I appreciate this. You've taken a huge weight off my mind. I know she'll be safe with you."

"I think this is the best thing for Claire. You know me. I

was never a big fan of Seaborne. Too isolated for my tastes." That much was true. The old house literally gave him the creeps. Give him a penthouse apartment in New York any day. All that country house fever was nonsense in his opinion.

Once Richard had concluded the call, Justin made a second, to the housekeeper's son. He'd jotted down Nathaniel's cell number off the board in the utility room the last time he'd been at Claire's home. He had Mrs. Godwin's number as well, but contacting Nathaniel seemed the most sensible thing to do.

The taciturn groundskeeper twanged an "Ey-ah?"

"Nathaniel Godwin?" Justin asked.

"Speak up. Who did you say it was?"

"Is this Mr. Godwin?"

"Ey-ah. Who is this? Sounds like you're talking through a drainpipe."

"Mr. Warren. Justin here. Mr. Bishop wanted me to contact you and your mother. He's out on the West Coast, so he asked me to call. Due to weather conditions, Mr. Bishop wasn't happy with Claire being alone at the house, so he asked me to pick her up. She'll be staying at a hotel in Bangor for the week."

"She won't be at the house?"

"No. I'm taking her to Bangor this evening."

"I was planning on being back there no later than . . ." The rest of Nathaniel's sentence was cut off.

Damn this cheap over-the-counter phone. Justin rapped it twice against his hand. "What was that?" he asked. "Poor reception. Must be the storm."

"I said I'd be back tomorrow," Nathaniel said. "Next day at most."

"No need for you to rush. Mr. Bishop suggested you take a few days personal time."

"With pay? I'm a working man. I can't afford to go—"

"I'm certain you'll be paid," Justin assured him. "Now can you contact your mother, or should I call her myself?"

"You say I'll get my full check?"

"Yes, I guarantee it. Do I need to call Mrs. Godwin's—"

"No need. Ma's sitting on the seat next to me. Lotta heavy traffic. We've been bumper to bumper for—"

"Enjoy your time off." Justin cut him off. He had no interest in where she was or what she was doing, so long as she wouldn't be returning to Seaborne early or calling Claire to confirm his story. Justin offered a hearty goodbye, dropped the phone on floor and stamped on it. The case crumbled, and he scooped up the pieces, started the car, and drove to the edge of the lot.

The heavily grown-up property dropped off sharply from the parking lot to the river below, but there were scraggly trees and underbrush. He didn't want some kid coming upon the cell phone, broken or not. Reluctantly, he got out of the car and walked a few yards through the rain and mud to a spot where the edge of the road met the bridge. He tossed the phone high in the air, and although he couldn't see the surface of the water below, he knew the evidence was going to end up in the bottom of the river.

Mud seeped into Justin's shoes, ruining a four-hundred-dollar pair of Italian loafers and a new pair of silk socks. He hadn't had the shoes more than two months, but you couldn't make an omelet without breaking eggs. He promised himself that he'd replace these with two new pairs. Once the technicalities were worked out, money wouldn't be a problem for him ever again.

It was all Claire's fault. If she'd only been reasonable, none of this would be necessary. He would have played the role of noble, devoted husband to his grossly handicapped wife. The sympathy vote alone would have ensured that he was never without feminine company. After all, a man as wealthy and obviously virile as he was, trapped in a marriage with a human vegetable, he would have nubile women flinging themselves into his arms and begging to comfort him.

And now that he'd been forced to resort to more permanent measures, no one would ever suspect that he had a role in Claire's tragic end. After all, Justin had driven all the way from New York City to see to the safety of his dearest ex-wife. What a pity that he'd arrive too late, some hours after the botched burglary, and discovered Claire's body.

He got back into the car and checked his map. He didn't trust the new satellite direction finders, couldn't abide the idea of some robot voice giving him orders about where to turn or what highway to take. He much preferred the old-fashioned way. Not that he didn't know the way to Seaborne; he did. He just didn't want to miss a turn in this rotten weather. He might end up driving miles out of his way to reach the house. And it was important to arrive sometime after midnight, well after Claire was asleep. He had a key to the kitchen door and the code to the security system, also compliments of Nathaniel's carelessness.

He decided to leave the Glock in the trunk until the last moment. There was no sense in having some do-gooder policeman stopping him without reason and seeing the pistol case on the seat beside him. Justin felt certain that he could do what had to be done without fuss. Not that he was any Rambo, but he knew the basics of using a firearm, and his contact had assured him that there was no chance of anyone tracing the weapon.

His last meeting with Carlos flashed across his mind. He was sorry that he'd had to ensure Carlos's discretion so violently. Yet, it would have been foolish to leave a witness or to pay so much for a handgun that might be defective. He might not have a second chance to deal with Claire. So, it had all worked out for the best. Sooner or later, Carlos's occupation would have been the end of him. The worst of it was that now Justin would have to deal with some other scum when he needed something that wasn't strictly above-board.

CHAPTER 27

"Alex?" Claire shivered as the pulsing light flashed and then faded, taking the image with it. Then there was nothing there but a pot of ferns and a blank wall. She laughed nervously. Is this what one bottle of beer did to her now? Was she so far gone that she was seeing specters in the night?

A blast of wind rattled the doors, and she jumped at the sound. The temperature in the room seemed to have dropped by twenty degrees. It had been pleasant when she'd carried her chowder to the table. Now . . . Now she wasn't hungry. She couldn't have eaten a bite. Gooseflesh rose on her skin, and she rubbed her arms against the chill.

Ridiculous! How could she be so childish? She might be brain injured, but she wasn't crazy. She turned the chair and prepared to wheel out of the breakfast room. She'd clean up what was left of her meal in the morning. She'd go upstairs, call someone, anyone. Have a chat about nothing important and put a romantic comedy in her DVD player.

"Claire . . ."

Her heart skipped a beat. The hairs on the nape of her neck rose. "Who's there?" she demanded. "This isn't funny."

"Claire."

The voice was the faintest whisper, hard to hear above the force of the wind and rain . . . difficult to know if it was real or her imagination. "Richard? Is that you?" If this was his idea of a joke, she'd make him wish—

Something warm and wet touched her arm. Her breath caught in her throat. Not something—someone. She could feel large fingers grasping her wrist, but she couldn't see anything. "Stop it!" she cried. She tried to pull her arm free, but it—he was too strong. She felt an overwhelming male presence. "Let go of me!" she screamed.

Soft in her ear, someone whispered, "Claire. I mean you no harm."

Light flashed, so brightly that she involuntarily closed her eyes. Whimpering, she snapped them open to find Alex standing there inches from her chair. At least, part of Alex was visible. His muscular bare legs were only suggestions, but the kilt or loincloth or whatever he was wearing seemed solid enough. It appeared to be gilded leather or perhaps steel armor. Alex's chest was definitely solid. She could make out his hard muscled shoulders and the sinewy column of his neck. His face was not nearly as distinct, like a TV station without a proper signal. Still, she was certain that the image in front of her was Alex.

"What . . . what do you want?" she stammered, ashamed of herself for being so frightened, ashamed of herself for feeling the giddy excitement rising up inside her. She wanted this—welcomed this madness. Hell, she'd be happy if he came to kidnap her again and take her down the whirlpool to Morgan. "Where is he?" she stammered. "He's not sick or hurt, is he?"

"Mor-gan. Coming . . . . Wait for . . . Trust him."

The pressure on her wrist faded. In an instant, Alex was gone. She stared down at her arm, wondering if she had imagined it all, wondering if she was still in her bed dreaming or if . . .

If what? What explanation could there be? "Trust him." Trust Morgan. "Wait for him." That's what Alex had said. But this hadn't happened before. When Alex had appeared in her bedroom, he'd been solid enough to pick her up and carry her out of the house. He hadn't faded in and out like Casper.

"Alex. Are you here? Please. I don't understand."

Hands grasped both her wrists, and she heard Alex's voice once more, not in the room, but in her head. "Listen," he said. "Listen and feel."

"Feel what?"

Strong fingers pressed into her flesh. Instinctively, she closed her eyes and let her mind go blank. Mist swirled around her. She had a sensation of water all around her. Shadows of fish and the sandy sea floor . . . She could taste salt on her tongue, feel the pressure of the water again her body. "Morgan, where are you?"

It wasn't the same. It wasn't working. She could feel the wheelchair padding against her back . . . the straps that held her in. Her legs were frozen blocks of wood. In frustration, she tried to slap them and realized that Alex wasn't holding her arm anymore. But her legs were dead weight. Waves crashed over her head.

She was sinking . . . sinking. Water poured into her mouth . . . down her throat. Was this death? Was this how it was all meant to end? Strangely, she wasn't frightened by the prospect . . . only that she might not be able to reach Morgan . . . to hold him in her arms.

"Morgan?"

She sensed rather than saw him. Wherever she was, everything was dark, and it was almost impossible to breathe. She tried to rise from her chair, wanted to stretch out her arms and legs and swim, but couldn't. She was trapped by her disability, drowning with no way to save herself. "Morgan, where are you?" she cried.

A crash and the sound of shattering glass broke Claire from her trance. Raindrops splattered against her, and she felt the force of the wind blow against her face. A large limb had broken off the tree outside the breakfast room and crashed through one of the tall windows. One leafy branch jutted into the room and lay across the table.

There was no sign of Alex or of Morgan. No waves, no water other than the pounding rain. She was in her house, with what was left of her supper covered in dirt and leaves, partially in her lap, and partially spilled on the table.

"Morgan?"

She knew when she called his name that he wasn't here. Her head hurt, as if she'd had a migraine and was coming out of it. And the cold truth was she would never know whether or not Morgan had been here. Her ghostly sighting of Alex could have been nothing more than a misfiring of brain cells that had been damaged in the boating accident.

You have to hold it together, she told herself. *Reality is here in this room . . . reality is being confined to this wheelchair for the rest of my life.*

Doubt crept in. Had she slammed the door on a chance at happiness when she'd refused Justin's proposal? Had she traded a husband, friends, a child, and a life for a cold supper alone in a house with rain pouring through the window?

"Stupid is forever," she said, and then laughed out loud. She'd promised herself that she wouldn't go there again. She'd chosen not to allow a selfish, lying man to control

her life. She'd chosen independence, and if that meant dealing with ghosts and broken windows in a nor'easter, it
went with the package.

She turned her chair around and pushed her way out of
the breakfast room. With effort, she closed the double
doors behind her. There was nothing she could do about
the broken window or the tree branch tonight. Luckily, the
floor was tile. Nathaniel could clean it up and replace the
glass when the storm passed.

She made her way through the dining room to the hall
and the elevator. She hadn't eaten much, but she was no
longer hungry. Her bar refrigerator upstairs was stocked
with an assortment of snacks, juice, and water, so she
wouldn't perish.

She was convinced she'd made the right decision about
Justin, and she was well rid of him. If she'd considered his
offer simply because she wanted to be a mother, maybe she
should pursue private adoption. There must be some
woman who would see the advantages she could give a
child, regardless of her handicap. She might make an excellent choice for a baby or an older child with special
medical needs. Race or age didn't matter to her.

She wouldn't give up on finding her own birth mother
either. If the agency she was using couldn't help her, it
might be wise to consider switching to another. New de-
tectives might have fresh ideas or sources. The chances
were that her mother was out there somewhere, and she
might just be waiting for Claire to contact her.

If she put it to Richard when he was in the right mood,
she might even convince him to share more information
about her birth mother with her. She'd call him tomorrow
and they'd patch up their disagreement. Richard was
bossy and he'd never given up attempting to run her life,
but she'd never doubted his love.

Maybe she *would* consider that clinic in Switzerland, she mused as she closed the elevator door behind her and began the short roll down the hall to her bedroom suite. A change of scenery might do her good. If she stayed here much longer, they'd be scooping her up with a net and carrying her off to Pineview.

Whatever craziness had happened downstairs in the breakfast room, the second floor was perfectly normal. She felt exhilarated at the thought of actively pursuing her dreams rather than simply waiting for a phone to ring or someone to help her. She'd start checking adoption agencies on her laptop tonight.

She turned the knob on her bedroom door and was pushing it open when a particularly strong gust of wind hit the corner of the house. Wood creaked, the lights flickered once, and then went out.

In Atlantis, Halimeda lay moaning on the stone floor of a cell deep in the cellars of the palace. Never had she imagined such agony. She felt as if her insides were being slowly devoured by crabs or sliced partially away and roasted over hot lava while still attached. She curled into a fetal position on the stone floor and clawed at her face. To her horror, pieces of skin and flesh came away. Blood oozed out of her pores, and her hair fell out in clumps.

She tried to scream, but her tongue was swollen and she couldn't raise her voice above a strangled rasp. Her eyesight was dimming. The stench of vomit, urine, and feces hung in a cloud around her. "Poseidon," she croaked. "Take pity. I'm innocent. It wasn't me, I swear. It wasn't me."

Blisters rose on her arms and legs; her scales peeled away, and her skin curled. "Caddoc!" she begged. "Help me!" She tried to think of him . . . of her only son, but the pain was too great. She'd never imagined such suffering.

How could this happen to her? Who had betrayed her? How had Poseidon guessed what she'd done?

She tried to tell herself that it would soon be over, but she knew that it wasn't true. Without the antidote, the poison killed whoever drank of it, but death was lingering and excruciating. And the brain remained functional to the end, so that the victim would feel every drop of anguish until the heart stopped pumping.

Halimeda attempted to summon her protective spells, ancient and dark formulas that should have guarded her from such an end, but the searing fire burned and charred its way through her body and mind, rendering her helpless before the slow spread of the poison.

One last hope flared in her memory. Melqart. "Melqart." She panted, seeking enough strength to call out to him. "Lord of the darkness, help me. I pray you, heed my cry!"

Mocking laughter, deep and malignant, echoed off the walls and assaulted her wretched body. She whispered her plea into the void. "Melqart, do not abandon your servant. Have I not always been faithful?"

"Have you? Have you? Have you?" The booming voice was inside her head, but the thing materializing in her cell was real. The man was naked, silver-white and covered in tiny fish scales—a magnificently endowed male with two legs and two arms, a head of black curling hair, and eyes as red as pomegranate seeds.

For seconds, cold terror pierced Halimeda's skin as though from a hundred spear points. As she watched, the image grew blurry, and for an instant the beautiful man traded his nearly human features for a horned reptilian head, and an extra set of arms. Her scream became a gargle, and she wished she had died rather than call up this loathsome and evil creature. Hooded eyes stared at her, and it bared daggerlike teeth in a scarlet maw. "Do you know me?"

"Melqart?"

The laughter rolled over her once more.

"More or less. One of my simpler manifestations." A tail covered with tiny hooked spines coiled and lashed, curling around her bare leg.

Halimeda screamed as a long strip of raw flesh tore away.

"Does this mean you're reconsidered my previous offer?"

"Heal me, and I'll do whatever you want." She was beyond caring, beyond thought. Only the primitive desire to live mattered.

He came closer. A forked tongue flicked against her face. The stench of a thousand bodies rotting in the sun blasted into her nostrils. She gagged and drool spewed from the holes in her face.

"I can save you, restore your beauty tenfold. With a flick of my fingers, I can make you whole and give you eternal life. Will you pay my price, Halimeda?"

"Can you . . . can you stop . . . stop the pain?"

"I can do better than that. I can promise that you will never feel physical pain again."

"Do it, then. Do it." In her excitement, she forgot how fragile her flesh had become and parts of her lower lip crumbled and fell to bounce off a ravaged breast.

"And your soul is mine."

"You can have it." Halimeda groaned. "My body and soul. Just take the pain from me."

"Do you think me a fool?" he blasted. "You summoned me! You need me! My price has increased." Again, the image wavered, and she saw not the demon but the silver-scaled man with the glowing red irises.

Her eyes widened. She tried to ask him what else she could offer, but she was too frightened to speak.

"It's your son I want. Give me Caddoc."

To her shame, she didn't hesitate, but nodded.

"His soul for your life!"

And my beauty, she thought desperately. *My beauty restored tenfold.*

"Done and done."

Again the laughter rang out, bouncing off the stone walls and floor, seeping into her bones. She should have felt some regret, some lingering guilt for what she had just sworn to, but already the pain was easing. As she stared down, she could see her limbs taking shape again, feel the thick hair growing in her scalp.

"More beautiful than ever," she crooned. She felt no guilt. What she'd done was necessary. In time, her son would thank her. How could it be otherwise? With Melqart's blessing, Caddoc's power would be limitless. He could have anything he wanted: food, jewels, women, men.

But then, the creak of hinges registered on her consciousness. The door to her cell swung open. She looked up at Melqart, questioning.

"What are you waiting for?" he asked. "Go, my precious. None will bar your way. None will even see you pass."

"I can't stay here? I can't be the high queen over Atlantis?"

He laughed again. "Why would you remain here? Come away with me."

He offered a cold hand, and with a sigh of understanding and, oddly, a deep sadness, Halimeda took it. "As you will, great lord. I am your servant in all things."

Richard let the phone ring six times, seven. Justin had made it clear that he didn't think Richard should call Claire yet, but he couldn't help himself. He was being an over-protective father. He knew it. And he knew how stubborn his daughter was. As stubborn as her mother had been. He didn't doubt Claire was sitting there staring at the phone, recognizing his cell number, and refusing to pick up. He let it ring three more times before giving up and glancing at his watch.

It was still daylight on the East Coast. Whenever Mrs. Godwin and her son were away, they always insisted that a nurse or one of the staff remained with Claire. And Justin would be there with her before the worst of the nor-easter hit. If Claire had agreed to go to a hotel with him, they were probably talking to each other now.

"Richard? Are you joining us?"

"Coming." He slid his cell phone back into his pocket. Claire was fine. Justin would see to her well-being. He'd always been too quick to try to protect her . . . with good reason. Her mother . . . He wouldn't think of Nina, not now, not ever if he could help it. She wasn't a part of Claire's life and would never be.

He'd try to reach Claire by phone again later. He'd have to fly up to Maine when he got back. He'd rent a car and drive out to the house. Apologize and try to make amends.

But she had to realize how dear she was to him. She was all he had. The two of them had to stick together. They were both reasonable adults. He was capable of compro-mise, but Claire had to be the same. Once the breach was mended, he'd talk to her about Switzerland again. She wouldn't have to fly to Europe alone. He'd take time off and go with her to talk to the physicians at the clinic.

They'd make a holiday of it: Geneva, Paris, perhaps even Florence. Claire loved Florence. When she was thir-teen, she'd spent the better part of two hours sitting in front of the sculpture of David. She couldn't turn down the opportunity to see it again with him.

"The car's waiting downstairs," his colleague said.

Richard told himself that he needed to stop worrying about his daughter and concentrate on this case. It wasn't going well, and he'd been called in to make certain that the corporation received a favorable judgment. If he failed, his partners might begin to start hinting about his retirement. He had to prove to them that he was as sharp as ever.

With a sigh, he rose and followed the two other lawyers out of the conference room and down the hallway. He glanced at his watch again. Tomorrow, he thought. He'd try Claire again in the morning. She was always more forgiving after her morning coffee.

Justin cursed as the back wheel made a flop-flopping sound. He was in trouble. A lumber truck had nearly run him off the road on the last curve. Actually, it had run him off the road, and swerving off the edge and back on had obviously done damage to his rear right tire. Why did everything have to happen to him? Bad enough it was raining like Noah's flood and he'd ruined his new shoes. Now he had to stand by the road and change a tire like some peasant. He had an auto club membership, but he didn't want to call them for the repair. It was important that he not leave a traceable time line. No credit card statements, no one to remember seeing him tonight.

The tire took nearly a half hour. By the time he was finished, he was soaked to the skin. At least, he wasn't far from Seaborne. He removed a second disposable cell phone from his briefcase and called the number he'd been given in San Francisco.

A woman with a Jersey City accent picked up. "Rita's Hair and Nail Palace. This is Faye. Can I help you?"

"I'd like to order a Philly cheese steak with extra onions and cheese whiz."

"You must have the wrong number, Mister. This is a hair salon."

"No, I don't have the wrong number. Is Dario there? He always takes my order."

"Oh. You want Dario. Hold a minute. He used to have this number, but the phone company changed it. You want . . ." She gave another number with the same exchange.

He waited until she ended the call and then punched in the new number. A man answered, and Justin repeated his order for the Philly cheese steak. "I need that delivered right away," he said, giving the hotel address, and the room number.

"You sure that's correct?"

"Positively," Justin assured him.

"You can depend on us. Service is our motto."

"No mistakes, no mix-ups."

"We don't make mistakes."

"Good." He hated using hired talent. But professionals were worth the extra expense, and he could hardly be at both coasts at the same time. Carlos had vouched for the organization and for their integrity, and Carlos had been generally dependable.

Justin used the tire iron to pound the phone into tiny pieces before tossing it into what looked like a cow pasture. Then, using his personal cell, he made a call to Claire. She answered right away.

"Justin. Hi."

"Sounds like you're glad to hear my voice." He mopped the water off his face with some napkins he'd snagged at the turnpike rest stop.

"You have no idea." She gave a wry laugh. "The power's

out. We've got a generator, but the switch is on the first floor, in the utility room. I'm stuck on the second."

"In the elevator?"

"No, luckily. But, technically, the elevator is my problem. It doesn't run without electricity, so I can't get downstairs. I'm in my bedroom, so there's no immediate emergency."

"That's right, you're alone, aren't you?"

"I am. If I'd let Jackie come, she could have walked down the steps and hit the switch for the generator. But I wasn't expecting a power outage."

"Not the best decision you've ever made."

"No," she agreed. "I hate to say it, but this is one time I wish you were here."

All the better, Justin thought. He'd been prepared to off the nurse if she'd shown up unexpectedly. He'd had fantasies of raping her, but he was afraid she'd be old or ugly. Besides, there was too much chance of leaving DNA around with bodily contact. But since Claire was alone, it made his job easier. He tucked the wet napkins into a plastic bag. If there was one thing he couldn't stand, it was an untidy car. "Is there a hint of sarcasm in your voice, Claire? Are you still harboring resentment over our last disagreement?"

"Should I be?"

"I've apologized. I acted like an ass. How many times do I need to say it?"

"You were an ass," she agreed. How was it that talking to Justin could make her feel so much better? She was still alone in the house, still without electricity, but just hearing another voice banished the childish fears she'd been feeling. "You were deliberately trying to hurt me."

"Guilty, but I was disappointed. I was beginning to like the idea of being a father. You know how I can be when I don't get what I want."

She sighed. "Don't I just? Admit it, you were already mentally planning a world cruise with my money."

"We could make it a honeymoon if you've changed your mind about marrying me," he teased.

"No, afraid not, but I wouldn't mind any human company right now."

"So you admit I'm human?"

"Afraid so. Obnoxious, but human. Wish you were in Maine instead of the city."

It was his turn to chuckle. "Coincidence. I'm not in New York. I'm about twenty miles from you. Your father called me and begged me to rescue you. He didn't expect a power outage, but on the chance you wouldn't sic that handyman of yours on me, I made reservations for us at that hotel you like in Bangor."

"I don't know about that, Justin. It sounds like a bad idea."

"No. It's a good idea. They have electricity and room service."

"You haven't reserved the honeymoon suite, I hope."

He laughed. "Two adjoining rooms. Even Richard would approve. I'm coming for you, Claire."

"I'll be here."

"Do you have any light at all?"

"Just a flashlight. Everything's locked downstairs, but there a spare key under the birdbath by the drive. Just past the rose arbor."

"I'll find it."

"You're going to get wet."

"You know, tonight, I doubt I'll even notice. See you soon, Claire."

CHAPTER 28

The elevator door opened and Richard stepped inside. The only other occupant, a pizza delivery boy carrying a large insulated pizza box, was standing in front of the control buttons. "Three, please," Richard said.

The boy in the Chicago-Style Pizza T-shirt, cutoffs, and ball cap half turned to look at him and smiled. He wasn't as young as Richard first thought, maybe mid-twenties, short and thin with a straggly goatee and a ponytail. Oddly enough, the kid was wearing thin leather gloves.

"Would you hit three?" Richard repeated.

"Three, it is," the man said. And as Richard stared at him in horror, he removed a handgun with a silencer from the box, shoved the weapon against Richard's chest and emptied three shots into his chest.

Richard felt nothing after the first bullet pierced his heart.

His assailant leaned down and removed Richard's gold watch and a wallet before propping the body in the corner where it would be the least visible from the door. He hit the button for the basement. When the elevator came to a stop, Leo got out, carefully stepped around the pooled blood on the floor, and heaved Richard's corpse to block the open door. He walked quickly away toward an exit without looking back. Just before he took a short flight of cement steps to the alley, Leo set fire to a pile of trash, smashed a fire box, and set off the alarm.

Chicago-Style Pizza tee, cutoff jeans, pizza container, ball cap, ponytail hairpiece, gun, and false goatee went into a bag for disposal in Dumpsters on the far side of the city. Underneath the shirt and blue jean shorts, Leo wore stretchy lime green shorts and a pink muscle shirt. He unlocked the chain holding his bike to a pole, jumped on, and pedaled away as the first sounds of fire sirens whined in the distance.

As Morgan approached the house, he was struck by the absence of lights. Always before, there had been outside artificial illumination when he'd come to Seaborne after dark. Usually, light shone through some of the windows, but this night there was nothing, not even the faint glow of an electrical appliance.

It had never occurred to him that he might come for Claire and she would be gone. He'd pictured her in his mind, waiting on the beach or sitting at her window. If she wasn't at Seaborne, how would he find her? The land mass in North America was large, not nearly as vast as the water world, but too big for him to search for her. And what if she wasn't on this continent? What if she'd traveled to Europe, even to Switzerland as her father had been urging her? How could he return to the court and tell them that his love had vanished? And what would the verdict be then?

But the power systems that humans used were puny and subject to failure. Perhaps the lightning or an automobile accident had cut off the electricity. He hoped that was what had happened. Lightning sometimes struck ships and destroyed them. He imagined that the force of this storm was enough to wipe out whole electrical grids.

Ignoring the wind and the sheets of rain, he climbed the

house to Claire's balcony. Surprisingly, it was more difficult than he'd expected. He'd accumulated far more time
out of the water in the last two months than was wise.
Breathing air and maintaining the illusion that he was
human put a tremendous strain on his body system. It both
weakened and temporarily aged him. But this was the last
time he'd have to leave the sea, this one time, and then
never again.

"Be there, Claire," he murmured under his breath. "Be
there waiting for me."

As he pulled himself over the railing, he could see what a
mess the storm had made of the area. Chairs and planters
were overturned, and flowers and dirt were spewed across
the deck. He went to the French doors and peered into the
room. All was dark inside. He couldn't see anything. No
music played, no television beamed pictures for Claire's
pleasure.

Lightning flashed behind him, and Claire screamed.

"Shh, shh," he called. "It's me. Morgan. Don't be frightened. It's just me." He couldn't wait. He turned the knob
and threw his shoulder against door. Something snapped,
and Morgan half fell, half vaulted into the bedroom.

"Morgan! Morgan!" Claire was laughing and crying all
at the same time. She rolled her wheelchair toward him,
and he bent and embraced her. "Let me out," she ordered.
"Get me out of this."

Heart slamming against his chest, he unstrapped the
belt and picked her up in his arms. She wrapped her arms
around his neck and covered his face with kisses as he carried her to the bed.

"Where have you been?" she cried. "Why didn't you
come?"

In answer, he pressed his mouth to hers and kissed her
passionately. "I'm here now," he said breathlessly when

they finally broke the embrace. "I wanted to be here with you, but I couldn't. I'll explain it all to you when there's more time."

How warm she felt, how alive! Love for this fragile woman seeped through his blood and bones. How precious she was to him. How lucky he was to have her. "By Zeus's cod, I missed you," he said.

"Are you real? I couldn't bear it if you aren't real." She grabbed handfuls of his hair and pulled his head down to kiss him again and again.

Hope soared in his chest. She loved him. It was more than sexual attraction, more than a quick summer romance. She really loved him. At least, he hoped she did.

He sat on the bed and cradled her in his arms. "We need to talk," he said. "Serious talk."

"Are you leaving me again?"

"Never."

"All right." She sighed and laid her head on his chest. "What are we going to talk about? Oh, your brother for one. He's been haunting me. At least, I think he has. Someone has, and it looked a lot like Alex."

"Alex was here?"

She made a sound that might have been laughter. "I think it was Alex. He appeared—well, part of him appeared in my breakfast room, just before the tree came through the roof."

"What are you talking about?"

"It doesn't matter. All that matters is you're here, and we're together." She caught his hand and kissed the backs of his knuckles, and then turned it over to nuzzle his palm. "Don't leave me again, Morgan. Please. I couldn't stand it if you—"

"You asked me before if you were dreaming," he murmured, stroking her hair. "Did it seem like a dream?"

"Yes, no . . . I don't know. How could it not be? You took me under the ocean. I can't breathe beneath the water. You showed me sunken ships and flying rays and magic caves and . . . So many wonderful things. It couldn't be true."

"It is true," he said, kissing her again. "Night after night you came with me into my world. We fell in love, and I realized that I don't want to live without you."

"If that's true, take me back. I *want* to go with you. I want to go with you. You can take me to hell for all I care, so long as you're there and you'll never leave me."

"Shh, shh." He pressed his fingers to her mouth. "Don't say that. Never say that. Your hell . . . my Hades is an evil place." He shook his head. "Not even as a joke."

"If this isn't a dream, I don't understand," she answered softly. "How is it possible? Who are you? What are you?"

"A man who loves you, who wants you to become his wife."

"For real?" She grasped his head between her two hands. "Do you love me?

"Yes, I do."

"Then, yes, I'll marry you. And yes, I'll go with you. Into the sea or into a catfish pond or anywhere you want. You mean everything to me, Morgan. More than my life, that's how much I love you."

He held her tight against him, cradling her, rocking her as he kissed her hair. "Claire . . . Claire."

"As long as you're not some kind of vampire or a werewolf or a serial killer."

"Vampires can't swim. You're safe from them in the water."

She giggled. "I'll keep that in mind. So that leaves werewolf or serial killer."

"Neither one, I swear. And my oath is my bond. I'm a prince, Claire."

"I knew that from the first time I kissed you." She
chuckled again. "And I should know. I've kissed a lot of
frogs. I was married to one, once."

He sat her on his lap and kissed her forehead tenderly.
"Seriously. I want you for my wife, but if you come with
me into the sea, it's forever. We can't come back."

He felt her shoulders stiffen. "You mean that? I couldn't
ever come back to Seaborne. I couldn't see my father?
Never?"

"I wish it could be different, but we only have a little
time. It's now or never, Claire. Either you come with me
tonight—now, or I can never see you again."

"You really, really want to marry me—like this, like I
am. Crippled?"

He laughed. "You won't be. Once you're in the ocean,
everything will be all right. You were whole before, weren't
you? Or don't you remember?"

"I remember everything," she said. "Our lovemaking,
the shaman, the valley, even the fruit your brother gave me
that—"

"Wabi? He gave you wabi? I'll kill him."

She laughed. "You almost had reason to. I think I was
tempted."

"Wabi does that to women."

"Only women?"

"I don't know. I've never felt the need to try it."

"I didn't *feel the need*, as you put it. Alex tricked me."

"We'll deal with him later." He could feel the weight of
the earth pulling him down, robbing him of his strength.
"We don't have much time, Claire. Will you be my bride,
come with me to a far country, and pledge your love to me
for all eternity?"

"I will," she answered. "Did you ever have any doubt?"

"Some." He chuckled. "We have to hurry. There's not much time."

"All right. I trust you, Morgan. But if you are a werewolf and you're going to bite my throat—"

"I don't have to be a werewolf to nibble that pretty neck, and other tasty parts," he teased.

"Isn't this the part where you're supposed to wow me with a two-carat ring?"

"You'll have a ring," he promised, "more rings than you have fingers and toes. I'm going to make you a princess."

She sighed. "If this is a dream, it's the best one yet."

"No dreams, and no regrets. Are you sure?"

"As certain as sunrise," she said. "Girl Scout honor."

Outside, the rain and wind still beat against the house, but it meant nothing to Morgan. He had what he wanted in his arms.

Justin used his key and a flashlight to enter through the utility room and throw the switch that activated the generator. The motor clicked and hummed before roaring into action. Lights, freezers, refrigerators, and other conveniences came alive. Justin took the back staircase. He wanted to surprise Claire, and a burglar wouldn't be likely to use an elevator in this house.

He was excited. What he had to do here were only the final steps in his well-thought-out plan. He'd considered doing away with Claire before her accident, but afterwards, he'd imagined it would only be a matter of time before she succumbed to her medical condition. When she'd stubbornly refused to die, he'd asked her to remarry him. And when that hadn't worked out, he'd come to the reasonable conclusion that he had to take matters into his own hands.

The will they'd made before they were married years ago, making each other sole beneficiaries of the other's estate, had been of great help to the expert forger whose services he'd hired. With both Richard and Claire dead, who would contest the new one? He'd even purchased an engagement ring to substantiate his story that they'd decided to remarry. The ring wouldn't be on Claire's cold finger though—obviously the intruder would have stolen that after he'd killed her.

Justin's wet shoes made squishing sounds on the carpet as he climbed the curving staircase. At first, he'd intended on strangling her, but he'd play it by ear. He'd take no chances. He pulled the gun from his inside coat pocket and clicked off the safety.

As he reached the top landing, he heard voices, Claire's and another's that he was unfamiliar with, definitely male. Another twist, but nothing he couldn't handle. Justin prided himself on being a man who could think on his feet. He simply tucked the gun under his jacket.

"Claire!" he called. "Are you all right?"

"Justin? I forgot you were—"

A stranger stood in her bedroom doorway, Claire in his arms. They appeared to be quite cozy with each other, and Justin wondered if he'd interrupted a lover's tryst. Kinky, he thought, and he eyed the man suspiciously. He was big and blond and way too good looking to be interested in Claire unless he was after her money.

"I thought you said you were alone."

"Justin?" Claire's eyes widened as she saw him in the hallway.

"What is this?" Justin asked.

"It's all right," she said. "It's not what . . . This is Morgan."

"I've heard about you," Justin replied as he moved to block the doorway. "Put her down. Now."

Claire felt Morgan's muscles tense. "We have to go

now." Morgan's voice had a steely note. "No time for introductions."

"Let us pass," she said. "Please, Justin."

"Where do you think you're going with this gigolo? And you, Atlas. I told you to put her down. I won't ask you again."

"Good," Morgan answered. "Because we're leaving."

"It's all right," Claire said, hanging on tightly to Morgan. "I want to go with him. I have to go. I'm sorry you had to come out here, but—" She flinched, gasping as Justin drew a gun from under his jacket. "Oh, my God! Justin, what are you doing?"

"Aim that someplace else," Morgan said.

"Not until you put her down. Back up. That's right," Justin said as Morgan took several steps backwards. "Lower her to the bed."

"This is a mistake," Claire protested. "I want to go with him. Please, Justin. Don't do this."

Justin squeezed off a single shot, striking Morgan. Claire screamed as the force of the bullet tore through his chest. He staggered and dropped her onto the bed. Still screaming, she reached out to him.

"Morgan! Nooo!"

Justin fired a second time and Morgan went down grasping his belly. Blood poured through his fingers. One of the bullets must have passed through him and shattered her bedroom window. Sheets of rain poured through the empty frame and salt wind blew into the room.

"Why?" Claire screamed at Justin. "Why?" Morgan was dying. She hadn't imagined that a man could lose so much blood. It spread around him, running across the hardwood floor in streams. She could smell his blood, acrid, sweet, and cloying. "No, you can't. Morgan!"

He struggled to rise, and then fell back. He reached toward her with a bloody hand. "Claire . . ." He gasped and then collapsed and lay still.

Justin came to the side of her bed. "It's your fault he's dead. You told me that you were alone."

"Why? Why would you shoot him?"

He removed a pair of medical gloves from his pocket and methodically put them on. "You should have agreed to marry me. I would have been happy with half. Now, I'll have it all."

"All what?" She stared at him. What was he doing? Why the gloves now?

Justin's gaze met hers, his eyes as emotionless as a shark's. "You see how it happened," he said. "A robbery gone wrong. Too bad I arrived too late to save you." He leaned over the bed, reaching for her throat with gloved hands.

"Get away from me! Don't you touch me!" She struck out at him. "You've gone mad. You can't murder me and get away with it!"

"Why not?" He smiled. "I killed Richard, and he's three thousand miles away. No one will suspect me."

"Richard? You murdered my father? You're lying to me. He left a message on the answering machine today. I—"

"Guess you should have picked up, darling. Rotten of you not to, seeing as how it was your last opportunity to speak to each other. A pity."

He knelt on the bed and wrapped his hands around her throat.

"No! Not Richard. You couldn't." Helpless from the waist down, she tried to beat him off, but he was so strong. His fingers tightened, biting into her flesh. Black spots danced behind her eyes. Her chest burned. Morgan dead. Richard dead. What did it matter anymore?

It mattered! It mattered if the bastard got away with it!

She let go of his hands, balled a fist and hit him as hard as she could in the face.

Justin swore and pressed down harder.

I'm dying, she thought. *This is what it feels like to die.*

Abruptly, Justin's fingers were torn away. She gasped for air, choking and gagging. Justin screamed as Morgan threw him across the room and he smashed into the French doors.

"Claire? Are you—"

She nodded her head, weeping now, unable to utter more than a rasp through her battered throat. "He killed Richard. He killed my father." She touched him. "Are you real?" she managed. "You're not dead?"

In answer, he picked her up and started for the door. She could tell by the way he walked that his wounds had drained his strength. "I have to get to the sea," he said.

"Go, save yourself," she urged him. "Leave me."

"Never again."

Outside, the storm had grown worse. The wind was coming off the ocean and the force of it hit them in the face as they crossed the lawn. "Take the elevator to the beach," she shouted in Morgan's ear. "The stairs are too steep. You can never make it down carrying me."

Ignoring her pleas, he passed the elevator platform and began the climb down the slippery stone steps to the sand. They were halfway to the bottom, and Morgan was clinging to the metal rail and attempting to catch his breath when another shot rang out. Blood and flesh exploded from Morgan's shoulder and he grunted in pain.

"Morgan!"

Claire looked up and her heart kicked against her ribs as she made out Justin's shadowy form at the top of the cliff. The muzzle of his gun spat fire.

CHAPTER 29

"Hurry," Claire cried. "He'll kill us." She'd never regretted the loss of her legs so much as she did at that instant.

Lightning struck the beach, momentarily deafening her. The shock of the bolt nearly knocked them off the stairs, and illuminated the landscape with the full force of the noonday sun. The stench of sulfur filled her nose. Her mouth tasted of metal. Half-blinded, she looked up and caught a glimpse of Justin's hate-filled face white against the dark cliff wall. He was coming down the stairs after them at a run.

The light faded into black, and Claire gripped Morgan's neck with all her strength. He was running too, his breath coming in hard, quick gasps with each step. Her pulse raced. She wanted to scream, but her terror was too great. *God, help us,* she prayed.

They'd reached the final turn on the stairs when a second bolt struck the beach pavilion. Wood and flames shot up to be whirled high in a howling gust of wind and driving rain. And in the glow, she glanced up to see Justin's feet slip on the wet stone. Frantically, he grabbed for the railing. His gun tumbled out of his hand, and then he was falling after it.

Justin's terrified shriek tore through her, turning her

blood to frost. Like a giant black bird, he turned over and over in the air as he plunged past them a hundred feet to smash on the jagged rocks below.

A dozen more steps and Morgan reached the concrete walk. He left the hard surface to cut across the wet sand toward the crashing surf. Without the lightning, it was so dark that Claire couldn't see the water, but she could hear it. In her mind's eye, she could picture the foam-churned waves rolling onto the beach. The sand would be littered with seaweed and shells.

The space between surf and beach would be a maelstrom, but beyond, in the deep, Claire could imagine the serenity of the ocean. She could taste the saltwater on her lips. "Keep going," she whispered hoarsely. "You can do it. Only a little farther."

Morgan wheezed with each step. Once, he fell, driving his knee hard into the sand. "Claire." He groaned. "I love . . . love you."

"Go on, damn it!" She yanked a fistful of his hair as hard as she could. "One more step." And when he staggered up and lurched on, she added to her lie. "One more. Just one more."

The roar of the waves was louder. Spray drenched their faces.

"Leave me!" she cried. "Go. Leave me."

Another step . . . another. She felt something cold and wet against her feet. Churning sand scoured her legs. It wasn't possible. But it wasn't her imagination. She could feel it.

There was so much water in the air that she could hardly breathe. It stung her eyes and ran into her nose and mouth, and—seeking shelter—she buried her face against Morgan's chest.

He gave a long sigh and went limp. His legs folded

under him and they splashed into the shallows. A wave rolled over Claire's head. She gasped and choked, then realized that Morgan was floating away. She grabbed at him, seizing his arm, instinctively knowing that she had to get him to deep water.

He was limp, unresponsive. "Morgan!" She shook him, but he was either unconscious or had passed beyond waking and was already dead.

"No! I won't lose you." She dug her heels into the sand and tugged at him. He was a big man, far taller and heavier than she was—or had been even before the accident—but she wouldn't let the sea have him. He was hers, and she would save him, no matter the cost.

Oddly, the sensation of cold had faded, and the saltwater felt smooth and soft against her skin. She kept walking, digging in and holding her ground as each wave struck her, then using the force of the outgoing water to gain a few yards. As the water deepened, it became easier to pull him. She caught her second wind and threw her muscles into the task.

Once, she thought she'd felt Morgan tremble, and she clung to that hope. He was hurt, yes, hurt badly, and he'd lost a lot of blood. But if she could get him help, she could still save him. The insanity of dragging a dying man into the ocean to heal him didn't matter. Deep inside, in some primitive part of her mind, she knew that this was exactly what she had to do.

The surf was the worst. The sand floor had given way to rock and shell and debris. The waves caught her in an iron grip and tumbled her over and over. Keeping Morgan from being ripped away from her took every ounce of her will, but when she'd been thrown back from the surf line a dozen times and was so weary that she barely had the strength to stand, something loomed from the blackness.

Something smooth and powerful . . .

Claire reached out and her hand brushed a large fin. Shark? If she'd had the strength, she would have laughed. What was it Richard loved to say? "There's no situation so bad that it can't get worse."

I've gone into the ocean to drown in a storm, only to be eaten by sharks, she thought. And then the thing bumped her ribs, hard, knocking the wind out of her, and she gasped once and let the sea wash her away.

She was dreaming again. And it was a good dream. Morgan was with her—Morgan whole and beautiful and strong—and he was kissing her with slow sweet kisses, kisses that conveyed such poignant tenderness that she was crying with joy.

Claire opened her eyes to discover that she was lying on a bed of kelp with Morgan sitting beside her and holding her hand. Blue-green water flowed above and around them, and hovering several yards above them was a large and handsome bottle-nosed dolphin. And, the dolphin was wearing what seemed to be a collar or harness.

"Am I dead?" she asked.

Morgan laughed. "No, not anywhere close to it."

She closed her eyes. She felt as though she'd been hit by a truck . . . but everything worked. She wiggled her toes and fingers, then reached down and pinched her thigh. She could feel it. She could feel it! "It's like before," she said, opening her eyes and laughing. "When I'm here with you, I'm not paralyzed."

"Never again," he promised.

She stared at him. Something about him was very different. He was still her Morgan, yet . . . more. . . . It made no sense. She looked down at her arms and her breasts. Her body was perfect, her arms no longer scarred and deformed by the accident, and for an instant, she thought she could make out tiny golden scales. She blinked. Scales? She must be dreaming.

"If we're not dead, explain this," she said, reaching up to touch his cheek. "A minute ago, we were both drowning in the surf. Actually, I was drowning. You were bleeding to death—if you weren't already dead. Justin shot you at least three times."

"He did. And you saved my ass. Again." He kissed her. "You're a handy woman to have around."

She glanced around. Columns of kelp formed deep green draperies on two sides, but the ocean stretched out endlessly in the other directions: sandy bottom sprinkled with shells, water rich with sea life. "No sharks?" she ventured.

"Plenty of sharks, just not here." He indicated the dolphin. "They tend to stay away from Echo."

"Echo? Its name is Echo?"

Echo clicked and gave a high-pitched whistle.

"Not it," Morgan corrected. "She's female. *Her* name is Echo."

"You have a dolphin buddy?" This had to be a dream. But then she remembered the manta rays. If he palled around with rays, why not dolphins?

"Actually, she's isn't my personal dolphin. She's my daughter Danu's." He shrugged. "Danu sent her along to watch over me when I came for you. And, as it turned out, we needed Echo. Badly. She pulled us out of the surf and brought us here to this sanctuary."

Claire sat up. "A daughter? You have a daughter? But you said you'd never been married? Is she the child of a—"

"Adopted daughter," he supplied, cutting her off. "It's a long story, but I hope you can come to love her too. She's an adorable child who's desperately in need of a mother."

Claire swallowed. "How . . . how old?"

"I'm not really certain. Four . . . maybe five. I'm no expert on guessing the ages of human children."

"Human? Wait . . . this is getting crazy. Where is she? This human child? Danu? You say her name is Danu?"

"It's what we named her. Danu was a Celtic earth goddess. She had another name when she lived on the land, but now she belongs to the sea and she needed a name to fit her. She's beautiful, Claire, sweet, and funny, and very smart."

Claire choked up, too full of emotion to speak. It was all too much—dolphins, daughters, and being here beneath the ocean with Morgan again. She didn't understand any of it and wasn't sure she cared. She would grasp what happiness she could and hold on to it as she'd held on to Morgan in the surf. She'd let the waves take her where they would, so long as she was with him and he was alive and loved her.

Thoughts of a motherless little girl—Morgan's little girl—dangled on the horizon of her hopes, but she wouldn't ask too much. Not yet. If she could have a child of her own, it would fill an ache that had grown under her heart since she was young, but it was too soon to take that in.

"Promise me that I won't wake up in my bedroom at Seaborne again," she begged him.

"You won't." He leaned and brushed his lips against her forehead. "I can't leave the sea again, not and live. I've used up my store of energy—for that, at least. You do remember that you promised to be my wife." He caught her hand and lifted it for her to see.

On her ring finger, on her left hand, was a braid of seaweed with a glistening pink shell for a stone. "Oh, Morgan. I love it!"

He laughed. "I promised you a real betrothal ring, set

with any precious stone you want. Ruby? Emerald? Diamond?"

"I'd rather have this one."

He grinned at her. "We'll see. I think I can provide an adequate substitution, but that will do until we reach Atlantis."

She stared at him. "We're going to Atlantis? It's real?"

"As real as I am," he said. "Remember when I promised to make you a princess? I really am a prince, Claire, crown prince of the ancient kingdom of Atlantis. Someday, you'll be queen of it all."

She looked at him suspiciously. "And Alex, is he real too?"

"All too real, I'm afraid. And Orion, and Poseidon, my father. I've a large family, Claire. Wait until you meet them. They're going to be surprised."

"That you're marrying a human?"

He laughed again. "No, that I've found an Atlantean woman on land. You shouldn't be able to breathe under the water without my assistance, but you can. You should have drowned in the surf, but you transformed, and you saved me as well."

"Now, you've really lost me." She slid her feet over the edge and stood. When she looked down, she saw that she was wearing a short tunic of leaf-green seaweed and that her bare feet had a fine web between her large toe and the next. "So, what you're telling me is that I've always been a mermaid? Like the one in the Disney movie?"

He shook his head and pulled her into his arms. "This isn't a fairy tale, Claire. Atlantis is a real place and, somehow, you carry Atlantean blood. You know Richard was your adoptive father, and you never knew who either of your birth parents were. At least one of them, probably your father, was an Atlantean."

"So, you're telling me that if I have a mermaid for a father, that would make me one too?"

Morgan chuckled and kissed the top of her head. "What I'm saying is that you carry the DNA of the sea people. It's impossible for you to drown in the ocean. In saltwater, your body knows how to make the changes necessary to live underwater." He pushed her back a step and tipped up her chin. "But you can't return to land, not even for an hour. Your system is too fragile. But this is your element. You're not an alien species. You're one of us come back to your home."

She shook her head. "I'm supposed to swallow all this? It sounds like a fishy tale to me. If I'm a mermaid, where's my tail? The one with the scales and fin?"

"You aren't a mermaid, and neither was your father. You're an Atlantean. Even if it wasn't a parent—if it was a grandparent—who carried our genes, that's all it takes."

"Then how could I have been a normal baby? How could I breathe air? It makes no sense," she argued.

"How do you know what you were like as a baby? Do you remember? All you have to go on is what Richard told you. I can't explain how or why. I'm only grateful that you don't have to pass through a normal transformation. I can't believe it didn't happen before this. . . . It's a wonder you didn't transform to an Atlantean as a child, when you were swimming in the sea off Seaborne's beach. You should have—"

"Richard wouldn't let me in the ocean. He was deathly afraid of the water. At least, that's what he told me." Memories of her childhood were sketchy, even memories of her father. She had to stretch her mind to see his face . . . to remember the sound of his voice. Even her beloved Seaborne seemed like something from a dream.

"We need to return to the palace as soon as—"

Abruptly, the dolphin swooped over them. She gave a loud series of squeaks and a whistle.

"We have to go," Morgan said. "Echo says that there is a pod of killer whales feeding nearby. We don't want to be here when they pass over."

"But you said this is a sanctuary," she protested, glancing around worriedly. "How could they come here?"

"Killer whales don't respect boundaries or treaties. If we travel fast, we should reach a way station in less than an hour. We'll use that to journey to the outreaches of the city." He took her arm. "You hold Echo's harness. I'm not fully recovered, but I can keep up with a dolphin carrying a passenger."

Claire closed her fingers around what were clearly handholds made of some white substance that felt like plastic but obviously wasn't. The dolphin clicked several times and began to swim through the water, carrying Claire with her. Morgan swam close beside them.

The ride would have been fun if it hadn't been for Morgan's mention of killer whales hunting them for dinner; still Claire found the experience exhilarating. They passed through barren stretches of rock and sand filled with human trash and shadowy forests of giant kelp. Claire recognized schools of codfish, as well as enormous tunas and several smaller sharks. Once she saw a manta glide by, but the creature didn't approach and it was soon out of sight. At intervals, Echo had to swim to the surface to breathe, and Claire caught glimpses of a calm and moonlit sea.

After they descended the last time, Morgan swam close to her, and she saw that he'd drawn his sword. "Not far now to the station," he said. "We'll go on alone. Echo can't use the . . ." He hesitated. "She'll meet us at Atlantis. We have to go deeper than is comfortable for her."

"But surely Atlantis has to be deep," Claire questioned.

"Otherwise, it would have been discovered by ships long ago. How can a dolphin breathe there?"

"Air providers. You'll see. We just have to leave her now. We'll be fine. The killer whales are behind us."

"That's what I'm afraid of."

He grinned. "Trust me, babe. I've got your back."

Claire was strangely reluctant to part with the dolphin. Her large and friendly presence had been comforting and she was anxious to know her better. "She's such a beautiful animal," she confided to Morgan as Echo swam away. "Are there others like her?"

"Thousands. Some wild, some bonded to our people. You'll have your own dolphin. My last one passed away of old age last year, and I haven't had the time or inclination to bond with another. We'll do it together."

She tilted her head and tried to decide if he was teasing. "I'll have my own dolphin?"

"Or, she'll have you. We're never sure. They are faithful and devoted. Absolutely invaluable. Better than a horse, because they feed themselves and you too, if you want them to." He grinned wryly. "The only problem is that they don't have a long life span. It's close to a human's forty years."

"That seems like a long time to me."

He shook his head. "You have a lot to learn, darling. An Atlantean's life span is somewhat longer than a human's."

He took her hand and they swam deeper still. The light grew dimmer until she was peering through the darkness at a shadowy world filled with strange shapes and forms. A squid, nearly five feet in length, flashed by. Behind it, in hot pursuit, came a fish sprouting glowing antennae and a mouth full of jagged teeth. Claire shuddered.

"Not to worry," Morgan soothed. "A klates. It only dines on squid. And the occasional octopus."

Without warning, a school of eel-like creatures swept

around them. Claire threw up her elbow to protect her face and something hard sliced her arm. She cried out in pain as a man carrying a pitchfork loomed ahead of them.

"Get behind me!" Morgan ordered.

She saw the outline of a second man materialize to her left and heard the clash of steel on steel. A bulky brute flung a net at her. It slipped over her head and shoulders and she ducked to wiggle out from under it.

Another assailant rushed at Morgan from the rear and she screamed a warning. He shoved her aside and slashed at Morgan's right shoulder. Morgan twisted aside and the attacker charged past, nearly colliding with one of the men in front. Morgan's sword gleamed in the semidarkness, and Claire heard a yelp of pain. The backstabber's sword fell and drifted downward through the murky water.

Claire dove to capture the sword and the man with the net swam after her. She'd counted at least three—perhaps four. Morgan would have no chance against them. She kicked and rolled, dodging the throw of the net once more. Still, the sword eluded her, but she followed the shining blade in the blackness.

Another squid passed over her head, momentarily delaying her pursuer. Terror made her limbs feel wooden. What if she couldn't reach the weapon? What if she became lost in the Stygian night and couldn't find her way back to Morgan? What if they killed him before she could come to his aid?

But then her hand brushed the hilt of the sword. She grabbed it, spun and swam, not away, but toward the man with the net. He threw up his arms to tangle her in his rope but she drove the point of the sword low and felt it pierce flesh and grate against bone. He fell away, and she swam up toward the spot where she'd left Morgan defending himself against overwhelming odds.

When she reached him, one man was floating away, obviously seriously injured, and Morgan was holding off the one with the pitchfork and another with a sword. Claire circled the man with the forked weapon. Seeing her, he crouched and threw it like a fishing spear. Claire moved aside, and the weapon passed and vanished into the darkness. The man pulled a dagger from his belt and swam toward her.

She heard a scream and turned to see Morgan pulling his sword out of his fallen opponent's side. As he swam toward her, the thug with the knife turned and fled, leaving them alone and victorious.

"Are you hurt?" Morgan called.

"Who was that? And why did they want to kill us?"

"The one with the knife—the one you chased off—was my half-brother Caddoc. He'd like to see me dead so that . . ." He shook his head. "It's a long story."

"And the one you killed?"

"One of his cronies. They all were." He looked down at the sword in her hand in disbelief. "How in Hades did you manage to—"

She grinned. "There's a lot you don't know about me. Not only was I a member of our college fencing club, but I worked summers at a Renaissance Fair. I was Maid Marian, and I honed my swordplay against Prince John's villains."

"A college fencing club and an actress? Against trained warriors? It's hard to believe."

Her grin widened. "You didn't know Richard. He flew me to Italy for lessons with a world champion fencing master. He never liked to do things halfway."

Morgan grabbed her and hugged her against him so tightly that she thought her ribs would crack. "How many secrets are you hiding from me, Claire? And how was I lucky enough to find you?"

Epilogue

Among Atlantis's many splendid palaces, breathtaking temples, glorious halls of state, great amphitheaters, and awe-inspiring edifices of learning, the Place of Joining should have been outshone in beauty. But, in Claire's eye, this small, exquisite building was a jewel box of perfection and the shining glory of all Morgan had shown her in the city.

The white marble building stood at the summit of a stepped pyramid at one end of a vast square, and was reached by a series of broad steps. The outer walls of the structure itself were not composed of solid blocks of marble, but magnificent Corinthian columns that cast a pattern of light and darkness on the inner sanctum.

The interior room glowed with light provided by hundreds, perhaps thousands, of tiny crystals set into the marble walls, and the starkness of the marble stone floors was offset by patterns of brightly gleaming tiles forming joined rings. The water here was a breathtaking blue and swirling with schools of tiny multicolored fish and sea horses that brought a smile to her lips and reminded her of flocks of birds.

It was here, in this sacred spot, in the Place of Joining, that the kings and queens of Atlantis had taken their vows of marriage for thousands of years. And it was here, with shaking knees, that Claire waited for Morgan to come and pledge his eternal love and devotion to her and her to him. But before the ceremony could begin, the custom was for the bride and groom each to meet privately with the highest-ranking priestess of the temple to make certain they were ready to take such a momentous step as marriage.

Lady Athena, not only a high priestess, but a member of the High Court and the Council, had already spoken with Morgan, and now it was Claire's turn. Claire was so nervous that she was trembling from head to toe. She was terrified. What would this great lady ask of her? What would she say? What if the priestess found her less than qualified to marry the crown prince? What if Lady Athena denied her permission to become Morgan's wife?

When the regal woman with the coronet of blond braids appeared, Claire was even more taken aback. She hadn't expected someone so young, with features so sweet and appealing that Claire was drawn to her immediately. She didn't know whether to curtsey or offer her hand, so she waited with bated breath.

The lady opened her arms and smiled, "Welcome, daughter."

Claire took three steps and found herself in a warm and genuine embrace. "Your ladyship . . . I'm sorry, I don't know what to call you."

"Lady Athena or simply Athena will do." She clasped Claire's hand and squeezed it. And when Claire gazed into her beautiful green eyes, she saw that they were clouded with tears. "I've heard of the death of your father. I am so sorry."

"Yes." Claire nodded. The ache remained, but faded more with each day. Richard seemed far in her past. She

hoped she would never forget him, for despite their differ-
ences, he had been a good and loving father. "Wherever he
is, I hope that he's safe and happy."

"He is," the priestess assured her. "If I have learned
anything in my centuries of study in the temples it is that
our souls are immortal. Surely, someone as well-meaning
as Richard will find happiness."

"I wouldn't want him to be alone. There was just the
two of us for so long and now . . ."

"Now you have Morgan."

Claire nodded. In a minute, she'd be crying as well.
"And little Danu. Do you know her? She's a precious
child."

"Yes, I know Danu and love her as well. She is as dear
to me as you are."

Claire blinked. "Me? But you don't know me. I'm not . . ."

Athena's sea-green eyes looked deep into Claire's own.
"My child, I do know you. Not as Claire, but as *Rhiannon*, the name I gave you when you were born."

Claire swallowed and clutched at Athena's warm hand
as though it were her lifeline. "You knew my mother? It's
true that I do have Atlantean blood?"

"What I tell you here and now must not go beyond
these walls. Do I have your solemn promise? It will not be
a secret to Morgan. I've already shared it with him, but no
other must know the truth."

"Of course," Claire agreed. "I swear I won't say anything. Please, tell me if you know anything about my birth
mother."

Tears overflowed the green eyes and sparkled on her
cheeks as she took Claire's palm and pressed it to her belly.
"I carried you here in my womb, my darling. And because
I was too cowardly to admit that I had fallen in love with

a human and bore his child, and because I was afraid for you, I gave you to him to raise. Richard was your biological father."

Claire's eyes widened in shock. "You? You're my mother? You gave birth to me? And Richard was my father?"

Athena nodded. "I knew you would come back to me in time. We Atlanteans are drawn to the sea always. But I have thought of you every day of your life, wondered how you were, and if Richard was a good father."

"He was." A knot that had held tight beneath Claire's heart for as long as she could remember came slowly undone and she threw herself into Athena's arms. "My mother? You really are my mother?"

Athena held her tightly. "Yes, my beautiful child, I am, or I was. And I would like to be again, if you can forgive me for abandoning you."

"There's nothing to forgive," Claire whispered. "But why didn't Richard come to you in the sea? Why did you remain apart if you loved each other?"

"I loved him. I think I still love him. Perhaps that's why I've never taken a husband among my own people. But I wasn't as strong as you, Claire. Our love wasn't as powerful. It's why I know you will make the right wife for Morgan. . . . And the right queen for our kingdom in the far future." Athena stepped back and wiped the tears from her face. "But you didn't come here to see me lose all my dignity. You came to be married, and your bridegroom awaits."

Claire nodded, too full of joy to speak.

"Are you certain that this is what you want? Marriage among Atlanteans lasts a long, long time."

"Yes," she managed. "I . . . I love him."

"And he loves you." Athena hugged her again and

kissed her cheek. "So we will begin again and try to get this mother-daughter thing right. And if you will allow me, I'd like to be a grandmother to Danu, as well."

"But you said no one should know."

Athena nodded and her eyes reflected the sadness in her voice. "There is always a price to pay for cowardice. You cannot call me *mother* or publicly acknowledge our relationship without risking a great deal for all of us. Mostly me, I'm afraid. But no one will think it strange if we are the best of friends. After all, I'm a woman without children of my own. It's natural that we might become close, because everyone knows how fond I am of Morgan and of Danu."

"Yes," Claire agreed. "If you think that's best."

"It is. It would be too . . . difficult for me to reveal the truth now. I would lose my place on the High Council and my seat in the court, and I am silly enough to believe that I am often the voice of reason among those esteemed nobles." She squeezed Claire's hand again. "But if you would humor an old woman, could you say it just once, so that I have something to treasure in my heart? Could you call me mother?"

"Yes, yes, Mother. *Mother*. Thank you."

"No, it is I who thank you, my daughter. You'll never know how many nights I dreamed of hearing those words from your lips."

"Lady Athena!" Morwena called from an antechamber. "Danu and the bridegroom are getting anxious. Will you be much longer?"

"No." Athena winked at Claire and placed a slender finger over her lips in a bid for secrecy. "We're ready for you."

And then Morgan was striding into the chamber, and Claire had eyes only for him. How magnificent he was in his golden kilt and vest and high-laced sandals. His beautiful eyes glittered with excitement, and he was smiling at her as if she was his heart's desire. Upon his head, he wore a thin circlet of pure gold.

Vaguely, she was aware of Danu and Morwena, Orion, and Alexandros, as well as the king and queen and a few other witnesses. But for her, during this short and beautiful ceremony, there was only the man she loved more than life itself.

Claire's hand trembled as Morgan slid a crystal ring on her finger and swore eternal faithfulness to her. Then he took her hand in his and Lady Athena bound their wrists together with a single braid of apple-green seaweed and recited the ancient ritual that made them man and wife. And finally, Danu came forward with a cushion bearing a coronet of crystal set with diamonds, and the king himself placed it on her head.

"You can kiss him, now," Danu urged. Everyone laughed but Claire and Morgan. Again, he filled Claire's heart and mind and world.

They kissed, and Claire's joy was beyond anything she had ever dreamed of. Her happiness overflowed as Morgan took her hand and led her out to the portico, and the cheers and well-wishes of thousands of Atlanteans rang in her ears. "I love you," she murmured breathlessly.

"And I love you," he replied, "and I always will." Then he clasped her hand and they stepped forward. "Be brave," he whispered. And raising his voice, he declared, "My friends, my family, my fellow Atlanteans, I give you the light of my heart, my beloved wife, the Princess Rhiannon."